"*Huron Breeze* is destined to blow the reader away wi
labyrinthine complexity. Landon Beach's hauntingly realized tale of murder,
treachery and deceit strikes at our hearts as well as our minds along a twist-laden
landscape. Beach perfectly straddles the mystery-thriller line in a tale that evokes the
likes of Michael Connelly and John Hart, proving yet again that he is an author to
be reckoned with."

- Jon Land, *USA Today* Bestselling author

"An exhilarating, can't-miss, one-sit read that'll stay with you long after turning the
final page!"

- Ryan Steck, The Real Book Spy

"Will helping a PI solve a local murder give a stalled writer the plot for her next
thriller? A crazy idea, but it works, but then there's a ruthless killer who knows she's
out there. Have fun with *Huron Breeze.*"

- Catherine Coulter, author of VORTEX

"It's impossible for a writer not to be instantly taken with this tale of an author so
desperate for a plot idea that she becomes an apprentice PI after a man turns up on
her beach with a knife in his back. You'll thoroughly enjoy this unique page-turner."

- Lisa Black, NYT bestselling author of the Gardiner & Renner series

"A blocked writer in search of her next novel idea teams up with a PI to solve a twisty case in hopes it'll get the words flowing and the book done. C'mon, what's better than that? That's the premise of Landon Beach's *Huron Breeze* ... and he nailed it. What a fun read. What sharp insights into the floppy muddle of a writer's mind. Loved it!"

- Tracy Clark, author of the Cass Raines Chicago Mystery Series, and winner of the 2020 Sue Grafton Memorial Award

"Landon Beach does a fantastic job of propelling the reader along the twisty path he creates in his mystery thrillers, and *Huron Breeze* is the best yet! I couldn't resist the 'book-within-a-book' premise of a floundering author desperate to find her next novel and ending up embroiled in her own real-life murder mystery! A guaranteed good time."

- Liz DeWandeler, A Novel Escape in Franklin, North Carolina

HURON
BREEZE

Landon Beach

Landon Beach
Visit my website at landonbeachbooks.com

Printed in the United States of America

First Printing: December 2021
Landon Beach Books

ISBN-13 978-1-7322578-7-0

For my mom and sister—two beacons of light in my life.

HURON BREEZE

"There's so much of me in that kid. Confident. Stupid. I don't know…protected. Playing life like a game without consequences. Until you can't tell the difference between a stage prop…and a real knife."

—Harlan Thrombey, *Knives Out*

"Three can keep a secret, if two of them are dead."

—Benjamin Franklin

"Yeah, but he didn't see it. He played something else and he lost. He must have regretted it every day of his life. I know I would have. As a matter of fact I do regret it, and I wasn't even born yet."

—Harry Moseby, *Night Moves*

"Writers are always selling somebody out."

—Joan Didion, *Slouching Towards Bethlehem, preface*

PART I

The Beach House

Landon Beach

I

South of Hampstead, Michigan, June 2022

The bonfire on the beach was almost dead—a circular carpet of red embers left on the white sand after tongues of flame had murdered the logs and kindling. Christine Harper ran a hand along the smooth, brown skin of her left forearm and then picked up her plastic cup of wine. She was ready to call it a night and should have felt relaxed, but there was something elusive, perhaps just beyond the realm of her reasoned awareness, that had her feeling uneasy. What it was, she couldn't say. Her intuition only whispered that forces as strong as the fire, which had consumed itself, were at play.

The last few drips of Chardonnay hit her tongue, and she swallowed, savoring the taste. She glanced at her watch. 10:45. It had been nice to sit and enjoy her drink and the fire without any company, well, at least the company that would be arriving in another week: her family.

The company she was supposed to have with her by the fire tonight had been caught in bed with their dental hygienist a month ago, which had ended her 3-year relationship with Danny Lee. The virtues of living together without the legal binds of marriage had been liberating, relaxed, with a come-and-go-as-you-please philosophy. It was uncomplicated with no restrictions. No pressure to settle down and have kids from parents because *"the relationship could end at any moment,"* according to her mother. If anything, the pressure was leveraged in the opposite direction: *"Don't have any kids until you're officially together."* The money situation had also been simple and straightforward. He had his checking account, and she had hers. He was a financial planner, and she ran her own book reviewing and promotion company, Harper's Highlights. They split the rent, went out to eat most nights during the week, and had no pets or other items to tie them down. The future? Well, when you were twenty-nine and twenty-seven, the future was a long way off. The only condition that they had discussed and agreed upon was monogamy. And so, in a life of freedom and choice, the only restriction had been the first one tested; Danny's eye had wandered from the comfort and security of Christine to their 23-year-old hygienist, Alyssa, and her glowing smile of perfect teeth, short golden hair, and cute laugh.

Looking back, the relationship had become stale over the past year, from the lack of quality time to the virtual elimination of their morning workouts together to the uninspired sex. She had lived in denial, knowing that the magic had fizzled but not knowing how to end the relationship. They had only had one major argument during the stretch, which had ended with him saying, *"Hey, I'm sorry. Let's just forget it and get counseling when we're like forty or something, okay?"* She had laughed, and the disagreement had been pushed away, but his words lingered, never quite exiting her thoughts. Now, on the cusp of turning thirty in a month, she felt free again. He had kept their apartment, and, as soon as she was out, the hygienist had moved in. Best of luck, sweetheart.

Her new place was a second-floor apartment in a complex on the other side of town. But, because her job was one-hundred percent online, she considered the move temporary. Escape wasn't the right word, but she had grown bored with living in Detroit. Yes, she would miss the summer evenings at Comerica Park and the nightclub scene with her network of friends that she and Danny had established; the term *young professionals* had been coined by someone, and it fit. However, what she wanted now was solitude—time to think, time to re-center, and time to consider what thirty to forty might have in store for her. And, minus her family, who would be showing up next week, there was no better place to contemplate her next move than the Harper family beach house that was here, fifteen miles south of Hampstead, on the shore of Lake Huron, where the summer breezes seemed to rejuvenate, inspire, excite, and calm all at once.

Speaking of the Huron breezes, the wind had picked up since she had started the fire. It had been from the west but had shifted and was coming out of the southwest now. She turned her attention to the large waves hitting the beach; the blaze of her fire had now been replaced with the roar of whitecaps breaking on the shore. Her flat-ironed, black hair blew away from her face, and she closed her eyes, feeling the cool wind on her face and neck. She heard a fresh set of waves reach the beach and visualized the sheen of water sliding across the wet sand toward the cool, dry sand above, like an athlete stretching her arms up toward the ceiling, trying to touch it with her fingertips, and then lowering her arms back to her side. She would unlatch and raise her bedroom window tonight and fall asleep to nature's finest lullaby.

After another full breath, she opened her eyes and gazed out over the water. Ten miles directly offshore was Beacon Island, a paradise that was privately owned by the Knight family. The closest she had ever been to the island was on summer sails in her father's 28-foot O'Day before he sold it. She swiveled her head and looked south. The white strip of beach extended for half a mile and then bent inward. Half a mile after the bend was the Knight's beach estate—a place she *had* visited.

She faced the water again and pondered going down to dip her feet in. Then, she saw the familiar glow of Beacon Light in the distance and watched as the light shined brightly for three seconds and then went dark. She counted off ten seconds in her head, and, right on cue, the light lit up for another three seconds straight and then went dark again. The lighthouse was located on the northern tip of Beacon Island and had served as an eternal night light for her as a child as she would leave her second-story window open and look out from her bed at the light as she drifted off to sleep. She planned to do the same thing tonight.

One more look.

The light came on, and she counted to herself, "One, tw—"

The light went out.

She set her plastic cup in the sand and then rubbed her eyes. *I've had three drinks, but I can still count.* She blinked twice and then looked back at the far end of the island. *Okay, 3 seconds. Let's go.* She narrowed her eyes and waited, but then a dark shadow of movement caught her attention.

Something had emerged from the water.

She stood up and observed the dark silhouette of a person against the clear, moonlit sky. The shadow started toward her. At this distance, perhaps twenty yards, she couldn't tell whether it was a man or a woman. Whoever it was moved irregularly—a mix of stumbling and limping. A drunk? She leaned over and grabbed her heavy-duty Maglite with her right hand. Her left hand had closed and become a fist.

Before she could turn the flashlight on, she heard the first moans from the unknown person.

She stepped to the side of her chair, giving herself a clear path to sprint back to the house. She turned the flashlight on and aimed it at the silhouette that was now fifteen yards away. "Who are you?" she said.

The flashlight's white beam illuminated a man wearing shorts and a collared shirt that were drenched. The man's hair was also wet and matted against his forehead. His eyes did not flinch from the sudden spotlight but rather opened wide as he pleaded, "Heeellllppp, muhh." He staggered to one side, held up only by his left leg. "Mmeeee." His eyes rolled back, and he fell forward, his chest and head hitting the sand with a thud.

Her altruistic instincts kicked in, and she rushed toward the man to help. A few yards away, though, her survival instincts hit right back, and she stopped. The man did not move as she started to circle his body, aiming her light at his bare feet and working her way up to—

She stopped.

Sticking straight out from in between the man's shoulder blades was the stainless-steel handle and curved butt of a knife.

Christine screamed, but there was no one to hear her cries.

2

Over two hours later, Christine Harper stood next to Hampstead Police Chief Corey Ritter as they watched the forensics and K-9 units finish up and then walk past them, heading toward their vehicles in Christine's driveway. The German shepherd, named Mario, stopped right before the sand ended and took a big dump.

As the handler started to guide Mario away, Ritter yelled, "Hey, pick that up!"

"Sorry," came the reply as the handler reversed course and scooped up the pile of feces with a pea-green colored bag.

Ritter looked down at where his feet should have been but only saw his bulging belly covered by the tan-colored summer uniform shirt of the Hampstead Police Department. He'd lost fifty pounds by Halloween on some kamikaze diet plan of celery, pills, sparkling water, and black coffee. Before that victory, he'd tried every diet plan known to the human species—Weight Watchers (the hell with counting points), Atkins (the fifth day of two steaks for dinner had led to an accompanying bottle of red wine, which had led to a second bottle, which had led to…), South Beach (when he hit phase two, his justification for adding back things he had deprived himself in phase one was 'I can handle it.' He couldn't handle it).

Anyway, after his latest diet had succeeded, his moment of triumph had come when he had paused thrusting and told his on-again, off-again girlfriend that he could finally see his cock again while having sex—'He's back!—which had immediately stopped their tryst. Then, like all perfect autumns up north with the leaves in full bloom and the smell of hot apple cider around every corner, Corey Ritter's return to glory had ended. The winter had snuck up on him like a strung-out burglar, and the good old Michigan time swap of spending one-third of your day inside and two-thirds outside from April to October to two-thirds inside and one-third outside from November to March sabotaged his food and drink intake.

The return to fast food, raspberry mochas, Sweetwater's donuts—of course—and a six-pack of longnecks before he drifted off to sleep in his burgundy recliner had been gradual at first. Six pounds in two weeks. Then, he played the mind game of, "You're fine. You just gotta work out to eat." The fallacy of riding a stationary bike for an hour each morning to work off the previous day's calories became apparent after an additional ten-pound gain after three more weeks. The morning biking came to a halt with the declaration, "I'm gonna return this piece of shit and get my money back!" He stopped weighing himself until a week ago; he was now right back where he had been last summer. The monster truck tire was around his waist again, but he had vowed to his lady that this summer he meant business—even called his nightly walk around the neighborhood his "constitution." The revival was on, and he was on day eight of *clean* eating, whatever the hell that meant. The internet nutritionist had introduced him to the term, and he'd been telling everyone about it when he announced that Corey Ritter was back on the weight-loss wagon, riding shotgun, and headed back into the wild west of hunger pains, hot sweats, and night terror about chocolate cake. He'd even upped the stakes and taken a break from the cancer sticks, which was like lopping off a limb—coffee and cigarettes in the morning, brandy and a cigar on his back deck at night. Then, tonight, he'd received the call about the body on the beach, and his car had swerved into

9

Walmart on the way over, where he picked up a dozen donuts from the bakery. This was followed by a stop at the Shell station for gas, coffee, and a pack of Marlboros. It was a twenty-minute drive out to Christine Harper's, and there were nine donuts left in the box when he had arrived.

Ritter said, "Asshole," and kicked a shoe full of sand in the direction of the K-9 and his handler, but they were twenty yards away now, and the only thing the theatrics of the kick did was make the overweight police chief almost lose his balance and have to grab Christine's arm to save himself. "Sorry," he said, taking in a few deep breaths.

Christine looked away and rolled her eyes. He had been overdramatic since arriving. When the body bag carrying the corpse of 35-year-old Kaj Reynard had been carried away by his deputies, Ritter had said, "Let's go," about a hundred times and had kept snapping his fingers and adjusting his pants. The body was now with the medical examiner, and Ritter had explained to her that his deputies were back at the station filling out paperwork. *"They're pretty much useless, but they'll get it filed before morning,"* he had said.

When conducting his official questioning of her, every question had been asked with his head cocked to one side, and his eyes narrowed as if to say *Corey Ritter was now in charge, and thoroughness flowed as easily through his veins as the blood that flowed out of Kaj Reynard's back.* He was pushy, impatient, and she judged that if a person was robbing the Hampstead bank and Corey Ritter was the only police officer to give chase on foot, then the robber would never get caught.

She'd told him everything, which wasn't much.

Two cars started in her driveway, and she could see the lemon beams illuminate the woods to the right of her house. Then, the beams swung in an arc and faded down the driveway. She and Ritter were alone now on the beach, and Ritter turned toward her. "So, you were sitting here enjoying a fire, your family," he said, pausing to open his pocket notebook, "mother, Roberta Judith Harper, father, Stanton Daniel Harper, brother, Keagan Michael Harper, who all live in Florida, and uh—" he flipped a page "—your aunt, let's see here, yeah, your mom's sister, Gail Leigh Kimball, and uncle, Alan Robert Kimball, who live in Seattle, are all arriving a week from now and haven't been here since last summer."

Jesus, the middle names. He was a slow writer, and it had taken him forever to scribble down the names earlier—making sure he had every single one spelled correctly. When she had asked him why the full names were so important, he had eyeballed her and said, *"Gives me perspective—and gets me inside their heads."*

What? Talk about amateur hour.

He walked closer to the fire, but the light from the pulsating embers was fading. He switched on his flashlight. "Your folks moved away from Hampstead eleven years ago when you graduated high school. Your older brother went to college in Florida and decided to stay down there. And your aunt and uncle moved out to Seattle before you were born." He flipped to another page. "But, they all—your mom, dad, aunt, and uncle—graduated from Hampstead High School. Dad and uncle, 1982. Mom, '83, and aunt '85—same as me. I remember all of 'em. Wanted to date your aunt, but..."

Are you serious?

"You didn't see anything in the water. No boat, no canoe, no kayak, no one else swimming, nothing." Ritter pointed at the ebony-colored water and started gesturing with his arm as if re-enacting the scene. "You saw Mr. Reynard, who you claim you've only seen a few times before but don't really know—" he raised an eyebrow "—emerge from the water, scaring the shit out of ya; he hobbled a few yards on the beach toward the fire, and then did a faceplant on the sand. You see the knife handle coming out of his back; you scream; you don't remember anyone else noticing your scream—no neighbors who turn on their lights or ask you what's wrong; you sprint to the house, go inside, and call us." He closed the notebook, put it back in his pocket, and locked eyes with her. After staying silent for a few seconds, he raised his right eyebrow. "You stay inside until we arrive twenty minutes later."

For the third time tonight, yes!

Christine gave a devious smile. "Not much to go on."

Ritter rubbed his goatee. "No, it isn't. His tracks come straight from the water and end where he fell by your fire; forensics went up and down the beach and didn't find a thing. And, it looks like the murder weapon won't help us either. A stainless-steel Cuisinart 8-inch chef's knife with an ergo—" He flipped open his notebook again. "Ergonomically designed handle. No prints, and that knife is common enough to make it impossible to track down."

"Not even a partial print?" She'd seen the forensics team member approach Ritter before heading out.

"Nope. Whoever stabbed him was probably wearing gloves. Evidently, Kaj Reynard got away from his assailant, which, I think, rules out the murderer asking him to pause for a minute while he or she wiped off the handle." He exhaled. "So, if it's gloves," he said, miming putting on a pair, "we're talking about, then this was most likely a premeditated murder." Ritter tapped the top of his notebook, apparently happy with his conclusion.

Christine nodded and remembered her mother's fifteen-piece Cuisinart knife set on the kitchen counter inside the beach house. Now that she thought of it, a few of the knives were missing, along with the scissors that had come with the set. She knew about the scissors because she had been in the kitchen when the plastic handle had snapped off when her mother was trying to cut a zip tie. *Was one of the missing knives a chef's knife?* "For sure," she said.

Ritter looked away from her and scanned the dark water offshore. "Going to be a tough one to solve."

Even if it was an easy case, you couldn't solve it. She closed her eyes and rubbed the bridge of her nose with her right thumb and index finger.

Don't be a bitch. You're still in shock, and he's just doing his job.

"Anything else, Chief?" she said.

Ritter pulled up his pants again, smoothing the shirt wrinkles above his belt with his thumbs. "Not right now."

They left the beach, and he offered to send a deputy back to stay outside her house for the rest of the night. She declined, even though her entire body felt as tight as a drum. It was unlikely that she'd get back to sleep, and part of her didn't want to. She'd stay up the rest of the night, and when the safety of a Lake Huron sunrise arrived, drift off then. She had already spoken to her mother and would call her back after the police chief left. During the last call, words of comfort had been given and offers had been made for the family to change their travel plans and arrive early, but she had said she'd be all right.

Will I?

Ritter swung his enormous gut into the patrol car, and she swore the vehicle almost touched the ground when he sat down. After starting the car, he rolled down the window. "Sure you'll be okay?"

Absolutely not. She lied by nodding yes.

"I'll be back out this way tomorrow just to take another look. By then, I'll know if forensics or the medical examiner have been able to come up with anything else. Instincts tell me no." He turned on the radio. Eighties greatest hits. *Ugh.* "My guys have already interviewed your next-door neighbors. And they—"

"Didn't hear or see anything," she said, cutting him off.

Ritter frowned. "Sorry. I know we've been over it a lot." He lit a cigarette, inhaled, and blew the smoke out of the open window. It smelled delicious. Maybe she'd buy a pack tomorrow. "We'll probably interview them again. Get some rest."

She thought about her friend, Rachel Roberts, who lived a few houses south of her. They'd probably talk to her sometime tomorrow.

He pulled out of the driveway, and as the golden bloom of his headlights disappeared down the road, she felt a tingle of fear slide up her spine. The woods on both sides of the house were a mixture of swaying black tree trunks, reaching for the sky, with a maze of gray tunnels between them. She shivered.

Get inside and get it together.

She listened to the little voice inside her head and jogged to the front porch.

The sound of a box fan at the top of the stairs greeted her as she stepped into the foyer. After locking the door, she turned on every light in the downstairs, grabbed a beer from the fridge, and turned on the TV, finding a *Lost* re-run marathon.

An hour later, she was snoring away on the couch—unaware of the vehicle that had stopped at the end of her driveway for a few seconds and then continued off into the night.

3

Rachel Roberts buried her head underneath her soft, down-filled pillow as her cell phone continued to ring on the nightstand. She knew who it was, and she did not want to answer.

An onshore breeze rattled the wind chimes outside her open bedroom window, and the sound overpowered the phone's annoying ring for a few seconds before the wind died back down. She had woken up at just after five to go to the bathroom and had opened the blinds and window then, getting a sense of the morning. Then, she had returned to bed and fallen back asleep. Now, the sun was a warm ball of orange just above the horizon, signaling the start of another beautiful Michigan summer day. The waters of Lake Huron remained dark and choppy but would lighten to a bright blue as the sun continued to rise.

The phone stopped ringing. Rachel lifted her pillow, exposing one of her blue eyes. The evil phone rested as still as a concrete block.

Stay right there, you little bastard.

It started to ring again.

"She just doesn't give up."

Rachel slithered her left hand through the maze of silk sheets and fluffy comforter until it emerged, and she reached for the phone.

She looked at the screen. The ID: Topaz Kennedy.

She had been right. It was her longtime agent, the most powerful agent in the business, calling from New York City.

She slid her index finger across the screen. "My sleeping hours yielded no ideas," Rachel started.

"Good morning, thespian," Topaz replied, her voice like rocks that had been smoothed by centuries of water rushing over them.

"I told you last night that I didn't think it would work, and it hasn't. Eating Fruity Pebbles before bed did not give me any 'adventure dreams' to spur my creativity."

"Well, it works for me. Maybe you should try again tonight. Eat a second bowl."

"I don't think I can. That stuff is pure sugar—took me forever to fall asleep. Must've been just before ten. The last time I looked at my phone was around 9:30, then, I was out."

"So you had no dreams?"

"Not that I remember."

"Well," Topaz said, "we need you to start producing pages."

She sat up in bed and exhaled. Then, her black cat, Hemingway, nicknamed Hemy, jumped onto the bed next to her, almost causing her to scream. *Sneaky shit still knows how to pull off the perfect ambush.* The sleek creature walked over her legs and laid down, snuggling against her left hip. She rubbed him, and Hemy began to purr.

"Rachel? Are you still there? I heard that huff, miss."

"I was just sitting up to let Hemy on the bed," she lied.

"Ugh. Cats. Get a dog, miss majestic. And when has Hemy ever needed you for anything?"

She was right. Hemy had marched to the beat of his own drum since he was a kitten. But he did like to cuddle—only on his terms. "Never," she said.

"Of course. Cats are mischief to begin with, but that fella you've got is pure evil."

"He is not, and you bought him for me, remember?" *And it was the least you could have done after taking 15% of the generous advance I got.*

"Worst mistake I ever made. Now, you're stalling. Where's the story? You *have* to deliver."

This is what Topaz hadn't mentioned last night, but Rachel had felt it coming. The publishing industry was slowly recovering from near disaster, and it needed hits—and needed them *now*. And Topaz had told her that it needed Riley Cannon.

Her agent's greeting of "Good morning, thespian" was not just a nod to Topaz Kennedy's favorite Humphrey Bogart film, *In a Lonely Place*. It was an appropriate way to refer to her one-time juggernaut of a client. For 40-year-old Rachel Roberts was not a coder who worked remotely for a major player in Silicon Valley—the lie she had perfected over the past decade. She was, in fact, the greatest mystery in publishing history.

Mega-thriller phenomenon author Riley Cannon (Rachel Roberts's pen name) had struck gold in her 20s with three runaway bestsellers in what had been labeled 'The 'Round the Clock Series.' One reason was because people weren't eating or sleeping, literally reading her books around the clock. The second reason was that they were the first three novels in a 6-novel series, featuring the unconquerable, indelible, enemy-eating heroine, Adrienne Astra—the 'character of the decade' according to the pearly gates of the publishing world, the maker or breaker of careers, the *New York Times*.

Her debut, *Morning Glory Mayhem!* had been a surprise national bestseller, which had prompted the high court of Doubleday to come a-knockin'. With the fabled dolphin and anchor power behind her, coupled with the gleaming and intimidating deal-brokering prowess of mythical agent Topaz Kennedy and the keen insight of the number one acquisition editor in the business, J. Rudolph Hightower, Riley Cannon's sequel, *Late-Afternoon Associates*, climbed the mountain and landed on the *New York Times* Bestseller list. Two years later, the Riley Cannon team reached the summit with *Enemies in the Evening*, hitting number one—and staying there for an incredible fifty weeks.

Enemies sat on the peak of Mount Everest compared to the rest of the books that launched and couldn't climb out of the valley. Then, as if to guarantee that no one else made it to the summit, Topaz pulled out her daggers and moved in for the kill, preparing for the contract negotiations for the final three books in the series: *Dark After Midnight, 3 a.m. Phone Call*, and the finale *Sunrise Kama Sutra*. She had already secured legendary audiobook narrator Suzanne Elise Freeman, who had performed the first three books as a favor for Topaz, to perform the final three. Like when Ian Fleming first met Sean Connery and said, "You *are* James Bond," Topaz had sat down with Suzanne, stared into the narrator's brown eyes, and said, "You *are* Adrienne Astra."

Then, as it was only thought to happen in a Shakespearean tragedy, the bard's plot eased itself forward on the publishing stage, and Riley Cannon disappeared through a trap door. And since Topaz Kennedy was the only person who knew the author's true identity and wouldn't tell because Rachel had it in her contract that her name would never be shared, the conspiracy theories had taken off and dominated the newspapers, cable news networks, and internet.

Theory #1: There was no single person who wrote the books. There were three top-name authors who had each taken on a novel and were now swimming in money. The problem with this theory, the conspiracy gurus admitted, was *Why didn't the three authors just keep going and finish out the series?* A weak argument had been offered: There had been contract disputes over who would write the 4th book.

Theory #2: There was a single person who wrote the books, but it was a major author who wished to remain anonymous. This was known as the

"Grisham wrote them" theory or the "Rowling wrote them" theory. But if this was the case, then why had the books stopped? The theorists who believed this explanation reasoned that the renowned author had fulfilled his/her escape from the pressure of his/her usual genre and was now done with this brief tangent to a storied career. This hadn't stopped a few mid-list authors from attempting to boost their sales and notoriety by claiming that they knew who Riley Cannon was but couldn't say—they'd been friends for years, and their solemn bond wouldn't allow for such a betrayal. This had led to wooing by rival publishing houses and agents, social media outbursts, and viral campaigns to get to the truth. Eventually, the mid-listers backed away from their claims, greedy lawyers had gotten involved—some saying that *they* knew Riley Cannon—the initial bump in sales died off, and the trail went cold. However, one author *had* successfully lassoed the hot air money balloon and was making a fortune off her backlist because her style was close to Cannon's and had people speculating that *she* was Riley Cannon. Events hit a fever pitch when, swarmed by the media outside of her Malibu beach house for the millionth time, she paused on her front porch steps, turned toward the cameras, red in the face, and said, "Believe me, I know who in the hell Riley is, okay? But it's not me, and I can't say, so leave me the fuck alone."

Theory #3: There was a single person who wrote the books, but they died after the third book was complete, and Topaz Kennedy, J. Rudolph Hightower, and Doubleday were keeping it secret while they looked for a suitable replacement. The theory gained traction when their joint statement was released to the public after the platinum deal for books 4, 5, and 6 fell through.

Riley is taking some time off for health and family reasons. It is unknown if she will ever pick up the pen again. And, since she holds the rights to the character of Adrienne Astra, we owe it to her fans to say that there may never be another novel in the series—let alone all three of the remaining books. We hope, with time, that Riley is able and willing to bring Adrienne back. You will all know something when we do.

This statement had, of course, generated even more hysteria and been labeled as a publicity stunt to drive book #4's sales through the stratosphere. The publishing world had seen it before. Big-shot author is worn out or bored or needs more time to write the book. Publishing house, agent, and publicist team up to take control of the narrative, offering a slim chance that the next book will happen, then go completely dark on the subject for however long it takes the author to finally finish the book, and, when the book is ready, seize the moment with an exclusive press conference to announce that the book is finally going to happen. Let the hype and publicity machine take it from there.

So, when the statement had been released twelve years ago, the legion of Riley Cannon fans and even the casual observer had suspected that within a few years, the announcement would be made. Hell, it had taken Dan Brown six years to release *The Lost Symbol*—the book that had ended *Enemies in the Evening*'s fifty-week reign—after *The DaVinci Code* had come out. Surely, they wouldn't have to wait *that* long. But as two years became four and four years became eight, the fans slipped into deep loss-of-Riley-Cannon depression and felt the symptoms of an Adrienne Astra withdrawal. Psychologists saw an increase in patients suffering from what they termed 'Riley Cannon Separation Anxiety,' and online support groups were formed that were similar to the keeping-your-beard support groups—ridiculous, quirky, and undeniably honest. The 10-year mark hit, and mock funeral services were held with grown men and women openly crying as they stared at the cold cemetery ground after placing a wreath by a cardboard headstone that had Riley Cannon's name with the dates "? – 2008" on one side, and Adrienne Astra's name with the dates "1978 – 2008" on the other. There was even a candlelight vigil at a sorority on the campus of The University of Alabama where sorority sisters wore crimson t-shirts with white lettering that said, "Adrienne was one of us." The sorority president had flown in Suzanne Freeman from L.A., who read the last words of dialog that Adrienne Astra had said in *Enemies in the Evening*, which brought the entire sorority to tears. The live stream of the vigil on YouTube had six million viewers, and one year later, it had fifty million views.

And now, twelve years after the last book had hit the shelves, the Riley Cannon army was back in a frenzy. On Christmas Day, six months ago, Doubleday had announced that book #4 *Dark After Midnight* would be published within two years. Present at the live announcement in front of the Rockefeller Christmas tree was the head of Doubleday, Suzanne Freeman, J. Rudolph Hightower, and Topaz Kennedy, wearing her signature topaz-colored suit with matching scarf, earrings, and high heels. The publisher had explained that they could not set a firm date for the release because the book still had a lot of hoops to go through. The launch was going to be bigger than Brown's and Rowling's books combined, and they wanted to get it right. No questions were taken, but before ending the press conference, Topaz had stood behind the podium and left the tasty morsel of, "What I can tell you is that it's Riley's longest, scariest, and *best* book. Get ready to be charmed, wowed, and thrilled by Adrienne Astra once again. After all, everyone knows that it is …" Her voice had trailed off as Suzanne Freeman suddenly rose, holding a microphone inches from her lips, and said in the most perfect, sultry voice ever, "Dark after midnight."

The crowd packing the Rockefeller Center had gone berserk, and the cheering had continued for over a minute.

But that was Christmas, and it was now June.

And Rachel Roberts, pen name Riley Cannon, hadn't written a word.

"Like I said last night," Rachel said, "nothing is working."

"Let me explain something," Topaz shot back. "You were paid the largest advance in the history of publishing. And we knew it might take some time for the work to come, but December is now ancient history, and you've missed outline deadline one, and you're about to miss outline deadline two. I've got Hightower begging for pages, well, begging for *anything* you have, and I've had two calls in the last week from numero uno at Doubleday. I can't hold them off forever, kid. You *have* to get going."

She had dreaded this moment. No one believed in her more than Topaz. No one had done more for her than Topaz. But now, her agent was telling her that it was time to deliver and there could be no more delays. And this was serious because if there was anyone on the planet who could haggle a publisher for more time or change a book's course with one phone call, it was Topaz. And now she had heard words from her champion, mentor, defender, and guardian that exposed the impossible: Even Topaz Kennedy's power had its limits. Of course, it was more than that. If Rachel missed the second deadline, the publisher could take back the money. Topaz was inherently "Team Author," but threaten to take back *her* money, and she became "Team Publisher" in a heartbeat. Rachel knew that the transformation had just occurred. In terms of Joseph Campbell's Hero's Journey archetypes, a literary agent was one of the traditional publishing industry's cornerstone Threshold Guardians—a gatekeeper, who kept unpublished, barbarian writers away from the cherished castle of book-deal majesty. What Rachel did not need right now was for Topaz to turn her legendary Threshold-Guardian-mercenary attitudes toward her any more than she already had in terms of getting the book finished. Rachel didn't need to outwit Topaz because Topaz ultimately wanted the book to get done. What she needed to do was harness Topaz's energy and absorb it.

Rachel had to give her something. "I'll take a look at the outline again."

"You've looked at it enough," Topaz said. "The idea is dead. Get it out of your head."

Her agent was, of course, referring to the outline she had written for book #4 twelve years ago. The idea had been sound, and Topaz had even applauded the twists and surprises that Rachel had sketched out, but that was then, and audiences were expecting more now. And the book had to be longer. Much longer. The old outline would result in a thriller of around 100,000 words. Her new contract stated that book #4's length needed to fall between 120,000 and 150,000 words. *"We need a whopper for this one, not a cheeseburger,"* Topaz had said.

Rachel had already spent January, February, and most of March trying to lengthen the original outline by adding one and then two subplots to cover the additional word count requirement. But the subplots threw off the pacing and timing of certain reveals and bogged the middle of the book down with needless scenes. In April, she had scrapped the subplots and had tried adding a new character to complicate Adrienne Astra's ever-blooming love life, but after sketching out a few scenes, the new character had grown too strong and was taking the focus off Adrienne's main love interest. The new character was also starting to influence the direction of the plot, which again threw off the calculated twists that Rachel had planned.

Topaz had added that *"Your fans will expect some classic beats that you've established in the first three books, but they will also be looking for some new ones. In terms of timeline, we need to set this book about ten years after book #3 so that fans wonder what Adrienne Astra's been up to for the past decade. After you're done with the first draft, we'll make an announcement on social media to ratchet up the hype."*

The wind chimes clanged and whistled as a fresh breeze came in through the screen, and Rachel slid back down under the sheets and comforter. "Topaz?"

"Yes, my child?"

"For the first time in my career, I'm scared."

There was a long pause, and the chimes rang louder as a gust blew through them and reached Rachel Robert's face, which, along with her hand holding the phone, were the only parts of her body not protected from the cold by her comforter.

"I know," Topaz Kennedy replied.

Besides being the only person who knew her identity, Topaz Kennedy had become more than Rachel Roberts's agent. She had become her parent as well. Shortly after a smooth-talking lawyer strode into town and whisked Rachel's mother away when Rachel was two, her father moved them out of their family home in Kalamazoo to Midland, Michigan. There, he raised her and watched her graduate with a full scholarship to Bryn Mawr. And it was there that she developed her love of writing and wrote the first draft of *Morning Glory Mayhem!*. Then, a month after graduation, the stars aligned. She queried Topaz, also a Bryn Mawr graduate, and Topaz scooped Rachel up. However, the agreement stated that Rachel would take on a pen name and that no one would know who she really was. *"I don't want my mother to ever find out that I am an author. The lure of money does strange things to people, and if she comes back to me one day, then I want it to be because she is owning her mistake and not because of what I do for a living. The chances are slim that this will happen anyway, but I've already discussed this with my dad, and he agrees. Maintaining my privacy is also very important to me. Topaz, I have no designs on living large or becoming a celebrity."* Topaz pleaded but eventually gave in. *"We could have made you into a star, darling!"* she said right after signing the document. Looking back, Rachel realized that her own reasoning was the product of her mid-twenties mindset—mature, guarded, and cautious on the one hand, unrealistic, angry, and with a slight bit of vindictiveness on the other. After Rachel had stayed firm with her decision to not write under her own name, it was Topaz who had shown a quick change of heart and come up with Rachel's pen name. *"I gave your reasoning a few minutes to buzz around in my head, and you're a genius, darling. Roberts would have been all wrong for you—already a Nora Roberts, so you'll never be the biggest Roberts on the block. I've got something better: Riley Cannon. Explosive, assertive, catchy, and, best of all, last name's a 'C.' Pretty much every 'C' has become an A-list author. Going to put your books strategically on the shelf right next to Chandler, Child, Christie, Clancy, Cornwell, Coulter, Crais, Cussler, and company. Believe me, you'll get read more, bright brain."*

Three books in, and the mystery of who exactly Riley Cannon was had only grown more. Book #4 was outlined, and Rachel was ready to begin the initial draft. Hightower was ready to sign on for books 4, 5, and 6, Topaz was squeezing the Doubleday brass for every penny in the negotiations, and then it had happened. Clark Roberts fell over dead while raking leaves in the fall of 2008, right after the release of *Enemies in the Evening.* Her rock, her role model, the man who had sacrificed everything he could have been to give her a stable upbringing, was gone. Overcome with grief, frustration, and anger, she told Topaz to stop the contract negotiations. *"Just give me some space. I'm certain the work will come with a little more time off to deal with this,"* she had said.

After two years, she had Topaz quietly tell Hightower and Doubleday that Riley Cannon was never coming back. However, Topaz had told her that she was not giving up on her prized possession. A year later, knowing from phone call check-ins with Rachel that she desperately needed something to take her mind off of her father, Topaz had hired her as a ghostwriter for three prominent authors that Topaz represented—two legends and one rising star. And because Rachel had nothing else to do, she took the covert writing assignments but reiterated to her agent that this did not mean that Riley Cannon was coming back. Topaz had said, *"Of course, darling—wouldn't dream of it,"* and continued to play the long game by respecting Rachel's wishes but also handling the contracts quietly. She had to: The authors' brands were so important to the publishing house that it absolutely could never be known that the authors were no longer writing their own books. Only the author, the head of the publishing company, Topaz, and Rachel knew about the agreement. And, if somehow speculation started, Topaz was to handle any question about the touchy subject with: There is no ghostwriter. *"There are estate writers, co-authors, and ghostwriters, my dear. Well, for these three books, you're none of them. You don't exist."* In fact, Topaz had told Rachel that her name would not even appear on the publishing contracts; the authors would give Topaz a portion of their advances, and, after taking her cut, Topaz would funnel the rest of the money to Rachel.

The up-and-comer was a newly retired Green Beret colonel in his forties for whom the red carpet was being rolled out: endorsements, gear companies hiring him as a spokesman, hundreds of thousands pouring into building him a massive social media following with top-notch videos regularly produced showing him hunting and then preparing his kills for a large family meal. A lot of work went into the narrative of establishing the colonel as a soldier-scholar who eliminated enemy combatants without remorse, showered, and then read Shakespeare with a red-lensed flashlight in his tent at night. Another promotional video showed the ex-serviceman seated behind his home office's desk, looking out a set of huge windows at the hills of Tennessee for a ponderous moment, and then turning his attention to the manuscript pages in front of him while unsheathing a red flair pen to begin the editing process. Of course, the kicker was that the public would never know that he didn't write the books. Rachel Roberts did. She laughed hysterically the first time she saw him via Facebook live at a book signing event, talking about the writing process, making small talk with the large number of fans who had shown up, and finally signing the last book while announcing that he'd love to stay and talk more, but he had another book to write.

The first legend she wrote a book for was an established mega-author named Trisha Parker, who had a stable of co-authors that allowed her to crank out about ten books a year. But the book that Rachel had been hired to ghostwrite was a special project. The story that would be sold to the public was that the mega-author had teamed up with a United States Senator to write a political thriller from the point of view of a fictional senator who got in way over her head as a spy on the senate armed services committee. There were snapshots of the author and senator, sitting by a fireplace with legal pads in their laps and pens in their hands, provided to the press by the author's publicist to show the women hard at work, making the novel as authentic as possible—within the bounds of what could be shared to the public of course. In an interview conducted just outside the hallowed Senate chamber, the senator had said, *"Well, we can't include every event I'd like to in the book, because if we did, then I'd be court-martialed for releasing sensitive intelligence. But, believe me, we're going to give you a great thrill ride."*

Would the author and senator write one word of the "co-authored" political thriller? Nope. Rachel Roberts would write every word. There was also a fifteen-state book tour—half of which were swing states for an upcoming election—scheduled for the author and senator "co-authors" to promote the book, their supreme collaboration. Trisha Parker had joked, *"If congress only worked together as well as the senator and I did, then we'd actually get some things done in this country."* When the advanced reader copies arrived at the bookstores, they were accompanied by a short letter from the mega-author who ended the note with, *"My hand is hurting from so much writing and revising of this book—the senator is a beast to work with—that I better stop this letter and put my hand on ice. Signed, Trisha Parker."*

The final author was the hardest to accept the job of ghostwriting for—no matter how much money Topaz had negotiated the deal to Rachel's advantage. The author was a former judge who had traded in her black robe for a shawl and become a seventeen-time #1 *New York Times* Bestselling author. And she was one author who Rachel had started reading in high school and never missed the author's annual spring release. She had even mentioned to Topaz how dirty she felt when she had written the book about the treasonous senator, which had received glowing reviews and even bolstered the actual senator's public approval so much that she was considering a run at the White House in the next election. Topaz, being an old lefty, had sighed and said, *"Well, that book tour moved the needle, and we got some of those yahoos out of there. Whatever it takes, darling."* Then, Rachel had mentioned that at least Judge Macy Ashberry would never stoop so low. In her opinion, the judge's last two novels were two of her best, and it appeared that the judge had recovered her old form. The critics agreed, *"This one reminded me of why I fell in love with the judge in the first place,"* and, *"If you have missed early Macy Ashberry, then this novel will take you back. The judge has never been better."* Hearing Rachel's passionate defense of her beloved author, Topaz had replied, *"Of course, my angel."* So, it came as a great surprise when Topaz called her and explained that Judge Ashberry didn't write her own novels anymore—the last one written by her being five novels ago. Rachel had wept. Her feisty former female judge, who had gotten in and mixed it up with the male-dominated thriller market and delivered beat down after beat down to the boys…had sold out.

Rachel wrote one book, watched it climb to #1, watched Judge Macy Ashberry on the morning talk show circuit explain how good it was to write about her mythical town of Shepherd, Georgia again. Rachel also read the reviews where everyone in the book business gushed about how tight of a thriller the judge's latest book was. Then, Rachel told Topaz that she couldn't do this anymore. She had enough money but was grateful that her agent had brought her some work to help her get through a couple of tough years. No, she wouldn't be revisiting Adrienne Astra anytime soon.

That was three years ago. When she had turned 40 this past November, she had picked up the phone and called Topaz. She was ready to write again. It was time to finish the last three books.

The wind chimes had stopped, and Rachel could hear the waves rolling against the beach. The phone felt slippery in her sweaty palm. There was no backing out of this, but she had to be honest. She owed Topaz that. "I'm ready. I know I am. But I've never had such an issue with coming up with a plot that Adrienne could navigate, grow as a character, and still wipe out the baddies. I'm—"

Shit. I am going to say it.

"—lost."

She could hear Topaz say, "Oh, fuck," but it was muffled as if Topaz had tried to cover the phone so Rachel wouldn't hear.

"I'm sorry," Rachel said.

"Oh, Jesus. Did you hear what I said? Well, there's no time for any of that now. You need to find it and find it fast, thespian. The sharks are circling."

She could feel the conversation already coming to an end. *Might as well be absolutely blunt with her. She always is with me.* "Topaz, I don't *have* an idea."

Her power agent did not hesitate. "Find one," Topaz said and ended the call.

Rachel sat back up and looked down at the phone's blank screen. *Find one? Where?* She loathed wasting time surfing the internet for news stories, did not have a lot of people she could call, and had already read every book in her beach house's library.

"C'mon, Hemy," she said to the black ball of fur next to her.

Hemy didn't move.

"Fine."

She rose from her bed and stretched while viewing the waves roll in toward her white sandy beach. A lone jogger passed by, heading north, and her eyes followed him as he disappeared behind a large grass-covered dune and then appeared moments later. He was too far away to guess his age, but he moved swiftly with the gait of a younger man. She continued to watch until he disappeared behind another dune that rose before the stretch of beach that was behind Christine Harper's house. Christine was a book blogger who Rachel had drinks with on occasion at The Buccaneer Pub, known to locals as "The Buck." She wondered if Christine had arrived for her summer visit yet. Sometimes they would talk books—Christine had no idea who she was—and sometimes, Christine's annoying boyfriend would join them on the beach for an evening glass of wine. *Maybe I should call her.*

She dismissed the thought as quickly as it had entered her mind. Her heart rate was starting to increase, not only because of her circadian rhythm at work but because of the situation she had put herself in. She needed coffee, and there was no time to waste. She had to start the book. Throwing on her crimson-colored L.L. Bean robe, she exited her bedroom and walked down the dark hallway toward the kitchen. The smooth, wood floor felt cold on her bare feet, and soon she could hear the waves and wind again through the cracked-open living room windows. The blinds were all the way open. She shrugged, realizing that she had forgotten to close them last night.

She entered the kitchen and began to make coffee, for she wanted it fresh and was not the type of person to pride herself on the efficiency of preparing it the night before so that all she had to do was push the start button in the morning. As she went through the motions of preparing her pot of morning lifeblood, the weight of Topaz's words became heavier and heavier. What had started out as easing back into her role as Riley Cannon had turned into something much more difficult than she had anticipated. And she knew why. The first three stories had come so easily for her. The psychological term for what she had experienced was *flow*, coined by Mihály Csíkszentmihályi—the ability to completely commit to an activity where one's skill level and the challenge of the activity are high. She had lost herself in the writing of the novels, wielding her artistic talents and, even though the novels were written in third-person, she felt at times like *she* was Adrienne Astra. She knew her movements, her motivations, her desires, her fears, and her sense of justice. Because of this luxury, she was able to develop plots that highlighted her main character's strengths and yet pushed Adrienne Astra to overcome her vulnerabilities. If she had continued with book #4 and followed the outline she had created, then the state of flow would no doubt have continued. She'd even felt a sense of flow on the individual ghostwriting projects—a certain level of pressure was eliminated because she did not feel the weight of responsibility in developing and challenging a character whom she had created. She supposed it was like guest-directing an episode of your favorite television show. One felt the freedom and advantage of using characters and settings that already existed but also felt the weight of responsibility to the fans who had certain expectations and standards.

She pulled the pot out of the coffee maker and poured the heavenly liquid into her favorite light-blue-colored Life is Good mug that had a red Adirondack chair with the word "Unplug" in black lettering on the front. After one whiff and then a sip, she felt the first hints of her body starting to catch up with her already racing mind. She needed a plot for a ten-year-older Adrienne Astra that would both satisfy her diehard and casual fans but also bring in new fans. Staying at her beach house today was out of the question—the comfort, scenery, and solitude had not helped her yield a single idea. As she sat on her living room couch with her cup of coffee, her eyes glanced up at the ceiling, and she pictured her writing room on the second floor. There were built-in bookshelves that lined two of the walls; the third wall had a supply closet with paper, pens, pencils, notebooks, and a locked filing cabinet inside; the fourth wall had large windows that faced Lake Huron above a built-in knotty pine desk that ran the entire length of the wall. An enormous brown leather office chair on wheels, which threatened to swallow her petite 5'2" frame every time she sat in it, was behind the desk. The only other things in the room were a chair and ottoman in a corner with a floor lamp behind the chair and a small table next to it. She would have to face the room soon, but she would not enter it until she had the idea.

Her eyes lowered from staring at the ceiling and steadied upon the dark water off her beach. If she couldn't stay and work here today, then she needed to find a place where she would have access to story capital—anything that might ignite her imagination. So far, she had taken the introverted route, reading books, watching television, and combing the internet for ideas. All of which hadn't worked. She decided that it was time to try the time-honored tradition that most writers employed: people-watching and people-listening. Around the area, she knew of a litter of establishments that would allow her to do this. But, there was a place where she had never been, only heard about, that stood above the rest: Darwinger's gas station, which was north of Hampstead on US-23.

She would begin her search for an idea there.

5

It was 9 a.m. that same morning when Rachel Roberts pulled her midnight blue Ford Expedition into the gravel parking lot next to Darwinger's gas station. She'd heard over the years that this was the epicenter of local information and gossip, but she did not expect the parking lot to be nearly filled this morning. But then again, maybe it was like this every day. She had to drive to the end of the last row of pick-ups and park halfway on the strip of weeds that bordered the lot.

As she exited the vehicle and walked toward the gas station's entrance, gravel crunched under each of her steps. A huge orange sign with the green letters spelling *Darwinger's* hung over the front door, and there were similar signs on the corners of the roof covering the gas pumps. Across the street, a small motorboat was moored to a dock, and she could see the sun shimmering across the surface of Lake Huron in the distance. The strong morning wind had died down to a gentle breeze.

She wondered what she would hear this morning. Her method for collecting information when she was ghostwriting was to visit a bar or restaurant, sit down, and scroll through her phone, completely ignoring everything on the screen while she listened. Topaz had given her the idea when she had been struggling with the dialog for a few scenes. At first, she had felt dirty eavesdropping on private conversations. But, to an extent, writing *was* a dirty, cruel business, mimicking real-life dichotomies like telling a friend to his face that his mind was still sharp while thinking, *he's lost a step.*

As she drew close to the door, she began to doubt her instincts about what she might be able to gather from a small-town gossip mill. Hampstead was a tight-knit, blue-collar community where life carried on at an easy pace, which had appealed to her when she was looking for a place to hide out after the first three Riley Cannon books had taken off. The fact that Hampstead was also a quiet and peaceful vacation destination for the wealthy and middle-class alike who flocked there by the thousands over the summer months gave the town a vibrancy and undercurrent of culture that celebrated the fine arts, fine dining, and also water sports. It also meant that there was a normal amount of ugliness like divorces, bankruptcies, petty crime, DUIs, and heated city council meetings. But, it also meant that there was not a high number of felonies. There hadn't been a murder in the Hampstead area for fourteen years—something about an old ship and treasure that had been found...she couldn't remember the exact details. Hence, the chances that she would hear anything this morning that would help her plot Adrienne Astra's next adventure were rare.

She reached the front door and was surprised by the commotion coming from inside. From the number of vehicles outside, she had expected a good measure of chatter, but this sounded like a full convention hall. Through the windows to the left of the door, she could see people piled into booths, drinking coffee, and leaning close so that they could be heard as they competed with noise coming from the nearby booths. One man was gesturing wildly with his hands above his head; then, he stopped and put one hand on his coffee mug and one hand behind his back. Slowly, he acted like he was pulling something from his waistband, and then quickly, he mimed stabbing his mug with an invisible knife.

Something has the locals stirred up.

The smell of fresh coffee hit her as she opened the door, and the volume of voices rose. To her right, a stately woman in her fifties stood behind a cash register and gave a receipt to a male customer who had purchased a 2-liter of Mountain Dew and a Snickers bar. The man tipped his cap to the woman and slid past Rachel toward the door. In front of her were a half-dozen aisles that contained the usual gas station items for sale, and on the far wall was a row of refrigerators containing drinks and a minimal amount of emergency, over-priced grocery items. To her left was the destination for this morning's creative idea search: Eight booths that formed a U, three against the windowed wall that faced the gas pumps and US-23, three against the opposite wall, and two at the far end. In the middle was a rectangular island that had eight coffee pots, two towers of paper cups, and a spread of coffee accessories: a metal napkin dispenser, tiny straws, a half-gallon of creamer resting in a champagne bucket filled with ice, a huge can of sugar, and then an assortment of sweeteners in different colored packets. The booths were filled to capacity, and patrons were standing around the island talking, only pausing to refill their cups.

"You want some coffee, hun?"

Rachel turned and saw the woman behind the register smiling at her.

"Yes, please," Rachel said.

The woman yelled, "Baby Lloyd!"

As if summoned by the President, a man wearing a cowboy hat turned away from a group he had been chatting with by the coffee island and sped to the register. As he neared, Rachel guessed that he was roughly the same age as the woman, and then she noticed that he had a belt around his waist with a holster that held a six-shooter on each hip.

"Yes, angel," he said to the woman.

She gave a grin back that said this was the proper greeting and acknowledgment of her status. "Get this nice lady a cup of coffee." She turned to Rachel. "What do you like in it?"

"Black is just fine."

"Black it is," the man said, winking at Rachel, and then left.

The woman moved around the counter and extended her hand, which Rachel took. "Agatha Darwinger."

"Rachel Roberts."

"Welcome to our store. That coffee bitch is my husband, Baby Lloyd Darwinger, third-generation owner. Dad was Little Lloyd, and his grandpa, Lloyd Darwinger Senior, built this place. Now, I saw you eyein' Baby Lloyd's pistols. No worries. Got a permit. Never seen him use 'em before. I think he just likes the feel of 'em or somethin'. Like, 'nobody's messin' with me' or some stupid shit. Well, he's harmless enough."

They watched as Baby Lloyd arrived at the coffee island. The crowd parted, and he grabbed a cup from the stack. Rachel's eyes drifted to the ceiling, and she could see a tell-tale line that ran all the way across and down both opposite walls, telling her that the four booths farthest away from her had been part of an addition at some point. Originally, there must have been only the four booths. And as she took a quick survey of them, she could see that those four original booths had much older people in them as if there was a seniority system at play and these booths were reserved for the tenured gossip high court members.

"Haven't seen you in here before, sweetie," Agatha said. "You new to Hampstead?"

"No, I've lived in the area for a while, just never been inside here before." She motioned out the door toward the pumps. "Usually just swipe my card when getting gas and then head out when I'm on my way back from a trip up north."

Rachel watched as Baby Lloyd made his way through the crowd with her cup of coffee. "Nice and cozy in here. Is it usually this busy?"

"Oh, we've got our regulars," she said, "but this morning is something else. There was a—"

"Here we are, ma'am," Baby Lloyd Darwinger said, placing the cup in her hands.

"Thanks," Rachel said.

"Pots three, five, and eight are running low, mister," Agatha said, pointing at the coffee bar. Her husband nodded and headed back.

"Takes orders well, doesn't he?" she said, snickering.

Rachel nodded and took a sip of the steaming cup of coffee, mentally filing away Agatha's words for possible use in a novel one day. Thinking that she would wince at the taste of gas station coffee, which had only served as a laxative in her early college days when on a road trip with her girls, she was stunned at how good the hot liquid tasted as it left her mouth and warmed her insides. As she took another sip, she watched as Baby Lloyd Darwinger emptied the remains of three pots of coffee into a stainless-steel sink and threw away the used filters. He refilled each pot with fresh water, put a new filter in the three makers, dumped two heaping scoops of coffee into each filter, and then started the makers.

"Efficient system," Rachel said.

"Got a pot for each booth. Got 'em labeled too. Tradition is that when a booth fills up, a coffee maker is voted into service for that morning, and each table polices its own coffee refills. Today, however, is a different animal." She leaned close to Rachel. "Had ourselves a little murder last night, hun." Her eyes opened wide and then closed back to a conspiratorial squint.

"Here?" Rachel said.

"Ha!" Agatha laughed. "That'd be the only thing that'd top it. No, it was south of town in that little uppity oasis called Lakeview."

Rachel almost spit out her coffee.

"You okay?" Agatha asked, grabbing her arm.

Rachel swallowed, coughed, then nodded that she was fine.

Lakeview was the most expensive neighborhood within a few hundred miles of Hampstead, and it was also where Rachel Roberts's home had been for the past decade. Located fifteen miles south of town, the Lakeview subdivision had two gated access points, one mile apart, off US-23. The entrances were announced by large wooden signs, painted turquoise and carved into the shape of seashells, with the word "Lakeview" in bright white lettering. Beyond each gate was a respective road that ran toward Lake Huron—Spring Drive, the northernmost road, and Ferry Drive, the southern border of the subdivision. Both weaved a quarter of a mile before they branched off at Shoreside Lane but continued to stretch all the way to Old Beach Road, which ran parallel to the lake and spilled into paved driveways that led to massive beachfront homes. Ten miles directly offshore was Beacon Island, owned by the wealthiest beachfront inhabitants: the Knights.

She liked to describe Lakeview as one large rectangular loop, the long sides being US-23 and Old Beach Road, and the short sides being Spring Drive and Ferry Drive, which were bisected by Shoreside Lane, breaking the large rectangle into two smaller rectangles. The exception to her description was at the northern end of the subdivision at the intersection of Spring Drive and Shoreside Lane. Whereas the southern stretch of Shoreside dead-ended into Ferry Drive, the northern portion continued north across Spring Drive for another quarter mile, ending in a maze of cobblestone streets called Lakeview Village. At the northern terminus were tennis courts, an outdoor pool, an indoor fitness center with a saltwater lap pool, certified trainers, whirlpool, massage room, sauna, healthy snack bar, and state-of-the-art luxury locker rooms. The heart of the settlement, however, was "The Shoppes at Lakeview Village." The Buck was located there, as was Sunrise Grill, Deep Blue Coffee House, Bakery, & Café, and Lexi's Catch. There was Lakeview Village Jewelry, Lakeview Village Barbershop, and Lakeview Village Spa & Salon. A farmer's market took place every Saturday morning from 8:30 a.m. – Noon, rain or shine. Capitalism was alive and well at Huron Waves Gift Shoppe and Fouled Anchor Liquors & Fine Wine, and one could even visit The Absent-minded Professor's Corner Market, which was a small, over-priced grocery store and pharmacy if you forgot something while shopping in downtown Hampstead. Lakeview Village hosted three popular festivals a year: The Lakeview Jazz Festival in October, "Lakeview of the Holiday Lights" in December, and the Lakeview 4th of July Freedom Week & Fireworks Show.

For Rachel and the other residents of Lakeview, the convenience that Lakeview Village offered was well worth 1) the price they paid to live in the neighborhood and 2) the exorbitant homeowners association fees. And she suspected that for these and many other reasons, Agatha and the Darwinger's crowd did not care for the uppity, pampered, and perfumed Lakeview crowd. And, truth be told, neither did she. Other than bending an elbow at The Buck or takeout from Lexi's, she had never become a member of the Village crowd. The purchase of her beach house in the gated community had been for one reason only: privacy.

The privilege of living with the rich could ignite passions and desires and provide the means and opportunity to act out fantasies usually reserved for erotica novels. But, evidently, the surroundings were not immune to other passions— like murder.

"What happened?" she asked Agatha.

The wise gas station matriarch leaned her head back as if taking the measure of Rachel, then took a sip of coffee. She tapped her fingers—more manicured and delicate than Rachel would have imagined—on her paper cup. "Fella by the name of Kaj Reynard was stabbed in the back last night. Came right out of the water and fell face down on the beach. Some book blogger...don't even know what the hell that is...was sitting her pretty little rich ass by her beach bonfire when Mister Kaj plopped down a few yards from the damned fire." She gave a smirk, one that said, 'I just let you in on a little secret.'

Book blogger. My God. That has to be Christine. She remembered the jogger disappearing behind the dune, but that was it. She had turned away from the window at that point. Rachel had seen a police car rolling down her street as she was heading out to Darwinger's but hadn't thought much about it. There was always one passing through. She would probably be interviewed soon. The police might even be knocking on her door right now. Last night, she hadn't seen or heard a thing. But she was a sound sleeper, always had been. Additionally, the local force was small and overworked. "How do you know this already?" she asked.

"'Cause Corey Ritter can't keep his mouth shut." Agatha pointed to the large uniformed man who was seated in one of the two back booths and gesturing with his hands at his booth companion, a massive seated figure whose beard reached the tabletop and whose bald dome seemed to reach the ceiling.

Rachel watched as Ritter paused his gesturing long enough to eat half a glazed donut in one bite. *Corey Ritter…right, the Hampstead Police Chief.* She hadn't heard much about him other than his on-again-off-again diet and his penchant for tall tales. He finished the other half of the donut and grabbed both of the men's large travel mugs. Then, he tried to squeeze out of the booth. She wondered who the giant across from Ritter was.

"That mountain is Obadiah Ben-David," Agatha said. "Saw you starin' his way." Then, she giggled. "Didn't think Corey Ritter was gonna make it out of that booth. Look at him headin' to the island for more coffee and fat pads."

Rachel watched as Ritter tried to weave through the crowd. She turned back to Agatha. "Who is Obadiah Ben-David?"

"Been a legendary private investigator around here for thirty-two years. He gonna be sixty later this summer. The Ben-Davids been in Hampstead for over a century—started out in the timber business and then shifted to construction. Asked if he wanted to continue his family's business, that bigun had the sack to say no. So, he up and started his own private detective business and been at it ever since. Does good work, that big ole boy."

From the booth, Obadiah Ben-David cocked his head toward them for a moment, observing Ritter, who had finally made it to the coffee bar. His eyes were intense and his face a wall of concrete—rough, solid, and unmoving.

"I feel like I'm on the set of *Iron Man*," Rachel said. "Beard's too long, though."

"Iron Man—he sure is," Agatha said in a tone that was a little too complimentary. "Oh, the *movie* Iron Man. Right. Funny you say that, 'cause he thinks he *is* Obadiah. Used to wear his hair in a combover, but since that movie came out, he started shaving his head. Used to trim his beard just like the character's, even wore a tuxedo to the gas station's annual New Year's Eve party. Had us all in sticks over that. Kept puttin' his arm around Baby Lloyd and saying, 'Tony, Tony.'" Her smile widened as if bringing a private memory into full focus. "In the past few years, though, he looks more like one of them Duck people. Keeps the shaved head, but I wish he'd trim that salt and pepper field underneath his chin."

"I imagine he'll be working the murder case."

"Oh, hell yeah. Already been hired by the Reynards. They called him up this mornin'." She put her hands on her hips and nodded at Ben-David's booth. "Probably gettin' all he can outta 'Crooked Corey' over there, and then he'll be on it like a bloodhound. He follows his instincts like seein' what direction his beard blows when them Huron breezes come in."

She thought about it for a beat. *Kaj Reynard wades in toward the beach with a knife stuck in his back. He trudges across the sand and dies feet from Christine Harper's bonfire.* The questions came faster than the caffeine kick she had received from the damned good coffee. *Who stabbed him? Why?*

She took a sip. *Whatever had happened, it had happened offshore in Lake Huron*, she thought. *A boat? Most likely. But who had been on the boat?* She tried to tone down the excitement she felt rising in her stomach, the kind she hadn't felt in years—when ideas form faster than she can process them. *Get a hold of yourself. Someone*

41

was just murdered. She took a breath. Still, the pressure was on from Topaz, Hightower, and those who resided in the golden tower of Doubleday management. She had not expected to come up with anything at Darwinger's when she had left her beach house in Lakeview this morning. She had almost not gotten out of the car. But now she had something, and she *had* to pursue it. For a split second, she felt like she was in the middle of an Adrienne Astra novel, ready to castrate the murderer of Kaj Reynard.

She turned toward Agatha. "I'd like to meet Mister Ben-David."

She grinned. "Sure, sugar." Then, playfully, her grin became a pair of pursed lips, and the large brown eyes were squinting again. "Whatchu up to?"

"Can't help it," Rachel said. "Guess the gossip bug bit me."

"I *like* an honest answer. Gotta way of sniffin' out bullshit—honed from years of callin' out Baby Lloyd when he's speakin' outta both sides of his mouth. I can tell I trust you already, honey. Now," she said, taking Rachel's arm, "let's get you introduced to our big celebrity. Might even scare off Police Chief Ritter, which would be good—sonofabitch's eatin' all my donuts."

If there was ever a vehicle that suited its owner's personality, then Rachel Roberts thought that Obadiah Ben-David's black Chevrolet Express van was it. She followed behind the giant of a man who had told her inside the gas station, unsolicited, that he was six-foot-eight and weighed two hundred and eighty pounds. She found her own five-two and one-hundred-and-ten-pound frame dwarfed by his stature as they walked side-by-side toward his van. There was not a cloud in the sky, but the wind had picked up, forcing her to take a hair tie out of her purse and put her shoulder-length auburn locks in a ponytail.

After introductions had been made inside and Agatha had been pulled away by Baby Lloyd to speak with Corey Ritter, Rachel had asked Ben-David for a word in private. *"I only talk new business in or near my van,"* he had said, and so they had both left a generous tip in the famed Darwinger's 'tip jar,' which was a black five-gallon bucket with faded red letters spelling Beecher Hardware on it, and headed outside.

Ben-David arrived at his van and leaned on the left-front corner of the hood. Rachel took up station behind the right-front, and the hood served as a makeshift table between them.

"So what's on your mind, ma'am?"

43

"I have a proposition for you, Mr. Ben-David."

"First," he said. "Is it okay with you if we use first names?"

"Sure," she said. "But you haven't heard my offer yet."

"Doesn't matter. I like to use first names. Gives me a sense of the person, and I find people are more honest when they use first names."

Could be the opening line of my new novel, she thought. "Agreed."

"So, let's hear it, Rachel," Ben-David said, giving a toothy grin.

She found his manner welcoming, and it was difficult to concentrate because of his beard blowing in the wind. This was a man who was on his home turf and comfortable. "Before we get to it, though, why couldn't we talk inside at your booth?"

"I don't know you, and when I don't know someone, I like to eliminate distractions. You can bet your heinie that I was talking business in there," he said, motioning to the gas station with his eyes, "but that's with people I know and somewhat trust."

"Fair enough," Rachel said. "Well, here's what I have in mind. You've got a new murder case that you're working on. I would like to tag along and learn from you, maybe even help out."

"Now, why do you want to do that?"

I have a book to write. I need ideas. I'm near my second deadline. My agent will kill me if I don't deliver. "I'm looking for a little adventure and figure this might be it for me."

The toothy grin turned into an abbreviated chuckle. "No way. I work alone." He shook his head. "What do you think this is, ride-with-a-cop for a day?"

"I'm willing to take the risk—"

"Nope," he said, cutting her off.

"I'll also pay you!"

The patronizing smile disappeared, and he rubbed his weathered hands through his beard. "What do you do for a living, Rachel?"

"I'm a coder, *Obadiah*." She frowned. "Sit behind a computer all day."

"And you need some excitement?"

"Maybe." She paused. "Or I'm looking for a career change. Perhaps both."

"You live around here?"

"I do."

"And you're thinking about becoming a professional investigator?"

"I thought it was private investigator."

"Not in Michigan. It's professional investigator."

"Oh," she said. "Well, if you think I'm moving in on your turf, I'm not. Just interested in learning."

"I've never seen you before, and I pride myself on knowing everyone around here."

"I keep to myself. Coder stereotype that's actually true."

He tilted his head and stared down at her, sunlight reflecting off the top of his head.

On the way to the booth to meet him, Agatha had told her that he had been married once, but that was a long time ago. His wife had died of cancer when they were both in their twenties, and he had never remarried. Rachel was not interested in him but wondered if, perhaps, he was interested in her or could use some company or was at least curious enough to let her accompany him for a few days and see how it went. Their time together could actually be over in a matter of hours if the murderer was caught. The police probably had the best picture anyway, and it was likely that she and Ben-David would be nowhere near any danger—especially when the murderer was apprehended. Hell, Ritter's deputies could be making the arrest right now. Inside, she had heard him yell across the room, *"The boys are blanketing Hampstead as we speak!"*

Ben-David said, "Did you know Kaj Reynard?"

She thought he might go here. Made sense. Had to clear her off the list of possible suspects before there was even a chance he would let her join him. She answered immediately. "No. I've never even heard his name."

His eyes didn't move from hers. "You sure?"

She continued to meet his stare. "Yes."

"Where were you last night?"

"Home."

"All night?"

"Yes. I got home from the grocery store at 4 pm and didn't leave the house again until I drove here this morning. I also have Blink security cameras that cover every side of my house. You are more than welcome to watch them."

"Got an alibi?"

Well, she had her phone conversation with Topaz, but she didn't want him to know about that or start prying. "I live alone," she answered.

"I can probe further into who you are, you know," Ben-David said.

"I know," she said. "Feel free to. But I had no idea there was a murder until I showed up here and Agatha told me."

"Why *did* you show up this morning?"

Shoot. Right back to throwing him off the trail again. She couldn't decide whether she was talking herself into these tough questions or if Obadiah was just good at probing. She decided on a half-truth. "I've been hearing about this place for years and finally decided to check it out."

He raised one of his thick eyebrows. "You picked a good day to do that."

"Is the crowd in there usually that large?"

"Occasionally."

She felt that she had proved to him that she was in no way connected to the murder of Kaj Reynard. But, of course, that was just based on her word. He could dig deeper if he wanted to. But, maybe he did suspect her, and, by taking her on, he would be keeping her close to observe her. *Fine by me*, she thought.

The fact that she lived a few houses down from where Kaj had stumbled upon the beach…she'd keep that to herself for right now. Time to push for an answer. "Well, now that we've got that out of the way. How about letting me watch you investigate?"

Except for the wind and the sound of gravel popping underneath the tires of an old SUV that had pulled up to get gas, it was silent as they eyed each other. She was ready to use some of the money Topaz negotiated into each book for research. If John Grisham could travel to Italy and gain ten pounds researching football for a book and get paid for it, then Doubleday could fork out research money for Riley Cannon.

Ben-David stroked his beard and finally said, "I don't know."

She sniffed a story or, at the very least, a character. Whatever she found would probably not be the story for *Dark After Midnight*, but it would get the creative gears turning—and, right now, that is what she needed. Nothing else was working. If Ben-David was Sherlock, then she could be Watson. "How about twenty thousand dollars?"

He stood up and then used the bottom of his t-shirt to wipe a bug off the van's hood. "You could hire your *own* professional investigator for that, buy a four-wheeler, and then take a vacation to Tahiti."

"I am hiring my own—*you*. And you're the best around here." She guessed that he was also the *only* one, too—didn't see the Hampstead economy supporting more than one professional investigator.

He leaned against his van, seeming to evaluate the compliment. "You usually throw that amount of money around?"

"Remember, I'm a coder, and I'm single."

He let out a derisive bark. "Yeah, you tech people."

"It's a living," she said.

"It's fake. Computers are stupid; you punch a button, and the machine automatically does somethin' without even askin'. That's dangerous. You and I wouldn't do just anything that someone told us to do."

"They don't always work so efficiently."

"They work efficiently enough for me to have no use for 'em." He frowned as if in defeat. "Gotta have this fella, though," he said, holding up his smartphone. "For business only."

His hairy paw was so large that the phone looked like a credit card in his hand. "And my offer?" she asked.

He slid the phone back into his pocket. "I'll do it for thirty." He crossed his arms. "I'm not slowin' down, but I am startin' to feel the hours more than I used to, and that amount of money gets me closer to retirement. Sounds selfish, but it's the truth."

"Twenty-five," she shot back. Compared to the money she had made on the first three Adrienne Astra books, this was pocket change. But, if she could get Ben-David to agree to an amount, and if the partnership helped her break out of her writing funk, it would make Topaz ecstatic. *"Love it! Dish out the green to the big oaf. Anything to get this story written. We're not going to give the money back to the publisher. Know why? Because you're going to get the fucking thing done!"*

He looked over at the hood, and then his eyes popped up, meeting hers. "Okay, twenty-five. But I'm going to have my lawyer draw up a short agreement. Ninety-nine percent of my work is pure boredom, but the one percent is sheer terror. There's always the unknown, and with this being the first murder case in fourteen years, well, I'm taking every precaution." With that, he pulled up his shirt and patted a Glock 22 that was in a holster on his belt. "As you saw in Darwinger's, everybody's a little spooked, and everybody's a little excited." He paused. "How do I put this? You seem like a straightforward person to me, but I don't need any lawsuit if we run into trouble and you end up injured or worse. I want you to know what you're signing up for." He started walking toward her.

48

"That being said, I'll do everything I can to keep you out of danger, but there are no guarantees."

"I understand," she said, feeling butterflies circle in her stomach.

"You got a concealed pistol license?"

Actually, she did. Publicly, Topaz Kennedy was one of the loudest gun control advocates in New York City—every 5th tweet seemed to be *"Round 'em up!"* This, of course, was in line with the views of her fellow agents. However, *privately*, she never went anywhere without her gold-plated Saturday night special in her purse. *"I know what I say publicly, mega-author, but you have your secrets, and I have mine—and if you burn me, then I'll deny all of it,"* she had said. *"Arm yourself, darling. You can't be too sure about people. Anyone tries any funny business with me, and I'll blow them to the moon with this pocket rocket. Now, the way we navigate this professionally is that if the public ever finds out who you are, then we'll hire private security to guard you. Being pro-security is still acceptable in our circles, and, hell, if the public ever knew how many anti-gun authors had sniper nests on their properties, they'd flip out. It's not that your fellow writers are pro-gun; it's just that they're so filthy rich, they think the rules don't apply to them. Dear God, now I may be talking about myself. Ah well, mucho moolah still trumps ideology. You know what I mean, right, one-percenter?"* Heeding her power agent's surreptitious counsel, she had contacted the Michigan State Police and had taken the necessary steps to get a concealed pistol license. Her weapon of choice was a Sig Sauer P365, which had been recommended to her by a manager at Cabela's. When she had reported this all to Topaz, Topaz had replied, *"Now you're just like your main character, my sweet. Lock and load."*

"Rachel?" Ben-David said.

She returned from her thoughts and said, "Yes, I do have a license."

Ben-David raised his eyebrows. "What do you carry?"

"Sig Sauer P365."

He nodded. "I approve. You packin' right now?"

She opened her purse and showed him the Sig.

"I'll have it noted in the contract that I'm aware of it."

"What for? I'm allowed to have it on me no matter what."

"Just protection for you. In case we step into some nastiness, and you've got to use that thing, I want it clear that I knew you had the weapon on you and that I assume my share of the risk. Fair enough?"

"I appreciate it." Her hands were shaking as she zipped her purse back up.

"You okay?"

"A bit nervous."

"Well, the chances of us running into the murderer are pretty slim, I think."

"Why?"

"Inside, Ritter told me that they didn't have much. Can't say that I'm surprised. Kaj Reynard came in from the water, and nobody up and down the beach saw anything. Not even Christine Harper, who had been sitting at her beach bonfire for over an hour. I also heard that there are no prints on the murder weapon. I doubt that they'll get anything off of Reynard's clothes either."

"What kind of knife was it?" Rachel asked.

"Cuisinart. Stainless-steel 8-inch chef's knife with an ergonomically designed handle. Thought we might get some prints or at least a partial print."

"But, Kaj came out of the water, right?"

"Actually, the odds of fingerprints surviving submersion is quite high. The forensics lead, Justine Grazer, and I grab dinner now and then, and she has told me that the probability of a strong latent print on most metals is somewhere around 70% even after a few *months* of submersion. Now, if the knife wasn't in the water and the murderer wasn't wearing any gloves or hadn't wiped the handle clean, then maybe we'd be in business. He or she would have been gripping the knife awfully tight to plunge it into Kaj's back. And that amount of force is going to produce tons of friction between the knife handle and his or her fingertips, causing a lot of potential for transfer. And, if it hadn't been submerged in the water, then there are amino acid tests that can be performed to determine the sex of the murderer."

He looked past her, seeming to study the deep blue water of Lake Huron. "But, no, we don't have any prints. I think our murderer had gloves on, which means this stabbing was more than likely planned." His eyes returned to her. "Tough case to solve. And it's also going to be a pain in the ass because word will continue to spread. When people get wind that you're hanging around with me, be ready to get asked a shit-ton of questions by the locals and summer visitors wherever you go. A murder in a quiet little beach town like ours brings out the amateur detective in a lot of people. Seen it before. There'll be suspicious looks given by everyone from the local bookstore owner to the cashiers in Walmart. I've already spoken with the mayor. Don't want a panic. How long have you lived in Hampstead?"

"A little over ten years."

"Then you know that we live and die by our summer population. Last thing we need is a bunch of people canceling their reservations at the state park or the other RV parks, campgrounds, and beach-side cabins for rent. Pressure's on. Ritter is feeling it too. We've got to find who did this, and fast."

As she listened to him speak, she decided that whatever Obadiah Ben-David felt about the world, one thing was certain: He was loyal to Hampstead. "Where does that leave us? You basically admitted that we don't have much of a chance. Not much for the hope business, I assume."

"Hope business? What in the hell is that anyway? It's business and always only business."

"God, don't tell his parents that."

"Already did, but I'm going to do my best regardless."

She nodded. It wasn't the answer she wanted, but it was a truthful answer.

"It'll be easier if we travel in my vehicle." He patted the hood with a note of affection. "Got all my equipment in here but also some creature comforts, so you'll be relaxed while we travel around on the job. You okay with that?"

"Sure. What about my car?"

"You can leave it here. I trust Baby Lloyd and Agatha. I'll tell them to keep an eye on it, especially if we're working late. See that two-story house across the road?"

She looked where he was pointing and saw a cabin nestled between two patches of pines.

"That's their place—a multi-generational household. Baby Lloyd's dad and mom live downstairs, and he and Agatha live upstairs. The Darwinger family has always operated like that; younger generation takes care of the older one. When you get to the downstairs, you're king and queen of the house but also one step closer to the coffin. Anyway, if you feel safer leaving your car in their driveway, I can arrange it. Been friends with the family forever."

"What kind of hours do you think we'll be keeping?"

"Who knows? Depends on the leads we get. Today and tomorrow will be straightforward because those are the interview days. Probably wrap up before dark. After that, I can't predict. We'll have to analyze the information we gather from the interviews and see where it points, if anywhere." He itched the part of his beard directly beneath his right ear. "Every job is different."

He then went on to tell her of the job he was on last night. It was 3 a.m. when he had returned from the surveillance of a local attorney who was sleeping with a Hampstead High School gym teacher, who, naturally, was not the attorney's wife. He'd been hired by the attorney's wife two weeks ago and, until last night, had had a helluva time coming up with any evidence of the affair. But, finally, the lawyer, who claimed to be "everyone's trusted friend" on an ugly billboard outside of town, had crept out of his house at 1 a.m. and gotten into the gym teacher's van three blocks down the street. An hour later, hanging in a harness attached to a telephone pole thirty feet above the ground, Ben-David had snapped photographs of the two having sex in an open field on the twenty acres of hunting property that the lawyer owned. Ben-David had already e-mailed the photos to the wife, and he was sure that she'd already confronted her husband and leveraged the d-word. Ben-David told Rachel that he didn't like thinking about the aftermath that resulted because of his work. By his count, he'd already expedited around ninety divorces over his career. At this, he explained that a professional investigator has to take the emotion out of it. One is hired to do a job, not show empathy. The moment one gets caught up in caring is the moment that one needs to find another line of work.

Her mental steno pad was filling up quickly—partly because she was interested in the psychology of being a professional investigator and partly because she was trying to find the inspiration for the plot of her novel that was due soon. Then, Ben-David quoted a line from one of her favorite films: *Rear Window*. *"What people ought to do is get outside their own house and look in for a change."* He explained that he tried to balance this with Harry Caul's philosophy from *The Conversation*, namely, that whatever surveillance work he did, it had nothing to do with him. He was simply doing the job he was hired to do. The aftermath of his work was out of his control, and he should try not to think about it. In principle, it sounded good, but it was another thing to hear about a husband getting arrested for domestic violence because he had gone off the deep end after his wife had shown him incriminating pictures or played him a recording that implicated him in an affair. And to know that this had happened as a result of Ben-David delivering the devastating evidence to the wife still created a sense of unease in the 59-year-old P.I. This was another reason why he had stopped purchasing *The Hampstead Record* years before and had ceased surfing Hampstead.com. He was no longer interested in the results of his work. Instead, he focused on his craft. This segued into a mini-lecture to her, as if she was a student of his. *"Do a quality job of investigating, submit your findings, and forget about the rest because it has nothing to do with you. Move on to the next case and improve. It's all about the work and not about the human beings involved. Speaking of that, don't ever get involved with a client or become personally attached to anyone you're investigating. This job is all about professionalism. So, be professional. We're not to blame for some dead-beat husband sticking his dick somewhere it shouldn't be. When they get caught, they all want to blame the investigator—take the heat off them and transfer it to someone else. Lawsuit, counter lawsuit, counter-counter lawsuit. They're all the same. Keep your shit squared away, be quick but don't rush, get in, get out, and move on. I used to get flack when I started out, but once I removed myself from my cases emotionally, I don't get messed with anymore. Stick with it, and you'll be there one day."*

She had given a quiet clap, and then Ben-David had provided her with a joke to reinforce the concept of detaching from clients. *"There's a veteran psychologist and a rookie psychologist that work across the hallway from each other. Every day, the two men show up to work looking refreshed, carrying their travel cups of coffee and briefcases. However, at the end of each day, the young psychologist looks worn out and disheveled while the veteran psychologist looks the same as he did in the morning and whistles a happy tune on his way out to the car. Finally, after almost a year of working together, the young man can't take it anymore and asks the veteran, 'How can you look so rested and calm and peaceful after an entire day of listening to disturbing confessions and stories of personal trauma?' At this, the old psychologist puts a reassuring hand on the rookie's shoulder and gives a slight grin. Then he says, 'Oh, I don't listen anymore.'"*

So much for getting to work fast. Well, he said he was better at it now than he was when he started, but there was still something about peering into other people's lives and collecting evidence to be used by one party to smack down the other with that made him uneasy.

She nodded as if she understood, which, in some way, she did. Her job as a novelist was to observe human behavior and report it in an entertaining way.

He acknowledged her nod, and it snapped him back into the present. "Sorry about that. The teacher in me eases forward on center stage every now and again even though I try to keep him in the shadows." He stared down at the ground and dragged his left boot across the gravel. "Never had any kids to pass on what I know." He looked back at her. "Promise I won't bore you with any more of that stuff unless you ask."

"I didn't mind it," Rachel said, and she watched him for any sign of relief. She had heard the pain in his voice and guessed that he was embarrassed for letting some private feelings slip out. His body, especially his face, didn't move a millimeter.

"I'll pop over to my lawyer's office, get the contract hammered out, and then grab takeout for us from my usual spot, The Sunrise Saloon. I'm buyin'. You ever dined there?"

Her body language must have supplied the answer because before she could answer, he said, "Pretty good eats. Mostly pub fare, but they're known for their brunch. Just on the other side of Beecher Hardware."

He had been right. She had never been there or to the hardware store before. There was a maintenance man named Don Garvin who serviced most of the homes in Lakeview, including hers. He made weekly rounds, checking the exterior of each home, and monthly rounds, checking the interiors. After his inspection, he would e-mail her a spreadsheet with any maintenance recommendations, costs, and his fee for taking care of everything. For as long as she had lived in Lakeview, she had simply paid his invoice and never given it another thought. His work was good, and it was nice having him around. "Brunch sounds delicious," she said.

"Basic brunch takeout combo is an omelet, toast, hash browns, pancakes, and coffee. That work for you?"

"Not a picky eater. The combo it is."

He smiled. "Good. I like uncomplicated orders. How about I meet you back here in two hours? Then, we'll start the interview circuit. Before I arrived this morning, I spoke with Kaj Reynard's family. Already got a list of a few people to check out."

"What should I do in the meantime?"

"Whatever you want." He looked over at the gas station, then back at her. "You could head back in there and mingle. The people are friendly. Always a chance that you'll hear something we could use. I got everything I'm going to get out of Ritter, but I'll check in with Amos later."

"Who's Amos?"

"Deputy Amos Meyer. My best friend, and, in my opinion, the only reason that Corey Ritter hasn't been fired numerous times."

Then, Ben-David, against his promise made moments before, went on another tangent, saying that he was a film buff who occasionally still used lines and themes from the big screen to guide his life, which explained the *Rear Window* quote earlier. He'd seen many films but owned few. In fact, he beamed with what Rachel thought was silly pride at the fact that his film registry included three and only three films. *The Searchers*: He thought he was Uncle Ethan reincarnated. *Rocky III*: Ben-David believed that he and Amos Meyer, one of a handful of African-Americans that lived in Hampstead, were Rocky and Apollo—forever training together on the beach. *Iron Man*: He admitted that he had never read the comics but had fallen prey to popular culture and believed that he literally *was* Obadiah Stane after watching the film in the Hampstead Family Theater downtown. He even wrote a letter to Jeff Bridges but never heard back.

She brought the conversation back on-topic. "Okay, I'll head inside. See you when you return."

"Sorry. Did it again, didn't I?"

"Don't give it another thought. We're going to be spending a lot of time together, and I want to find out everything I can about being a professional investigator. After all, I'm paying you, right?"

"Twenty-five thousand big ones."

"You use Hampstead Bank?"

"Have for over forty years."

"Good," she said as she got out her checkbook and started writing on a blank check.

He walked toward her.

She finished and ripped off the check. "Here, deposit this at the bank before you visit your lawyer. That way, you'll know my money is good."

He took the slip, folded it, and put it in the front-right pocket of his jeans. They exchanged cell phone numbers, and he said, "Okay, I'll see you back here."

As she watched his van pull away, she felt the dreary clouds of uncertainty that had been hanging over her since December start to disappear. Her morose disposition was changing to one of motivation and energy, fueled by curiosity and focus. Before she went back inside to hit the booths with the locals, she needed to write down her thoughts. She strode toward her car, dust billowing into the air with each step across the gravel parking lot. On the passenger seat was her notebook, and she intended to make good use of it.

Her adventure had started. But as she reached the car, her excitement became tempered by the memory of Obadiah's assessment. There wasn't much to go on. In fact, the murderer or murderers were probably long gone by now. There would be some initial excitement around town, but as the trail got colder and colder, life would return to normal. She'd be out twenty-five grand and probably have made no more progress on her novel.

She stopped next to the passenger door and looked down at her black Moleskine notebook on the brown leather seat—a chocolate square on a molasses cookie. Most likely, she'd be back home in a day.

"Jesus. Don't start doubting yourself," she said, opening the door.

Little did she know that her doubts would vanish in the next few hours when they interviewed their first suspect.

7

"Ready?" Obadiah Ben-David asked as they approached the heavy wooden doors of The Buccaneer Pub.

Rachel Roberts wasn't sure. The early morning confidence and hint of excitement had dulled, and she had returned to the game of second-guessing herself. *What if I ask a stupid question and Ben-David wants to call the whole thing off after the first interview? What if the case goes nowhere and I don't become inspired to write my novel?*

"Absolutely," she replied.

"That's what I like to hear," Ben-David said, not looking at her and reaching for one of the door's stainless-steel handles.

She had already picked up on his mannerism of speaking to people without looking at them—maybe every third exchange, she would get a glance. In one sense, it was impersonal behavior; in another sense, his way of communication exuded calmness, like everything was happening the way it should. She thought that the character trait could be used to make one of her minor characters stand out a little more in her upcoming novel.

Maybe this was working.

Ben-David grasped the handle.

Still time to call it off, girl. What if you come face to face with a murderer, and that murderer wants to harm you? Can you handle yourself? She looked at the gigantic hulk that was Ben-David. *He could handle a bloodthirsty murderer, right?*

Just before he opened the door, she heard a murmur of voices, clinking glasses and plates, and caught a whiff of fried food—fish, onion rings, fries, something delicious—through the open window to the left. *No turning back now*, she thought.

The Buccaneer Pub was the final outpost in the Lakeview Village beachfront dining lineup. Aged with creaky floorboards, small booths, weathered stools at the bar, and sparse lanterns hung on the wall that kept the dining area in perpetual shadow, "The Buck" and its owners did not pretend that the pub was anything other than a place for its patrons to unwind with family or friends, eat tasty pub food, and drink refreshing brews. The mixed crowd of wealthy well-dressed summer residents and local blue-collar types gave the restaurant a sort of cross-section-of-American-life vibe. The closest restaurant to the Village's entrance was the flagship of the establishment: Sunrise Grill, which was an expensive steakhouse with crafted and comfortable cuisine and happy hour that ran every day from 3 to 6. Next door was Lexi's Catch, which boasted the best-tasting seafood on the eastern coast of Michigan and had both indoor and outdoor dining. All three did good business, but "The Buck" remained the heart and soul of Lakeview Village, and Ben-David had told Rachel that it was the *only* place in Lakeview Village that he would step foot inside. The exception being if business demanded that he enter one of the other uppity holes as he called them.

Rachel felt both comfort and unease as she and Ben-David walked in through the front door at just after five in the afternoon. She was comfortable because of her familiarity with The Buck—*"A Long John Silver's for adults,"* she had answered Ben-David when he had asked her what she thought about the place earlier. He had laughed, saying he still ate at the Long John's north of Hampstead at least once a week. He also admitted that he still read *Treasure Island* every summer and then had pulled a tattered copy out of his glovebox. In addition to her other anxieties about starting the case, she also felt butterflies in her stomach because Ben-David would draw some attention when they got a table—hard to avoid when you're almost seven feet tall—and that meant that *she* would draw some attention by accompanying him. Some of her fellow beachfront estate owners were nosey, and so far, she had been able to live in Lakeview flying under the radar. They had tried to snoop, but when they had found out that she was an introverted coder who spent most of her day behind a screen and that she did not have many visitors, they had moved on to someone else. Christine Harper had told her that the word down the beach was that Rachel Roberts was boring, not social, and not worth the effort of getting to know. Christine had also said that most of the well-off neighbors were intimidated by someone who knew a lot about computers, thinking that techies like that had an unfair advantage over them and that *they* were vulnerable to having their lives pried into by Rachel. Best to leave the coder to her code writing—and not cross her. Secrets about people were fun to learn and maybe keep, but the summer gossip game stopped being exciting when someone found out *your* secrets. But, when a person in the prime of his life emerges from the water and dies on the Lakeview beach—Christine's at that—with a knife stuck in his back, then everyone in the posh subdivision becomes paranoid about their secrets getting revealed because of the inevitable investigation. Rachel wondered how her book-blogging friend was holding up. No doubt, they would be questioning her in the next few days, and she could imagine Christine's reaction when she saw her computer nerd of a friend tagging along with the local mountain-of-a-man investigator. 'Shocked' was her guess. In any event, Rachel just wanted to give her a hug. She couldn't imagine what her own reaction would have been if Kaj Reynard had fallen to the beach in front of her.

The paperwork had taken longer than expected, but the brunch had been worth the wait, and the extra time had given Ben-David the opportunity to tell

Rachel about Kaj Reynard's wandering eye with the ladies. His parents had admitted that their son had discovered the joy of sex early in high school when they had opened his bedroom door with a plate of cookies and two mugs of hot chocolate, thinking that he and his next-door neighbor classmate Ashley were having a study session for freshman science, and discovered that a different science was being studied. After a series of failed sit-downs with Kaj about how what was in his underwear was overpowering the logic in his brain, they decided to let go and let their son roam. Girlfriends had come and gone—their son had always been respectful, they had claimed—and instead of giving more lectures, they had invested in condoms. This had led to a discussion about his most recent girlfriend, Ingrid Bara, who was a hostess at "The Buck" and the reason that Rachel and Ben-David were here. The veteran investigator's philosophy was, in the absence of any substantial leads, to start with the romantic attachments.

The only tension in their afternoon discussion of the mating habits of Kaj Reynard had come when she told Ben-David that they could drive separately to Lakeview because she lived there. He had almost come unglued at that point, wondering why she hadn't told him that she lived a few houses down from where Kaj had come ashore. She had explained that she had nothing to hide and assumed it would come up eventually. His anger had simmered down after conducting another interview with her about anything else he might need to know. They both agreed that her beach house's location would be a liability— more attention would come her way—but also an opportunity: She could take a stroll down the beach and stop by Christine's to talk with her and also watch her neighbors from her second-story, lake-view room. Every walk down the beach would no doubt bring suspicious looks along with new theories about who could have killed Kaj Reynard. And, since Lakeview was a gated community, it would be a somewhat controlled atmosphere to observe. Ben-David had said to expect unusual boat traffic offshore as every fisherman, sailor, and pleasure boater in Hampstead would be taking a pass by the Lakeview beachfront.

The chatter inside the restaurant was a pleasant ambient noise, a packed house of people quietly sharing stories, woes, achievements, or the well-needed joke to either cut the tension from a full day of work under the hot sun or keep the spirits flowing from a day of yachting or sunbathing on the golden sands of Lake Huron's beaches. There was standing room only at the bar that ran the length of the large room's left wall, and the high-top tables were mostly full of the under-thirty crowd. A half-wall separated the bar area from the rest of the room as if to announce the demarcation line of civilized dining around the dark round tables in the main room and controlled chaos in the bar. Fishing nets and small red and green buoys were affixed to the wall on the right, and a handful of coveted booths ran along the floor-to-ceiling windows that allowed an unobstructed view of the darkening blue shades of Lake Huron.

Rachel could make out a Bob Marley tune coming from the bar area as they approached a podium that looked like it had been built by a carpenter who had eyeballed the cut of each wooden board and then nailed them to the two-by-four frame, leaving a scattering of creases between the boards. The wood had been painted a battleship gray color, and the top of the podium was an out-of-place wrought iron artistic maze of lines and seafaring knots. At present, there was no one behind the greeting stand.

"There's still one corner booth open," Ben-David said. "I'll try to get us seated there so we can question her in private."

Rachel nodded and looked across the room, seeing the half-moon booth furnished with blood-red cushions that Obadiah was referring to. The adjoining booth was filled with a family of four, all zoned into their cell phones and not talking, and the nearest table on the other side of the booth was at least ten feet away and had a group of three couples sharing pitchers of beer and laughing. Christine Harper was still on her mind, and a memory of them sitting at the corner booth that Ben-David would try to get them seated at popped into her head. It was of Christine recommending that Rachel should really try out the three novels by Riley Cannon, *"They're can't miss, girly-girl!"* Rachel had grinned and told her that she would if she had time. *"Ugh, you coders. Get your buns down to your beach and get some use out of it. I swear you'll love her main character. For Chrissakes, I want to be Adrienne Astra."*

The memory was interrupted by a female hostess who materialized out of the bar crowd and took up her post behind the podium. She wore the standard Buck uniform of black wedges, black slacks, black belt, and black blouse with a name tag that was a mock gold coin. The name 'Ingrid' was engraved in black lettering on this particular coin.

She seemed to recognize Ben-David immediately. "I thought I'd see you here today," she said.

Ben-David placed his huge hands on the podium. "Pretty good assumption," he said, studying her face. "We'd like the corner booth. Can someone cover for you while you join us for a quick chat?"

Ingrid's blue eyes elevatored down to meet Rachel's. "Who's she?"

"She's assisting me on this case—and that's all you need to know."

Rachel extended her hand. "Rachel Roberts."

Ingrid paused and then shook the hand. "I've seen you in here before."

"I live just up the beach."

After seeing a picture of Kaj Reynard from Ben-David earlier—effortlessly handsome with chiseled facial features, black hair, and green eyes, tall, Ben-David said he was six-three and in-shape, which she could tell by the fit of his clothes, Rachel thought that he would be the perfect aesthetic complement to Ingrid. A few inches taller than Rachel, she had brown hair pulled back with a few barrettes, exposing a tanned face with straight, gleaming white teeth and a soft shade of red lipstick that was just enough to highlight her beauty without drawing too much attention to her mouth. Her slim figure was similar to Rachel's. Whether or not the relationship had had any substance to it, they'd have to find out.

"I'll seat you and then ask my manager," Ingrid said.

Five minutes later, they were all seated in the corner booth with waters in front of them. Rachel squeezed her lemon over her glass and then stirred it with the knife from her place setting. Laughter rose from the couples' table as another joke found its mark, and a server had just arrived to deliver the food to the family in the booth next to them. The server said, "Okay, steak and fries?" There was no reply as the mom and dad continued to scroll through their social media feeds, and the children nervously pushed buttons while playing games. After hearing the server a second time, the father held up a finger, not in acknowledgment that the steak and fries were his but rather as a signal for the server to pause for a second.

Outside, whitecaps had formed on the lake, and the windsock attached to the top of a metal pole in the corner of The Buck's back deck was streaming parallel to the ground.

Ingrid took a sip of water and said, "The Huron breezes have arrived."

This was the second person in one day who had mentioned the Huron breezes. Of course, she knew there was wind that came in off the lake—she'd listened to her wind chimes rattle this morning—but this phrase seemed to mean something beyond what she had experienced. "What does that phrase mean?" she asked.

"You heard it before?" Ben-David said.

"This morning. Agatha said the same thing at Darwinger's. What am I missing here?"

Ben-David looked at Ingrid and gave a slight bow along with motioning toward her with an open palm that said, *"Might as well get this out of the way before we question you about Kaj Reynard. Please, enlighten us."*

Ingrid cleared her throat and began. "First of all, the breezes I'm talking about are not the usual lake breezes you get over the summer where the land temperature becomes warmer than the water." She straightened her fingers and then moved her right hand in a wave motion over the booth's table toward her left hand; at the same time, she raised her left hand slowly, shaking her fingers while doing so.

"The warm air over the land rises and is replaced by the cooler air that is just above the lake surface, creating an onshore breeze, which means that the wind blows from the sea toward the land. Because of this, people flock to the Huron beaches to escape the inland heat, which can bake you when it gets over ninety. These breezes are around ten miles per hour and usually form a couple of hours after sunrise and then fade away by early evening. The larger the difference between the land and water temperature, the more likely it is for a lake breeze to form. Also, if the wind speed is slow, then a breeze is more likely to form. As I'll explain in a minute, most of our summer winds are westerly, but they aren't that strong, which allows the wind to shift near the beach, and the breeze becomes easterly. Now, when the westerly or offshore winds are too strong, then lake breezes won't form until the speed drops. With me so far?"

"Yes," Rachel said. *There are two kinds of people in the world*, Rachel thought—*those who speak while using body language and those who don't.* Ingrid Bara looked like someone who had an encyclopedia of hand gestures.

Ben-David nodded in something that seemed stronger than acknowledgment—more like approval.

"Wind direction is reported by the direction from which it originates and usually using cardinal direction or degrees. For example, a northerly wind blows from the north to the south and would have a direction referred to as either zero degrees or three hundred and sixty degrees. Similarly, a wind blowing from the west would have a wind direction referred to as two hundred and seventy degrees. In terms of wind speed, over eighty percent of the summer months have winds that are between zero and eight miles per hour. They're nothing, which allows the lake breezes to form and means that a very small percentage of days have winds that are between eight and twenty-five miles per hour—say, only around fifteen percent. But winds that are twenty-five miles per hour are extremely rare because that number is basically your wind gust high for Lake Huron. Hence, there are seldom any days over June, July, and August that reach that force. Now, in November, December, January, and February, it's a whole different ballgame; in those months, you've got around a fifty percent chance of having a day with eight to twenty-five mile per hour winds. No surprise there because that's when we have all of our big storms."

"I don't mean to call into question what you've said so far, but how do you know all of this?" Rachel asked. She thought it was a fair question and knew that after Ingrid brought her up to speed on what was meant by the phrase 'Huron breezes' that Obadiah would take over the questioning as they moved into the murder investigation. At least, she hoped he would. *Enough of the science lesson already.* But, then, as if J. Rudolph Hightower's mighty red editing pen streaked across the manuscript of her last thought, she withdrew the complaint. Research was key for any novel—and a pain in the ass—and perhaps Ingrid had just given her material for a short scene. She could have also given Rachel another characteristic to deepen a character: always going into excruciating detail when asked about something he or she knows.

"No worries," Ingrid said. "My dad was a lifelong fisherman. Needed to know the winds and day and water temperatures every day—taught me more than I ever wanted to know." She took another sip of water. "And not just recreational fishing. He worked at the Hawthorne Fish House for thirty years before retiring."

"So, he worked for Gary Hawthorne," Ben-David stated.

"He did."

"Not a day goes by that I don't miss him. Showed me all the good spots before he passed away."

Ingrid nodded in understanding. "Still remember the day that my dad came home and broke the news to me. Gary was like a father to him."

They were all silent for a moment. Rachel knew that the Hawthorne Fish House was still in business because she picked up fresh fish there every Monday. Beyond that, she knew nothing of the business's past.

Ingrid resumed. "So, if you average the data, the winds are usually westerly at nine miles per hour for the summer months, and the water temperature average is high sixties during the day and low sixties during the night, although we've had highs around ninety and lows in the thirties before. All that being said, every once in a while, you get what my dad and others around here call the Huron breezes, which are summer winds that behave like it's the middle of winter and last for a few days in a row or even a week. Fifteen-mile-per-hour sustained winds with gusts at twenty-five that not only turn the lake into a frenzy but also heat the blood and stir people's emotions to the point where they take risks and do things they wouldn't normally do. I don't know about either of you, but I don't remember jack from my high school education. It was pretty pathetic. But." She leaned forward on her elbows. "The one thing I do remember was that I *hated* Shakespeare. And I mean *everything* about the man and his plays. Which is why it is ironic that one of the only things I remember from those misspent days of youth is that my senior English teacher told my class that Shakespeare was one of the first writers to link bad weather to behavior and use it as a plot device. I mean, in like *Macbeth*, day was night, and night was day, and there were horses eating each other, apex predator birds being hunted by their prey, and—" she paused, looking away from them, "—good people committing murder."

Never did Rachel want to join the conversation more. Reading, watching, and acting Shakespeare was where her writing career had started. Harold Bloom's *Shakespeare: The Invention of the Human* had convinced her that Shakespeare was the world's first psychologist and that Freud's entire body of work was just a coda to the bard's. But, she felt she could not join the conversation as it would expose her taste and thirst for both literature and literary discussion. No coder she had ever studied when working on establishing her current persona had ever shown affection for Shakespeare's works. In fact, Silicon Valley was doing a pretty solid job of drawing attention away from the literary aesthetic in favor of promoting the surveillance of other people's lives with the touch of a button or tap of a screen on a myriad of their high-tech machines. No, she would look disinterested instead. *Wait, there was one question she could, and should, ask.* "So, you think that when the Huron breezes come in, some people in Hampstead fall into a trance and start to act differently, perhaps even achieving regrettable destinies?"

Ingrid gave an embarrassed grin. "Possibly. The winds started yesterday and aren't forecasted to stop for another three days. Look around here," she said, motioning her hand across the room. "This place is always busy, but not like this. The only reason you got this booth was because it was vacated right before you arrived, and those who entered before you headed straight for the bar."

"So, we've got a few days of the Huron breezes in store?" Rachel asked, committing what she'd just learned to memory. The topic had become more than just accumulating research or using Ingrid's desire to tell everything she knew about something as a character trait. The bard's plot device had officially re-emerged—people doing things they wouldn't normally do because of the weather—and she might use it in her new novel. Then, another forgotten writerly piece of advice appeared: When you've got writer's block in a scene, just change the weather. She could feel the gears in her creative engine start to turn faster, faster than they had in years.

Ingrid's grin disappeared. "Just sayin'. And if we get an old-fashioned mid-western tornado along with it, then stand the hell by."

At that moment, a gust of wind blew over a table on the outdoor patio, and the three watched as a server opened the sliding glass door, exited, and fought against the wind to pull the table back up. Another gust hit, and two more tables went over. This time, the manager braved the elements and helped the server tip all of the tables on their sides and shove them against the railing. The server tripped on a corner of one of the tables, and down he went.

68

"Oh!" yelled the bar-goers.

With a helping hand from the manager, the server got to his feet, and they stacked the chairs on top of each other and then eased the stack on its side. They returned to applause from the bar area, and the music was cranked up. Drinks and conversation continued to flow—now with more intensity.

Rachel sensed that Ben-David would use the high winds as a natural segue. She would if she was writing a novel.

He did.

"Think the Huron breezes had anything to do with the death of Kaj Reynard?" he asked.

"I don't think the breezes killed him, but someone obviously did," she said.

"Where were you last night?"

She liked Ben-David's approach. Straight to the point. In fact, now that she thought about it, she wondered if there was a place for a P.I. character in *Dark After Midnight*. *Interesting. I could take it in that direction. No, Topaz would veto the idea: "There's only one person doing any investigating in your novels, love, and that's Adrienne Astra investigating how to eliminate the villains."*

"I closed last night. Came on at eight, and we shut down at two. I didn't leave until two-thirty." She pointed to the cameras mounted on the ceiling. "You can check our digital recordings to verify where I was and also check with my manager."

"I will," Ben-David said. "But it sounds like you've got a credible alibi." He made some notes on a pad of paper and then started in again. "Kaj's parents said you two dated for over three years, were even engaged at one point."

"That's right."

"His philandering ruin it?"

She looked away, fixing her eyes on the lake once more.

Rachel made eyes with Ben-David for a second and then followed Ingrid's gaze out the window.

A couple was trudging up the beach with their windbreakers over their heads, no doubt trying to keep the hail of sand grains from needling them as they tried to reach the inland safety of the parking lot. The pure sand was pretty to look at in contrast to the deep greens of beach grass contrasted with the blue water and red beach fencing that marked the two boundaries of The Buck's beachfront. However, with winds like today, the innocent-looking strip of sand became nature's weapon that stung bare legs and blinded eyes.

"In a way," Ingrid said.

"What's that mean?"

"It means that for most of our time together, he kept it in his pants—outside of his time with me. But then he met someone. Blew up our engagement and ended our relationship."

"When did it end?"

"Two summers ago."

"Did you ever find out who the 'someone' was who he cheated on you with? Someone local?"

Her eyes stared straight ahead as if drilling two pin-sized holes through Ben-David's skull.

Rachel recognized 'the stare.' It was one reserved for having to remember the person who had gotten between you and your significant other. She was impressed with Ingrid Bara's version—cold, menacing, and yet, controlled. *Look at Bara going all Adrienne Astra on Ben-David.*

"That would be Daria Knight."

This answer immediately changed the stakes of the investigation. She knew it, and Ben-David leaned back and exhaled, giving her the impression that he knew it too.

achel Roberts watched as Ingrid Bara let her words sink in and take up vacancy in Obadiah Ben-David's brain. His glass of ice water almost disappeared in his large paw of a hand as he tipped it back and drank for the first time since the drinks had arrived. When the server had offered him a straw, he politely declined, mentioning that he only used straws when he picked up fast food.

After he put the glass back on the table and wiped the water that had spilled onto his beard with the sleeve of his shirt, Ingrid said, "So, you know the Knights?"

"Never met one of them, but, yeah, I've heard of them," he said.

So had Rachel. Christine had filled her in on Rachel's back deck a few summers ago. Daria Athena Knight was the daughter of billionaire couple Saul and Pamela Knight, who lived at Lakeview's southernmost beachfront property in what was jokingly, yet enviably, referred to as The Knight Compound. Rachel had witnessed its construction over a three-year period as it was about twenty lots down from her beachfront home and marked the turn-around point whenever she took a walk on the beach at night. There was a 13,000-square-foot main house, heated pool, jacuzzi, tennis court, basketball court, and a 4,000-square-foot guest house with its own pool and jacuzzi. Next to the basketball court was a helicopter pad for their big Sikorsky, which was named *Knight Sky*. Because of their love of watersports and cruising the Great Lakes, they had paid an ungodly sum to have their own L-shaped dock put in to house their three watercraft: a two-hundred-foot mega-yacht named *Knight Moves*, a fifty-foot cabin cruiser named *Knight Dive*, and a twenty-five-foot speedboat named *Knight Jet*.

Daria was in her early thirties, about ten years younger than Ingrid, Rachel guessed, and her older brother Brendan was mid-thirties, around the same age as Kaj Reynard. Like the Ewing family from the epic nighttime soap opera *Dallas*, the two adult Knight children still lived at home as it was rumored that the Knight family membership came before all else. Daria and Brendan each had their own wing of the mansion with a private entrance where they could come and go as they pleased. In terms of Lakeview gossip, Christine had gone on to explain that the Knights were the favorite topic of discussion year-in and year-out for the mere multi-millionaires that lived around and down the beach from the compound. No doubt someone over in the bar or at one of the tables in The Buck's main room was talking about the Knights right now.

Christine had never been invited to one of the Knight's exclusive parties, but she had explained to Rachel that if she could promote a few more books and get her name out there more, then…maybe. Before their chat had ended that night, Rachel had learned that the Knight family also owned Beacon Island, which was ten miles directly offshore of the Lakeview beach. The island was shaped like an upside-down trapezoid. In the northeast corner were Beacon Island Light, the old keeper's house, and one of the island's two helicopter landing pads. Beacon Road stretched southwest across the island and ended at a dock in Hideaway Cove, which was formed by a curved index-finger portion of land that 'hooked' into Lake Huron at the Southeastern tip of the island. At the base of the finger was the 5,000-square-foot Knight beach house where the family would escape to for a part of the summer. There was a beach on one side of the house that bordered Hideaway Cove, and there was a beach on the other side of the house that dropped off into Lake Huron. The second helicopter pad was inland, next to the house. Nosey Lakeview residents were known to take their yachts and drift off the southwestern shore, where they would use their binoculars to try and see which celebrity was being dropped off at the helicopter pad in *Knight Sky*. Most of the boaters stayed clear of the inlet to Hideaway Cove, as there was a reef with razor-sharp rocks that lurked beneath the surface, ready to slit or puncture a hull in an instant.

"How long did Kaj and Daria see each other?" Rachel asked.

Ben-David looked at Rachel and then back at Ingrid. They waited for her answer.

"It was almost a year, if you can believe it. Daria is known to just take what she wants and then trade whatever she possesses for something better. Kaj is charming, and, well, you've seen pictures of him. Handsome and athletic. Not too much going on upstairs, but it was enough for me. I never thought he'd be enough for Daria, but just because she's rich doesn't mean she has much going on in the cranial region either."

"You see him after the break-up?" Ben-David asked.

Rachel wouldn't have gone there, but the question was already out.

"In a drunken moment of weakness one night, but it never happened again after that. And we never really ever became friends again either. For most of that summer, he was out on his boat, and no one saw much of him. He'd pop in here every once in a great while with Kevin Shelby."

The conversation then drifted for a few minutes, and Ben-David gave a brief biography of marina owner Kevin Shelby, whom he had known since Shelby had been born. Kevin's father, Ralph Shelby, had owned and operated Shelby's Marina until passing away, when ownership transferred to his son. A known alcoholic and rumored drug user and drug dealer, Kevin Shelby ran a decent marina with pretty fair prices. Nowadays, he didn't spend much time there as he had just finished wrapping up his third divorce and was spending the majority of the winter months down in Florida surf fishing at Melbourne Beach. Shelby was forty-four…and looking sixty-five.

"He spend a lot of time with Shelby?" Ben-David asked.

"They drank their share of brews here together, that's for sure. Kaj told me that Shelby had a falling out with Randall McCleod and wouldn't set foot in McCleod's anymore. Said Shelby liked it better down here, mingling with the well-to-do."

"I don't get it. There's plenty of well-to-do summer residents up at McCleod's. Hell, that stretch of beach up by Leonard Shaw's old place is just as nice as Lakeview." He turned toward Rachel. "No offense."

Rachel had driven past the road that led to the stretch of houses Obadiah was talking about but had never turned in to take a look. On the way over, he'd told her that he lived just south of that stretch. She'd heard about the multi-millionaire Leonard Shaw and his beach castle before when some of her current neighbors were comparing the Knight's compound to Shaw's one-time residence. Last she had heard, there was an NFL coach who had bought Shaw's estate and was using it as a summer house.

She motioned to him that she was fine with his comment.

Ingrid said, "You've got me. Making sense of anything that Kevin Shelby thinks or does is wasted time."

"Why was Kaj hanging out with him?" He paused. "Drugs?"

Ingrid exhaled. "I don't know. Maybe. We smoked up a few times with Shelby when we were dating, but I never saw anything stronger than pot when we were together."

"You said he spent a lot of time out on the water last summer. Any idea why?"

"No, but it is a bit strange because in the three years we were dating, we hardly ever went out on his boat. I don't know what he was up to."

"Fishing? Solitude?"

"Not likely. He enjoyed being around people too much."

"Scuba diving?"

"Not that I ever knew of."

Rachel joined in with, "What about Kaj and Brendan Knight? Were they friends?"

"Best," said Ingrid. "It's my theory why Daria kept Kaj around so long."

"What about when they broke up?"

"Well, the night that I regrettably spent with him after Daria had broken his heart, he confided to me that while he was in Daria's good graces, he was in really good with the family—especially Brendan. But, once Daria dropped him, they all immediately distanced themselves from Kaj—like they didn't even know who he was. Brendan was cordial at first and was the last to cut ties, but once he did, they never spoke again. After we had sex, of course, he told me that he hated to admit it—he was raised blue-collar like me—but he missed the lifestyle even more than he missed Daria. He'd gotten used to the vacations in Italy and Switzerland and spending time at the family's home in Key West. They had given him extravagant gifts—clothes, jewelry, cologne—and given him access to their suites at Comerica Park and Michigan Stadium. Then there had been the wine tasting in California and the nights at the beach house on Beacon Island. I cut him off at that point, and the evening ended there. But," she said, pausing to take a sip of water, "I could tell that he was really hurting."

"You think the Knights had anything to do with his death?"

She answered immediately. "Not a chance. That was over a year ago, and the Knights are the kind of people that just move on. They didn't care about Kaj anymore, but they wouldn't have meant him any harm."

All Ben-David did was give a "Hmmph" in reply.

"Look, I know that people like the Knights have a public image that has been refined and sculpted to present one thing but hide another. They get everything they want because they can pay for it. But, there is not *one reason* that they would want Kaj dead. Even if he had some kind of dirt on them, he had over a year to expose it or be bought off. I saw both Daria and Brendan in here a few weeks ago. Daria was with a young stud who was in his early twenties, and Brendan had the gorgeous daughter of his father's mistress on his arm."

Rachel didn't know that Saul Knight had a mistress. Christine hadn't mentioned it. "Who is his mistress?"

"Nina Raquel Lawford."

Rachel and Ben-David both raised their eyebrows.

"Yes. *The* Nina Raquel Lawford that we've seen on the silver screen for twenty-five years now. Kaj told me about her. I guess that Saul has been seeing her for most of those years. Pamela Knight is a real drama queen, fashions herself as a selfie star—a real attention-craving, self-absorbed bitch. But, since she still enjoys the life, she allows Saul's fling to continue. I mean, Kaj said he could be a real patriarchal asshole when he wants to be, but he's easier to deal with than her. So, yeah, from what I saw of the whispering and small pecks, I'd say that Brendan Knight was seeing Nina's daughter Lilly."

"We'll have to question them," Ben-David said. "Good to know the background information." He wrote something in his notebook while saying, "I agree with your assessment, though. It'll probably be a quick interview. I'm assuming they're still around."

"I would think so. It'll be interesting to see your impression of them."

"Why is that?"

"Maybe Brendan will act like he's sad that he's lost his old friend. Maybe that's the right play for him: Show the community that the usually aloof Knights care about their local friends. But does he care? Then again, maybe he won't show what he's feeling. Or maybe he'll claim that they weren't the best of friends. The natural human reaction when faced with adversity is either fight or flight. Flight would have Brendan taking off to Hawaii and disappearing into some sort of paradisiacal vista to numb his loss. Fight would be him trying to exert some kind of control over the aftermath of his onetime friend's death—cooperating with the two of you and law enforcement to find the killer. Well, whatever side of himself that he decides to show, it won't bring back Kaj." She turned around, and the three of them saw Ingrid's manager, who tapped on his watch and smiled.

She faced them again. "I need to get going."

She started to ease out of the booth when Ben-David said. "Just one more question before we verify your whereabouts last night with your manager."

She sunk back down into the cushions. "Yes?"

"How did you feel when you found out that he was murdered?"

"Excuse me?"

"You heard me right. How did you *feel*?"

"Mister Ben-David—"

"Obadiah," he said, cutting her off.

"Obadiah, I hope you find out who did this. No matter how Kaj treated me, we shared a lot, and he didn't deserve to die."

"He might not have deserved to die, but are you necessarily sad to see him gone?"

Rachel watched as Ingrid began to squirm in her seat. She couldn't tell if Ingrid was sad, having to recall emotions that she had buried years ago, or if she was angry at this sudden departure from the tone of the other questions, *or* if she was hiding something and afraid of showing it.

"I—I, well, of course, I'm…well wouldn't you be sad?"

"I'm asking *you*."

"Let me be absolutely clear: I did *not* want him to die, and I was sad to hear the news this morning. Jesus, give me some time to process!" she snapped.

Ben-David and Rachel let the words hang in the air. "You're right," Ben-David finally said. "I think that's enough for today."

They all slid out of the booth and stood for a moment, facing each other.

"Thanks for your time," he said and then gave a lawyerly shrug. "Can't guarantee that I won't have to touch base with you again, but I appreciate your help. Please let me know if you think of anything else."

Ingrid exhaled, seeming to calm down, and said, "You know where you can find me," and she turned away and headed toward the restrooms by the bar.

They checked with the manager, who corroborated Ingrid's statement about where she had been last night. They thanked him and left.

Outside, Rachel asked, "That last question. Why did you ask her that?"

They started to walk across the parking lot, the wind whistling through the trees that bordered the entrance.

"I'll tell you when we're in the van."

O
badiah Ben-David turned the wheel of his massive black van, and when he was lined up with Shoreside lane, he floored the vehicle, and it shot out of the parking lot like a hockey puck slap-shotted across the ice. Rachel Roberts winced as two golf carts drove onto the shoulder to avoid the oncoming van. She could see the red wine leave the bottle that a man was fumbling with in the passenger side of the closest cart.

"You always speed out of the parking lot like that?" she asked.

"They won't report me." He looked in the rearview mirror. "Not supposed to be driving around in those things with open bottles of wine. All your neighbors do it. I just like to give 'em a little scare now and again."

"Is that what you were trying to do inside with Ingrid Bara? Shake her up?"

"It's just the way I work," he said. "I keep the questions short and to the point and see where the answers lead me. If, over the course of those questions and answers, I get a sense of where they're at emotionally, then I don't press. But if I don't hear what I believe they really think or haven't seen a hint of what they feel, then I'll nudge or needle to get something. Saves time."

This was great stuff. *I should model a character after Ben-David.* "Did you do that with Kaj Reynard's parents?"

"I'm not that cold-hearted," he said, laughing. "In almost forty years, I've only had to push close family members twice. Once, I had to be tough on some parents, and once I had to zero in on the wife who had hired me to find out if foul play was involved in the death of her deceased husband. Both times led me to the suspect. In the second example, it ended up being the wife. She'd hired me to try and throw the police off her track. People do that more than you think." He took a pull from his travel mug. "Anyway, I'm always cautious before I go there in an interview." He set his mug down. "Let me ask you: Did you think she was telling us the truth?"

Rachel hadn't thought about it until now. Maybe it was because she'd been through a bad breakup before and felt for Ingrid Bara. Maybe it was because she didn't like it when men pressed women for answers, which is why her heroine, Adrienne Astra, did all the questioning—usually after a punch, kick, or Glock upside her adversary's head. And yet, she respected Obadiah's experience. You didn't last almost forty years in the business by being an asshole, especially in a small town where everyone knew you. It was their first day together, and she needed more time before she made a judgment call regarding the professional investigator sitting next to her whose head was almost touching the ceiling of the van and who, moments ago, had almost run over some of her neighbors. "I think she was telling the truth. But this is my first time on the job, so I can't be sure. What do you think?"

"Sounded pretty genuine. But that last part made me wonder if she knows more. People are weird when they are interviewed. I call it my diary theory."

"And what's that?"

"Most people write diaries with the intent that they be read someday, which means that they can't escape their own human nature to make themselves look as good as possible, even while supposedly sharing their private thoughts. I'm not saying that there isn't some truth in diaries; I'm just saying that it's never the whole truth of what that person believes or knows. I've found interviewing people to be the same as reading someone's diary. They tell you some of the truth and some of the story, but there's always, *always* something else." He looked at her. "And it's up to us to get it." He focused back on the road. "My philosophy is to try and pull whatever we need out in the first interview. Believe me, I didn't start there. In my first few years of doing this, it would take me three or four interviews to get the good stuff. I learned my lesson. Now, it takes at most two, because nowadays I won't leave a second interview until I get it."

"Think we'll need a second one with Ingrid?"

"Depends on what Brendan and Daria Knight have to say."

"Won't they lawyer up?"

"Hell no. They've got enough money to have been coached that hiding behind a lawyer ends up creating more suspicion, and if and when they need one, they know they'll be taken care of. Also, the rich people I've encountered are so confident and cocky, they like being questioned and giving Ivy League answers."

"What about the Knights, though?"

"I admit, I've never been in the ring with anyone as well off as them, so they're a different animal—but from the same zoo."

"There could also be a third reason why they won't immediately lawyer up," she said. It had come to her while he was giving his explanation of the first two reasons. She had to be careful, though, because the answer had come from her first novel *Morning Glory Mayhem!*, and she shouldn't mention where she was getting the idea from. In the novel, a diabolical hedge fund manager named Samuel Ingraham Michaelson starts murdering his mistresses one by one and watches cable news relentlessly as each body is found…every Monday morning for a month. At first, no one can connect the women to each other, and the case starts to dry up. But, as investigations wrap up, drifter Adrienne Astra comes to the Big Apple and stumbles upon a frightened woman in the corner of a dark barroom who happens to be Michaelson's final mistress. Now alerted that the corpses may all be traced back to him, Michaelson comes forward and admits to the affairs but claims he has nothing to do with the murders. In fact—and this is where she got her idea from—he starts to *help* with the investigation.

"And what's that?" Ben-David said, turning the van onto Old Beach Road.

"Whether they are guilty or not, it could turn them on to become a part of the investigation by offering their help. You know? Like playing a high-stakes game."

"For thrills? Adrenaline fix?" He tilted his head, then shook it. "I don't see it."

"With all of that money, think how bored these people can get. They can buy anything or purchase any experience that they want to have. However, murder and becoming a player in a real-life game of Clue is harder to make happen. And. If they are guilty, then it's a game to see if they can get away with it. If they're not guilty, then it's about getting some positive press for offering their deep resources to help bring someone to justice, which, if they're successful, they start a charity or gift a sum of money to the victim's family. Philanthropy pays." And now, she expected the question.

He delivered.

"Where did you get that idea from?"

If I wrote what I just said into a book, no one would believe it. But, sometimes, truth is stranger than fiction. "Is it a good one?"

"Yeah. It is."

She wondered if he would drop the question now. She had tried the trick of answering a question with a question. This could either distract someone long enough to forget what the original question was—attention spans were getting shorter every day—or it could take the conversation in another direction. As she waited to see what would happen, she remembered that in her novel, Samuel Ingraham Michaelson had proved to be a worthy adversary for Adrienne Astra and for Riley Cannon's plotting abilities. Just when the happy author had the slimy hedge fund honcho cornered, his lawyer, Brandon Gold, entered the story and her subconscious alerted her that Brandon had started his own affairs with the women when he would visit them with monthly payments to keep them quiet. Hence, as Riley's fingers danced on the keyboard, her antagonist became stronger, and a subplot that she hadn't seen before came alive on the screen before her eyes: Samuel Ingraham Michaelson had planned all along to pin the murders on his lawyer.

"But where did your idea come from?"

Shoot! He hadn't forgotten. Relax. She did. *Now, deliv— Wait! Another opportunity!* "I wonder how Christine is doing?" she said, pointing at the beautiful two-story house with white vinyl siding, red shutters, and black roof.

"We'll get around to talking to her."

Her plan seemed to be working, but he was a professional investigator. For good measure, she threw in, "Why didn't we start with her?"

"Ritter told me everything I needed to know this morning. I don't think it was her, or at least she's not at the top of our shortlist. If I had heard something that sounded off this morning, then we'd be talking with her today." He snuck a peek at the house. "However, it doesn't mean that you can't have a chat with her if you want to give her a ring tonight after we're done."

"I might do that."

They rolled past a few more houses, and her beach house came into view through the scattering of tall pines.

"But, seriously, that idea of yours is a good one. Where did it come from?"

He wasn't giving up, but she didn't suspect that he was on to her goal of avoiding the question. "Just came to me while I was listening to your answers." It wasn't a lie. She added, "My mind is just scrolling over the details of the case so far, and all sorts of things are popping into my brain. Is this what it's always like?"

"Welcome to the club," he said, giving a toothy grin that was surrounded by the enormity of his beard.

His smile was actually attractive. The contrast of his straight white teeth against the sea of steel wool made it impossible to look away. It was like some mysterious magnet that kept her in a trance. She wasn't attracted to *him*, per se, but there was something about the whole package—his larger-than-life persona, stature, beard, and van—that made the entire show so ridiculous, puzzling, and unknown that she felt compelled now to see where the case went. At first, she had thought that the money she had paid him would be the motivating factor for her to see things through, but that had all changed now.

In fact, she was proud of her answer because it was truthful but didn't give away exactly where her idea had come from. The more she thought about it, investigating a murder was like writing a nov—and then, like it hadn't happened since the writing of her third book in the series, the first nugget of a story idea for *Dark After Midnight* formed. "Yes!" she shouted, raising her hands and hitting the van's ceiling.

Ben-David hit the brakes, and the van screeched to a halt.

"Shit!" he yelled.

Realizing what she had actually done, she scrambled for answers. "Oh, I'm sorry. I—"

"What in the hell was that?"

You've done it now. Think! "I'm just connecting things and got a bit excited. Sorry." Again, she wasn't lying. This was exactly what happened to her when ideas began to form for a book, and she hadn't felt it for so long that her emotions had taken over for a moment.

"Thank God no one was behind us. In these parts, no one exchanges insurance information over a little fender bender and goes his separate way. No, no. They claim whiplash, psychological trauma, the whole kit and caboodle. Of course, no-fault insurance would cover us regardless, but who wants to deal with all of that? We were just lucky, ma'am." He eyed her.

Even his angry stare was captivating.

84

"Now, what did you connect?"

The van began to roll down the street again.

What she had connected was that Adrienne Astra would be betrayed by an old friend in *Dark After Midnight*. Readers had latched on to a minor character named Rose Varga—Rachel had come up with the name looking at RVs online—who was supposed to only be in an early scene of her second book *Late-Afternoon Associates*. However, as it sometimes happened in the writing of novels, one scene became two, and two became three, and soon, Rose was shouting at Rachel to have a more prominent role. And so Rose Varga, the college roommate of Adrienne Astra, came alive and almost stole the show before Rachel trimmed some scenes, cut others, and gave her heroine more obstacles to overcome. But readers had still gone bonkers over Suzanne Freeman's creation of Rose's sassy tone in the audiobook version. *"They want more Rose, darling,"* Topaz had told her after a focus group was formed to give Rachel feedback before she started book three. And so when Rose came to Adrienne's rescue in *Enemies in the Evening*, the readership was both shocked and rewarded. Shocked because Adrienne Astra had never been more vulnerable—*"A risk of the highest order,"* her editor J. Rudolph Hightower had said. Rewarded because the intricate plotting had provided the perfect opportunity for Rose to help Adrienne in a way that was plausible, satisfying, and unpredictable.

And, now, Rachel realized that because Rose was so likable, it had blocked her for the past ten years from seeing that Rose would not be better as an even stronger ally, but that her dear darling would be delicious and better as an *enemy* of Adrienne Astra's.

The Moleskine notebook felt heavy in her left hand. She needed to start writing some of this down. She tapped the tip of her Frixion erasable pen against the pad. Topaz had mailed her a pack of them—*"Erases the marks completely. I couldn't believe it. You can't wear the eraser down, but try! Why? Because at least that will mean that you're writing something, star child!"*

A small branch, carried by the forceful Huron breeze, hit the windshield and brought her out of her writerly trance. She watched as the limb bounced off into the wind. Then, she remembered Ben-David's question: *What did you connect?* She looked at him. "Just that Christine might be able to tell me some more about the Knights. For some reason, seeing her house and knowing where we were headed reminded me of her fascination with them." It wasn't a complete lie.

"Oh," Ben-David said. "Makes sense. Make sure to ask if you talk with her before we stop by for our interview."

He bought it.

"I will," she said, opening her notebook.

"I'll write it in mine too when we stop."

She wrote down the note and then flipped halfway through the remaining empty pages. Rachel gave a sideways glance at Ben-David. The road ahead held his complete concentration.

As she started to write, he said, "There's the gate."

She looked out the windshield and watched as Old Beach Road came to an end. To their right, Ferry Drive started, which would take them back to US-23. To their left was a private drive that led to an expansive gate with a gigantic 'K' engraved into a circle in the middle.

She closed the notebook.

Ben-David said, "Ready?"

The butterflies returned to her stomach. "Yes."

And they turned into the private drive.

10

As the van traveled down the asphalt drive, the Knight mansion loomed before them like a giant ogre. Whereas most of the Lakeview beachfront was defined by a scattering of Cape Cod, Mediterranean, and Modern-styled homes, The Knight family had broken with their neighbors and gone with a Victorian architectural style, highlighted by a circular tower in each of the four corners. It was one thing to hear from Christine that the place looked like the world's largest haunted house, but it was another to actually see it up close. Other than the towers with their bay and bow windows that had half radius tops with grids, the defining feature was the wrap-around porch that was so expansive it seemed like there was a deck built around the house rather than a porch. The window and door frames were cinnamon in color and popped against the light blue siding and white trim. Only the window size betrayed the pure style. A classic Victorian had tall and narrow windows; the Knights' home had large windows that belonged on the Modern-styled homes down the beach. In fact, as the van crept closer to the massive castle, Rachel thought that the perfect way to describe the house would be Victorian, but Modern when it wants to be, which moved her overall assessment of the mansion's aesthetic quality to gaudy.

Ben-David took a sip from one of the to-go coffee cups they'd gotten at The Buck, then said, "Now, I just live in an old A-frame house on the beach north of Darwinger's, and I'm certainly no design critic, but this place doesn't know what it wants to be."

They passed by the tennis courts, Olympic-sized pool, and pool house.

"When you have this kind of money, I think you make your house whatever you want it to be."

"I'm starting to agree with your friend Christine," Ben-David said. "The bold colors don't take the haunted edge off this place one bit." He leaned forward in his seat. "And those towers are four stories high. No way they're within the legal height specs according to the building code."

"Great view of the lake, though. Maybe they'll let us go up in separate towers, and we can wave to each other through the windows."

"Doubt it. We won't get past the sitting room." He played with his beard, this time twirling the hair around his fingers like a fork in spaghetti. "However, they've had a few minutes to prepare because we had to get cleared through their gate guard. That means we might need longer with them to get what we need, and they could try and wow us with a mini-tour to distract us."

"Why longer?"

"I'm not saying that I get off on surprising people, but there is a certain advantage in ringing the doorbell and knocking on the front door when someone doesn't expect you. I can tell a lot by the first reaction I get when they open the door. So, when I have to wait at the gate to get cleared to even come down the driveway like we just did, I lose the element of surprise. And that's not an insignificant thing."

"What you mean is that they'll have had time to put on their faces."

"Exactly."

Ben-David parked the van in front of a 4-car garage, and they walked across the concrete parking pad and then up the stone steps to the porch. From far away, it was hard to judge both the scale and craftsmanship of the place. But, up close now, she saw that the evenly-spaced square porch pillars were enormous, and the railings were made of ornate spindles that could have been hand-carved.

They reached the top step, and before she could push the doorbell, the massive front door opened. An older man wearing a dark suit and tie walked through the doorway and shook their hands.

"Good evening. I'm Abernethy, the Knight family butler. Let me show you to the Cosette Room, where Brendan and Daria will be joining you shortly."

She met eyes with Ben-David, and his look told her that they were probably thinking the same thing. A servant showing them into the house spoke of hierarchy, social class, privilege, comfort, efficiency, and, most importantly to them, layers. Layers in terms of who has access to Brendan and Daria, when this access is granted, and how long it is granted for. Abernethy was a gatekeeper of sorts, but his presence had also delivered the wordless opening statement from the two siblings to them that, if spoken, would have said, "You are lower on the social ladder of importance than we are. Therefore, you will wait, in a place that we designate, for us when we are ready to talk with you." It was one of the oldest and easiest methods of establishing or maintaining the superior-to-subordinate relationship. When you're the superior, make your subordinates wait so that they know where they stand. Until now, the closest she had come to experiencing this was when Topaz had flown her to New York to meet with her publishing team for the first time. They'd kept her and Topaz waiting outside a conference room for an hour. At that point, Topaz had burst into the room, shut the door behind her, and Rachel heard five minutes of yelling and what sounded like a chair being thrown across the room. This was followed by a minute of silence, and then Topaz had opened the door and said with a smile, *"Come join us, angel."*

They entered the foyer, and Abernethy led the way down a short hallway that spilled into a living area. Rachel thought that if the outside of the house, minus the large windows, spoke of a previous century, then the inside spoke of the current century. There were large open spaces with high ceilings, modern art pieces, and other lavish décor, small LCD displays on the wall that no doubt controlled a variety of the home's functions. She had one such screen in her own house that controlled her security system. They had already passed three screens, and that was just the foyer and hallway.

She tried to get Ben-David's attention twice, but he was fixated on the old man, and she wondered what her partner was thinking.

Beyond the large living area was a longer, darker hallway with small lanterns affixed to the wall that lined the sides. There were no windows, and Rachel thought that the hallway was at least six feet wide and wondered why the architect decided on that design. As she tried to come up with answers, the wide tunnel curved to the left, and after a few more paces, they reached a large wooden door that reflected the lantern light off of its sheen of varnish.

Abernethy pulled a gold key from his pants pocket and unlocked the door. "The Cosette Room," he said, ushering them in.

Rachel followed Abernethy and Ben-David into the room. They were in the bottom room of one of the four towers. Next to the door was an elevator, which Abernethy explained ran up to the third floor. To access the tower's fourth floor, one had to climb up a circular staircase. This was because the fourth floor had a three-hundred-and-sixty-degree view through its large windows. "Each level of this tower is a wonderful place to disappear with a good book, or to watch the sunrise, or to see a summer storm come in over the lake," he said.

They moved into the room, and Abernethy seated Ben-David on one end of a large blue leather couch and Rachel on the other end. Across from the couch were two leather chairs with ottomans, and against the east wall was a wooden writing desk with a leather office chair behind it. Like Rachel's own writing station on the second floor of her house, the past and future occupants of the chair had an unobstructed view of Lake Huron.

As they sank into the couch, the old butler moved around the room like he'd seated people here for a hundred years—a quick wipe of the tabletop, a flip of a switch to light the gas fireplace, and an effortless stroll to a serving table that had a silver tray with a stainless-steel pitcher of coffee, four cups, and saucers, creamer, and sugar.

Ben-David looked around the room. "Why the 'Cosette Room'?"

Grinning like he'd been asked his favorite question—or at least the one he trapped guests into asking—Abernethy brought over the coffee tray. "Coffee?" he asked.

They both nodded, and as he began to pour, Abernethy launched into his brief explanation of the room's name. "Madame Pamela Knight's father, Roland, was American—raised in New York City—but her mother, Cosette, was French. During World War II, Madame Cosette's family were all members of the French Resistance, and, tragically, she lost her father and brother right before Paris was liberated. But, her mother, Eloise, and her three sisters, Gemma, Solange, and Valara, all survived. After the war, Mademoiselle Cosette, a fierce, independent spirit, immigrated to America and settled in New York City where she met Roland." He passed the delicate cups to Rachel and Ben-David. She decided to take her coffee black and watched as Ben-David poured cream into his cup, followed by a spoonful of sugar. While he stirred, Abernethy continued. "Once Madame Knight was born, the family traveled back to France and then did so once a year for Madame's entire upbringing. And during these visits, she became very close to her grandmother and her three aunts. When this house was constructed, Madame Knight chose to honor them by naming rooms of the house in their honor. As you saw, no doubt, in your approach to the house, there are four towers. The lower room in each tower is named after one of them. And so, this room was named after Madame's mother, Cosette, which in French means: victory. The southeast tower's room is named after Gemma, which means jewel, the southwest's after Solange—dignified—and the northwest's after Valara—

strength. And, finally, there is a grand ballroom at the far end of the estate, between the southeast and southwest towers. It is named after Madame's grandmother, Eloise, which means 'famous in war'—ironic, isn't it?"

About to answer, she stopped as a stream of information unexpectedly flooded her mind: memories from a long-ago college seminar on Shakespeare and the French humanist Michel Eyquem de Montaigne, arguably two of the greatest writers who were alive at the same time—they'd never met—during the Renaissance period. It was the towers that had prompted her recall. Yes, Montaigne had a substantial collection of books in a third-floor room of a tower in his château, and in a small study next to the library in his home, he had inscribed a resolution on the wall. *How did it go?* It came to her, preceded by the memory of a boisterous declaration from the professor of the course who said, *"This beautiful man gave us a gift that we can never repay him for! Now, listen to this inscription. Drink Montaigne. Feel Montaigne. Live Montaigne."* And it read:

In the year of Christ 1571, at the age of thirty-eight, on the last day of February, his birthday, Michel de Montaigne, long weary of the service of the court and public employments, while still entire, retired to the bosom of the learned virgins, where in calm and freedom from all cares he will spend what little remains of his life, now more than half run out. If the fates permit, he will complete this abode, this sweet ancestral retreat; and he has consecrated to it his freedom, tranquility, and leisure.

In a way, she was like Montaigne—retiring early, albeit prematurely. But in another sense, she was different than Montaigne; she had not retired to spend the rest of her life reading and thinking. Her mind snapped back to Abernethy's question regarding the name of the room, *"Ironic, isn't it?"* Rachel thought it was, but her brain was now too busy filing away this information for a future book. The naming of rooms could be seen as touching, but it could also be seen as corny or a bit pretentious. Topaz would get a kick out of the fact that the Knights named rooms in their mansion. Then, the floor plan to Rachel's house unrolled in her mind, and she wondered what room she'd name the Topaz room. Probably her wine cellar.

Seeming to play along too, Ben-David asked, "How about her grandfather and uncle who died in the war?"

Abernethy nodded as if he had expected the question, and he pointed out the window toward the churning waters of Lake Huron. "The Knight estate on Beacon Island features rooms named after them. Madame thought it appropriate as the island house is a bit more remote, rough, and secretive—like the cause her grandfather and uncle died for. Her grandfather, Rene, was a reader of the first class and a man of letters before the war stirred the blood in his veins, and he traded in his pen and paper for a knife and gun. Hence, the Rene Library is located just off the grand atrium and, other than the beach when the weather permits, the library is the place where all of the Knights go to read—leather armchairs, leather couches, a coffee bar, the temperature kept cool so that a sweater is recommended, a chest of wool blankets, banker's lamps placed throughout, and silence." The slender old butler paused, seemingly lost in his own reverie of the bibliophile oasis. The wind howled outside and brought his attention back to them. "There is only one tower at the island house, but it is much larger and even higher than the four here." He grinned at them, regaining his old-world charm. "The view from the top room is sublime, and Mr. and Madame Knight do a fair bit of entertaining up there over the summer. Why, just last summer, the Governor and her husband came for a weekend stay." He saw Rachel's half-empty coffee cup. "A refill, my dear?"

She held up her cup, and he continued his explanation while he picked up the pitcher and poured. "Now, in the war, Madame's uncle, Julian, whose name means 'youthful,' was a derring-do sort of chap who not only performed surveillance from great heights but also assassinated a substantial number of Nazi officials—really a first-rate spy. Made perfect sense for Madame to name the highest point between the two houses after him. Hence, the circular top room of the five-story-high island house tower is referred to as Julian's View. The Knights tell a longer version of what I just told you to the guests that they entertain up there. They start with a few specific stories of Julian's early adventures in the south of France, and later, move on to the ones about his involvement in the Brotherhood of Notre Dame, where he helped provide the allies with photographs and maps of the German forces stationed along Hitler's Atlantic Wall. There's a framed picture of the old boy and an engraved label for the room on the pedestal that sits next to the staircase leading up to Julian's View. Smashing tribute."

Rachel went to take a sip of her coffee but was interrupted by a voice in the direction of the Cosette room's entrance.

"Still boring the guests with our family tales, Abernethy?"

Rachel turned her head in time to see a man and a woman, roughly her age, walk into the room.

"Ah, Mister Brendan and Miss Daria," Abernethy said.

If Rachel was writing a first draft of *Dark After Midnight* and Brendan and Daria were two characters, she would note that the siblings resembled the crooked brother and his evil sister in *The Incredibles 2*—well-dressed, fit, and an unmistakable air of being affluent, which not all wealthy people displayed during a first encounter. But that would be lazy first draft vomit, and by the final draft, she would describe Brendan as a tall hybrid of a young professor and a cross-fit coach. His green eyes pierced through the designer glasses, which were rimmed in black and matched the thick, perfectly swept-back hair on top of his head. The belt around his waist looked like the ones that were molded and painted on one of her Ken dolls from childhood; it didn't move and highlighted his narrow waist. The tight-fitting Polo shirt exposed his muscular arms, which had just the right amount of black hair to highlight his masculinity without making his forearms look like they had fur sleeves over them.

Daria was slender—Rachel thought too slender—and with the heels she was wearing, almost as tall as Brendan. If her brother's physique was defined by muscles that flexed with every movement, then her form could be described as a symphony of wire appendages that bent and moved with ease and purpose. Her white leggings exposed tanned ankles and feet, and her toenails were painted bright purple. A light summer sweater was pulled up past her elbows, and the bottom barely went past her small tush. Whereas Brendan only wore a diver's watch with a silver bezel and orange strap, Daria displayed her affinity for jewelry: gold earrings, gold necklace, gold watch, and an assortment of gold rings—one with a colossal purple stone that caught the light from the ceiling just right and sparkled like a single star in a jet-black sky. Her blonde hair was styled in a choppy pixie cut, and her eyes were the same color as her brother's.

Abernethy motioned his pale, bony fingers toward Rachel and Ben-David. "May I present Mister Obadiah Ben-David and Miss Rachel Roberts."

Whereas Brendan had a smooth, confident gait that displayed both power and control, Daria glided toward them as if she was standing on one of the moving treadmills between terminals at large airports.

The handshakes were pleasant, firm, but quick.

They know why we're here.

Brendan fixed his eyes on Rachel's for an extra moment, and then they all took their seats. Abernethy poured two black cups of coffee and placed them on the glass tabletop in front of Brendan and Daria, who were seated on the couch across from the one where she and Ben-David sat.

Ben-David started things off. "Thanks for carving out some time for us."

Rachel liked it because the statement contained at least two possible subtexts. One was both complimentary and deferential to the Knight's social status; it said *We know how busy you are, and, yes, you made us wait for your grand arrival, but we're glad that you didn't make us wait too long.* Another was sarcastic; it said *This is a murder investigation, and we don't care how well-off you are…thanks for taking time out of your delicate, luxurious, and precious day to help us with the murder case we're working on. We really aren't worthy of being here, but you're so generous for letting us interview you. Such a privilege.* What made the statement work both ways was Ben-David's honed delivery: even tone, eye contact, professional.

Without pause, Brendan replied, "Sure. We'll do anything to help."

Daria took a sip of coffee. "Before we begin," she said, "we'd like to know a little bit more about Ms. Roberts."

They had discussed this topic in the van. The Knights would know who Ben-David was, and a check of his credentials would be easy. But, they would not be able to find out a lot about Rachel Roberts. Perhaps that she was their neighbor down the beach. Maybe a phone call to see what she did for a living or how long she had lived there. Not much past that. Ben-David had told Rachel that he gave the gate guard both of their names on purpose. He wanted to see what the Knights were able to come up with before the meeting—said it would tell them more about the multi-millionaires' curiosity and resources.

Ben-David took her question in stride and quickly provided the basics of who she was and what the arrangement was between them—minus the part about the fee Ben-David was collecting from Rachel.

Daria gave Rachel a smile, one that Rachel read as condescending and patronizing, and then said, "If you're a coder, then you should be in for some fun the next few days."

"Why the next few days?" Rachel asked.

Rachel watched as Daria's smile vanished while her eyes panned over to…Abernethy?

The old butler gave a slight grin and then ambled over to the serving table to grab a tray of cookies.

Daria then eyed Brendan as if she wanted his attention.

He was staring at Rachel.

Daria exhaled and brought her gaze back to Rachel. "Well, hopefully, you both find the murderer sooner, but I imagine it could take a few days." She crossed her legs. "Maybe weeks or months, or maybe we'll never know what happened to Kaj. That's what I meant."

Rachel nodded. "Thanks. I'm new at this and didn't know. Thought you might know something we didn't."

"We do," Daria said. "That's why you're here, right?"

Rachel hadn't meant to stir up the interview, but she wasn't about to be talked down to either. She thought of the library out on Beacon Island and remembered an article in Politico about a book service called 'Books by the Foot' run by the bookseller Wonder Book. 'The Washington bookshelf' was famous in the nation's capital, where both Republican and Democratic politicians would place orders according to their ideology to serve as décor or a Zoom backdrop to make them appear well-read. She figured that the Knights had probably placed an order to fit their image—whatever that was—and it had most likely been a long time since Daria Knight had picked up a book.

As she contemplated what to say back, Ben-David said, "Wouldn't be here for any other reason." He let the statement find its mark. Then, he added, "So now that you know who we are, let's get down to business."

She noticed that Ben-David was still eyeing the butler and wondered why.

Abernethy arrived at the coffee table and set down the tray of cookies. "Freshly baked this afternoon."

"Thank you, Abernethy," Brendan said.

The old man bowed and then began his retreat to the serving table.

"Speaking of Abernethy," said Ben-David, "I think it's best if we're *all* honest with each other, agree?"

Rachel watched as the old man froze and then carefully turned around. There *had been* something to Ben-David studying him. *My powers of observation are getting back into shape.*

"What do you mean?" Brendan asked.

"What I mean is that his name isn't Abernethy." Ben-David stood up, towering over the old man, then leaned over and squinted at the butler's glasses. "Yep. What I thought." He sat back down. "Abernethy's real name is Jayson Jasper, and he's your father's longtime personal attorney." Ben-David frowned at Brendan Knight. "This was really unnecessary, don't you think?"

The room remained silent for a few agonizing seconds. Then, Daria said, "Really, I think—"

Brendan cut her off. "Okay, so we were being a little overly cautious. You know how many times a year this family gets sued?"

"Don't really care," Ben-David said. "You trying to pass off your dad's lawyer as your butler just makes the two of you more suspicious."

Then as if his backbone became a steel rod, Jayson Jasper stood up and took off his glasses. He addressed Ben-David and Rachel as if he was persuading a jury that would be voting soon. "Okay, okay. Let's relax. It was my idea. I can't help it if I feel protective over these two," he said, waving his hand with much more dexterity than before. He suddenly seemed ten years younger. "I've known them since the day they were born, and they've always been a weakness of mine. They wanted to speak with you alone, but I insisted."

Daria rubbed her heart. "Jayson—"

"No, no, Daria. It's all on me, my dear. I just know that the two of you were here the other night when Kaj Reynard showed up on the beach, and I wanted to make sure that there were no problems with this interview. And now, look at me, I've gone and complicated things."

Rachel watched the drama in amazement. She wondered why the Knights just didn't have their lawyer join them in the first place.

Jayson Jasper continued. "Well, now that we know who everyone is—"

Rachel swallowed.

"—let's let the interview commence." He pulled up a chair and poured himself a cup of coffee, loading it with cream and sugar.

"Any other surprises planned?" Ben-David asked.

Brendan gave a sly grin. "No more games," he said. Then, he leaned forward with almost child-like excitement. "But, I've gotta ask. How did you know who he was?"

Ben-David rubbed his beard and picked up his coffee cup, which looked ridiculous in his huge hand. "I know a little bit about your family and its associates. Hard not to. After Leonard Shaw left years ago, you've become our biggest celebrities. Mr. Jasper here has stayed out of the limelight for a while, but even with those fake glasses, I can still make out a face." He took a giant swig of coffee, finishing it, and then turned it upside down and then back upright again. He held it out toward Jasper. "More, please?"

Jasper's eyes narrowed, but he bent over and poured Ben-David another cup. However, after Ben-David said, "Thanks," Jasper rose.

"I'm calling for Abernethy," he said to Brendan and Daria.

"Won't be necessary," Ben-David said. "I'll get my own coffee from now on. Just wanted to see what would happen if I asked."

Jasper's face was turning red as he sat back down.

"Now, that's the face of a lawyer," Ben-David said, laughing. The giant snatched up three cookies and placed them on his lap. He shifted his focus back to Brendan. "He's a pretty good actor too. Didn't even ask us about the case, which would have been a dead giveaway. Butlers are notorious for eavesdropping and for knowing family gossip, but they are tight-lipped with outsiders."

A part of Rachel was enjoying watching Ben-David turn the tables, but there was another part that felt betrayed because he had not told her everything that he knew about the Knights. She would bring it up with him later. Meanwhile, her creative juices were flowing with ideas. *A fat cat family lawyer posing as a butler!* As she felt the ideas and coffee flow through her, she decided that she would need to make a full pot when she arrived home and then go upstairs and start typing as fast as she could. Ideas were appearing in her brain by the minute now. She'd never had a character use a disguise before in any of her novels. Well, maybe it was time for Adrienne Astra to go Sherlock Holmes on someone.

"Enough, all right?" Daria said—her face almost as red as Jasper's.

Ben-David ignored her. "So, you said they were both home on the night that Kaj Reynard showed up on Christine Harper's beach?" he asked Jasper.

"That's what I said."

"How do you know they were home?"

"Because I live in the compound, and I saw them at dinner. Then, we had drinks on the back deck before I saw them heading down the hallways to their respective wings in the main house."

"Respective wings." He turned to Brendan and Daria. "How old are the two of you?"

"Thirty-seven," Brendan said.

Daria rolled her eyes. "Thirty. What difference does it make?"

"You both live here, though, right?"

Daria looked away, but Brendan nodded for both of them.

"So when was the last time you actually saw them?" he asked Jasper.

"When they walked down the hallway, it was around seven-thirty."

"And you didn't see them after that?"

Jasper squirmed in his seat. "No, I didn't lay eyes on them again, but they were in for the night, for Chrissakes."

Ben-David scribbled something in his weathered notebook and shifted his attention back to Daria and Brendan. "Tell me about your respective wings."

Daria looked at her watch and started tapping her right foot on the floor. Brendan answered for both of them. "I have the wing on the lakeside that includes the southeast tower. Daria has the one next to mine, which faces west and includes the southwest tower. Both wings are twenty-five hundred square feet and include a full kitchen, two bedrooms, a guest suite, three baths, living room, office, dining room, and bonus room." He paused, taking a sip of coffee. "Plus the tower and its four levels. There is a door off of the bottom floor of the tower and French doors off of each master bedroom that lead out onto a private deck. My deck connects to the main deck and outdoor living area; Daria's is more private."

Ben-David scribbled notes, trying to keep up with the information. When he finished, he brought the eraser end of his pencil to his mouth and tapped it against his bottom lip. "So, two possible exits from each wing?"

Brendan nodded.

"Any way to exit the upper floors of the tower? Say there's a fire on one of the bottom floors." Rachel asked.

Ben-David gave her a look that she interpreted as saying, *"Good question. Hadn't thought of it."*

"There's a rope ladder bolted to the floor under the largest window on each level. To maintain the aesthetic aspect of each room, the ladder is stowed in a large trunk with a blanket on top. If there's an emergency, you simply open the window, open the trunk, and push the ladder out the window. It unrolls quickly. Then, all you have to do is step outside and climb down."

"So, three more exits per tower," Rachel said.

Brendan gave her a flirtatious smirk. "Yeah, I guess that's true when you put it that way."

She felt a little bit more a part of the conversation now, and she felt that she had contributed something to the investigation. The Knights were shaping up to be a dead-end, but she admitted to herself that she was enjoying the atmosphere. She'd underestimated Ben-David. He was good and knew how to make people comfortable when he needed them to be and also uncomfortable when he needed them to be. She also found Brendan Knight attractive, more pleasant, and more approachable than his younger sister, who she saw as more of a thirty-year-old teenager.

Ben-David was back to writing in his notebook.

Jayson Jasper fidgeted in his seat as if he needed a tall glass of scotch to calm his nerves.

Daria Knight kept tapping her foot on the floor.

"So," Ben-David said. "Three more possible exits for each wing, giving us a total of five per wing." He turned his head toward Jasper. "And where are your quarters?"

"When I stay here, my room is on the second floor in the main wing."

"What's the main wing?"

Brendan jumped in. "The main wing is the rest of the house—the other eight-thousand square feet, which includes the other two towers."

"Could you see them leave the estate from your room?" Ben-David asked Jasper.

"Only if they left via the driveway. My room is on the west wall, and my windows face the pool and tennis courts."

Rachel raised her hands in front of her face as if mapping out the floor plan in the air. "But you could see Daria's deck from your room, right?"

Jasper glanced at Daria. There was perspiration visible on his forehead. He swallowed and then said, "I can see some of her deck from my bathroom window." His hands were shaking, and Rachel watched as he brought his hands together and then rested them in his lap.

"How long are you staying here?" Ben-David asked.

"I'm here for my usual summer stay, which is about three weeks. Saul and I have always treated my summer visit as a mid-year retreat of sorts. Some work, a little fishing, a lot of golf."

"Jesus Christ. Are we almost done?" Daria asked.

Ben-David took a bite from one of his cookies and then washed it down with a gulp of coffee. Then, he eyed both of the Knights. "Did you both stay home last night after Mr. Jasper saw you exit to your wings?"

"Yes," Daria said.

"Yes," Brendan said. "Too much of the joy juice before dinner. We were tired."

"Is there anyone who can confirm your whereabouts after seven-thirty?"

"We each have a cook and housekeeper for our wing," Brendan said. "Since we had dinner in the main wing last night, our cooks helped the head chef. I didn't see them after dinner."

"Where do they live?" Ben-David asked.

"The main wing houses the staff quarters. Our butler, three maids, and three cooks live there. The groundskeeper and gatekeeper live in a finished suite in the pole barn."

"Did either of you see your housekeeper when you returned to your wing?"

Daria said, "No, I never see her after seven unless I'm having a late dinner or entertaining. She does the dishes after dinner, turns down my bed, leaves a mint on the pillow, and heads for the staff quarters."

"Same for me," Brendan said.

Ben-David looked up at the ceiling and let his eyes wander around the room. "I'm assuming this place has a state-of-the-art security system. Alarms, motion detectors, cameras, the works."

"We do, and I'll answer the question you are about to ask."

Rachel's money was on the security cameras. *Where were they positioned? Did they cover all of the possible entry and exit points of the estate—especially the wings where Brendan and Daria lived?*

Brendan sat up a little straighter and cleared his throat before beginning. "We did have a top-flight security system, but it was time for an upgrade. So, for the past three days, our gate guard and head of security, Jacques Renault, has been tearing down the old one and installing the new one. It was supposed to be installed last week, but the new system was late in arriving. He told me this morning that it would be up by tomorrow, which is good because we're having our first party of the summer next Saturday night. Fifty guests are coming."

She had been right. As Ben-David took the information in, she asked, "So, there's been no surveillance footage of the estate for the past three days, including today?"

"Unfortunately, there is no footage. Believe me, when we found out about the murder this morning, my father was beside himself because if the security system had been up and running, then it could have been used to clear everyone." Brendan shrugged. "Murphy's law at work again, I guess."

"So, *for the record*," Ben-David said, pausing to make eyes with Jasper and then glaring into Brendan and Daria's eyes, "neither of you left your wings or your property last night?"

"I went to my kitchen, got a bottle of water, took some ibuprofen, and then went to bed," Daria said.

"I stupidly had another scotch in my living room by the fire, made a phone call, and then took a shower and went to bed." Brendan glanced at his watch and then the ceiling. "It was probably around nine-thirty when my head hit the pillow."

"Hope the mint is still okay," Ben-David needled.

She watched as Brendan Knight's calm demeanor slid into one of annoyance.

"Now that you know where we were," Daria said, "are we done here?"

Ben-David smiled for the first time in the interview. "Hell no. Ms. Knight, we're just getting started."

11

Seemingly stunned by the large professional investigator's statement, Daria Knight looked to legendary family safety valve Jayson Jasper to stop the pain. "Jayson, can't you take care of the rest of this? I mean, I was in my fucking wing all night. End of story."

"He can't," Obadiah Ben-David said. "Since you both can't prove where you were after Mr. Jasper saw you, I need to ask some more questions."

Rachel Roberts spotted Jasper's hands starting to twitch again as he unclasped them and wiped the sweat off of his forehead. It looked to her, more than ever now, like the old battle-worn lawyer needed something amber-colored in a liquid form that burned on the way down your throat.

Brendan Knight finally put Jasper out of his misery. "Jayson, why don't you go over there and pour us all a drink." He looked around the room. "Thirty-year-old scotch okay with everyone?"

Nods all around except for Ben-David, who said he'd stick with coffee. Rachel enjoyed a good scotch now and then, mostly because of Topaz. *"Nectar of the Gods, my love! Warms your heart, soothes your soul, and paves the way for real conversation."* After two short ones with her beloved agent, she saw the attraction but stopped short of losing the magic when she declined a third. However, in all of their scotch chats over the years, Rachel had never tasted anything over an 18-year-old single malt.

As Jasper happily strode to the serving table, Brendan casually stated that the Knights only kept "parent" scotches, which meant 30-year-olds and older. Anything under 30 was considered a child's scotch.

Ben-David refilled his coffee and said, "Before I get to you, Ms. Knight, let me start with Mr. Knight."

As Ben-David was talking, Rachel watched as Jasper quickly filled a heavy glass halfway full and downed it in two gulps. She heard him say, "Good, good," to himself, and then he poured the rich honey-colored liquid into all of the glasses.

"Was the person you called last night Lilly Lawford?"

Brendan's head twitched backward, and Rachel could see that the question had surprised him. He waited until Jasper had delivered the scotches before answering. "I'm impressed with your preparation," he said. "I assume you've spoken with Ingrid Bara."

"That's a good assumption."

Brendan raised his glass. "To your health."

They all drank. From the moment the liquid entered her mouth, Rachel felt like she had just fallen into a bed of infinite cushions that made every part of her body relaxed and supported in the perfect way. Then, she did as Topaz had instructed her. "You let it wander around your mouth for a good two or three beats before swallowing, child. Roll your tongue through it and inhale slowly for as long as you can." When she swallowed, she felt like the inside of her throat was being pampered and massaged, and she unintentionally let an "Mmmm" escape.

"I agree," Brendan said.

Jayson Jasper was already taking another sip. The sweat was gone from his face, and his right hand could now win a steadiest-in-class award.

"Mr. Knight?"

"Yes. I called Lilly last night."

"You two seeing each other?"

Brendan brought the glass to his mouth but did not drink; instead, he took a long whiff. "I love the smell of this stuff too." When he finally brought it down, he said, making eye contact with Rachel instead of Ben-David, "Until last night we were."

"Find someone else?"

This time he brought the glass up, and he drank. "Not yet," he said, smacking his lips. "How's Ingrid? Tough on her when Kaj started dating Daria."

Daria smirked, finally seeming to enjoy something that was said.

"She told us that you and Kaj were best friends until your sister broke up with him," Ben-David said.

"We were. And I always liked him. But, well, you know how it goes. When things end like that, you sort of stop hanging out."

Jasper broke in with, "He was a good kid," and then took another sip as if he had just added some profound statement.

"How did you feel when you heard the news this morning?"

"Terrible. I know that we weren't close anymore, but what happened to him is just awful. Looking back, I regret not staying in contact."

Daria let out a grunt of disbelief.

Rachel paid close attention. She wondered if they were playing some sort of complicated game here or if she was observing their true brother-sister dynamic.

"It's true," Brendan said to Daria. "I shouldn't have lost touch with him after you two split."

"Well, I never stopped you from contacting him," she replied.

"Why did you break up with him, Ms. Knight?" Ben-David said.

"Why is that important, you sonofabitch?"

"Daria, Daria," Jasper said, playfully shaking his head.

Ben-David's face was a monument to stoicism.

After a few seconds of silence and a prompting head tilt from Jasper, she said, "Okay, Jesus, sorry." She threw back the rest of her scotch. "There was someone else."

"Who?"

Daria motioned to Rachel. "Her friend, Christine Harper."

Stunned, not by the fact that Christine had had a relationship or at least fling with Daria, but that her book-blogging friend hadn't mentioned it to her when she had told her all about the Knights.

Ben-David said, "I see."

"Tell her I said hi," Daria said to Rachel.

"I will," Rachel said and took another sip of scotch. The second one always went down smoother.

Ben-David scribbled in his pad again and then asked, "How did you feel when you heard the news of Kaj Reynard's murder, Ms. Knight?"

"It didn't really affect me." Then, she saw all of the reactions and added, "No, I'm not being cold-hearted. Not at all. It was just that we were over, and I hadn't thought about him in like forever." She turned her hand over, and the purple-gemmed golden ring caught the sunlight again.

"You put that ring up in your lighthouse, and you could paint Hampstead the color of Barney the Dinosaur at night."

"Are you jealous, Mister Ben-David?"

He ignored her. "So, you didn't mind that he had been murdered?"

She exhaled and started tapping her foot again. "Don't start twisting my words around."

"I'm not twisting your words around. Did you want him dead?"

"Of course not."

And with that answer, Rachel thought that the weird charade of an interview was over. They were both home last night; the security system had been down for a few days; neither of them wanted Kaj dead.

"It's obvious that you both spent some time with Kaj Reynard, and let's say everything you both told us is true," Ben-David said. "Do you know of anyone who might have wanted him dead?"

The room was silent, and Rachel chastised herself for not thinking of her partner's logical follow-up question. The interviews were not just to see if someone was guilty or not; they were also to collect any information that might lead them to who *was* guilty. She'd forgotten this because of the unorthodox nature of how this entire interview had started. But, the visit had given her one key piece to her story puzzle that had eluded her for the past six months: Misdirection, when properly deployed, was a powerful plot device. Her earlier brainstorming sessions and abortive outlines had relied too much on the linear nature of her first three novels—Adrienne Astra is having a nice day…wham!…something bad happens…she's called to act…and, for the rest of the story, she exacts her revenge. A leads to B leads to C. But for *Dark After Midnight*, she now not only had Rose Varga turning enemy on Adrienne Astra, but Rachel would throw in a complication in the second act to ignite the misdirection and hide Rose's identity as the true enemy. Perfect. And it would help lengthen the novel as well. Her ever-keyed-up editor, J. Rudolph Hightower, had been adamant that *"Your fans have been waiting forever. This novel has to be in the 120,000 – 150,000-word range. Don't worry, we'll get the font and margins set so that it doesn't look like Lord of the Rings. But it's got to be thicker, Cannon."*

"What kind of question is that?" Brendan asked.

And, like that, she was pulled back into the interview.

"Do you know anyone who didn't *like* him?" Ben-David said, leaning forward.

Daria suddenly became assertive and said, "I knew Matty Joshua didn't care for him."

"Who is Matty Joshua?" Rachel asked.

"Didn't know you were still a part of the interview, sweetie," Daria said.

What a bitch. She held her anger in. "Still here," she said. "Who is he?"

"When I first started dating Kaj, he was hanging out with Matty and Kevin Shelby."

At this, she saw Ben-David sit up and not move. It was as if someone had slipped a few pills of Adderall into his coffee, and his attention was presently at an all-time high. He asked, "Friends or business associates?"

At this point, Brendan re-entered the conversation. "I don't think it's a Hampstead secret that, other than running his marina, Kevin Shelby also deals drugs on occasion."

"Been doin' it since high school," said Ben-David.

"Kaj told me that he had been business partners with Kevin and Matty before he broke with them."

"When did that happen?"

"Around the time Daria started dating him."

"Ever see him with any drugs?"

"We smoked some pot together, *which is legal now*, but, no, I never saw him with any hard stuff."

"Why did he split from Kevin Shelby and Matty Joshua?"

"Because I told him I couldn't be involved with someone who was doing drugs or selling them. Knight family rule," Daria said.

"And Matty didn't like that," Ben-David stated.

"No. Kaj told me that Matty thought they had a good thing going—referred to the three of them as the power triangle or something stupid like that. Anyway, I guess Matty got upset because, at the time, Kaj was dating Ingrid Bara, which meant that he had access to the Lakeview crowd—a market with an appetite for the kind of stuff Matty and Kevin could get for them. They already had the area north of town out by Shelby's Marina and the beaches covered, but they needed an 'in' down here, and Kaj was perfect. Then he started seeing me, and they lost some of their clientele because Kevin and Matty were too well known, and every time they came down to hang out at The Buccaneer Pub, the owners made it uncomfortable for them. I think because Ingrid worked there and was dating Kaj, they never suspected him of dealing—just thought he was there to see his girl."

"Then you entered the picture, and Kaj parted company with them."

"Pretty much," Daria said.

"Kaj start working with them again after you broke his heart?"

"I don't know."

"What about you?" Ben-David asked Brendan.

"I still saw him around Lakeview Village on occasion, but I couldn't say if he was back with them or not."

Ben-David consulted his notepad. "So, Matty Joshua was angry with Kaj when he stopped working with them. How about Kevin Shelby?"

Brendan said, "He told me Kevin didn't seem fazed by it. Apparently, Kevin has been dealing for so long that associates just come and go. But, we want to make clear that we officially have no idea what Kevin Shelby and Matty Joshua do. It was all hearsay from Kaj."

"Who happens to be dead now after having a knife thrust into his back last night," Ben-David added.

"Again, wish we could help you with who did that, but the only thing I think we're going to be able to give you is that Matty Joshua was pissed when Kaj started dating Daria and stopped hanging out with him and Kevin. Hardly a motive for murder, I would think." Brendan finished his scotch and then uncrossed his legs and folded his hands across his lap. "And, Daria broke up with Kaj a year ago. If Matty really wanted Kaj dead, then why did he wait a year to do it? Doesn't make any sense."

Rachel watched as Brendan presented his thoughts. Whereas Daria had become more and more of a flake during the interview, Brendan had remained calm. Meanwhile, Jayson Jasper had already risen to the serving table, poured himself another tall scotch, and returned to the circle, nodding his head more and more often now as if he understood every aspect of the relationship web being discussed.

Certified alcoholic.

"Do you know where we might find Matty Joshua other than his house?" Ben-David asked.

"Not a clue," Brendan said. "I'd say start at Shelby's Marina, but you already know that."

Ben-David closed his notebook and gave a nod to Rachel. "You have any more questions for them?"

Naturally, she wanted to know more about Daria and Christine, but that would be better handled with Christine. She didn't think she could handle being in the same room as Daria for much longer, regardless of the heaven-sent, 30-year-old "parent" scotch. Now, if Brendan had wanted to speak with her for a bit more, then that would be different.

"No," she replied.

Ten minutes later, the van was rolling down the driveway toward the gate when Ben-David hung up his cell phone. He'd placed a call to Shelby's Marina right after starting the engine.

"Well?" Rachel asked.

"Time to interview Matty Joshua."

12

O badiah Ben-David turned the van onto US-23, and Rachel Roberts watched the speedometer climb until it read sixty miles per hour. She had thought that he was a five-mile-per-hour-over-the-speed-limit type of driver.

Ben-David hit the cruise control button, and the van traveled north along the scenic waters of Lake Huron. The wind had died down some, and the water was like a mammoth deep blue-colored bedspread that needed to be straightened. It would take around twenty minutes to reach Shelby's Marina, and, still feeling a rush from interviewing the Knights, Rachel was anxious to find out what Matty Joshua knew. She was now also interested in contacting Christine Harper to see if they could get together tonight. But, first, she needed to clear the air with Ben-David.

She started off with, "I have a hard time believing that you don't know who Matty Joshua is."

"Go on," he said.

"Well, you've worked this area for decades, and you knew who the Knights' attorney was. I don't know who Matty Joshua is, but I've heard of Kevin Shelby before. No one in Lakeview likes the guy; that's why they keep their boats at the state dock."

"I would too," Ben-David interrupted.

"So, it's obvious that you know who Kevin Shelby is and who he hangs around with. So, you have to know something about Matty Joshua."

"Sound reasoning," he said.

"Do you?"

He laughed. "Yep. Know exactly who that absolute train wreck of a human being is."

"Then why act like you didn't know who he was when we were with the Knights?"

"I wanted them to think that I didn't know who he was for two reasons. One, they'd feel more in control and frame their impression to suit themselves, and two, their answer would possibly give me a better gauge on what percentage of the truth they had told during the rest of the interview."

She was impressed with his answer. "And how much of the truth do you think they told us?"

"Well, they sure were cocky with the whole lawyer disguise bit. Normally, the rich folk have their lawyer there, say very little, and that's about it. But when you think that you're beyond the law, or know how to at least work around it, then you get bored and pull stunts like they did. The fact that they tried that told me more than what they said in the interview."

"What did it tell you?"

"It told me that they have no respect for us or for the investigation. It also told me that they didn't care that Kaj Reynard was murdered."

"So, you think they lied?"

"Everyone does. Whether it's what you say, or what you embellish, or what you leave out, it's all the same. With people like the Knights, I always like to start with what truths they told and then work from there. Problem is," he said, looking at her, "I don't know what the truths were that they told us. And that's dangerous." He concentrated on the road again. "Now, were we dealing with a room full of zeroes today who had nothing to do with Kaj Reynard's murder and wanted a little juvenile excitement by trying to pass off their alcoholic family lawyer as their butler? Maybe. We'll have to keep their story front and center as we interview more people."

"What you're saying to me is that you lie when you investigate."

She watched as he tapped his large fingers on the steering wheel—each pat like the stroke of a typewriter, crafting his response. His mannerisms were magnetic. "All part of the game," he said.

"You did it with Ingrid Bara—saying that you didn't know anything about the Knights."

"I wanted to know what she really thought about them. Unless people have such strong feelings about someone where they either think that they've got to tell you how horrible that person is so that you're saved from any further pain or how wonderful someone is so that you should try to get to know them more, it's better off not telling them what you know and what you think about the people whom you're asking about. I always try to come across as if I don't really know anyone—even if I'm asking about a friend like Corey Ritter, who people know I must have some sort of relationship with because of the nature of our work. I just say something like, 'Well, I know him professionally, but that's about it.' See? Puts someone right at ease, and I'll have a better chance of finding out what they really think about him."

What he was saying made sense, but since they were investigating the murder together, she wanted to be more in the loop. "I'd like it if you let me know what you knew and what your approach was going to be ahead of time. When you revealed that you knew who Jayson Jasper was, I couldn't hide my surprise, and that doesn't make me—*us*—look good."

"But, it makes us look out of sync, and people tend to relax around people who they think they're smarter than."

"Great. You were playing me too," she said, her face turning into a scowl.

He glanced over at her and then said, "I'm sorry. Didn't mean to use you to get what I needed. Might have backfired anyway because the Knights already thought they were better than us. What I don't know, however, is if I shook them up enough by exposing Jasper. I could have let the charade play out, but in the field, you've gotta make decisions—sometimes, right in the spur of the moment—and I thought it best to hit back."

It was a half-apology, she decided, but better than nothing at all. "You'll tell me more from now on, right?"

"My trust in you is growing, and I'll fill you in on what I can when we're alone." He took a sip from his coffee mug. "But. There still might be occasions when I've got to make a call about something that we haven't discussed. You'll have to trust my judgment. Fair enough?"

She wanted to pull a Topaz Kennedy and demand to know everything, but, at this point, she couldn't. She said, "Fair," and concentrated on the road ahead.

The van traveled another quarter of a mile, the trees hiding Lake Huron from sight. When they reached the next bend, the trees thinned, and she watched as Ben-David's eyes scanned back and forth between the road and the water.

When he had done it at least ten times, she said, "See something out there?"

"Wait for a few seconds," he said.

She did, and then the trees disappeared for a long stretch, giving them a clear view of the water.

"See that boat out there?" he asked, pointing.

She followed his finger and, in the distance, saw a solitary boat on the water.

"Someone you know?"

"Yeah, an old salt named Abner Hutch. Lives out past the bight, north of Shelby's and north of my place. Probably out there with his grandkids. They're up visiting this week." He met eyes with Rachel. "Good guy."

Rachel nodded, then stared out at the boat until it disappeared behind a wall of trees.

"But Matty Joshua is not one of the good guys, right?"

"It's going to be an ordeal interviewing that fucker," Ben-David said.

Her eyes opened wide, and her head tilted back, surprised by his language.

"What?" he asked.

The language didn't bother her—God knows she'd had Adrienne Astra use the handy little f-word on occasion—but having Ben-David say it defied one of her assumptions about him. "I'm not offended, but…gosh, I don't want this to come out wrong—"

"You thought I was Jewish, right? Well, Jewish people swear too. Hell, with a name like Obadiah Ben-David, I would have thought I was Jewish too."

"Are you? I haven't seen you wearing a kippah."

"I am, or at least was. I don't know. Haven't worn a kippah in over thirty years."

She was immediately interested as religion had always held a sort of fascination for her. But she didn't want to push. "Is there a synagogue in Hampstead?"

"One. It's about two miles west of town." He paused. "Don't attend anymore."

She wanted to ask why but waited instead.

He took another drink of coffee.

"I don't and won't talk about it, but a long time ago, something happened in my life that threw everything into question shall we say."

She gave the typical nod of understanding, without understanding, and let the silence do the talking for both of them. He could be both elusive and straightforward at the same time. *First, I need to clone him, then perform literary plastic surgery on him so that no one will make the connection, and then inject him into Dark After Midnight.*

They traveled through town and then followed US-23 north until they came to a sign with an arrow beneath the words MARINA.

They turned, and Ben-David said, "Okay, let's see what Matty Joshua has to say."

13

If marinas were armpits, then Rachel Roberts determined that Shelby's Marina would be first among equals. From the moment that Obadiah Ben-David had pulled his black van into Shelby's massive dirt parking lot, she had seen no less than three broken boat hoists, two ramshackle buildings that looked like they would fall over at any moment, weeds sprouting everywhere, an ice cooler outside of the main building that had missing doors, and absolutely no one who even resembled her version of what a boater should look like.

The van passed by a large barn that had no doors and no lights on inside, which only allowed her to get a glimpse of the looming dark hull of a massive sailboat resting on a trailer. This entire place looked as if twenty years ago, a siren sounded, and every person either ran out the front entrance or boarded a boat in the marina and took off forever. Once past the barn, she could see a litter of sailboats, cabin cruisers, and yachts in the rows of slips. Still, not one person, though.

"Where in the hell is he?" Rachel asked.

"Dory said he'd meet us in front of the main building."

"You don't sound too sure of that."

"It's 'cause I'm not. Dory tells the truth about half of the time, and I'm guessing that Matty Joshua tells her the truth half of the time."

The van rolled the final yards toward a decrepit two-story building that had once been painted red but had so much of the paint flaking away that it looked pink with gray streaks. An old office chair with stuffing coming out of the seat cushion sat below a bay window with only one shutter.

Ben-David parked the vehicle in front of the building's solitary door, which had frosted glass on the top half and a brass kick plate on the bottom. Above the door hung a wooden sign with white letters spelling SHELBY'S.

Rachel looked around Ben-David's enormous frame. The dinner-time sun cast long shadows across the dirt driveway, and the wind rippled the water in the basin. So far, the case continued to parallel her development of the story. She thought about it for a moment and then decided that even though she was writing a novel, the best way to describe her process was to imagine it as if she was the writer, director, and stage manager of a new play being performed in her mind, except that she was performing all three jobs simultaneously. As she sat in the first row of the theater with her pen and legal pad in hand, characters appeared on stage as she thought them up. When she wrote their dialog, they performed their lines and interacted with the other characters present. As she described the setting, it faded in, and props appeared wherever she wanted them. And stage right, with a spotlight illuminating her, was Rachel's narrator, wearing a microphone and headset to privately communicate with Rachel as she wrote the story and told her narrator what she had in mind. Hence, for her current project, *Dark After Midnight*, the yellow legal pad had a beginning written down along with a rough outline of where the first third of the story might go. Adrienne Astra and Rose Varga were onstage, Adrienne center stage and Rose stage left. Adrienne was tapping her right foot, impatiently waiting for more direction, while Rose seemed to be taking in her surroundings and studying the props as they appeared onstage. There were a few other minor characters starting to interact, and because some of the scenes were set to music, an orchestra had now appeared in the pit and was trying some of the tunes that Rachel had mentioned as atmospheric touches. In the balcony, to Rachel's right, was Topaz Kennedy, drinking a martini, blowing her kisses, and laughing with Suzanne Freeman. In the row behind her was her editor, J. Rudolph Hightower, who occasionally leaned forward, looked at her notepad, and whispered things like, *"That's good. We can make that work,"* and, *"No. The readers have seen that before,"* and, *"You haven't written anything today. I need pages, dammit!"* Even, *"Sure you want to have Adrienne do that? How many times do I have to tell you: Show, don't tell."*

Finally, there was the Doubleday brass, who were stationed at every exit with the president and chief executive officer at the fuse box, threatening to throw the breakers and cancel the play at any moment.

"You see something out there?" Ben-David asked.

The playhouse disappeared, thankfully—she didn't need Ben-David in there—and the marina came back into view. "No," she said, unbuckling her seat belt.

They approached the door, and Rachel noticed that the brass kick plate had a large dent right in the middle of it, and the upper right corner screw was missing. The welcome mat looked like two English mastiffs had fought over it.

Ben-David didn't bother to knock and opened the door.

Before she could concentrate on the small woman seated behind what looked like a simple metal desk supplied by the U.S. Government, Rachel noticed the piles and *piles* of magazines and newspapers haphazardly stacked on the floor. The carpeting had large holes in it, and there was a tangle of lines thrown on a broken wicker chair in the right-hand corner with two buoys resting on top of the maze. To the left of the desk was a slim hallway that led off into darkness. Next to the desk was an ancient oscillating fan that jerked unevenly through its cycle, threatening to break at any moment. She thought she could smell coffee, but the room's musty odor overpowered what would usually be a pleasant scent.

If she had to give a short description, she would have said that Shelby's Marina's front office looked like a travel agency that had closed thirty years ago.

"Hey, big stuff," Dory said to Ben-David.

The marina's administrative assistant had short hair and was wearing a dark tank top, the color impossible to determine because there were no lights on in the room.

There was a flicker of red-orange light and then a steady flame as Rachel watched Dory light a cigarette. Speaking of the cancer sticks, as they approached the small utility desk, Dory's skin looked like a cigarette bomb had gone off inside her, and the charring had slowly oozed to the surface, creating ripples of crusty wrinkles.

Ben-David gave Dory a quick grin and then peered down the hallway. "Kevin in?"

Dory inhaled, and the end of her cigarette glowed—a pinpoint of red against the room of shadows. "At home," she said, exhaling. "Be in tomorrow morning." She paused, watching the smoke rise from the cigarette. "Late morning."

"Was he in today?" Ben-David asked.

She took another drag, eyeballing Rachel, and then exhaled. "No," she said. "You here about the murder? All anybody's talkin' about."

"Matty Joshua been talkin' about it?"

Dory grinned and tapped her cigarette over a golden-colored ash tray. "He's always talkin' about somethin', that boy."

"Is he around?" Rachel asked.

Dory's grin disappeared as if she had a sensor telling her that Rachel was not a local. "Haven't seen you around before," she said to Rachel.

It was hard to determine the woman's age. She could be anywhere from forty-five to sixty-five, Rachel guessed. "I live south of Hampstead and am not up this way very often."

"You a lifer?"

Ben-David chuckled.

"I'm sorry. What's a lifer?"

"Ha! You just answered that one!" Dory shouted.

Rachel made eyes with Ben-David as if to say, *"What in the hell is a lifer?"*

"Being a lifer means that you were born in Hampstead and have stayed here. Lifers like this fine lady," he said, pointing at Dory with his coffee mug, *"think* it gives you seniority around town."

"Does," Dory said, correcting him. "Always has. Always will. You should know that 'cause you're one of us."

"I forgot," Ben-David said, shrugging.

"Lucky I like you so much, you tall bastard."

Ben-David laughed and waved his thumb toward Rachel. "You should like her too. Good people. Learning the P. I. ropes."

"That true?" Dory asked Rachel.

The woman was something else. Now she rose to her full height of perhaps five feet and walked around the desk, exposing her cut-off jean shorts and thick stubby legs. Rachel saw that her hair was gray and the tank top was black. And now that she had a better look, she noticed that part of the tank top was untucked as if Dory had been trying to tuck it in but got interrupted by their entrance. Rachel could also see sweat stains on the shirt under Dory's armpits, and Dory's forehead was beaded with sweat. She had one flip flop on but quickly kicked it off as she playfully snatched Ben-David's coffee mug out of his hands and went over behind one of the mammoth stacks of magazines that were resting on top of a wooden table that had been behind Ben-David when they entered the room.

Soon, Rachel could hear her pouring liquid into the mug. The only thing visible was a tuft of gray hair above the top magazine. Then, Dory started whistling the national anthem.

"Murders make you feel patriotic?" Ben-David said.

123

There was no reply, and a few moments later, Dory wheeled around the stack of magazines and gave the mug back to Ben-David before resuming her perch behind the metal desk. She stopped whistling and took a final drag on her cigarette before stubbing it out in the ashtray and then lighting another one. "Just want justice served," she finally said.

Ben-David took a drink. "You still make the second best coffee in town."

"Darwinger's still number one?" she asked.

"Unfortunately so, but it's damn good," he said, giving her a small toast.

"I'll let the comment pass."

"You always do."

Dory put her bare feet up on the desk. "So, you want to talk to Matty, huh?"

"You said he'd be out front waiting for us."

Dory blew a smoke ring. Rachel still had no clue how people did it. When Topaz had briefly taken up smoking during a rough patch, *"The stress, darling,"* she had figured out how to do it. *"Make your villain do it at least twice in the next book. You have to!"* She didn't.

"That's what he told me," Dory said.

"Any idea where he might be?" Rachel asked.

There was a low thump from somewhere down the hallway.

Dory tried to sneak a glance before they noticed, but she was too late. "Maybe back there?" she said.

Ben-David rolled his eyes. "Follow me," he said to Rachel.

"Tell him I said hi," Dory said, snickering.

There were three doors in the hallway. Ben-David pointed to the first and said, "Supply closet." They walked another step, and he pointed to the door on the other side of the hallway. "Restroom." Then, they took three more steps and stopped outside the door at the end. The word "Manager" was stenciled into the door frame, and the doorknob looked like it was about to come off. "This is Kevin Shelby's office. I think Matty's in here."

She turned around. Dory had poked her head around the corner but pulled it back when Rachel looked at her.

Ben-David knocked on the door then opened it.

Inside, standing behind a gargantuan desk, was a bare-chested man of around thirty with a towel around his waist. Matty Joshua had a big smile across his face, and a quick glance down at the bulge in his towel told her what was going on in the office right before they had entered. He rubbed his hands through his shoulder-length mane of blond hair, pulling it back into a ponytail. Proud of his physique, which was nothing to be proud about, he rubbed his chest hair and then motioned them to sit in the two chairs on their side of the desk.

"You running the marina now, Matty?" Ben-David asked as he sat down.

Matty sat too and then poured himself a short glass of Jack Daniels from a bottle that he pulled out from one of the desk drawers. "Pretty much," he said.

"Shelby know you walk around his office in only a towel?"

"I don't see him around. Do you?"

"Do you always conduct business dressed like that?" Rachel said.

He took a drink and cocked his head to one side. "I think better when I'm relaxed."

Ben-David pulled out a large Swiss Army knife from his pocket and popped open the main blade. "Think about this."

Matty bit his lower lip.

"I'm sure you've heard by now that a blade bigger than this made its way into the middle of Kaj Reynard's back last night." He rotated the blade and then closed it, putting the knife back in his pocket. "You weren't south of Hampstead last night, were you?"

"Maybe I was, and maybe I wasn't. Not talking to you without my lawyer."

"Why do you need a lawyer?"

She watched him swallow twice and then start to fidget, tapping his knuckles on the tabletop.

Ben-David leaned forward. "Run out of answers already?"

Big-time marina owner Matty Joshua took a shaky sip then set the glass down. "I was south of Hampstead last night."

"With Kaj Reynard?"

"How'd you even get my damn name?"

"Answer the question."

"I wasn't with him last night," he said and then paused, seeming to weigh his next words carefully—*if that was even possible*, Rachel thought. "But I saw him."

"Where?"

"He was leaving the Lakeview subdivision as I was arriving. You see his new wheels?"

Ben-David shook his head no.

"Brand new, fully-loaded Bronco, man. Serious swag. Can't believe Ford brought it back. Glad they did, though." He put out his hands like he was revving up a motorcycle, which made no sense to Rachel. "That sumbitch is a serious load. Kaj's color was, get this, *antimatter blue*. What the hell does that even mean? Don't matter, 'cause it was tight as shit."

"Those aren't cheap," Rachel said, remembering researching the new Bronco as a possibility for Adrienne Astra's wheels in *Dark After Midnight*. *"Time to trade in the Mustang and get rough, darling!"* Topaz had commanded.

"They sure ain't, baby," Matty said.

"Don't call me that."

He held up his hands. "Whoa, whoa, whoa, I'm sorry, ma'am."

She knew he didn't mean a word of it.

"Any idea where he got the money to pay for the Bronco?"

Matty Joshua suddenly seemed to find the floor very interesting.

"He hanging around with you and Kevin Shelby again?"

Matty kept his head down. "Don't know anything about that, Obadiah. He's just a friend."

"What time did you see him leave the Lakeview subdivision?" Ben-David asked.

"Around seven."

Rachel jumped back in. "Why were you in Lakeview?"

Matty looked up, studying the open door to the hallway. He lowered his voice and said, "I was seein' someone."

Rachel rose and closed the door.

"Thanks," Matty said.

"Who were you seeing?" said Ben-David.

"My girlfriend, Ingrid Bara."

Rachel turned her head toward the door and then back at white trash playboy Matty Joshua. "Your girlfriend?"

"Well, yeah, she is my steady, but we've always kept things kind of...*open*, you might say."

"Does she know that?" Rachel asked, feeling like Ben-David had momentarily jumped inside her body.

Matty poured himself another short glass of Jack Daniels and took a drink. "Yeah, I mean, I guess so. We're still together after all this time, right?"

"Not really a straight answer, Matty," Ben-David said and then looked at Rachel. "We'll have to speak with Ingrid again."

"Again?" Matty said.

Ben-David motioned for the bottle and a plastic cup from the stack that was on a bookshelf behind Matty.

After shrugging, Matty passed over a cup and the bottle.

Ben-David set his coffee down and then filled up his plastic cup with whiskey. He took a sip and then said, "Yeah, we spoke with her today. Funny thing though, she never mentioned you." Ben-David stretched his long legs and then crossed his feet on top of the desk. He drank again. "But you know who she did talk about? The Knights."

At this mention, Matty Joshua lowered his own legs from the desk top and would not make eye contact with Ben-David. Rachel wondered why the mention of the Knights had spooked him. "You know the Knights?" she asked.

He glanced at her for a second and then studied the amber liquid in his cup. "Not personally. But I know *of them*." He downed the rest of his drink. "What did Ingrid say?"

"What do you *think* she said?" Ben-David asked.

"No clue. I mean, Kaj used to date Daria and stuff, and he and Brendan were besties."

"Besties?" Ben-David said.

Matty Joshua laughed. It was not a pleasant laugh like the kind that makes other people smile or let their guard down; it was more of a patronizing guttural hack. "You're such a dinosaur, Obadiah. We gotta get you caught up with all the new lingo. Besties means best friends."

Ben-David's face was stone. "I see," he said. "Were you *besties* with Kaj Reynard? You know that I know you hung out with him and Kevin Shelby."

"I do odd jobs for Kevin around here—"

"Like screw his secretary?" Ben-David interrupted.

"Man, lay off, Obadiah."

Ben-David's expression didn't change. "Continue."

Matty motioned for the bottle.

"No. When I think you've answered enough questions honestly, I'll give you this back. Might even head out so you can continue your fun with Dory—if she's still here."

Matty exhaled. "Kaj and Kevin were golfing partners on Monday night league. My partner was and still is Brett Slater. Every now and again, we'd get matched up with Kaj and Kevin, but that was all I ever really saw of Kaj."

"How'd that go? You know he was pokin' Ingrid before he dumped her for Daria Knight."

"Man, fuck you. I'm not answering anything else if that's the way you're gonna be, bruh."

"What did you call me?" Ben-David asked.

"Forget it," Matty said.

"I won't forget it, and you better start telling me the truth before I give Ritter a call."

"I've told you the truth—"

With agility that surprised both her and Matty Joshua, Ben-David lowered his legs, leaned forward, and slammed his fist on top of the table. "No, you haven't!"

The 'No' was in his usual low, measured, and direct tone; the 'you haven't' came out like someone had dropped his vocal cords into a blender, flipped the switch, watched the transformation, and then poured the new, menacing and deafening enhancement into the air. Rachel blinked and shivered.

Matty froze in his seat.

"I've seen all three of you at least a dozen times together, and it wasn't at the golf course. Local tennis courts ring a bell?"

Matty's cockiness had left him, and Rachel watched as he readjusted his towel so that it would stay around his waist. "Okay, we used to hang out a little. Nothin' wrong with that, right?"

"But you stopped hanging out, correct?" Ben-David asked.

"Yeah. We did."

"Because of Ingrid?"

"I still want to know what she told you."

"You'll have plenty of time to ask her tonight. That is, if you didn't have anything to do with Kaj Reynard's death."

"Why would I want to kill Kaj?"

Why do you do anything that you do? Rachel thought

"I don't know," Ben-David said. "Why would you?"

"I didn't kill him, man. Now, can I please have another drink?"

"You weren't with Ingrid Bara last night because she worked the night shift until closing at The Buccaneer Pub. We've already verified that and seen the surveillance footage from inside the bar." Ben-David filled his plastic cup only half-full this time and then passed the bottle over to Matty Joshua, who took it with relief. "So. Where were you last night?"

Matty filled his glass and took a shaky sip. "Okay, okay, here's the truth. After I saw Kaj exit Lakeview in his new wheels, I went down to The Buck for drinks with Kevin."

Rachel interjected. "If you saw Kaj leave Lakeview at seven, then you probably arrived at The Buck around seven-fifteen. You see Ingrid when you got there?"

"Yeah, she was looking hot."

"You're lying," Rachel said. "Ingrid didn't start her shift until eight."

"I—"

"It's easier if you just tell the truth," she said, crossing her legs.

"Looks like you picked a good partner, Obadiah. She don't mess around. You two dating?"

"Get your shit together," Ben-David said.

"Okay, man, easy. Now I remember. I saw Kevin at the bar, and we had a few drinks. Then, Ingrid showed up, and she visited with us for a few minutes before starting her shift." A quick sip. "Around eight-thirty, Kevin blows out of there. Says he has somethin' to take care of at the marina before heading home. Now, off the record, that's always been his code for going to hook up with his lady friend on the side." He smiled as if pleased with himself for imparting a piece of information that they did not have. Rachel just wanted the interview over with. "I stayed for one more ice-cold tall boy and then headed home for the night. End of story."

Ben-David jerked his thumb back at the door. "Can *anyone* verify that you were at home last night?"

Matty frowned. "Naw. We only do it here. She's never been to my house."

"So, no one can verify that you were home last night?" Rachel pressed.

"No. I don't have any way of proving it."

"Make any phone calls? Get on the internet from your home computer?"

"Hey, that would have been a good way to show where I was." He gazed at the ceiling after taking another sip. "Fuck. Never crossed my mind."

"So, you used to hang out with Kaj Reynard, and he used to date your current girlfriend, Ingrid Bara. Then, you stopped hanging out with him. Last night, someone murdered him, and you have no alibi for where you were. That about sum it up?"

Matty Joshua's eyes darted side to side as if two velociraptors had ambushed him and were about to pounce. "You make it sound like I could have done it."

"You could have," Ben-David said. "Now, let's say that you didn't. Is there anyone else that you know of who would have wanted him dead?"

Matty got his eyes under control and leaned back to the point where Rachel thought he would fall over, but the man in the powder blue towel managed to stay upright. "I might know someone," he said. Then, Matty leaned forward and got serious. "A week or so ago, I was in Darwinger's grabbing a morning coffee and looking for Baby Lloyd. We sometimes share fishing information on where the bastards are bitin'. Anyway, Agatha tells me he's down at the dock. I head outside, cross over twenty-three and then stop. There's Baby Lloyd and Kaj standing eye-to-eye at the end of the dock and arguing. It's so heated that they don't see me, and I figure I'll eavesdrop for a minute before I enter the conversation." He looked back and forth between Rachel and Ben-David one time. "You know, if I can tell what they're arguing about, then maybe I can help smooth things over and stuff."

Rachel begrudgingly gave him a nod of affirmation. *Anything to move the clown along.*

"I'd only listened for a few seconds when I see Kaj turn away from Baby Lloyd and stomp down the dock toward me. Then, I hear Baby Lloyd yell, 'I'll kill you, you sonofabitch!'" Matty paused, the master storyteller apparently in his zone. "I gotta tell you…I think he meant it."

"Did you speak with Kaj about it?" Ben-David asked.

Matty rubbed his eyes, his fists twisting like corkscrews. "Naw. I friggin' turned around and ran." He pulled his hands down, and Rachel couldn't tell if he had been hiding tears or if the rubbing was another one of this dufus's nervous tics. He continued. "Wasn't gettin' in the middle of that war."

"How about after?"

"Nope. Didn't see him again until last night."

"How about Baby Llyod?"

"No. Haven't been in for coffee all week."

Hearing the word coffee prompted Ben-David to take a drink from his mug, and Rachel filled the silence with, "Why not? He didn't have a problem with you."

"I know, but I've never seen him so mad before. And, I didn't know if he had seen me or not. I'm pretty sure Kaj did, but I didn't care."

"So, you wanted to give Baby Llyod some time to cool down in case he did see you. That right?" she said.

Matty's face lit up like a boy who had just been given his first Happy Meal. "Yeah. Yeah. You see why, right?"

And now seemingly full of confidence, the questionee became the questioner as Matty asked, "Obadiah, you're close with Baby Lloyd. You ever seen him blow his top?"

"Never heard him threaten anyone before," Ben-David said.

"I know. Me either! I 'bout had shit runnin' down my legs crossin' twenty-three."

"Ever find out why Kaj was there?"

Matty shook his head. "No. It was weird because I seriously had never seen them on the dock before. Kaj would swing by Darwinger's for coffee sometimes, but who doesn't in Hampstead?

Until today, me, thought Rachel.

"So why do you *think* he was there?" Ben-David asked.

"I got nothin', man," Matty said. "Just doesn't add up."

Rachel asked, "Do you think Baby Lloyd could have killed Kaj Reynard?"

For the first time since they had met him, Matty's playboy act vanished. "I don't know." He tightened and then smoothed his towel again. "I hope not."

Baby Lloyd Darwinger stood behind the helm of his Boston Whaler and motored away from the small dock that had been in the family for generations. As he took a quick peek back at his beloved gas station, he felt the uneasiness that accompanies regret. After being inside all day, hearing the locals continue to gossip about the murder, he had pulled his wife aside half an hour ago and told her that he needed to get away. Knowing what he meant, Agatha had approved, for she was aware that there had been words exchanged between him and Kaj Reynard but didn't know *what* had been said.

Unless Kaj told someone, then I'm the only one who knows what I said to him that day, he thought.

The waters of Lake Huron had been his sanctuary since he was a small boy, and he figured that it would take an act of God to pry him away from the things he enjoyed: the deep blue hues of calm water on a summer's day, the seagulls gliding across the sky above, the taste of fried Walleye, fries, and ice-cold beer after a day of fishing, seeing the orange ball of fire rise above the horizon in the morning while sitting on his dock, drinking strong coffee, and, most of all, the cool summer breezes on ninety degree days that refreshed his body and nurtured his soul anytime he felt lost.

And right now, that is exactly what Lloyd Darwinger the Third felt.

As the Boston Whaler left the protection of the small inlet, the lake's waves started to slap against the hull. The Huron breezes were here again, and there was a small craft advisory out. Baby Lloyd Darwinger didn't care. He needed to be out on the water; he needed clarity; he needed to get his mind right—even if he had to stay out here all night. His wife wouldn't worry; he'd done it before, and she would know where he was.

What she didn't know, however, was where he had been last night.

14

"Think Agatha's telling the truth?" Rachel Roberts asked Obadiah Ben-David.

They were each leaning against their respective vehicles in Darwinger's parking lot. The sun had gone down, and the lights on the roof over the gas pumps were now on, bathing the rectangular area in a soft yellow glow.

"I think she is," Ben-David said and then pointed at the dark, churning waters of Lake Huron. "He's out there, but he'll be back." He turned toward Rachel, the increasing winds blowing his beard away from his neck. "We'll talk to him tomorrow morning when we meet here for coffee."

"I don't get it," Rachel said. "We just heard from his wife that she can't account for his whereabouts last night because she went to bed early. Then, when we ask her about Baby Lloyd's relationship with Kaj Reynard, she tells us that they used to be fishing buddies but that there had been an argument last week, and her husband wouldn't tell her any more about it. Now, Baby Lloyd takes off in a boat for who knows how long tonight. And last night, Kaj Reynard comes in from the water with a knife in his back. Don't you think it's a bit suspicious that Baby Lloyd and Agatha didn't mention a thing about this when we were both here in the morning?"

"It's too early to rule anyone out for sure, and we need more info, but I don't think he killed Kaj Reynard, Rachel."

"How can you say that? We need to talk to him as soon as possible."

"And we will. Just not tonight."

"You said you had a boat. Why don't we get on it and go find him?"

Ben-David laughed. "You feel this wind? We've got a major storm comin' in tonight." He glanced up at the sky. "And God's gonna be pissin' on us in less than an hour. No way I'm takin' *Grizzly Adams* out in this."

"*Grizzly Adams* is the name of your boat?"

"Most underrated television show—ever."

"Let me guess, you've got a bear at home?"

"Close. Got a bloodhound. Have had four of 'em now, named 'em all Ben after the bear." He took a peek at his watch. "Reminds me, old Ben's probably mad because I haven't fed him yet. Should have swung into my place on the way back from Shelby's, but I guess the Jack Daniels and what Matty Joshua said about Baby Lloyd distracted me."

"He's probably left you a puddle or a pile by now," Rachel said.

"No, Ben's got a dog door from my bedroom to the back yard—can do his business when he pleases. You got a pet?"

"My cat Hemy."

"How long you had him?"

"He's eight. How old is Ben?"

"Seven. Slowin' down more every day."

She gave a nod of understanding. Then, the front door of Darwinger's opened. Agatha stepped out, saw them, and then headed back inside. This brought her back on topic. "See? She's nervous. We have to go out there and find Baby Lloyd."

"Rain would blind us, and being on the water during a thunderstorm is not smart. All we'd do is get wet, get seasick, and maybe drown if it gets as bad as the weather report says it's going to."

"But *he's* out there," Rachel said.

"Never said Baby Lloyd was the sharpest knife in the drawer." He pulled the key fob out of his pocket and unlocked the van. "But he knows the waters, even when they're rough."

She shook her head in disappointment.

"Look, he's got nowhere to go. Not gonna leave Agatha and the gas station that's been in his family forever. Know him too well. Whatever he knows, he'll tell us tomorrow morning. Now, we had a good day. There's always a chance that you get lucky on the first day, but it didn't happen. People don't always tell the full truth—like Ingrid Bara. Would've saved us a whole other trip tomorrow if she'd told us that she was dating Matty Joshua. But now we've got to find out why she didn't mention it. See? This business is not an A leads to B leads to C kinda deal." He opened the driver's side door. "I'm gonna head home, take care of Ben, throw a big steak on the grill, and call Corey Ritter. I'll get some information from him—won't tell me everything he's got—but then I'll give Amos a buzz, and he'll come over and fill in the rest over a tall Dewar's. They both know you're with me, so they're in no rush to interview you."

"What about staying here until Baby Lloyd gets back?"

Ben-David paused. "I can't stop you, but all you'll do is lose a good night of sleep."

"But what if he is the murderer? He could kill again." As the words left her mouth, she realized that she was now thinking like a pulp novelist instead of a detective. Who was Baby Lloyd going to kill now? Before Ben-David could reply, she said, "Okay, that's far-fetched, but he has to be a priority, right?"

"Absolutely, he is. Right now, we've got Brendan and Daria Knight, Matty Joshua, and Baby Lloyd Darwinger connected to Kaj Reynard with no alibi for where they were last night. We've spoken with the Knights and Matty, so we'll start with Baby Lloyd tomorrow."

"Then move on to Kevin Shelby and finally circle back around to Ingrid Bara," she said.

"It's what *I* had in mind."

"How about me? What can I do tonight?"

"If you're up for it, maybe you can talk to that book blogger friend of yours, Christine Harper."

"I'll give her a call when I get home."

"Good," said Ben-David. "Now, here's the rule for nights: Unless it is something that can't wait until morning, we both sit on it." He pouted. "Yeah, I'll have my damned cell phone next to my bed in case something happens, but I won't like it. Now that you're a real part of this, I'd keep your phone handy at night too. There's always the chance that we will get something and have to act on it right away. Been a while since I've received a 3 a.m. phone call, but it does happen on occasion."

She bit her tongue, hearing Ben-David unknowingly reveal her next book's title. But she couldn't concentrate on *3 a.m. Phone Call* right now; she hadn't written one word of *Dark After Midnight* yet. She pulled her key fob out and unlocked her Expedition, then held up her cell phone. "I'll have it on my nightstand."

He started to get into his van, but she decided that she had to ask the question that had been on her mind ever since they left Agatha ten minutes ago. "Evidence aside, do you think you know who did it? Gut feeling?"

Hearing the words, he reversed course and stood between the interior and the door. "No clue. Could be someone we spoke with today. Could be someone we haven't spoken to yet." He paused, looking out at the whitecaps roll in toward the shore. "You?"

She thought about her quick conversation with Topaz while he was using the restroom in Darwinger's. *"Glad you're getting ideas!...Oh, yes, the best news of the day by far...Interesting, yes, why wouldn't she tell you that he was her boyfriend...Ah-ha! I've got it: It's the marina owner, darling!"* she had said. "I'm leaning toward Baby Lloyd, but that could be too obvious."

His eyes left the water, and he shrugged. "Can't rule it out." He climbed in and said, "Good night."

A minute later, his vehicle had left the parking lot and headed north on US-23. She climbed up into her SUV and started the engine. The purple accent lighting on her instrument panel calmed her nerves as she put the vehicle into drive.

Before she reached the end of the gravel parking lot, the first large rain drops began to hit her windshield.

It was time to get home—and find out what Christine Harper knew.

Landon Beach

PART II

Wind and Waves

15

Later that evening, Rachel Roberts sat on Christine Harper's sofa with a glass of white wine. An overhead ceiling fan blew cool air down on her legs as she took a drink and then watched Christine move from the kitchen to the living room to join her. The beach house was cozy and lived in, different from her newer home, and hadn't changed since the last time she was here the previous summer. From the family pictures on the mantle to the worn spots on the carpet, Rachel could feel the warmth of the home and almost see the generations of Christine's family members moving about the house. Like many of the older homes in Lakeview, there was not a distinct style or color scheme that ran through the house—it was more by room. Bright colors in the kitchen and bathrooms. Earthy tones in the living room with striped throw blankets for accent. Muted and understated colors in the hallways and den. She'd never seen any of the bedrooms.

"I'm glad we're doing this," Christine said, plopping down on the couch after placing an ice bucket that was holding the bottle of wine they were sharing on the coffee table. "I have to get my mind off last night."

She then proceeded to tell Rachel everything about it—the relaxing evening by the bonfire, finally free from her ex-boyfriend, the freedom that would be short-lived because her family was arriving soon, the feel of the night breeze against her skin, balanced by the heat from the bonfire on the beach, seeing the familiar Beacon Island Light blink in the distance, and then the sheer terror of Kaj Reynard coming ashore, pleading for help and then plummeting to the sand…dead—with a knife in his back. Just hearing the eye-witness account had made Rachel shudder, and Christine had passed her a fleece blanket, which Rachel was now covered with. As more of the story had come out, more of the wine had emptied from the bottle, and they were now on number two—a Chateau Grand Traverse Dry Riesling. It was a favorite of Rachel's and one of the bottles she had purchased last summer on her annual August tour of the 40 or so wineries up in Traverse City. She liked to pick up at least one bottle per winery to last the year, her preferred winery being Mari Vineyards, which was owned by treasure hunter Marty Lagina. She had never been the stereotypical blitzed writer behind the gargantuan desk writing at all hours of the night, but she did enjoy a nice glass of wine while staring out at the heaven that was Lake Huron's flat blues.

"But, enough about me and last night," Christine said, "I just hope they catch whoever murdered that poor guy."

"You didn't know Kaj Reynard?" Rachel said.

"No."

"Not at all?"

"No. Now, c'mon, let's shift topics, girl. I've been talking about this all day. You sound like a private investigator."

Rachel took a drink of Riesling and then laughed to herself.

"What?" Christine said.

"You're more right than you know." Rachel set her glass down and then curled back up under the blanket. "Ready for this? I'm co-investigating the crime with Obadiah Ben-David."

Christine spit the wine in her mouth back into the glass. "Get out of here. What?"

"It's true. I've been thinking about a career change for a while now. You know I never talk about my job."

"Computers. Boo. No offense, but thank you for sparing me." She rose from the couch. "But you might owe me a new bottle of Riesling. That spit-up you just caused probably cost me ten dollars."

"Sorry," Rachel said, watching Christine put her glass in the sink and then pull a clean one down from her rack of wine glasses underneath one of the cabinets above the granite countertop. She liked the design and would think about having a rack installed in her kitchen. "But, I will tell you, it's a lot more interesting than staring at lines of code every day."

"Anything has to be better than that, sweetheart," Christine said, returning to the couch.

"Can't argue with you."

Christine filled her new wine glass and then sat back down. "Fill me in. What did you find out today?"

She wondered how much she should tell. Her main reason for being here, besides spending time with Christine, whose company she enjoyed, was to find out anything she could about the Knights by using Daria and Christine's supposed fling as a starting point. How would Ben-David start? She decided to lay off a bit. "I'll tell you all about it, but first, you tell me how the book business is going."

"Good. I still have my stable of new authors who I'm editing manuscripts for around the clock, and I'm also promoting like crazy." She took a sip. "Here's some insider news: Judge Macy Ashberry has a novel coming out next summer, and her publisher wants me to promote the book."

No, the Judge's ghostwriter has another book coming out next summer, and the publisher wants you to help put money in the judge's pockets. "That's great! And forgive me for asking, because I haven't checked your website in a while, but have you ever promoted someone as high profile as the judge?"

"Never. I've wanted to cover her for years, but word is, Riley Cannon's book will be coming out at the same time, and the judge is pulling out all of the stops." She put up her hands in celebration. "Fine by me. Just gets Harper's Highlights more publicity."

Rachel raised her glass. "To you."

They drank.

"Now, don't get me wrong. I would love it if Riley Cannon's team reached out to me. I mean, c'mon, this is her first book in ten years. But I'm not counting on it."

"Why?"

"I'm not supposed to talk about it—and this never came from me—but it sounds like the new book is not going well." She crossed her legs, and Rachel noticed the bright red nail polish on Christine's knobby toes.

That's an understatement. "What do you mean by 'not going well'?"

Christine pulled her long, flat-ironed hair into a ponytail and used a pink silk scrunchie to hold it in place. "I heard from an agent, who knows her agent's daughter, that she hasn't written a word."

"Did you read her first three books?"

"Who didn't." She paused. "Oh, sorry, did you read them?"

Rachel smiled and tapped Christine on the arm. "No worries. I read them."

"They were so good. I just don't know where she goes in book number four."

"You know she'll come up with something. I wouldn't trust that agent."

"Yeah, the big ones always pull it together in the end. Plus, she's got mister perfect on her team."

"Who's that?"

"The best editor in the business, J. Rudolph Hightower."

If only she could tell Christine how imperfect this man and his ego really were. "Maybe you'll get a call from her team as it gets closer to next June."

"Doubtful," she said, taking a sip, "but maybe."

"Your coverage is top-notch," Rachel said. "You told me last time that your reach was now, what, half-a-million readers?"

"Four million now," she said. "Once a few of the big dogs hired me to help promote their books, my reach expanded. Five, six years ago, I wouldn't have even been an afterthought for someone like Riley Cannon. But now, since a few of her contemporaries have hired me and are getting results, she's in play. I'll tell you the key, though. It's her agent, Topaz Kennedy."

Rachel agreed and was impressed by Christine's knowledge of the publishing game. Everything that had to do with Riley Cannon went through Topaz, but the rub was that Topaz was never available and only returned calls to people who were in the short list of contacts in her cell phone. She was notorious for looking at her phone when it rang, seeing a call coming from someone who was not in her contacts, and then turning it off. The only time this had backfired was when the President of the United States had called to both notify and congratulate her on being selected to be awarded the Presidential Medal of Freedom for her leadership, philanthropy, and representation of diverse voices in the publishing industry for more than forty years. That call had gone down the Voicemail black hole. Later that night, after another failed phone call, an FBI special agent had shown up at her door and told her that the President would be calling in five minutes. *"Rubbish, sir. I know all the presidents of the big five, and they know not to call this late."* The agent then told her that it was *the* President, and her eyes opened a bit wider. *"Believe it when I hear his gravelly voice, mister."* Her meeting with the President in the oval office, months later, would go down in history. He had told her that he and the first lady were mega-fans of Riley Cannon and, after his trademark wink, asked her—just between old friends—the true identity of the thriller author phenomenon. Topaz had replied, *"If you have to ask me that, then our country's in dire trouble, darling. And, while I'm here, get us out of the Middle East, ban Hollywood from talking politics, and please remove your hand from my knee."*

"Then I'm certain Ms. Kennedy will be in touch with you," Rachel said. "Four million followers—impressive."

Christine gave a devious smirk. "I had a little local help."

Could she be referring to Daria Knight? Rachel thought. "Tell me about it."

"In some ways, it won't be a surprise because I've talked about them with you before."

"Someone in Lakeview?"

"Indeed," Christine said. "The Knights."

"Of course." Rachel gave it a few seconds to approximate the time it would possibly take for her brain to make a connection to previous knowledge. She opened her eyes and then squinted at her friend. "Wait a minute. Did you finally get invited to one of their famous summer celebrations?"

Christine scootched closer and leaned forward; Rachel could tell that she was enjoying the gradual unfolding of the tale.

"On the money, girl." She tipped her wine glass back and cut the amount left in half. "But there's more."

Rachel feigned excitement and shifted her position on the couch so that she was facing Christine. "Do tell."

"Okay, we talked about them before, right?"

"A little bit—the compound, Beacon Island, the constant gossip around here about the family and its fortune, but that was about it."

"Good. So, I'd never met any of them. Then, one day last fall, I'm at Sunrise Grill grabbing a quick glass of wine and an appetizer before I go home and continue editing a horrible novel from one of my clients—nice guy, but this thriller was a howler compared to his earlier stuff. I'm talking awful—had to call for a re-write of the entire last third of the book, and I *never* have to do that." She rolled her eyes.

"Did it turn out okay, though?"

"Oh, yeah. Ended up being the heaviest edit of my career. Paid off for him, though. Book shot to number two on the *Times* bestseller list. I literally edited every single line in that manuscript. Weasel. He got a new three-book deal out of it too."

Rachel did her best to nod understandingly. *The book business—so kind to a select few, including her, so cruel to everyone else.*

"I'm getting way off track here."

"I don't mind." And she was being honest. Learning how all of the pieces fit together and what it took to pull the different levers of power still intrigued her.

"Really?"

"Really."

"You're such a good listener! Way better than me. I even get bored hearing myself talk." Then, Christine paused before taking another sip. "You ever thought about writing a book? I know you're a computer nerd, so, something nonfiction? I mean, you probably wouldn't write fictio—hey, that's being unfair. Why couldn't you write fiction, right?"

"I've thought about it," Rachel said. "But—sounds like a lot of work."

"You've got that right. Every now and then, I'll have a friend who says she has an idea for a book, and I just say, 'Don't do it! Save yourself the pain.'"

They both laughed.

"But what about the Knights?" Rachel asked.

"Right! So, I'm in the bar area of Sunrise Grill, and in walks Daria Knight." Christine looked to the ceiling as if replaying a clip from her time with Daria. "God, so beautiful." She shivered and then looked back at Rachel. "She walks up to my table and asks if she can join me. I say, 'Sure. Why the hell not!' and she orders a bottle of the most expensive white on the menu. I know because I always look at it on the menu to see if they've raised their price. I know, weird habit. Stay with me."

At the mention of wine, Rachel held out her glass for more.

"Sorry! Being a bad host."

Christine refilled their drinks and put the bottle back in the chiller. "We have a few drinks, and I ask her why she's at the restaurant. Remember what I told you last time? That everyone was gossiping that she and her brother Brendan hung out mostly at The Buck? Yeah, so I never thought she'd be at Sunrise Grill."

"What did she say?"

"Get this. She said that she had seen me sunbathing on my beach a few days prior and wanted to meet me."

Rachel gave her best imitation of Christine's devious grin.

"Right?" Christine said. "I know, I know, I was dating my boyfriend at the time—and he never found out what I'm about to tell you. Doesn't matter anyway now. He cheated on me with our twenty-three-year-old dental hygienist."

"Ouch. I wondered why he wasn't around here," Rachel said. "Danny, right?"

"Yeah, *Danny*. Three years together...ah, whatever." She blinked as if the overhead light had temporarily blinded her. "I'm starting to get tipsy."

"Same here," Rachel said, giving Christine's arm a pat.

"Good, good," she said, nodding her approval. "That particular night, Danny was away on a three-day golfing outing up north with some of his useless college buddies." She regained her smile. "Well, Daria and I finish the bottle, order and finish another, and end up back at my house where she gives me the most mind-blowing night in bed of my life. For an entire month, we sneak around Dannyboy—mostly using her place, which, I have to say, is un-bah-leave-ah-ble. I feel this real connection with her and almost leave him."

"What about Harper's Highlights?"

"Right. She never told me exactly what she did—I'm assuming it had to be because of her networking—but in the month that we were having our affair, my followers on social media and my e-mail list exploded like...well, you know."

Rachel giggled and said, "I'm not sure I do."

A triumphant, gloating gesture came across her friend's face, and Christine said, "Hmmm. You might *not* know what I'm talking about. Wait. Who in the hell are you dating nowadays? You're drop-dead gorgeous, woman."

"No one at the moment. But forget that. How did it end with you two?"

"We decided that as fun as it was, we weren't serious about each other. She had recently broken up with…guess who? *Kaj Reynard.* And I thought that I was still in love with Danny, which, looking back, I wasn't. Funny how we stayed together for almost another year."

"So, it wasn't an adversarial parting with Daria then?"

"No. We're still friends."

"Think there's any chance that you might get back together?"

Christine gave her thigh a playful push with her left foot. "Listen to you, you little gossip."

"Remember, I'm a professional investigator in training."

"Ha! Almost forgot!" She brought the rim of the wine glass to her lips and rested it there for a moment. "I suppose there's always a chance we could start up again. Doubt it would be anything serious, though. I don't really know her that well. Our affair was mostly about the sex and the thrill of sneaking around. I'd like to get to know her, though. She still texts me every once in a while to see how the book business is going, and I did let her know that Danny and I are over." Christine drank and then adjusted her position again on the couch. "Now, tell me about this investigator business."

Rachel explained her itch to get out of the house and possibly change careers. The summer was just starting, and she needed something to focus on—something different. Nearing forty, she wasn't getting any younger, and if she didn't stop writing code soon, the Bouchard nodes in her knuckles would make it impossible to type before long. Christine was attentive at first but seemed to drift when Rachel mentioned meeting Ben-David at Darwinger's. Her attention returned when Rachel brought up the interview with Ingrid Bara.

As Christine reached for the wine bottle, Rachel said, "Then, Ingrid told us about Daria Knight," and her book-blogging friend dropped her empty wine glass.

16

Christine Harper reached over and picked up her Riedel wine glass from the living room's thick carpet. "Still in one piece," she said and proceeded to fill her glass.

Rachel Roberts watched Christine's shaky hand pour the wine and wondered if she should gently suggest that her friend cut off the joy juice spigot. Christine's next question postponed the intervention.

"What did that skinny bitch have to say about Daria?"

"Just that Daria had been the reason for her break-up with Kaj."

Christine sighed. "She would say that."

"So, it's not the truth?"

"No, it's mostly the truth, but she didn't deserve him."

"So you knew Kaj?"

"Not very well. I'd say it was 'Hi' or small talk now and again. Like Ingrid told you, he used to drop by The Buck. I stop by there every now and again, and that's where we would briefly interact."

"Why so sour on Ingrid?"

Christine rolled her eyes. "Because she's no angel herself. Made a pass at Danny last summer."

"But wasn't that when you were with Daria?"

"That's not the point," Christine scoffed. "Ingrid knew I was with Danny, and she still came on to him."

Rachel wondered if Ingrid Bara had known about Christine's affair with Daria.

"And have you heard who she's dating now?"

"Matty Joshua?"

Christine's eyes opened as if someone had just turned a dial all the way to max intensity. "*Ex-act-leeeee.*" She took a large gulp of wine—*sipping time was over.* "How did you know about that?"

Rachel detailed her interview with him at Shelby's Marina.

"What a lowlife. Ingrid deserves him."

"Do you know Matty Joshua?"

"I put him in the same casual acquaintance lane as Kaj. But, the stuff I've heard about him. Well, look at what you just told me. Sleepin' with the marina secretary and sittin' in the boss's chair with only a towel on. Ridiculous!"

She decided to press a bit further before switching back to Daria Knight. "Did you ever hear anything about him, Kaj, and Kevin Shelby selling drugs?"

"Who hasn't?"

"How did you find out about it?"

"You're pretty good at this, you know it?" Christine said.

"I took notes today."

"I'll say. You sure you don't want any more wine?"

Rachel had passed on the last two refill offers. But now that she had Christine talking, she decided to go along for one more. She held out her glass. "Oh, okay," she said.

"That's my girl," Christine said, pouring. "Now, where were we?" She set the bottle back in the chiller. "Right. How I found out. It was Daria. She said that Kevin was the main dealer but that Matty and Kaj did a job for him now and then. You know what? And I never said this to the police last night, or when they visited today—too much in shock, you know? But, it wouldn't surprise me if Matty or Kevin killed Kaj or had him killed."

"We plan on talking to Kevin tomorrow." Rachel took a drink. This bottle was even better than the others. "But let's go back to what Matty said earlier tonight. He told Obadiah and me that he saw Kaj coming out of Lakeview last night in a brand-new Bronco. Why was Kaj in Lakeview? There has to be some connection between his murder and what he was doing in our neighborhood, right?"

Christine nodded. "Seems like it. I have no idea why he was there last night. This is creepy."

"Who would he have been visiting?"

"Could've been Ingrid Bara."

"No, she was working the entire time. We've seen the video evidence."

"He could have seen her before she started her shift. Maybe they met somewhere else in Lakeview."

"I hadn't thought about that," Rachel said. She *had* thought about it but wanted to see what Christine would say.

"Sounds like you might need to speak with her again."

"I think we will."

"Hell yes, you should. She didn't even tell you that she was dating Matty Joshua. She's hiding something, I bet."

"Could be," Rachel said, indulging her.

Christine tipped back her glass once more. It was almost empty.

Rachel decided that it was time to talk about her interview with Daria and Brendan Knight—before Christine became totally sloshed.

"The other place I visited today was the Knight Compound."

Christine's glazed expression vanished. "You're kidding me."

"No, I'm sorry we got off track. But Ingrid told us that we might want to talk to Brendan and Daria because Kaj had dated Daria." She paused, letting what she had said sink in. "And, she told me that Brendan and Kaj had been best friends."

"They were," Christine said. "So, tell me all about the visit."

Rachel told her everything from the attempted Jayson Jasper butler charade to the attentiveness of Brendan and the detached vibe she had felt from Daria. It was challenging, but she tried her best to put Daria in a positive light—the wine helped—knowing that there was a high likelihood her words would get back to Daria via Christine. Perhaps, in an inebriated phone call after Rachel left tonight. Then, she mentioned how Daria had told her to say hi to Christine for her.

"She said that in front of everyone?"

"Yes."

Christine gave a smile laced with surprise. "Kind of sweet of her to remember me, don't you think?"

"Maybe she misses you," Rachel said.

Christine turned her head and focused on the massive waves rolling in toward the beach. The wind howled, and then thunder boomed. "I should call. What did you think of her?"

"She's not my favorite person in the world."

"Yeah, she can be kind of cold."

Rachel left it there. *No use stoking that fire right now.* "If you do talk to her, and she says anything about the case, you'll let me know, right?"

Christine's head snapped back around. "Oh, come on. Daria and Brendan didn't murder Kaj Reynard."

"I'm sure you're right, but they didn't have an alibi for last night, so we have to keep them on our list."

Christine leaned forward. "Look, I know they didn't have an alibi, and that amateur-hour shit with Jayson Jasper was, well, ridiculous. Okay, I'm plowed; I already said it was amateur hour, and that was enough." She took a power chug. "Did I tell you that Jayson Jasper, Attorney at Law, tried to make a move on me one night when I stayed over with Daria?"

Of course, Rachel nodded 'no.'

"Yeah, I told Danny that I had a book retreat that I needed to attend. He bought it. So, I drove the couple of miles to the compound, was let in, and parked my car in the garage so that it couldn't be seen. The fun and games with Daria began the moment we entered her wing. *Her wing.* So rich. Anyway, I found out that she has this weird habit when she's hooking up with people. She'll do everything with you and anywhere, but she always sleeps alone. So, once we finished up around midnight that night, I went to sleep in her guest quarters." She set her wine glass down on the coffee table. "Next thing I know, I'm being tapped on the foot at two in the morning. Jayson Jasper is naked and standing at the foot of my bed. He says, 'Ready for Jayson Jasper, my African queen?' Racist motherfucker!" she yelled, shaking her head and slapping the couch.

"Did you punch him?" Rachel asked.

"Should've," Christine said. "But I didn't know what kind of state of mind he was in. So, I rip off the covers, evade his grasping arms, and sprint out of the room. By the time I get Daria up and we return to my room, the old courtroom warhorse has disappeared. She asks me if I was sure that he was there or if it was a dream." Christine frowned. "We did some mushrooms right before our final tryst. I also had a ton of tequila. So, I couldn't be sure if it had happened or not. Like, how did that old fool get the key to her wing anyway?"

"Did you see him the next morning?"

"I did. He just smiled at me over his morning paper and acted like nothing ever happened, but I swear he was there. So gross."

"Daria say anything more about it?"

"Never came up again. I only stayed the night there one more time, and he wasn't around."

"Why do you think she broke up with Kaj? Apparently, he took it pretty hard."

"Maybe she got bored with him. They did date for over a year though, which from what she told me in a post-romp confession, was rare for her." She must have seen Rachel's surprised reaction. "Sorry, I get pretty raw when I'm bombed. I get a sailor's mouth when I fuck too!" She said, laughing.

"If Daria goes through lovers like Siskel and Ebert went through films, then—"

She stopped talking because Christine was roaring and clapping.

"My God, Rachel. You sounded like an author for a moment. Gotta remember that one for my next wanna-be author who hires me to help them make it. Jesus, girl."

Calm it down, Rach. Keep it simple, and no more similes! "Thanks. Maybe I'll have to try my hand at it. Don't know, though. The empty screen intimidates me when I've got code to write. I have no idea what it would be like if I had to write an entire novel."

Christine exhaled. "And you don't wanna know. Sometimes I think I'm more of a psychologist for my writers than an editor."

"Appreciate the warning. But here's my question. Why would Brendan and Kaj have a falling out? It doesn't sound like Daria made it hard for them to still be friends."

"You know what? You're right. I guess you'd have to talk more with Brendan about that. I didn't get to know him that much. He knew that Daria and I were together, but that's about it. Do you think you'll interview them again?"

"Hard to say at this point. We've got to talk to Kevin Shelby in the morning and then Baby Llyod Darwinger." She sat up and put her empty wine glass on the table, giving the slightest hint that the evening was almost over. "If I had to guess, I'd say that we'll talk to Matty Joshua or Ingrid Bara before we swing back around to the Knights."

As drunk as Christine was, she still picked up on Rachel's gesture. "Well, I just hope that this gets wrapped up soon. It was freaky as hell last night to see him materialize out of the water and then *literally* die right in front of me."

Rachel reached out her hand and gave Christine's arm an affectionate rub. "I'm sorry. I keep forgetting. You going to be okay tonight?"

Christine squeezed her hand and then released it. "I'll be fine. Got Corey Ritter's phone number in my favorites. Says he'll be here pronto if I need him, no matter what time it is." She pointed her index finger toward the ceiling and then made a circular motion with it. "Big deal. Don't know what that tub of donuts could do to help me out. But, I guess it's something."

"You've got my number too. Seriously, call or text if you need me."

They rose and hugged, and then Christine led the way to the front door, walking down the long hallway as if the floor was oscillating between canting ten degrees to the left and then ten degrees to the right.

Rachel entered her house. She was soaked, tired, and ready for a good night of sleep with a newfound respect for the daily life of a professional investigator on the job. Hemy came out of the darkness and rubbed against her leg. Feeling the water, he scampered away.

"You're so picky," she said to the cat.

As she turned on the foyer lights, her cell phone rang. Hemy started meowing from the shadows.

"Come back here, big guy."

Hemy went silent.

She pulled her phone out of her pocket and looked at the screen. It was almost 1 a.m., and the caller was Obadiah Ben-David.

17

"Wake you up?" Ben-David asked.

"No. I just got back from Christine Harper's." She locked the door and headed down the dark hallway. When she reached the utility room, she said, "Hang on for a minute, okay?"

He acknowledged, and she set the phone down on top of the dryer. Then, she removed her wet clothes and placed them in the washing machine. Naked now, she picked up the phone and headed for the hallway. "Okay. What's up?"

"Spoke with Corey Ritter tonight. Played our usual game of 'you give me something, I give you something.' So, I told him an abbreviated version of our interviews today, and he got silent on the other end of the phone—could almost hear him scribbling every word down that I said 'cause he's lazy and hadn't interviewed anyone that we had. In fact, I bet he stayed at Darwinger's most of the day waiting for clues to pour out of the coffee pots. But. He did have one key item for us. Ben! Get your ugly ass over by the fire and lay down! Sorry," he said. "Dog went out and came in drenched. He just shook water all over the wall and floor. I want the old boy to sit by the fire, get warm, and dry off."

She tried to be patient. "My cat didn't like my wet clothes when I entered the house," Rachel said.

"Pets," Ben-David grumbled. There was a pause, and then the professional investigator shouted again, "Ben! Goddammit! Sonofabitch just jumped up onto the bed with me. There, there. There, there. Well, it's my fault. He's always been allowed to hop up here whenever he wants."

C'mon. Out with it already. It's almost one in the morning—he's got to have something good.

"Okay, where were we? Right, Ritter's news. He tells me that Baby Lloyd had been complaining to Kevin Shelby about some money he had loaned Kaj. Sounds like he was pissed. Maybe even pissed enough to say what Matty Joshua told us he heard Baby Lloyd say. Shelby said that Kaj hadn't paid Baby Lloyd back—kept promising he would and that something big was in the works, going to pay him what he owed plus some fat interest. From my experience, any time people say that, it means that they don't have the money and are about to do something very stupid to try and dig it up."

Okay. Now we're getting somewhere. "Did Ritter say why Kaj was borrowing money from him?"

"No, but he got the feeling that Shelby knew. That's the thing with Kevin Shelby, though. He'll spill some of the beans, sometimes all of the beans if it's necessary to keep his ass out of jail. But. You have to pull whatever he's got in him out carefully, or he just clams up and disappears until whatever it is blows over. A few years ago, he disappeared for an entire winter after a bag of pot dropped out of one of his runner's pockets onto the street right in front of Deputy Amos Meyer—my best friend, remember?"

She entered her bedroom and walked across the soft carpet to the bathroom. There, she grabbed her robe and then sat on the edge of her bed. "Yeah. Did he stop by tonight?"

"In fact, he did. Good memory." His shift in tone told her he appreciated that she remembered that he and Amos were close. She hadn't heard of a companion of any sorts; she figured Ben-David lived alone. "It gives us a solid place to start with Kevin Shelby tomorrow, but Amos also delivered some news that made the case more difficult."

"What was it?" she asked.

"He examined Kaj Reynard's cell phone records for the past two years. Lots of calls to and from Ingrid Bara and Daria Knight when he was dating them and a large volume of calls with Brendan Knight when they were friends."

"Anything recently?" she asked, breaking in.

"I was hoping that there would be, but, get this, since he broke up with Daria last summer, he's basically only called home or numbers from town like the golf course, the hardware store, stuff like that. There were a few calls to Shelby's marina last summer and another couple to Matty Joshua, but that's about it. Zero breadcrumbs for us. I honestly can't believe it."

"Another phone?"

"That would make the most sense, especially if he was in business with Kevin or Matty, but Ritter's already been out to his house and searched it with Amos. They even brought Bill Mooney out there with them to search."

"Who's Bill Mooney?"

"A deputy that's basically just collecting a paycheck. Amos hates him."

"And they didn't find the phone or anything else that might help?"

"Not a thing."

"Think they'll let us search his place?"

"Ritter might let us in a few days. He's got it locked up, so nothing's leaving there."

"If Kaj had a second phone, do you know of any place he would hide it?"

"Maybe at his parents'. Ritter is going to check there tomorrow. But I wouldn't bet on it. I got the feeling when I interviewed them that they didn't approve of their son's loose lifestyle. Told me that they didn't see him much. And, after all, he was thirty-five."

"Do you still want to interview Baby Lloyd first? Or should we head to Shelby's before then?"

"I thought about it, and I'm inclined to do as you say and switch things up. Let's still meet in the parking lot at Darwinger's, and then we'll head back over to Shelby's together."

"Eight a.m.?"

"Let's make it nine. That'll put us at the marina around nine-fifteen. Shelby will never be there before then."

"Got it."

"How did your meeting with Miss Harper go?"

Rachel filled him in on most of it. When she was done, she felt exhausted, reliving the drama for a second time.

"Well, at least the case is moving in the direction that most do."

"And what's that?"

"Everybody's telling some of the truth, hiding most of it, and worried about what everybody else is saying." There was a pause. Her wind chimes clanged outside as if they were a swing that someone kept giving underdogs to. "Got one last thing for you."

She crossed her legs and rubbed the sole of her right foot in small circles. "Ready."

"Matty Joshua is missing."

"And you didn't lead with that!"

"Doesn't matter. He wasn't gonna be found in the fifteen minutes we've been talking. And if he was, my phone would've started blowin' up. Ah, shit."

"Ben roll over on you?"

"Ha. No. I just said a phrase I heard Matty Joshua say earlier. Right after our interview with him, remember when Matty and I both headed for the bathroom? Yeah, well, in the stall next to mine, he kept singing the line, 'I miss you blowin' up my phone' over and over. Can't believe I just said that."

"Secret's safe with me," she said, giving a tiny laugh.

"Anyway, Ritter went out to his house, and Amos went everywhere Matty usually is. He's gone. Even when Amos went to speak with Ingrid Bara, she tried calling and texting him, and there was nothing back. Now, she's worried, and Amos has been checking in with her every hour. She called the marina, and Dory told her that he said he was meeting up with someone and would be out on the water for a while. No one's seen him since."

"You think he went out with Baby Lloyd?"

"Maybe. Point is, he said that he'd meet up with Ingrid when she got off work at The Buck at ten, but he never showed up. And speaking of boats, Ritter and Amos checked Kaj Reynard's boat out a few hours after he was murdered. Kept it at a small set of docks across the public access ramp on the Hampstead River, which empties into Lake Huron. The owner of the docks, Mac Schmidt, said Kaj hadn't been on the boat in a few days and that Kaj certainly didn't take it out the night he was murdered. Amos told me that he and Ritter went aboard and didn't find anything that raised an eyebrow. In fact, they said it was smartly tied up to the dock and that everything onboard was stowed and clean. Not something either of them expected with Kaj. Anyway, they checked on it again when they heard Matty might be out on the water. Boat's still there and hasn't been touched. Maybe we'll take a look at it tomorrow. I know Mac Schmidt pretty well."

"If Kaj had a boat, why did he go fishing with Baby Lloyd? And has Baby Lloyd come back yet?"

"I called Agatha, but it went straight to Voicemail. When we get to Darwinger's in the morning, I'll poke my head in and see if he's there. If he is, I'll tell him not to go anywhere before we've had a chance to talk. Christ, Corey Ritter will probably be there talking to him for half the morning anyhow."

"What do you think about these developments?" It was like a novel's plot unfolding before her, and now her brain was alive again, synapses firing and circuit cables illuminating with more ideas for *Dark After Midnight*. She doubted she would be able to sleep before she wrote some of them down. As she had forgotten, writing was mostly hard work and frustration. It was struggling to find inspiration, and, when it appeared, usually not knowing what to do with it. You just didn't wake up and have a million-dollar idea, which was why now, she had to stay up and get her ideas on paper. Because that was another guaranteed rule of writing: If you did not write the idea down, while it was still fresh in your mind, it would disappear and not return—or return long after you needed it, like, when the book was already on the shelf being sold.

"Don't know. But somethin's cookin'. Your doors locked?"

She felt a shiver. "Yeah. Why?"

"Just checkin'."

She swallowed and felt as if her stomach was a cave that had suddenly emptied, and the last few bats were circling, trying to find a way out. *Relax. No one is going to hurt you*, she thought. "I don't have anything to worry about, do I?"

"No. Sorry for droppin' that on you. I just—well, see you in the morning. I'll bring coffee." He hung up.

Rachel put on her slippers and went to the kitchen, where she made a cup of coffee in her Keurig machine. Then, she headed for the stairs. She would not leave the second-story writing room until she had finished jotting down her new ideas for the novel.

With each step, she felt herself climbing the mountain of both mysteries where the solutions awaited her at the summit—the answer to who killed Kaj Reynard and the answer to what the plot of Adrienne Astra's newest adventure would be.

She entered the dark room and closed the door behind her, taking a sip of coffee. About to flip the switch to the overhead light, she decided against it.

You've got to change your routine.

For years, she'd turned on every single light in the second-floor writing room at night, and she imagined that the bright light emanating from the massive windows acted like a lighthouse along the stretch of darkened beach houses. No, tonight, she'd use the desk lamp instead. Perhaps it would be better, cozier, more focused. She approached the desk and looked out the window. Some of the clouds that had burst for the past few hours had cleared out, and the moon had found an opening to cast a glowing beam down on the churning waters of Lake Huron below.

A few of the towering pines between her house and her neighbor's house swayed as the wind whistled through them. It had always been a concern that they would topple over and crash through her roof. But now was not the time to be worried about that.

She sat down and looked out at the choppy whitecaps, taking another sip of her strong coffee. Her wind chimes were at it again, and the waves almost got in sync with their ringing. About to turn on the lamp, a question entered her mind, and she found that she could not set it aside.

So, where is Matty Joshua?

18

By the time Obadiah Ben-David and Rachel Roberts pulled into Shelby's Marina just after 9:30 the next morning, the sky looked like it had never seen a storm before. White, puffy clouds were scattered across the blue canvas above, and the sun's warmth had dried everything that had been soaked by the never-ending rains of the night before. Rachel sat in the passenger's seat of Ben-David's van and tapped the notebook in her hand with the bottom of her empty paper travel cup of coffee. She'd written until 2 a.m., and the rain had stopped by the time she had brushed her teeth and climbed in bed at a quarter after 2. She wasn't as rested as yesterday, but she'd had 6 hours of sleep, which she could function on.

Ben-David pulled the van into the same spot as yesterday. No doubt they would see Dory again once inside. However, as they got out, the front door opened, and Dory stepped out, followed by a man approximately 6 feet tall with a greasy mane of gray hair. *This must be Kevin Shelby*, she thought. He was wearing flip flops, torn jean shorts, and an untucked Hawaiian shirt that could still not hide his gargantuan gut. They got out of the van.

"Mornin', Dory, Kevin," Obadiah said.

Dory gave a half-smile but averted her eyes.

167

Shelby yawned, scratched his belly, and then extended his hand to Ben-David. "Good morning, your highness," he said.

The men shook hands, and Rachel walked up to them and stood to Ben-David's right side.

"This the new investigator everybody's talkin' about?" Shelby asked.

"Who's *everybody*?" Ben-David asked.

"I don't know. People."

Rachel put out her hand and said, "Rachel Roberts."

Shelby took it and gave it a quick shake as if he was the kind of man who was intimidated by a confident woman. "What can I do for you both?"

With the morning sunlight at its peak intensity, her eyes glanced around, getting a better look at the grounds compared to the gloomy afternoon visit yesterday. Ben-David had told her that Shelby's was both a Hampstead treasure and the place where old boats went to die. It was a treasure because as long as you didn't need anything from the marina other than the slip that you purchased for a dirt-cheap price, then absolutely no one bothered you. It was the place where old boats went to die because there was absolutely no effort from the marina staff to aid in the boats' upkeep. The owners knew this too, and the marina's laissez-faire spirit eventually numbed them, feeling nothing for their boats and spending more and more of the summers sitting on the rickety docks drinking beer and then slipping below decks for a long nap.

"Sure you heard about the murder by now," Ben-David said.

Shelby put his front teeth on his lower lip as if he was a preacher about to deliver the eulogy for Kaj Reynard. "Yeah. Decent kid. Good kid." He shook his head, overacting the part, and looked out at the crystal blue bay of water beyond the marina. "Don't know what happened."

"What about Matty Joshua?" Rachel asked.

Shelby gave Dory a sideways glance and then focused back on Rachel. "What about him?"

"Think he had anything to do with the murder?"

Shelby closed his eyes, exhaled, and then re-opened them. "Look, the last time I saw Matty Joshua, he was being removed from McCleod's pub a month ago by three police officers while shouting, 'Do you know who the fuck I am? Do you *know* who the *fuck* I am?'"

"That's not what she asked," Ben-David said, taking a step closer to Shelby.

Shelby's posture and tone changed. *Sexist asshole. Why did it take the hulk of Ben-David to make Shelby shape up?* Well, Shelby's treatment of Rachel spoke only of him and nothing of her. She readied her next question.

"I'm not sure. I mean, I. Don't. Know. Obadiah. He's unreliable, been acting as strange as the weather." Shelby pointed to the massive puddles in the parking lot. "We got swamped last night, and the breezes are supposed to be back tomorrow and even stronger." He took a pack of cigarettes out of his pocket, shook a white stick out, and then lit it. "What I need to do," he said, glaring at Dory as if she was responsible for what he was about to say, "is have the damned parking lot paved."

Dory glared back at him defiantly. "If you've got the money to do that, then you've got the money to give me a raise," she said, putting her hands on her tiny hips.

"Always askin' for money," Shelby said and turned back toward Ben-David.

"So, when's the last time you saw Kaj Reynard?" Rachel asked.

"She's a viper," Shelby said to Ben-David.

"Well?" Ben-David asked.

"Quite a while ago, actually. He hasn't been out to the marina since last year, in fact."

"Social call? Moving some product for you?" Rachel shot back, enjoying the game more than yesterday.

At the word 'product,' Shelby took a long drag, his chubby right hand looking like it would spasm at any minute. "Well, I don't know anything about any *product.*

Now, he did some remodeling work on my home a few years back, but that's the only business I know of." He took another long drag and exhaled a steady stream of smoke as if he was trying to see how long he could keep blowing. His display was cut off by a coughing fit, which Dory snickered at. Finally, he got his breath back and said, "And, no. He wasn't making a social call. Did some work on his boat last summer."

"What kind of work?" Rachel said.

"Needed a new engine, and he also wanted me to refinish part of the hull."

Rachel made eyes with Shelby and then slowly looked around the ragged marina, darting her eyes back at Shelby's every few seconds to make sure that he was following hers. When her survey was complete, she gave him a smirk. "And were you able to fix his boat?"

He dropped his cigarette on the ground and squashed it with his right foot. "We do good work here," he said. "That boat left here looking brand new, and he's never been back with a complaint."

"Know why he wanted it fixed?" Ben-David jumped in. "He usually just fishes with Baby Lloyd."

"No clue," Shelby said. "But he paid me in full, all upfront in fact. I gotta say, he was handy too. Stayed out here and helped my boys work on it. Guess he needed to stay away from southern Hampstead after that rich chick dumped him."

"Daria Knight?" Rachel said.

"Yeah, that was her name. Fine lookin' lady—see her a couple of times each summer when I head down to The Buck."

"You ever meet Matty Joshua and Kaj Reynard there for a drink?"

Shelby lit another cigarette.

Dory cleared her throat, and Shelby shook one out for her and lit it.

"No law against havin' a drink with someone is there?" Shelby said.

"Matty and Kaj get along?"

"Far as I could tell. Nothin' more than just a few old boys gettin' together to transfer some pitchers of beer to the urinal."

"Where'd he get the money to pay for the boat repairs?"

"Never asked him."

"Maybe the money from the *remodeling* he did for you?" Rachel asked.

He smiled, seemingly happy to use her suggestion for his lie. "Come to think of it, I bet that's it." He winked at her. "I know one place he didn't get the money from."

"Enlighten us," Rachel said, immediately wondering if Shelby knew what enlighten meant.

"Daria Knight. Once they broke up, she cut him *off*. Asked him how much he had mooched off her when they were going out. Told me that he had some nice clothes and had lived the dream while he was with her 'cause she paid for everything, but when they split, he had nothin'—no jewelry or cash from her."

"And now Matty's disappeared," Ben-David said, letting his words sink in for a moment. "Unless, that is, either of *you* knows where he is," he said, pointing at Shelby first and then Dory.

Dory swallowed, and Rachel watched her raise a shaky hand to her mouth for some quick relief from the cigarette.

"What do you mean *disappeared?*" Shelby said. He turned toward Dory. "He was here last night, wasn't he?"

"I told you he was," she said.

Shelby shrugged and said, "Well, maybe you've got yourself a suspect."

"That's a pretty quick turnaround," Rachel said.

"I call it like I see it," Shelby stated. "There's no reason for him to be missing right now. Not with him dating Ingrid, aaannddddd," he said, twisting his head to look at Dory, "not with him hooking up with this fine lady."

"Since we spoke with him here yesterday—"

"You spoke with him *here* yesterday?"

"For Christsake, I told you that too," Dory said.

"Yeah, we did," said Ben-David. "And the last we heard, he was meeting up with someone on a boat last night."

"You check Kaj Reynard's boat?"

"Ritter and Amos did. Hasn't left the dock."

Shelby rubbed his chin and peered out at the calm surface of Lake Huron as if the answers were out there underneath the glistening surface. "They might have had an argument."

Enough with the show, Kevin.

"Who?" Rachel demanded.

But Kevin Shelby was still in The Actors Studio, and he pursed his lips and looked like he was about to announce that he'd been sober for sixty-one days.

When he finally spoke, he said, "Kaj and Matty."

19

Kevin Shelby delivered his statement with both subtlety and authority—eye contact, but not a stare-down; firmer tone, but not shouting; body posture…well, as regal as Kevin Shelby was capable of, which meant he wasn't passed out on the ground.

Rachel Roberts had to move her hand over her mouth to cover the grin that would have ruined the moment. She thought that if they were all actors on a set of the hit series *Game of Thrones*, then Kevin Shelby acted like he had just walked over, sat down on the iron throne, and supplied them with his proclamation. So, his two wayward pupils and rumored partners *had* gotten into a quarrel. *Perhaps about Ingrid Bara? Daria Knight?*

"When? And what about?" she asked.

"Last week—"

She saw Ben-David's mouth opening, but she beat him to cutting Shelby off. "You said the last time you saw Matty Joshua was a month ago."

"Did I?" Shelby said. "You must have heard me wrong. It was last week."

"Thanks for clarifying that," she said.

Ben-David gave her a nod of affirmation.

Shelby shook his head as if to say, *"Why's everybody messin' with me?"*

173

"Continue," said Ben-David.

"Anyway, I was helping an old high school buddy, who comes to Hampstead for the beginning of the summer, fuel up his sailboat." Shelby pointed to the refueling slips in the marina but then drifted off, seeming to get lost in remembering the encounter. After a few moments of silence, he said, "Man, his son looks just like him. But he's got blonde hair like his grandpa di—" His voice trailed off.

As Rachel watched him, a different feeling came over her, for Kevin Shelby, ace marina owner, appeared no longer to be acting. Whatever was going through his mind meant something to him because the 'I don't give a shit about life' façade was gone, replaced by something else. Perhaps he had jogged loose another memory, a lot further back in his mind, that was related to seeing his high school friend and that friend's son. They didn't have time to let him stare at the slip forever, but for some reason, she decided to ask him about his friend instead of focusing on the argument between Kaj Reynard and Matty Joshua. "Who is your high school friend?"

Shelby tiptoed his eyes toward her, possibly caught off guard by her question. "Tristian Norris. His mom still lives up here, and he visits a couple of times a year—brings his family. Wife and two kids."

"He still up here?" Ben-David asked.

"Yeah," Shelby said. "You know him, right?"

"I do. Knew his dad and uncle too."

There was silence for almost a minute, and the storyteller in her immediately gathered that there was a lot that wasn't being said. She wondered what it was, but then Ben-David got the line of questioning back on track.

"So you're helping Trist fuel his boat, and?"

"Right," Shelby said. "Kaj and Matty storm out of the office, and the f-bombs start flyin' outta Matty's mouth while Kaj walks away from him toward his new Bronco."

"Were they arguing inside?" Rachel asked Dory.

"Wasn't there," Dory said. "Day off."

"Why were they out here?" Rachel asked.

"Kaj showed up ten minutes before Matty. Said he needed an old chart for Baby Lloyd."

"Is that normal?"

"Oh, yeah. We've got stacks of 'em in there," Shelby said, pointing to the office. "Sometimes, Baby Lloyd needs a particular chart for his fishing trips, and he sends Kaj here to get it."

"Did Kaj walk out with a chart?" Rachel asked.

"Yeah, he had one rolled up and in his right hand—looked like he was holding a Christmas wrapping paper baton," Shelby said, laughing.

"Why was Matty out here?" Rachel said.

"I figured to see Kaj. As soon as he pulled up, he asked me where Kaj was, and I nodded toward the office. He jogged over and entered, and then a minute later, they're outside havin' a spat."

"You catch what they were arguing about?" asked Ben-David.

"Couldn't understand Matty, 'cause he was talkin' too fast and, like I said, hittin' the hell out of the expletives." Shelby rubbed his chin, the actor regaining his mid-play form. "Did catch one thing though, but don't know what it meant. Just before Kaj got in his new wheels, Matty said, 'What's out there?'"

"What's out *where*?" Rachel asked.

Shelby motioned toward Dory. "Had this fireball ask him just that, and he wouldn't say shit about it."

Ben-David took another step closer to him. "Well, Kevin, you're a *creative guy*. What do you think he *meant* by that statement?"

"I honestly don't know, Obadiah," Shelby said. "I admit I was curious, but I didn't see him again. And Dory said he didn't say anything to her about it either."

"But he was meeting someone last night to go out on a boat, right?" Rachel asked Dory.

"He was," she said.

"So, do we all think that 'out there' may have meant Lake Huron?" Rachel said.

"Could be," Shelby answered. He warmed up to his statement and said to Rachel, "I like how you work."

She ignored his compliment. They'd already caught him in a lie, and who knows how many else he had told. However, admitting that his high school friend had been present for the argument between Kaj and Matty—and that he was still in town—gave that story some credibility because Shelby knew they could go visit Tristian Norris and ask him what he saw and heard that day. If Lake Huron was the 'where,' then *what* was out there? And why had Matty Joshua gone after Kaj Reynard about it? As she pondered the questions, she noticed that they were all staring out at Lake Huron.

A boat's motor at the far end of the marina came to life, and it brought everyone out of their trance. Shelby said, "Well, that about it?"

Then, Ben-David proceeded to do something that he told Rachel in the van ride over that he hardly ever did. He summarized things in front of a possible suspect. "So," Ben-David began, "a year ago, you fix Kaj Reynard's boat. He'd done some remodeling work for you, and he pays you cash all in advance for the work. You don't know where he got the money to pay you from, but you're sure that he didn't get any from Daria Knight. Then, a week ago, you witnessed Kaj and Matty having a fight, and Matty yelled, 'What's out there?' Then, you don't see Matty again, but you know that he's dating both Ingrid Bara and Dory. We come to your marina yesterday and talk to him, and after we leave, he says that he's meeting someone on a boat. And now," Ben-David said, looking at his watch, "no one has seen him since last night. He's not here. He's not home. He's not at Ingrid Bara's. He's not at Dory's. We show up today, and you say you don't know what Matty meant by the words he shouted at Kaj that day. And you also say that Matty could be the murderer. That about sum it up?"

Shelby shrugged. "Suppose so."

Ben-David looked at Rachel. "You have any other questions for them?"

She studied Kevin and then Dory. Ever since they had started questioning them, the marina secretary had remained mostly quiet and avoided eye contact. For a moment, the novelist in her came out, and she wondered if this was how Rose Varga would be in *Dark After Midnight*, avoiding suspicion and then coming out of nowhere to claim her place as the mastermind villain. Dory put out a shaky hand for another cigarette from Shelby, and Rachel determined that Rose Varga may be able to deceive everyone, including her best friend Adrienne Astra, but Dory could not. Rachel crossed her off the list of possible suspects. "No more questions from me," she said.

They extended their thanks to Shelby and Dory, and as Ben-David pulled the keys out of his pocket, he said to them, "Don't leave town. We might be back."

A minute later, Dory and Shelby were back inside the marina office, and she and Ben-David were in the van heading out of the parking lot.

"Why did you do a recap at the end?" she asked.

"I normally don't because I want the person that I'm interviewing to be thinking about what he or she said." He turned to her. "Want 'em wondering what I remember about what they said too." He turned the blinker on, and they took a right out of the marina. "But in Shelby's case, I wanted him to hear what he had said so that it was crystal clear that *I* had heard everything. And I did it so I could watch his reaction while I played it all back for him."

She nodded, approving of the technique. "You notice anything?"

"I've done it enough times to know that he knew he would be held accountable for what he said. In fact, you helped me when you called him out on the Matty Joshua inconsistency. That was top-notch."

"Thanks. Do most people get caught up in a lie that quick?"

"Some. I'm not surprised that we caught him, but we had to call him on it right there, and we did."

They reached the stop sign, and Ben-David stopped the van, checking the traffic on US-23. A huge convoy of vehicles was headed north. She wouldn't have tried it, but, apparently, he thought he had enough room and gunned the van, turning right and then continuing to accelerate. Rachel watched the lead car in the convoy through the rearview mirror. It got closer and closer, and she dug her fingernails into her knees as the car almost hit the van's bumper. But Ben-David continued to test the van's engine, pressing the gas pedal all the way to the floorboard. The van started to gain some separation, and Ben-David, who had also been watching the events unfold in the mirror, smiled.

"Nothing like the US-23 grand prix in the summer months. A little bit of a rush, huh?"

She relaxed her fingers and began to rub where her nails had pressed against her legs. "That's enough excitement for today," she said.

"We *did not* want to get behind that train of vehicles," he said, patting the steering wheel. "And, excitement? Well, hang on. Because you might get just that when we try to find out why Lloyd Darwinger put out to sea last night…and who he may have been with out there."

20

By the time Obadiah Ben-David and Rachel Roberts pulled into Darwinger's parking lot at ten-thirty in the morning, there was only one open spot left. Without a cloud in the lively azure sky above, the sun's rays were like pulsating waves of heat that created one of those perfect summer days in Michigan, where the outdoor activities seemed endless. If not for working on the case—or working on her novel—Rachel would have been spending the day on the beach or hiking the trails out by the Hampstead lighthouse.

She knew, however, that the beautiful weather was due to change after dinner tonight, and the Huron breezes would be back in force—even more than last night.

Ben-David parked the van and went inside to fetch Baby Lloyd.

She looked at her phone and saw that she had a text message from Topaz Kennedy.

Morning, bestseller. Ejogo and Vergara signed on for film 4 last night. Affleck to direct. Rhimes and Kasdan to write. Team is back! No novel. No script. No problem. All betting on you, darling. Writing must start soon. Found your murderer yet? Call me after 3.

* * *

If Rachel Roberts had felt her seat getting warm a few days ago, she now felt it start to sizzle as if Topaz had just turned the burner to 'high.' There was definitely no turning back. Her agent had pulled off what many had deemed as impossible and bagged the trifecta again—the actresses, writers, and director she wanted.

When they had started working together, Topaz had explained that, normally, literary agents didn't handle anything to do with film, TV, etc.—they were focused only on the books—and that authors had separate agents for these items. Then, Topaz had said, *"But I'm not your normal literary agent, big show. I'm in control here. I handle it all, and I'll get you the best. Not finding another agent to take your fifteen percent. Got it? Only one other agent like me in the business, and he lost out on you. Going to make him regret that mistake, aren't we, darling?"* Rachel had agreed, knowing by that time that Topaz Kennedy was a powerful megalomaniac and that she would have taken control regardless.

The decision had paid off beyond her wildest imaginings.

More than a decade ago, after Rachel's novels had become bestsellers, every major studio had reached out to Topaz, and she had played them all against each other beautifully. By the time the ink had finally dried on the contract, Director Ben Affleck had been notified that he would have his pick of actresses to play Adrienne Astra and Rose Varga. But, instead of going with the most highly paid and biggest box office draws, Affleck had gone with who he thought would be perfect for the parts: Carmen Ejogo as Adrienne Astra and Sofía Vergara as Rose Varga. But, as Affleck knew, you had to have the perfect writers for Riley Cannon's alchemy of character-driven thrillers. After refusing the gig to write the scripts herself, Rachel had told Topaz her dream team: Shonda Rhimes and Lawrence Kasdan—only they could take the potential of the novels and draft a script that would deliver on the big screen. Two Oscars later, Topaz had beamed, *"You've got the instincts of Warren Buffett, lass!"* Another brilliant move had been to pick the right villain for each of the first three films. *Morning Glory Mayhem!* had

Donald Sutherland, who had gotten hot again from his role in *The Hunger Games*, as a monomaniacal oil baron who owned the sinister hedge fund manager Samuel Ingraham Michaelson, and *Late-Afternoon Associates* had Catherine Zeta-Jones as the femme fatale who seduces Byron Worth, the head of the secret off-the-books government agency that Adrienne Astra and Rose Varga work for.

Then, more magic had happened.

For the third film, Rhimes and Kasdan were tied up, and Affleck couldn't break a previous commitment. Because of that, as things have a way of working out when every great once in a while the stars align in Hollywood, a cultural phenomenon was born. For years, Peter Bogdanovich had tried to lure Cary Grant out of retirement, but Grant had not taken the bait. When Grant had died in 1986, Bogdanovich's dream had seemingly died with the legendary actor. But then, after a decade had passed, Grant's heir apparent finally surfaced in the form of George Clooney, and everyone in the world waited on the edge of their theater seats to see Clooney cast in a role that only he or Grant could play. When Affleck had been pulled away from the third film, Topaz Kennedy had pounced on the opportunity and arranged dinner with Bogdanovich and Clooney in the private dining room at Caravaggio's in New York City's Upper East Side. The possibility was almost too good to be true. *Enemies in the Evening*'s plot was like Hitchcock's *To Catch A Thief*—Clooney's debonair character, a retired art thief, was similar to Grant's in that he helped bring down the real thief. However, in the film version, Rachel had told Topaz that she thought Clooney's character should be the villain, and only Ejogo's Adrienne Astra, along with her friend Vergara's Rose Varga, could catch him. As only Topaz could tell the story, she had detailed what had happened in an event she had dubbed 'The Meeting in the Back Room': *"Now the film business usually doesn't work this way, my sweet child. When a hot deal emerges in Tinsel Town, it's terminator agents and pompous studio heads hacking away at each other—egos clashing like rams. But, as you'll recall, we still held a lot of power from negotiating casting and directing decisions from the success of the first two films, and with Affleck unavailable, they were open to suggestions. So, I found out when my dear loves, George and Peter, would be in town—lifelong friends, both of them—and made a reservation under the auspice of catching up with maybe a little business. I totally played on Bogdanovich's nightmares of not being able to make a picture with Grant, and, well, when we opened the second bottle of red, I hit them with the secret plot twist for the film. I said, 'George, darling, you're going bad in this one,' which excited him because he had read the book and wanted to know what creative freedom he would have with the character. He always plays the good guy, right? This information had him asking about when the filming might start; I knew we were onto something. And right about that time, Peter was pulling on his ascot and wondering, in that wonderful voice of his, what the budget might be. I mentioned some rough figures, and his eyes got greedy behind those dark glasses. On bottle three, knowing that Rhimes and Kasdan were committed to other projects, they both asked if Tony Gilroy would be available to pen the script. Of course, I had had dinner with Tony a few nights before and told him to stay hush about the whole thing. So, when I said that indeed Tony was available, those beautiful sets of eyes lit up, and God, they both smiled. Have there ever been two stimulating smiles like that? Anyway, we ordered champagne, and the whole thing was a go. Gosh, I'm getting warm just talking about it; both of the devils were single at the time too! No, no, my dear, one mustn't tell."*

When the film was released, it had shattered every record in box office history by having the perfect combination of opening like a *Star Wars* film and then having the legs of *Titanic*. Both Clooney and Bogdanovich had only signed on for one film—both men having agreed with Bogdanovich's sage-like wisdom, *"You only get one chance at this."* And as it had turned out, they only needed one chance. Ejogo and Vergara's chemistry as friends found its mark in the third film and catapulted them to the top of the profession. And Clooney rose to Bogdanovich's challenge to meet and surpass Grant, while the old battle-hardened director shot and assembled a masterpiece—the lighting, the angles, the surprises (audience members had screamed when Clooney went evil), the suspense, and to top it off, he'd brought in the legend John Williams whose work in *Catch Me if You Can* had intrigued Bogdanovich enough to hire him to score the film. It was deemed wise by most critics, risky by some, but Bogdanovich's fabled instincts proved correct. As if Bernard Hermann, John Barry, and Jerry Goldsmith had all smiled down on him from heaven, Williams wrote arguably the most touching, playful, and memorable composition of his unmatched career.

But now, Rhimes and Kasdan were itching to take their characters back. Affleck had grown powerful and was ready to give *Enemies* a run for its money, never publicly admitting though confiding to Topaz in private that the biggest regret of his career was the choice to not walk away from the previous commitment so that he could have directed *Enemies*. And, he was *hungry*. And she had assured him that Riley Cannon had a once-in-a-lifetime story to tell in *Dark After Midnight*—*"That's why it took a fucking decade, lustrous fellow,"* she had told him.

Rachel realized that her fingers were tapping madly on her legs as if she was typing at fast-forward speed. She stopped and then felt her chest. Her heart was pounding. She had to start writing tomorrow. If the case was not solved by then, she would gracefully bow out from her time with Ben-David. She took a deep breath, held it, and then exhaled. The foundation for the story was there. Adrienne Astra worked in the Rescue and Sanction Division of multi-millionaire Byron Worth's front company of Worth, Tipler, & Associates. Her best friend was Rose Varga, who worked in W, T, & A's Surveillance and Planning Division. Rose's assistant was Kristy Cummings, a resourceful techie who often traveled with the duo and was responsible for luring Sutherland's oil baron character into a trap in the first book. But now, Kristy's ambition had turned the better angels of her nature into a soul that resembled a pit of vipers. The other recurring character was the company's weapons expert, Ulysses King, a gay man married to the famous talk show host Dr. Michael, whose famous line at the end of every show, *"You've faced yourself today,"* had become a staple in the film versions of the books. With two more books after *Dark After Midnight*, Rachel couldn't kill everyone off in this one. But Rose would go down in the epic showdown at the end of the book, and probably Kristy too. Would Ulysses get to see book #5, or was Dr. Michael on borrowed time? She couldn't decide now, but what she had decided last night was that Rose Varga had secretly, over the first three books, fallen prey to the oldest job dissatisfier in any workplace environment: she felt undervalued, underpaid, and overshadowed by a fellow employee—Adrienne Astra in this case—whom she believed wouldn't be successful and would probably be dead without her. Rose wanted the perceived utopian and ever-eternal luxuries of money and power, which at the end of every life, always end up only as *borrowed*, not everlasting, luxuries. Rachel had a motive, but she still didn't have a plot. What would be a mission worthy of Adrienne Astra? Catching Clooney with his hands in the priceless art cookie jar had worked in book three, but now, a decade later, the world had changed. At a solitary new year's celebration in her home with Hemy six months ago, she had made the following list of words to describe her outlook on the coming months: uncertainty, division, fear, loss, spending, repair, hope, balance, utility, neighbor, calmness, skepticism, and change. Unknowingly, her list had not only described her feelings about the world but also about *Dark After Midnight*. When she had to take stock of what had suddenly exploded into everyone's lives and become much more upfront and overt, it was clear: politics. Her new book would almost certainly have to include the topic, but she would continue to resist writing a fiction book that took sides or was an attempt to prove points or change minds; let the pundits, columnists, and cable news networks handle that.

But, how to incorporate that ugly little word?

Then, it came to her as she saw Ben-David and Baby Lloyd Darwinger leave the gas station and start walking toward the van. Rose Varga, along with her capable assistant Kristy Cummings, would kidnap the President of the United States' daughter and hold her for a ransom. Naturally, Worth, Tipler, & Associates would be contacted, and Adrienne Astra would be given the mission to rescue Madame President Joan Callahan's daughter, Reese. And, of course,

Byron Worth would activate the entire support team of Rose, Kristy, and Ulysses. Then, when the timing was right, Rose's plan would be to eliminate Adrienne, forcing President Callahan to pay the ransom. She'd collect, wait a year, and then retire because of what she would claim as the overwhelming guilt and post-traumatic stress of losing Adrienne Astra. *Damnit, it was looking like Ulysses was going to die. But maybe not. Don't get ahead of yourself, ma'am. Remember the case you're on right now. People lie. People protect themselves. People are greedy. People try to get away with things.*

She flipped open her notebook, wrote a few more thoughts, and then closed it up. Ben-David and Baby Lloyd were almost to the van.

They stopped short, and Ben-David waved her out.

She opened the door and said hi to Baby Lloyd. His eyes looked like they hadn't seen sleep in forty years.

"Let's head over to the chairs that Lloyd's got set up on the dock," Ben-David said, pointing across the street.

She shut the door, and they headed toward US-23, where the traffic had picked up even more from when they had darted in front of the convoy earlier. It was bumper to bumper—campers, RVs, trucks trailering jet skis or boats, and cars packed to the gills.

A few minutes later, they were seated in lawn chairs facing each other. Baby Lloyd's face was hidden under an old baseball cap and Ben-David's bald dome shined like a beacon from the sun's unblocked rays. They each cradled a travel cup of fresh Darwinger's coffee, which Agatha had prepared.

"Well, let's have it, Lloyd," Ben-David said.

"I was out of my mind last night," Baby Lloyd said. "Headin' out into that storm like that. The breezes are coming back tomorrow, you know?"

"Yeah, we went over that inside," Ben-David said, taking a big gulp from his coffee cup. "Going to make yesterday look like a calm day. Now, keep going."

This was where it paid to be a professional investigator in one area for a long time, Rachel thought. You built relationships, got to know everybody, and when you needed straight answers, you could go to greater depths with the people you had known for most of your life. It saved time too, and you could be blunter like Ben-David was with Baby Lloyd right now. This told her that he was actually friends with the man, whereas he had approached everyone earlier in a more oblique manner as if he didn't know them.

"Well, thing is, I've been feeling really bad about Kaj. Sure you've heard by now that we were fishing buddies?"

They both nodded back at him.

"The kid had a nose for 'em. I swear." He took a sip of coffee, looked like he was going to continue, but then took a longer drink from his cup. He sat up. "I know my spots, which my dad and grandpa showed me, but this guy was somethin' else. And I liked hanging out with him even though we were thirty years or so apart. Kid was funny."

"Shelby said that he fixed Kaj's boat last summer."

Baby Lloyd grunted. "A minor miracle."

"So he did fix it?" Rachel asked.

"Against all odds, yes. And it was about time. He'd had that cabin cruiser for five years and never gotten much use out of it. Just sat next to the dock on the Hampstead River, and he'd go there to drink beer or bring his lady friends from time to time. Or so he told me. That's another thing I liked about him. Good storyteller. I knew half the stuff he said wasn't true, but I went along with it because he was fun to listen to."

"My understanding is that you and Kaj went out fishing in *your* boat," Ben-David said, pointing at Baby Lloyd's chest. "Why did he suddenly feel the need to have his own boat fixed?"

Baby Lloyd smiled, held it for a beat, but then frowned.

What was that all about? Rachel thought.

186

"We always used my boat, which didn't bother me because we caught so much fish, and like I said, I enjoyed his company. Sometimes, he'd pay for gas and almost always brought beer and sandwiches along for the outing. But then, last summer, his fling with wealth ended abruptly when Daria Knight let him go, and the kid was in a bad way. Showed up loaded at the dock in the morning more than once, and I wouldn't let him on board. Now, I don't mind puttin' away a few brown bottles now and again, but you're not goin' out in my boat blasted."

"What happened on those mornings?"

"I sent his ass home. Agatha gave him a jug of water and found him a ride. A couple more times, and he got the point. Then, one day, something changed in him. He showed up sober, and we went out and caught a ton of fish like the good old days. But on the way back in, he asked me if I could loan him some money to pay for the repairs to his boat—engine and some of the hull."

"What do you think made him change all of a sudden?" Ben-David asked.

Baby Lloyd took another long drink of coffee, and Rachel wondered if Agatha hadn't put a little something special in there for him—loads of sugar at a minimum, perhaps a touch of something stronger.

"I don't know. Still don't, and…well, I guess I won't ever know now."

"Did you lend him the money?" Rachel asked, and Ben-David gave her a nod of affirmation. In just a few days, they had found a natural rhythm together. She had to admit that she enjoyed his company, but there remained something private about him, like a hallway full of doors that were all slowly opening except for one at that end that had five or six locks on it and was guarded by his bloodhound, Ben.

Baby Lloyd's frown returned. "Yeah, I gave him the money."

Didn't think it came from Kevin Shelby's remodeling job, Rachel thought. She met eyes with Ben-David and could tell he was thinking the same thing.

"Sounds like he didn't pay you back," Ben-David said.

"No, he didn't. And here's the thing, I don't think he used the boat that much."

"Why do you say that?" Rachel asked.

"Because we continued to use my boat for fishing. Only went out once on his. Engine ran smooth as a baby's bottom. Had the inside clean as a whistle too—could tell he took pride in the boat."

It wasn't adding up for Rachel. Kaj Reynard has a boat for five years, then borrows money to have it repaired, and then…doesn't use it? She took a sip of coffee—*heavenly*—and then asked, "Not making much sense so far, is it? Why would he go to all of that trouble to get his boat fixed and then not use it? And of all the places he could have taken it to—Shelby's?"

"I've been trying to make sense of it for over a year now, believe me. Once I gave him the money to get his boat repaired," Baby Lloyd said, and then jerked his thumb toward the gas station, "and she's not ever going to let me hear the end of that, I'd never seen him so focused. He paid Kevin Shelby the money for the repairs all upfront, which I told him was a horrible idea, and then went to the marina every single day to make sure the repairs were on schedule. Then, I didn't see him touch a drink for the entire summer. When we were out on my boat, he was nice, but there was a newfound edge of professionalism to him. I mean, he was all business and took care of himself. Must've lost twenty pounds but bulked up. I used to kid him that he was getting a little pudgy when he was dating Daria, living the good life."

"Do you remember when the boat was finished?" she asked.

"Yeah, he drove it from Shelby's all the way down here. I took a bottle of champagne, and we had a little christening ceremony right here," he said, motioning to the end of the dock.

"What's the boat's name?"

"*Coca-Cola Classic*. Used to kid him about picking such a dumb-ass name. Yeah, you guessed it. The paint scheme was red with white trim."

Who names their boat that? Apparently, creatures like Kaj Reynard.

"And then, other than the time he took you out fishing, you never saw him use it?"

"That's right." Baby Lloyd paused—the kind of pause, Rachel thought, that people have when they were weighing information that they had either just remembered or had been sitting on for a while. "But someone did. It just didn't make any sense to me."

"Who?" Ben-David asked.

"His dock owner, Mac Schmidt, told me that a few nights last summer, he saw Kaj's boat leaving the dock after midnight. Mac had gotten up to take one of his midnight pisses—gettin' old is no fun, ma'am—and he saw the boat heading down the river toward Lake Huron. Now, Mac has been known to come up with a few tall tales of his own, like the one a few years back when he told me that he knew where the *Griffon* was years before Hutch discovered her."

Ben-David and Baby Lloyd shared a laugh.

"So, I suppose what he said could be all a load of bunk, probably why I dismissed it when he said it. But, then again, even if it was true, why would Kaj be taking his boat out in the middle of the night? Maybe to clear his head or somethin'. And now I sound like I'm projecting myself on him because that's exactly what I was doing out there last night."

She wanted to go there right away but decided to stick with Kaj. "Let's say he was taking his boat out in the middle of the night. What could he have possibly been doing?"

They all sat in silence for a moment. Then, Rachel heard the sound of a motor, and she turned her head to sea and watched as a powerboat passed by a few hundred yards offshore and headed north.

Baby Lloyd drained the rest of his coffee and set the cup on the dock. "I thought about that question last night. I know this sounds absurd, but the murder mixed with the Huron breezes, well, it made me do things I wouldn't normally do. Now, I've taken my boat to sea at night before to clear my mind or at least to try and get my mind right about something. Sometimes, I'll even anchor, throw on a tank, and just sit on the bottom for an hour to get away from everything. But last night, I went out there trying to find Kaj. No, not literally, but to try and see if I could put together what happened to him. He came in from the water with a knife in his back, right? So, I paralleled the coast and headed all the way past the Knight compound, then I headed out and circled Beacon Island a few times. All the time, I'm wondering, 'Why would he have been out on the water past midnight last summer?' and, shit, probably this spring and summer too. Also, 'Who would have wanted to kill him?' Well, as you can imagine, I didn't get too far in my thinking because of the storm. Was hell motoring out by the island. Didn't even get back until around four this morning."

"But did you come up with anything?" Ben-David asked.

"The best that I could figure is that if he wasn't going out there to do some thinkin', which is completely possible, then maybe he was meeting someone or looking for something."

And now, Rachel thought, *is the time to address what Matty Joshua said he heard.* Ben-David didn't disappoint.

"A week ago, did you say, 'I'll kill you, you sonofabitch!' to Kaj?"

Baby Lloyd coughed and then rubbed his eyes. "Who did you hear that from?"

"Who do you think I heard that from?"

The old gas station owner tapped his right foot on the dock a few times as he studied his folded hands on his lap. "Matty Joshua, right?"

Ben-David nodded.

"Thought that was him I saw scurrying away across twenty-three after I said it." Baby Lloyd let out a cleansing exhale as if he was suddenly relieved of the burden of keeping that particular statement to himself. "It had been a year since I had loaned Kaj the money, and I had been asking him when he was going to pay me back. All last year he had been saying that he was working on it. But, in the last few weeks, his tone had changed to, 'Don't worry, Lloyd, I'm gonna take care of you. Won't be long, I swear.' I had caved once again and said okay. I mean, he hadn't paid me in a year, so what was another few days or a week, which was the timeline he gave me, by the way." Baby Lloyd took off his hat and wiped the sweat on his forehead with the sleeve of his shirt. Then, he crossed his legs—his right foot going berserk in circles. "Then, he shows up in a brand-new Bronco, and that was the thing that sent me over the edge. I. Went. After him. Asked him how in the hell he could afford a new vehicle without paying me back. Asked him what he was doing out in Lake Huron after midnight. I'd had it."

"This all came out on the dock that day?" Rachel got in.

"Yes. And when I asked him all of that, he clammed up, looked like he'd seen a ghost, wouldn't say anything except for the fact that he promised he was going to pay me back with some interest for being a loyal friend and helping him out. I couldn't believe it, and I guess something in me snapped, and I said, 'If you don't, then I'll kill you, you sonofabitch!' He just nodded and turned away. It's the last I saw of him."

"What would you say if I told you that Matty Joshua went missing last night after he was supposed to be meeting someone on a boat?" Ben-David asked.

"Are you serious?" Baby Lloyd asked.

"Yep. Kind of gives a little credibility to your theory that he was meeting someone, doesn't it? Now, the question becomes, what would those boys be meetin' up about? And, since Kaj was dead, who was Matty meetin' up with last night?"

Rachel thought that it was a possibility that Kaj had been going out on the water to meet up with Matty Joshua—especially if any illegal activities were taking place. Minus the sociopaths in life, people got paranoid when they were breaking the law. Then, a question dawned on her: Was Rose Varga a sociopath? She didn't think so, but that could be fun to play with in her plot. It would definitely make fans look at the first three books in her series through a different lens. In fact, if she played it right, then when the new paperbacks of those books came out in coordination with the release of *Dark After Midnight*, she would probably get some additional readthrough because fans would want to go back and see if they could spot early signs that Rose was malevolent. Some fans would just dust off their hardcovers from their bookshelves, but some would go out and buy all three of the newly designed paperbacks. If there was one thing that rang true about book fans, it was that common sense went out the window when it came to book purchasing. *My gosh. I'm starting to think like Topaz.*

"I don't know who he'd be meeting last night," Baby Lloyd said and then abruptly stopped talking. His eyes shifted between her and Ben-David. "My God, you think he was meeting with *me*?"

"You were out on the water last night, and no one's seen him since," Ben-David said flatly.

"I never saw him. In fact, I didn't see anyone." He brought his fingers together underneath his chin. "On the eastern side of Beacon Island, I thought I heard a motor at one point last night, but it could have just been the thunder. It was pea soup out there."

"If not you, then who might he have been meeting with?"

Baby Lloyd uncrossed his legs and seemed to relax a little. He stared at Rachel, "I don't know you, so I don't know how long you've been here." He then shifted his gaze to Ben-David. "But you've been here forever like me, and I don't think it's a secret that Kaj, Matty, and Kevin Shelby have dipped a toe in the drug business now and then."

Ben-David nodded in agreement.

"So, from my viewpoint, it doesn't rule out Kevin Shelby as a possibility for who Matty was meeting last night."

"Makes sense," Ben-David said.

She thought it was now the perfect time to bring up what Matty Joshua had said to Kaj Reynard in the marina parking lot. Ben-David rubbed his beard, and, after waiting a couple of moments to let him bring it up, she went ahead on her own. "What would you say, sir, if I told you that a week ago, Kaj Reynard went to Shelby's marina to get a chart, and Matty Joshua confronted him while he was there, ending the fight by asking Kaj, 'What's out there?'"

Ben-David laughed.

"What?" Baby Lloyd asked.

"She beat me to it," Ben-David said.

She gave him a smile, and he responded to her gesture with a grin of his own. She felt they were getting close to something here. Ben-David had explained this stage to her as 'mystery fever,' a puzzle that, when put together, reveals the identity of the murderer. However, a professional investigator always needed to be careful at this stage because as pieces appeared, some that looked like they would fit together wouldn't, and others that looked like they didn't have much on them would start coming together naturally in another corner where you weren't even looking. *"Keep the whole puzzle in front of you. Don't zero in on some attractive pieces and combinations,"* he had said. Wise words not only for her, but also for Adrienne Astra when she started to suspect Rose Varga near the end of *Dark After Midnight*. Now, all of her creative synapses were firing, and the urge to write was almost pulling her off of the chair, into her car, and back to the second-story writing room.

"I'd say that Matty Joshua is looking more and more like a suspect. Should we go back to the gas station and talk to Corey Ritter? He's been here wolfing down donuts since six this morning. I'm kind of surprised that he didn't come out here with us."

"He knows I'll talk to him. We've both always kind of respected each other's turf," Ben-David said.

And again, it was silent, and Rachel thought that they had now covered everything with Baby Lloyd. They needed to find Matty Joshua.

Then, Baby Lloyd said, "There's more."

21

The morning's sun was starting to flex its strength, and Rachel Roberts's legs felt sticky against the aluminum frame of her lawn chair. She inched forward and felt a bit of relief. If this chat with Baby Lloyd Darwinger went on much longer, then she'd insist that they head indoors. The coffee was slowly waking her up, but it was also making her sweat.

Obadiah Ben-David opened his notepad and flipped to an empty page. "Okay, what else is there, Lloyd?"

The gas station owner was twiddling his thumbs while looking at Rachel's legs.

"Lloyd!" yelled Ben-David.

Baby Lloyd jumped in his chair, his right leg knocking over his empty coffee cup. He reached over and tipped it back up. "The murderer might not be Matty Joshua. What I said on this dock that day is nothing compared to the explosion between Kaj and Don Garvin four days ago."

Don Garvin? The Lakeview maintenance man? "My maintenance man?" she asked.

"Oh, so you live down in Richville?"

"I already told you that," Ben-David shot back at Baby Lloyd.

"You did?"

"Forget it. Yes, she's from Lakeview. How in the hell did you ever hear Kaj Reynard and Don Garvin arguing?"

Baby Lloyd looked at Rachel first. "No offense about where you live."

"Don't worry about it," she said. Minus the occasional drink with Christine Harper, she didn't run in the Lakeview social circle but knew she would always be associated with it because of where she lived.

Baby Lloyd shrugged and swiveled his head to Ben-David. "You know that Don's got a good reputation around town for being able to fix anything. Suppose that's why the Lakeview Homeowner's Association scooped him up to be their maintenance guy. Heard he works Monday, Thursday, and Saturday but is on-call for emergencies the rest of the time."

Another boat passed by, this time with a woman water skiing behind it.

Baby Lloyd continued, "It was a Monday morning, and I needed an estimate on how much it would cost for him to repair the columns on our front porch; we've had some wood rot, and I wanted to hire him to rip out the warped wood and replace it. I'm old school—like to talk in person—so I find out from his wife where he's working in Lakeview that day. She tells me Marty and Alisha Cantor's house. I head over there, and as I travel down the long driveway, the house finally comes into view, and I see Kaj and Don standing in the grass next to the far side of the garage away from the house."

"Was this before or after your confrontation with Kaj on the dock?" Ben-David asked.

"Before. Looking back, perhaps I channeled some of Don's anger when I lit into Kaj. Poor kid. He got it from both of us in the span of a couple of days."

Rachel jumped in. "Had you ever seen them together before?"

"No," Baby Lloyd said. "Surprised me. But, they were both my friends, so I thought it would be a nice chat. Boy, was I wrong. The moment I got out of my car, I heard the following, which was the end of their chat because Kaj took off right after, barely acknowledging me on his way out, and Don wouldn't talk about it when I asked him what it was all about." Baby Lloyd put his face in his hands for a moment and then exhaled. "I feel bad saying this. I don't want to get Don in trouble."

Ben-David was firm. "Lloyd, you need to tell us what he said."

Baby Lloyd took his face out of his hands and sat back. "Okay. I opened the car door and heard Kaj say something like, 'I could end your marriage right now, so don't tempt me.' And then Don said, '*You* screw with me or my wife, and they won't find *your* body. You've already stabbed me in the back once, and if I find out you did it again, I'll shove my knife so far in your back it'll come out your fuckin' chest. And that's after I rip off your head and shit down your throat.'"

"Did they physically touch each other?" Ben-David probed.

"They were eyeball to eyeball, but I didn't see anybody touch anyone."

"You sure?"

"Pretty sure. Anyway, at this point, they noticed me, and I was able to get out, 'Fellas, fellas,' but they ignored me. Kaj said to Don, 'Watch it,' and turned away from him. Don yelled back, '*You* watch it!'"

"Looking back now, do you know what they were arguing about?"

"That's the thing. I don't have any idea. Don just goes about his work and keeps his own counsel, and the only reason that Kaj has ever been down to Lakeview is because of Daria Knight or Ingrid Bara, and those relationships were over long ago. Now, Hampstead is a small town, so I guess Kaj and Don may have crossed paths before, but I would think only if Kaj had hired Don to do some work for him." Baby Lloyd took off his hat and scratched his unruly hair. "I suppose Kaj's parents could have hired Don in the past. But the way they were talking to each other that day, man, something went wrong."

From what Rachel had heard, it sounded like the classic case of someone getting into someone else's business. She'd written about it in her books.

Someone puts his nose where it doesn't belong and finds out something that he shouldn't. "It sounds like Kaj was a threat to Don and his wife," she said.

"That's the conclusion that Agatha came to," said Baby Lloyd, "but she knows Don's wife, Minnie—they go to our church and belong to the rotary club—and can't imagine how Kaj could be any threat to them. Affairs are hard to hide in a small town." He pulled his cell phone and waved it. "And now that everybody carries this little guy around with them all of the time, it's almost impossible to keep marital indiscretions secret. If Don and Minnie were having trouble, Agatha would have heard about it."

"Don't know Don that well," Ben-David said, "but that's a pretty serious threat he made. And, for Kaj to die in that specific way—"

"I know!" Baby Lloyd said, cutting Ben-David off. "I just can't believe he'd kill Kaj, though. Guy's got it made. Fixes rich people's stuff three days a week and then golfs the rest of the time."

"Has Don talked to you since the murder?" Rachel asked.

"I thought he might drop by or at least call because of what I had heard, but, no, he hasn't reached out. I also considered telling him that he should go see Ritter and let him know what had happened between him and Kaj. After all, he knew that I had witnessed the dust-up."

"Why didn't you? And why didn't you tell me this yesterday morning?" Ben-David said. Rachel could hear the annoyance in his tone.

"Sorry. I should have. Should've let Ritter know as well. Too much on my damned mind. Looks like Don's keeping it to himself too. But, if I was him, I would have talked to somebody already."

Doesn't make sense; this isn't the kind of thing you forget because too much is on your mind. Feels like he's hiding something or maybe planting a false trail.

"Says the guy who went out on his boat by himself all night, a day after someone who he had threatened a week ago was murdered."

Exactly!

The gas station owner looked like he had swallowed a canary.

Ben-David stood, and Rachel and Baby Lloyd followed suit.

"Looks like it could be Matty or Don," Baby Lloyd said.

Or you, Rachel thought.

"Now, don't go off flappin' your lips about any of that," Ben-David ordered. "We'll check out Don, but I don't want you startin' any rumors in the booths over there," he said, pointing his huge hand toward the gas station. "And I'll fill Ritter in. Not you."

Baby Lloyd nodded, and they exited the dock and headed back across the street.

Twenty minutes later, they were in the van heading south for Lakeview Village. The traffic southbound was thin compared to the parade of vacationers headed north.

"Did Minnie Garvin sound concerned when you asked where Don was?" Rachel asked.

"Maybe a little, but she knew where he was. And in this business, that's always better than not knowing where someone is."

"Matty Joshua could be our murderer, but he could also be in hiding, scared out of his mind."

"Could be," Ben-David said. "While you were talking to Agatha, I filled Ritter in. Wanted to send Amos over with us, but I talked him out of it. For Kaj Reynard to be killed in basically the same way that Don Garvin threatened him is too coincidental—doesn't feel right. I told Ritter he should focus on finding Matty Joshua."

"Does that mean that you're leaning in that direction? Is Matty our prime suspect?"

"He's definitely the most interesting option so far. But I've seen cases lean one way and then *smack*," he said, clapping his hands together before putting them back on the steering wheel, "head off in another direction you never thought of. That's what I'm always thinking on a case, 'What haven't I thought of?'"

"Well, there's always the possibility that Baby Lloyd did kill Kaj. He could have heard Don Garvin's threat and then killed Kaj in that exact same manner to frame Don."

Ben-David raised his eyebrows, the equivalent of headlights popping up on an old Ferrari. "We'll follow the evidence, and we don't have enough yet to go after anyone."

"Look, I know I have zero experience in actually investigating murders, but I've seen the framing move I just detailed on about every police procedural T.V. series that I've ever watched. Do Agatha and Baby Lloyd seem like the type to sit down with a few beers and watch *Law & Order*?" She paused. "Well, they sure do to me."

"Maybe. That show hasn't been the same since Jerry Orbach left. Although, I did like Jesse L. Martin a lot."

"Me too. My favorite was *SVU*, though. I'm still in love with Christopher Meloni."

"So, you think we should keep Baby Lloyd as a suspect?"

"I think we have to," she said.

"Good instincts. We'll for damn sure ask Don what he said to Kaj. Still don't think Baby Lloyd did it, though. But—doesn't hurt to keep him in mind."

She got out her notepad and wrote:

Have Rose Varga suggest a method close to the one that she used for the kidnapping of the President's daughter to Adrienne Astra. This will throw Adrienne off.

"What ya scribblin' there?" Ben-David asked.

"Just a note about Baby Lloyd." It wasn't a complete lie. Her point about him framing Don Garvin had given her the idea for Rose. She closed the notebook. "What's your plan for Don?"

"His wife said he's at the Thompsons' house replacing some plywood in the attic. We'll get him outside and talk to him on the side of their garage. Not the same house, of course, but I like to try and recreate the setting where someone said something of interest when I interview them."

She liked the idea—it reminded her of Shakespeare's use of a play within a play. Finding out insider techniques like this would be invaluable to her if she decided to go ahead and write a detective series, which Topaz had been begging her to start for years. *"Mysteries always, always sell, thespian. And you can never publish enough of them."*

"You'll have to excuse me, but even a coder can appreciate that creativity."

"Sometimes it doesn't work. But when it does, it can break a case wide open. One time, I was working a case—"

He broke off, and she felt the van start to slow. Rachel shifted her gaze from the passenger's window to the windshield. The Lakeview sign came into view. She had been so caught up in the narrative possibilities of exposing someone by recreating a scene that she hadn't noticed how close they were to the subdivision.

Ben-David turned on the blinker. "I'll have to tell you another time. You ready?"

"Born ready." *What had this come from?* A grin formed when she realized that it was Adrienne Astra's pet answer to Rose when they started a new mission. From time to time, she unknowingly became her characters after spending so much time with them. Her response was a good thing. Anytime she started saying or thinking like her characters it meant that she was ready to write about them. And she hadn't said or thought an Adrienne Astra line in a very long time. "Let's see what Mister Garvin has to say," she said.

They turned into Lakeview, and then, into something else unexpected.

22

The Thompsons' one-story house was located halfway down Lakeview Village's quiet interior street of Shoreside Lane. There was no view of the lake, but the lots were spacious, and Lakeview's public access for all of its residents to enjoy was only a quarter of a mile away, located adjacent to the entrance of The Shoppes at Lakeview Village. At the access was a nice section of beach and a ramp where you could launch a boat or a jet ski. Sometimes, Rachel Roberts would see a family, who lived on one of the interior streets in Lakeview like the Thompsons, walking down the street in flip flops and bathing suits, carrying an inner tube and cooler headed for the Lakeview beach. The Thompsons had purchased the wooded lots on either side of their house, which gave the property a more secluded feel. Most of the interior-street residents dreamed of one day moving into one of the coveted beachfront homes. As they pulled into the Thompson's long driveway, she wondered if they were one of these types or if they were content with what they had.

They parked and got out, and Obadiah Ben-David headed straight for the open garage.

"Shouldn't we knock on the front door?" she asked, following him.

"Not when who we need to talk to is in here," he said.

They entered the garage, and Rachel saw the ladder hanging down from the opening to the attic. The rest of the garage's floor space was covered in boxes, plastic tubs, camping gear, and Christmas decorations. The sound of a power drill could be heard as they reached the ladder.

Then, they heard the drill stop, and a weathered voice said, "Bitch is goin' nowhere now."

Ben-David seized the silence that came after the statement and called for Garvin to come down.

There was a shuffling sound, and then a series of creaks, like the ceiling was answering back to the professional investigator. A tanned face with a head full of gray hair poked down through the opening. "Who's ther...oh, hi, Obadiah," said Garvin.

"Hey, Don. Gotta minute?"

Garvin's head disappeared, and then his Wolverine work boots appeared on the top step. He came down: jeans, olive-colored t-shirt on a trim waist and big arms, and a carpenter's pencil behind his ear. If he was twenty years younger, he'd be starring on *Trading Spaces*, Rachel thought.

He reached out a hand and shook Ben-David's; he was tall, only a few inches shorter than her partner. Then, he was introduced to Rachel, and they shook hands—a little rough but also warm, and he didn't try to squish her fingers.

"What can I do for you both?" Garvin said.

"Wife said you're puttin' plywood down."

Garvin wiped the sweat off his brow with his wrist. "Yeah. Ted Thompson had half-inch plywood up there, which is all you really need, but when they brought everything down," he said, pointing to the stacks covering the garage floor, "in preparation for their garage sale in a few weeks, he decided to have me take out the half-inch boards—been up there for twenty years he told me—and replace them with three-quarter inch plywood."

"Make much of a difference?" Ben-David asked.

"It's what I use and recommend," Garvin said.

Rachel thought to her own attic. She didn't store much up there—a few boxes with high school and college memories—but she knew there was flooring that she now assumed was plywood. As for decorations, she didn't need to keep her Christmas items up there because her downstairs den was decorated for Christmas year-round—a luxury of living by yourself and not having company over. Or, when company was over, just simply closing the doors to the den to keep her everlasting holiday room preserved and secret.

It was silent in the garage, and the summer heat had them all sweating now. *The attic must be like a sauna*, Rachel thought.

"But I'm guessing that you aren't here to talk with me about plywood or attics," Garvin said.

"The Thompsons around?" Ben-David asked.

"Had to make a trip to Saginaw. Should be back around dinner time."

"Let's get some fresh air and talk," Ben-David said.

With some uncertainty, Garvin said, "Okaaaaay."

This time, Rachel led the way, and they left the garage, taking up station on the thick green grass that lined the side of the garage facing the street.

Rachel studied Garvin even more now. His self-assured carpenter-of-the-year demeanor had abandoned him, and he was alternating between rubbing his hands together or wiping sweat off of his forehead.

He's definitely nervous.

Ben-David wasted no time. "We heard from Lloyd Darwinger that you and Kaj Reynard had words about a week ago over at Marty and Alisha Carter's house." Then, Ben-David replayed the conversation for him.

Rachel watched Garvin turn pale.

"That true? You say all that?"

Garvin's mouth opened and then closed as if an invisible lawyer was perched on his shoulder, telling him to be quiet.

The veteran investigator continued, "Don, I've got a murdered Kaj Reynard. I've got a witness who says you threatened to kill him. And, as I'm sure you've heard by now, when Kaj fell facedown on the beach just a few blocks from here, it was with a knife stuck in his back, which is exactly how you said you would kill him. Now, if you don't talk to me, then Corey Ritter is next. You get me?"

Garvin's hands were starting to shake, and he looked like he might bolt for his truck at any moment. She noticed Ben-David's right hand down by his waist—near where he kept his gun, which was hidden by his untucked shirt. Then, a thought came to mind. *What if I stepped in as the good cop?* Her partner obviously had Don Garvin feeling uneasy, but maybe a shift in tone would get him talking. They had never discussed playing good cop, bad cop, but there was a reason the dynamic worked in all of the detective shows, and she suspected in real life as well. She decided to try it. "We're not accusing you of murdering Kaj Reynard, Don. But we need you to tell us where you were two nights ago. If you have an alibi that checks out, then you're all set." She gave him a reassuring smile. "What do you say?"

Garvin exhaled then wiped his eyes, which were tearing up. "I need to make a phone call," he said. "And, no, it's not to my lawyer. In ten minutes, you'll have all of your answers. Deal?"

They agreed, and Garvin walked over to the driveway and made a call.

Almost exactly ten minutes later, a woman on a bicycle rode down the driveway. As she got closer, Rachel recognized her as Alisha Carter, who lived two houses down the beach from her. They'd said hello before, but that was about it. Her husband was a retired Chief Financial Officer for some company out of Detroit who helped almost everyone in Lakeview with their taxes each year. Alisha was around twenty-five years younger than him; Rachel thought she remembered Christine telling her that it was a second marriage for both of them.

Alisha hit her brakes and put the kickstand down. She was wearing a white tank-top and a short white skirt with footie socks and Nike running shoes. Her blonde hair was in a ponytail, and her body was lean and tan—almost too fit.

Garvin met Alisha by her bike, and they talked quietly for a minute before waving over Ben-David and Rachel.

They went into the garage, and introductions were made. After taking a moment, Alisha registered who Rachel was and gave her a friendly, "Hi, neighbor."

Then, the silence returned, and everyone looked to Don Garvin.

"What Lloyd told you was true. I did say those things to Kaj that day, and he did threaten me and my wife."

At that moment, Alisha put a hand on his shoulder, and Rachel immediately guessed what he was about to say.

"I have an alibi for that night," he said, turning to Alisha. "Her husband was at a fundraiser dinner for his old company and was gone for the evening. I told my wife that I was finishing up some work on their porch, which was partially true." He turned back to face Rachel and Ben-David. "But, from around six p.m. until just after eleven p.m., I was in their house with her." He exhaled. "We've been together for almost six months now. My wife doesn't know, and neither does her husband."

"And Kaj Reynard threatened to expose the relationship to your wife, right?" Rachel asked.

"Yes," Garvin said.

Alisha gave him a side hug.

"But why would Kaj Reynard do that?" asked Ben-David. "How did he know about the two of you?"

It was then that Alisha took off her sunglasses and wiped them on the bottom of her tank top. "I was involved with Kaj before Don," she said. "When he was dating Daria Knight, they used to take walks on the beach past my house. I always thought he was good-looking, and he always waved when he saw me. They broke up at the beginning of last summer, and I didn't see him around for a while. Then, in August, I was home alone one weekend while my husband was doing some consulting downstate, and I saw Kaj pass by in a boat. Didn't even know that he owned one, but I waved to him, and he waved back. Then, on impulse, I waved him over, and I swam out to his boat. It was hot, and I needed to cool off and thought I would just say hi. Well, he dives in, and we swim around and talk for a while. Nice guy. So I invite him over for dinner that night, and we start seeing each other. Now, fast-forward to January, and Don starts doing some work on our house. By that point, I'm getting bored with Kaj, and I just start to feel this connection with Don—like nothing I've ever felt before—and we start seeing each other. Well, one night, Kaj comes over on Friday night, which is the night when my husband goes over to a friend's house for poker with the guys, and Kaj catches me with Don. I hadn't expected him over, and, believe me, I was going to break it off, but he showed up, and that was it. We talked a few times after that, but he's been mad at Don ever since."

"But why the confrontation almost half a year later?" Rachel said.

Garvin rubbed Alisha's back. Then, he brought his hands together in a more relaxed and confident manner. "A few weeks ago, Kaj shows up at my house out of nowhere. My wife answers the door and calls me over from the living room. My eyes get a little wider as I arrive, and the three of us stand together on our front porch for a moment. My wife goes inside, and he says that he would like to hire me to help him remodel a room in his house. I think about it and ask him when he needs it done by. He says that he wants me to drop everything I'm doing at Lakeview for a week and help him. Promises to pay me more than my usual fee. But, I can't just pause my jobs at Lakeview." He smiled at Alisha. "The well-off don't like to wait."

Alisha gave him a playful jab. Rachel wanted to throw up.

"I tell him that I could probably help him out on a weekend or two," Garvin continued, "but he just blows his top at that and says it has to be done *now*. I tell him sorry, and that's when he first threatens to expose my relationship with Alisha to my wife. I get in his face, and we almost go to blows right then, but instead, he storms off and tells me to think about it. I tell Alisha what happened, and we wait it out for a week with no contact from Kaj at all. Then, he shows up at her house that day, and we go at it again. And that's when Lloyd Darwinger shows up and hears my threat."

"Why do you think he was so adamant about having a room remodeled in his house?" Rachel asked.

Garvin exhaled, "Who knows. The guy was a loose cannon."

"He ever tell you what he was up to in his boat that day you swam out to him?" Ben-David asked Alisha.

"I asked because I had never seen him on his own boat before—always out with the Knights and their various yachts and toys—but he avoided the question."

"You have any proof that you were both at your house that night from six until after eleven?"

"Yes. We have cameras that cover every side of our property."

"And your husband never checks them?"

"He's a Luddite. I handle all of our tech stuff. But, he did ask me about the footage on our back deck the night of the murder, thinking there might be something that could help the police because Kaj came in from the water. So, I brought it up and showed him. Nothing but our neighbors taking their nightly walk on the beach. He didn't ask to see anything else, but if he did, then he knows that Don is working on our house." She met eyes with Don and then added, "I'd be happy to show you the footage if you want to see it. You'll see Don come in through the front door at six and then leave the same way just after eleven."

Ben-David and Rachel exchanged a glance that said they had what they needed for now.

Feeling the silence and possibly anticipating the end of the interview, Garvin asked, "Where does this leave us?"

"What do you mean?" Ben-David asked.

"I mean about you both knowing about me and Alisha."

"We don't plan on telling anyone. It's your business. I'll tell Ritter that you were at her house that night working. No lie there, just not the whole truth."

Garvin sighed. "Thanks."

"Thank you," Alisha added.

A few minutes later, Rachel was in the van with Ben-David heading toward her house. She had invited him over to review the case, which he had initially accepted but then declined after getting off of the phone with Corey Ritter. He wanted to see Ben-David at the station to compare notes and see where the investigation might head next. The townsfolk were getting jumpy, and some of the tourist population had thinned, joining the northern convoys past Hampstead for other small towns where no murders were taking place. Ben-David said that she was welcome to go along but that it would be boring and advised against it. She took it as a good sign—a few hours to get some writing done before dinner. He said he would call her after he spoke with the police chief, and he could pick her up after dinner if for nothing else to take her to Darwinger's to get her vehicle.

As the van neared Rachel's house, she couldn't help but notice Ben-David's change in mood. In fact, he looked like someone had stolen the wind from his sails and was threatening to sink his boat. She wondered if maybe he had thought that Don Garvin really had murdered Kaj Reynard. He certainly acted differently after the interview. However, the visual of Ben-David's frown while moping back to the van was not the picture that had stayed in her mind.

No, the image occupying her thoughts at the moment was of Don Garvin leading Alisha Carter by the hand back into the Thompson's garage after they had waved goodbye.

23

The cool wind from the ceiling fan blew down on Rachel Roberts as she dozed on her lounger in the second-floor writing room. Hemy was curled up on top of the blanket draped across her legs. A fifteen-minute, writing-break nap had turned into a three-hour deep sleep. She'd written for an hour and liked what she'd gotten down. More Adrienne Astra lines had popped into her mind, and now she was to the point where the snippets were starting to direct her attention toward *when* those particular lines of dialog would be spoken in the novel.

"The book is your monologue to your readers, dear. Don't muddle it up with a bunch of tomfoolery or tommyrot—and why create words that go after all the Toms. Totally unfair. Don't you think the name Tom has a nice ring to it, angel?" Topaz had droned on one day.

Then, she had tired, and Hemy had purred, and there was the small glass of red, and—

Her cell phone's ring tone growled at her like a monster underneath the bed, waking her up without warning. But this monster was real; the unique tone announced that Topaz Kennedy was in the waiting room, ready to be invited into the creative arena.

Rachel wiped the crust out of her eyes and focused on the time before swiping to answer.

6:45 p.m.!

She was supposed to call Topaz after 3. *Had Ben-David called? No time to check.* She answered the phone. "Hello, Topaz."

"Good God, my dear—starting to think you'd forgotten about me. Must be up to your neck in writing, I hope."

No, just taking a long, writerly afternoon nap. "Of course," Rachel replied. "Got your text. Fantastic news. Looks like the crew is back together."

"Affleck's meeting me for dinner tomorrow night. Wants to talk over where we might be headed in this one. Can you send me something?"

"I feel like I'm getting close to breaking the story, but I don't have anything typed up. Here's the nugget you can feed Ben with, though: Rose Varga will be the main enemy, turning on Adrienne Astra. A few beloved minor characters are going down, and the mission that Adrienne goes on will be high-stakes, worthy of a decade-long wait."

"Good girl! I'll rev him up with those tasty morsels."

"I'm definitely in a better place than I was before. Feeling my stride return. Everything virtuous on the publishing end?"

"It is absolutely not!"

Her legendary agent's tone was menacing.

"What's wrong?"

"What's wrong is that no deals are happening. The indies are raiding the book box office, darling, and they're fucking everything up. Agents aren't taking on anyone new, and publishing houses are in disarray—don't want to face the music that hardcovers are going away—bookstores are closing, and, you didn't hear this from me, if anyone finds out that the Judge doesn't write her own books anymore or that the good and right Green Beret colonel only writes about thirty percent of his books and then jets off to promote gear and his new brand of tequila while a ghostwriter—a *real* writer—does the heavy lifting, then we're all in deep trouble. I know, the irony, right? After all, you did some superb work for them a few years back." She sighed. "Truth is, though, my rock, the book business will never be the same because we did it to ourselves, and now we're cannibalizing each other on the way down. Nowadays, as soon as an author has a few hits, she sets up her estate to preserve her brand forever, so when she's tired of writing or dies, the stories live on. Always sounded like a good idea when we had gatekeepers and could control who we competed against. But those days are gone, and when her fan base dies, the fountain of new novels will be turned off."

"Didn't know it was that bad. Are *we* still okay?"

"Oh, heavens yes, child. Your backlist continues to travel the world 'round and reach new readers every year, and the entire damned business is banking on Riley Cannon's *Dark After Midnight* to part the seas and race to the top. Then, the big D is going to hemorrhage all kinds of dough to keep you there. Also, not to add any more pressure, but every agent and publisher in the business will be watching your book's release to see where the market stands. But they're dead wrong, dearie. Your book is guaranteed to make it—wrong model for them to use. But use it they shall, primarily to justify that everything is okay in la-la land when we all know that it isn't. Well, fun while it lasted, I suppose."

There was a pause as if for one moment, the book world's status became a collage of images and video clips: a frowning bookseller handing over an over-priced hardcover to a customer, an agent sending a form rejection letter to a potential client that, twenty years ago, would have been a request to see the entire manuscript, an executive shouting at the top of his lungs, "If I see another fucking cover with a muscular male holding a gun, I'm gonna blow! Our best covers were forty years ago when we actually had *artists* designing them," an editor not fully committing to the edit because he couldn't stay away from his phone, and a publicist who—

"So, how's the big case? Marina owner all along, right?"

"We've actually hit a roadblock, I think."

"Oh?"

"I took a look at my call log while we've been chatting, and there's nothing from the P.I. I've been shadowing."

Rachel used this to segue into a complete recap for Topaz, ending with Ben-David's promise to call if anything new had come up during the afternoon.

"Has to be dirtball Matty," Topaz said. "Probably show up soon. Guys like that always make mistakes, especially if they're hiding or on the run. Peanuts for brains—that sort of thing."

"Since Obadiah hasn't called me, I should have the evening to work on the book." Her stomach grumbled. "That is, after I get some dinner."

"Splendid. In fact, if you've got everything you need for the story, then why not bail out now and keep those fingers churning? Everybody knows Matty did it, risk-taker."

"I don't have *everything* yet, Topaz. And, there is a part of me that wants to see this thing through. If not to catch the killer, then to at least get more ideas for the book."

"Okay, but I'm only giving you three more days, tops, and then I'm going to need an outline. Hightower will want to weigh in, and the tidbit about Rose will be enough to keep Affleck occupied for now, but he's going to want details to start thinking about locales and such and such. Riley Cannon can't keep them waiting forever."

"Fair enough."

"That cat of yours deceased yet?"

"Topaz!"

"All right, sorry. Just keep the little bugger away from your work."

"I hope your dinner goes well tomorrow night—"

Topaz cut her off, saying, "You know he's going to ask me who you are for the millionth time."

"Just tell him 'hi' for me."

"Will do. Must run now, lady Riley. Talk in a few days, okay?"

"Until then, my guardian and protector."

"Ha! Now, *write*."

In typical Topaz Kennedy fashion, the call ended before Rachel could reply. She rubbed Hemy in soft, slow strokes, making him purr. But, after a minute of the pampering, the cat, seemingly satisfied that she had finally given him the proper attention, hopped to the floor and nudged the cracked door open enough for him to slide out of the room.

She debated calling Obadiah but then decided against it. If he had anything of importance, he would call her. A crack of thunder made her jump, and she looked out the large windows of her writing room. The sky had gone from sunshine and no clouds to a purple sheet. The water had become choppy as if its stomach had become upset again after being coated for most of the day with Pepto Bismol. As predicted, the Huron breezes were back and gathering strength. Any peace or tranquility that she had felt during the morning and afternoon had been replaced with uncertainty as she saw two separate bolts of lightning strike down from the sky near Beacon Island. How violent would the winds get? They'd been known to stir up tornadoes now and then. But she wasn't in Florida; no one in Michigan boarded up their windows when a storm hit. However, going outside was out of the question when the heavy Huron breezes commenced. She remembered being on a school bus headed for a high school basketball game when, in a matter of minutes, a funnel formed in a field to the right of the highway. The driver stopped the bus, and the coach nervously told the girls to sit tight and pray. They watched in horror as the tornado came straight at them but then mercifully turned, hopping over the road, and mowed a path through the woods on the other side.

Rachel's stomach turned again, and she grabbed her empty wine glass and headed downstairs to make dinner.

As she reached the first floor, her phone beeped, and she looked at the screen. It was a text message from…a number she didn't recognize. But, under the number it said:

Hi, Rachel. It's Brendan Knight. I…

She unlocked her phone and looked at the full message.

Hi, Rachel. It's Brendan Knight. I got your number from Christine Harper; she's an old friend of Daria's. Know it's out of the blue, but I was wondering if you'd be up for a late dinner tonight at my place? If you've already eaten, then maybe for a drink? Would like to see you again.

She read the message a second time and then continued to the kitchen, where she peered out at the gathering storm. "Great. Just Great."

She had felt some attraction to Brendan during the interview yesterday. The fact that she had no desire to live large and flaunt her wealth made the pairing interesting because out of all the well-off residents in Lakeview Village, she was probably the one who was closest to his tax bracket. And of the two Knights, he seemed to be the one closer to adulthood and showed signs of some degree of friendliness. But. He was still a suspect, and she was unsure how to proceed in a situation like this.

She dialed Ben-David's number.

24

The three-hundred-and-sixty-degree view from the tower in Brendan Knight's wing was stunning. The purple clouds had darkened to ebony, and the lightning over the lake acted like a strobe light, illuminating the candle-lit room for brief moments before returning it to near darkness. Jazz played from speakers in the ceiling, the scent of the fresh purple lilac flower arrangement on the beautiful wooden dining table filled the room, and a slight trace of Brendan's cologne also hung in the air. Rachel Roberts was seated at the table directly across from her host. In front of her was a white linen tablecloth and folded white napkin along with a water goblet, red wine glass, fine china coffee cup and saucer, and spotless silverware. The *real* Abernethy was present, dressed in a tuxedo, and had just seated her before ambling over to a small bar to fetch a bottle of wine.

"We're safe up here, right?" Rachel asked.

Brendan said, "When we built the place, my father made sure that the towers were erected to sustain hurricane-force winds. Cost a lot more, but, yes, I assure you we're safe."

As an apology for the Jayson-Jasper-as-Abernethy charade the previous day, Brendan had sent the old butler to pick up Rachel in the Knight's golden

Lamborghini. They had beaten the rain, and her white summer dress and styled hair had remained untouched.

The two candles on the table gave off enough light so that she could see his confident smile, which was the same one she had enjoyed yesterday.

Movement from her right side made her jump as Abernethy poured wine into her glass.

The old man grinned, seeming to enjoy the start he had given her.

Brendan played along. "You okay?"

"He's pure stealth. I didn't even see him leave the bar."

"Takes years of training, Miss Roberts," Abernethy said. He took a step back from the table and wiped the rim of the bottle with a white napkin that was draped over his forearm. "Test the wine?"

She swirled the crimson liquid and then took a deep breath while tipping the glass's enormous bowl up until the wine entered her mouth. It was glorious—a blackberry aroma with hints of mocha. She put the glass back on the table. "Approved."

"Excellent," Abernethy said and poured her a glass. Then, he poured Brendan's and disappeared behind her.

Brendan raised his glass, and his navy jacket bunched up around his shoulders while his smooth tan made his white polo shirt gleam almost as bright as his teeth. "To a new summer and a new start."

They touched glasses and drank.

As the wine entered her throat and then warmed her belly, she heard a noise from behind her.

"Appetizers have arrived, sir," Abernethy said.

Rachel turned and saw the butler taking plates out of a dumbwaiter.

"Bring them over," Brendan said.

Abernethy arrived with a platter of jumbo shrimp and calamari.

As they dug in, she wondered what Brendan was up to and thought back to Ben-David's advice about having dinner with the heir to the Knight fortune.

"It could be nothing. He's loaded, and you told me that you thought he was attracted to you. Might be as simple as that. Then again, we haven't cleared him or his sister; possible, he's snoopin' for info about the case. If he asks, you can tell him who we've interviewed, but don't give him anything else. See how he reacts. If he keeps prodding, change the subject—act like you're not that interested in the case, just testing the waters of what it's like to be a professional investigator. Or, you can say that I'm playing my cards close to my vest and not letting you in on much. If nothing he says or does raises an eyebrow, then I'll pick you up at your place around nine tomorrow morning. Projected to be a lull in the storm around then before it picks up and batters the shit out of us the rest of day and night. Thought about checking out Kaj's boat today, but it's not going anywhere, and the storm's picking up, and Matty Joshua is still missing in action, so we're kind of still in a holding pattern. But, if you do get something over at the beach hotel tonight, call me. I'll be up with Ben and Amos—gonna watch Rocky III again. Helps me think, and I need good thinkin' right now. Case has gone cold in a hurry, and that either means that we're losing the trail or somethin's comin' outta nowhere fast. Anyway, enjoy the dinner—I'm sure it'll be good, and I don't think you'll see his sister—but if you see Jayson Jasper, tell him to go fuck himself."

Ben-David had gotten off the phone roaring at his last statement.

They finished the appetizer with ordinary chit-chat. A sneeze by Brendan with Abernethy providing a tissue and then taking it away after Brendan was done. A question here and there about her job as a coder and what the summer work schedule looked like. A probing question about the Knight business and when his father planned to give him the reigns. A compliment about her dress. A compliment about his hospitality. A question about how the book business was going for Christine Harper. A joke about Jayson Jasper. It could almost be considered flirting, but because the depth never reached below surface-level questions or topics, it wasn't.

Abernethy cleared the appetizer plates and then returned from the dumbwaiter with the main course: filet mignon and lobster with garlic mash potatoes along with roasted vegetables. After their wine glasses were refilled, the butler asked, "Will you be needing anything else, sir?"

"Not at this moment. I'll buzz you when we're ready for dessert."

Abernethy bowed to both of them and then opened the floor hatch next to the dumbwaiter and disappeared below via the spiral staircase that led to the third floor where he would wait. There was a restroom there along with the elevator that would return her to the ground floor once the evening was over.

The hatch closed, and they were alone.

Then, rain began to splatter against the windows, and she could no longer see Beacon Island.

"Here it comes," she said, putting a heavenly piece of lobster into her mouth.

"There goes my plan of taking you for a cruise tonight."

"Won't get to see your island either," she said, playing along.

He stabbed a piece of steak with his knife and carefully pulled it off with his teeth.

"Pretty handy with a knife there," she said.

"Never stabbed a friend in the back," he said and took a sip of wine to wash down the steak. "But, speaking of that, how's the investigation going? Learning a lot from Obadiah?"

She cut a piece of her own steak. "We're making some progress," she said. "And, yes, he's a great mentor. Investigating a murder is something a techie doesn't do every day." She swirled the wine in her glass. "Don't know if I'll make the career change after this, but it definitely helped me answer a question that had been bubbling inside me for a long time."

"What's that?"

"We seem to be around the same age."

He pointed at himself with his wine glass. "Thirty-five—just turned old enough to be President."

"We're within five years of each other. I'll let you use your imagination to see which side of those five years I'm on."

"The lower side, of course," Brendan said. "Unless you want me to be on the younger side of you?"

His answers were smooth but a bit pre-programmed. But perhaps that's the way someone who probably grew up with his own Lego room was destined to act when they reached the Presidential threshold. She decided to give a non-committal grin and swerve back to answering his question. "I wondered if I would wake up in my fifties or sixties one day and regret not exploring other career options in my life. This summer, I decided to do something about it."

"What can I say? I'm impressed."

"I don't think I'll make the change, but at least I can cross it off my list and not bolt upright in the middle of the night sweating in a few decades wondering if I missed my calling."

"Peace of mind is important." Then, he casually ran his hand underneath his nose, and when he turned his head toward the bar, the light from the flickering candle hit his face just right, and she could see a glistening glob of liquid underneath his left nostril. Not noticing that she had seen it, he got up and walked over to the bar, where he grabbed a handful of tissues from a box that Abernethy had placed on the end of the bar. "Allergies acting up again," he said, wiping his nose and then depositing the used tissue in the wastepaper basket behind the bar. He washed his hands at the small sink and returned to the table.

They finished the main course, the conversation centering around Brendan's travel plans to Scotland, Banff, and finally St. Thomas at the end of the summer. Business was booming again, and she found him engaging and knowledgeable about the benefits of holding meetings outside of the United States. Abernethy returned, clearing the dishes and pouring coffee for them. Then, he brought in fresh raspberry pie that the Knight family cook had made that afternoon. Brendan had used up two more tissues, but Abernethy had slipped him a glass of water and two pills, and Brendan's runny nose had seemed to stop.

The raspberry pie did not last long as the conversation dropped off to almost nothing. But whereas she would have felt awkward with so much silence on a date in a restaurant, she felt relaxed, listening to the jazz, which Abernethy must have turned up because of the storm.

The rain died down, but the wind picked up and howled. Lightning continued to spark on the horizon, and thunder boomed, announcing that the storm was still raging outside the safety of the tower's glass windows. Rachel felt she was safe in the tower but also felt the risk of being so high above the ground while the wind bent trees over, threatening to snap them. Because the rain had let up, she could see the churning seas below as if there was a war between the sea and the wind to see which was the more powerful.

Abernethy poured two glasses of brandy and set them in front of Rachel and Brendan. "Your nightcaps," he said, bowing again. Then, he vanished down the circular stairway, closing the hatch behind him.

"We won't see him again tonight," Brendan said. He motioned to the leather loveseat on the far side of the room that was positioned so that those seated could gaze out at Lake Huron and Beacon Island in the distance. "Shall we take our drinks and move over to the couch?"

She nodded, and they sat down on the loveseat next to each other, holding their glasses of brandy.

"I feel as if you know something about my family, but I know nothing about yours." He took a measured sip. "Where do your parents live?"

She took a sip and held the brandy in her mouth, dipping her tongue in the sweet liquid before swallowing. *What was there to say?* Her mother had abandoned her when she was two years old, leaving her father—a grocery clerk by day and a community theater actor by night—to raise her. Later, in one of life's cruel twists, her father had fallen over into a pile of leaves on the side of their small home's driveway while raking. Heart attack. Fifty-three.

"They both passed away around ten years ago. I was an only child, so I've been on my own since."

"Sorry," Brendan said. "You lost them early."

"Heart attack and cancer," she said, telling the truth about her father's death and lying about her mother's—but it was a lie that years ago she had wanted to believe. It was back when she had been in pain, dealing with emotions that she had not been equipped to handle, and her father, as kind as he was, had been emotionally unavailable on the subject. She knew it had been because of his own trauma. And it was because of this that she spent much of her twenties and thirties wishing that her mother, wherever she was, was suffering. But, emotions as strong as those have a way of coming to the surface eventually, and when they did, she had found that she could not write. Hence, Adrienne Astra's adventures were put on hold, and Rachel had finally decided to reach out for help. The healing had been slow but cleansing, and now she no longer wished that her mother was suffering. Instead, she pitied her and eventually forgave the woman she had only vague memories of—images really—from the first two years of her life. It was because of her focused work on herself that she was able to write again. However, even though she was excited to revisit her main character, she knew that Adrienne would be different because she was different. The thought both energized her because she was excited to see where she could take the character, but it also scared her because the anger, resentment, and hurt that was lurking below her surface from the abandonment by her mother had driven her for the first three books. Rage was a powerful ally. Now, she would find out if peace, love, and acceptance were just as strong. For the past six months, she'd had her doubts, thinking that her perfect storm, which had helped her blaze a path and destroy anything that was in her way, could never be harnessed again, and her new book would fall flat. But the past few days had shown her that her hard-won mature perspective of realizing that hurt, disappointment, failure, and change gave life meaning and depth was starting to show her the way. Maybe this was where Adrienne needed to go. In the first three books, she was primarily an action figure, and the audience did not have a lot of background information about who she was or where she came from. *Yes. This was it. Thank you, Brendan Knight.* In an early scene, she had to have a character pry into Adrienne's defenses and start to unravel who she was before she became an agent. Perhaps, it was time to introduce a love interest—someone who could cross the moat and enter the castle of her mind.

"I'm sorry," Brendan said. "Other than Christine, do you have any friends or other family members who you're close with?"

Her father had been an only child too and lost his parents when he was young. He had told her that her mother's parents left the picture when she did and that her mother's only sister lived in Arizona and had never seen Rachel before Rachel's mother had split. Friends? She still had a few college girlfriends that she would text with now and again and once in a great while call, but other than that, there was no one. She was introverted, so she was not haunted by the constant urge to connect with people. "Not really," she answered Brendan. "I keep mostly to myself and my cat, Hemingway."

He tipped his glass back as if stymied by his charm offensive. He had not surprised her. He had not built any sort of an empathy or sympathy bridge. And he had not awed her with his wealth. If she wanted to, she could have her own tower and her own Abernethy waiting on her hand and foot. She felt in control. Yes, it had been months since she'd had sex, and if it was to head in that direction tonight, she'd consider it. But it would be because she wanted it and not because of anything Brendan Knight did. Perhaps, he sensed this too. However, as she moved her eyes from the dark skies outside the rain-streaked windows to his eyes, she noticed that he had moved closer.

"I'm still not over the shock of Kaj," he said. "When he was dating Daria, we got to be close. Like brothers." He shrugged. "I never had one. Don't know why either. Parents could have definitely supported another Knight."

"But you're close with your sister?"

He inched closer. Their legs weren't touching—yet. "I guess. About as close as brothers and sisters can be nowadays."

She sipped her brandy, watching him put his arm up on the back of the loveseat and then resting his head against his hand. "What do you mean by *nowadays?*"

"Too many distractions for real closeness. Even when we were in elementary school, we each had so many toys and gadgets to distract us that we hardly ever spent any time together." He closed his eyes and gave a short chuckle. "I just realized how snobby and...what's the buzzword everyone's throwin' around?"

"Privileged?"

He snapped his fingers. "Yeah, that's the one. Anyway, it was a glib thing to say."

"Is Daria at the estate tonight?"

He smirked. "She rubbed you the wrong way the other day, didn't she?"

Hell yes, she did.

"Not at all. The interview dragged on a bit, and I figured she wanted to wrap it up." She paused for effect. "Why do you mention it? Do *you* think she didn't like me?" Rachel realized that she was flirting back, and flirting annoyed her, but in a tower on a stormy night with a billionaire, well...

"She saw you as competition."

"For whom?" She swallowed a sip of brandy and couldn't resist. "Jayson Jasper?"

For what she thought was the first time that evening, Brendan Knight gave a genuine laugh. For some guys, their laugh knocked them down a few notches; for others, the laugh completed the package and got them onto the escalator

225

heading up to the floor of total attraction. Brendan had some advantages: the pretty face, the square jaw, the perfect, piano-key teeth, but those could all slip to the basement with a goofy or over-boisterous laugh. Thankfully, Brendan's was a becoming laugh—fun, energetic, vulnerable.

"You've got an answer for everything," he said, inching closer. "The wit of a writer."

Stop talking and do it already.

"Speaking of writers," he said, jumping off the couch. "I've got the perfect conversation piece."

Only the heir of a billionaire's fortune would ever state that out loud and kill the mood. But, she was forgiving.

"Have you ever heard of Riley Cannon?"

Instantly, she went into protection mode. "Not much of a reader," she said, watching him walk across the room to a large trunk with a blanket on top. Her palms started to sweat. *Do they know who I am?*

Holding the blanket, he opened the trunk. "She's my mom's favorite author."

What's he getting out of the trunk?

"She wrote three mega-bestsellers about ten years ago, but—are you sure you haven't heard of her?" He didn't wait for an answer. "In the past six months, it's all my mom can talk about after the big announcement that Riley's fourth book in the saga—a saga no one thought would ever be finished—is coming out next summer. Here we are," he said, closing the chest.

In his hand was a book. *Which one did he grab?* If it was her first book, *Morning Glory Mayhem!*, then she'd be fine. The picture was small, and it was on the inside of the dust jacket's back flap. But if it was one of the other two books, *Late-Afternoon Associates* or *Enemies in the Evening*, then the entire back of the dust jacket was a glamor shot of her sitting in a leather chair by a fireplace. But it was retouched, and she wore chic designer frame glasses with short blonde hair—like

Sandra-Brown-spikey short. She didn't think that she looked like any of the pictures now, but she supposed that if someone studied the back cover and her present profile long enough, they might see the resemblance. However, it was dark in the tower, they had been drinking, she was ten years older, and her hair was longer and dyed auburn. And Rachel had never had worn glasses.

Brendan sunk back down into the couch and showed her the cover for…

…*Morning Glory Mayhem!*

Thank. God.

"It's a first edition, signed by Riley Cannon herself," he said. "Heard it was worth a couple a grand. Pennies to me, but—shit, there I go again. Sorry. Money is one big pain in the rear."

She ignored him and took the book, amused at the fact that at some point around 13 years ago, she had sat down for three days in a hotel room in New York City that had been arranged by Topaz and signed around twenty thousand hardcover copies. She'd argued against the exclamation point at the end of the title, but Hightower had said that because she had so much underwater action in the book that an exclamation point might bring back memories of Clive Cussler's *Raise the Titanic!* And *Night Probe!*. It was a calculated risk, but because of the sales, Hightower could always hide behind his own theory that it had been the right call. No one could disprove it—or prove it—and those were the best theories to have in publishing. *"I know my goddamned numbers!"* Hightower would shout into his desk phone. The cover had always amused her: The top third was the title in bright white block letters; the middle third was a cover artist's rendering of a cabin cruiser on the surface of aquamarine-colored water with a female scuba diver beneath, diving down into the depths—the water fading to black until it became a white bedsheet with two sets of intertwined legs sticking out; the bottom third was her pen name, Riley Cannon, in an assertive font and in all caps. "Interesting," she said, opening the front cover.

And there, on the title page that was starting to turn yellow, was her signature. She did not attempt to take off the dust jacket and look to see if this was the signed copy that had her secret drawing. Topaz had come up with the idea: *"Draw a tiny picture on the inside of the front cover that will be hidden by the dust jacket's inside flap. What to draw? Who cares, Miss Anonymous! Draw two pigs in a compromising situation for all I care. Now, pay attention. On launch day, we'll announce that such a drawing exists, and your new fans can see if they've got the lucky copy. What will they win? Haven't figured it out yet, but we'll make it good. Maybe a Ben Franklin's amount on a gift card to their favorite restaurant. Something like that. Well, what do you think, shy one?"* She'd drawn a cat with a pair of sunglasses, holding a drink in one hand and a stiletto in the other. *Let Hemy's presence be felt!* *"Dear God!"* Topaz had shouted. *"Anything but that, Cannon!"* And she'd drawn the same picture—perhaps the cat gained a little weight each time—for her other two books.

She continued to flip through the pages, feeling the air from the fan of pages fluttering by, until she reached the back cover. She looked at the picture like a woman who was measuring herself against the photo and then closed the cover. On the back were the blurbs that Topaz had fought so hard to get: John Grisham, David Baldacci, Danielle Steele, Oprah, and Clive Cussler.

"Looks fun," she said, handing the book to Brendan.

"I even heard that Suzanne Elise Freeman is supposed to read the first line of the new novel on Facebook live on July 4th. I can't believe you haven't heard the news. When her new book was announced in December, it, like, *broke* the internet."

"Apparently, it didn't break mine, but then again, I'm hardly ever online anyway."

"I've noticed. You haven't touched your cell phone once tonight."

"Don't really have a reason to. Not a big texter, no one uses e-mail anymore, and the only news I'm interested in is if we're being nuked—and if that's the case, then I doubt I'd be notified before we all got vaporized. Other than that, the news really doesn't tell anyone that much anymore. It's like a soap opera. You can go a year without watching and then see one episode and be all caught up."

"What about the weather?"

"Now that I do check on my phone. But, tonight," she said, pointing to the storm outside, "I'm pretty sure what the weather is."

He held up his cell phone. "Gotta admit. I'm guilty tonight. I checked it when I went over to open the chest."

She gave a satisfied grin that said, *"You're weak."* "Anything important?"

"Of course not," he said. He thumbed through the book.

Don't concentrate on the picture.

He flipped all the way through and took a prolonged pause while looking at the picture.

Oh, God.

"No one even knows who she is. It's a huge secret that no one can crack."

Stop looking at the picture! "I bet that's not even her," Rachel said.

He closed the book, glanced at the blurbs on the back, and then turned it back over to the front cover. "Yeah, you might be right. They probably use that picture to throw everyone off.

Are you a mind reader?

"But," he said, glancing in the direction of the chest, "I think the other two pictures are different."

She was starting to sweat. *He might know. Well, does he? Maybe not. I have to get him off this subject.* She rubbed his arm. "Forget them," she said, giving him a sly grin. "What are they doing in that chest anyway?"

"My mom likes to come up here and read. Don't ask me why because she's got the rest of the house to choose from. And she's got multiple copies—hardcovers, quality paperbacks, mass-market paperbacks—in bookshelves all over the house. Plus, she loves to read along with the audiobook version up here—calls Suzanne Elise Freeman her close friend. Whatever. I don't understand it." He glanced over at the chest and nodded at it. "I guess she thinks the first edition hardcovers will be safe with me up here. Wouldn't dare trust them with Daria."

"Why not?"

"Because she's a hot mess when it comes to other people's stuff—doesn't treat anything that's not hers with respect."

He finally noticed her hand on his arm, placing his hand over hers and giving it a soft rub. She liked the feel of it.

"I'll try not to loan her anything," Rachel said. His hand pressed harder and then softened to a tickle, his fingers massaging her entire hand as if they were going over harp strings.

"Wise choice," he said. Then, as if they had mutually agreed to kiss after a three-second pause, their lips met.

For all of his shortcomings in tact about his wealth, he gained ground with his ability as a kisser. There was nothing worse than a man who did not know how to navigate a woman's mouth. The clumsy and untutored tried too hard— usually an ailment of the youth that could be corrected. But if you were beyond thirty and still couldn't maneuver and respond to what should be romantic excitement and discovery, then you were hopelessly doomed to walk the night alone—or at least not with her.

They stopped, repositioned, and started in again.

The evening had gone well, and she had confirmed that her attraction to him was real. Was it headed in a serious direction? Of course not. At least not yet, but she'd give him a second date and see where things went from there. The kiss felt good—basic human proximity and connection—but she backed away from her previous thoughts of sex. There was still an investigation going on, and, as easy as it would be to welcome young Brendan into her mastery of the Kama Sutra, she decided that this was not the proper moment. Besides, there was the rest of the summer; it was all ahead of them.

She gave him an intense finish and rubbed her tongue over her lips as she pulled away.

Then, the music cut off in the middle of Ella Fitzgerald's *Midnight Sun*.

Rachel watched as Brendan looked around; he appeared uneasy.

"Power's out," he said. "Generator should be kicking in any time."

There was a knock on the hatch.

"Come in, Abernethy," Brendan said.

The hatch opened, and Abernethy's ghostly head rose through the opening in the floor. "Everything okay, sir? Power is back on. Should I start the music again?"

"I better get home," Rachel said. "Need to check on Hemy and see if my power is out too."

Brendan gave a slight frown but recovered. "I understand," he said. "Do you have a generator?"

"Yes. Natural gas. Everything should be fine." She could sense his disappointment, but the power outage had made her exit a little easier. "Maybe tomorrow night?" she added.

He let out a sigh of relief. "Definitely. Thought I did something wrong."

"Not enough wrong," she teased.

"That's a start." He turned toward Abernethy, who was now standing by his side. "Abernethy will drive you home."

"It would be my pleasure, Miss Roberts," the old butler said.

"Thanks for the great night," she said and gave him a peck on the cheek.

She caught Abernethy's grin before he had a chance to make it vanish.

Ten minutes later, she was inside her house and watching the lemon beams of the Knight limousine disappear down her driveway. Hemy approached cautiously as usual as if testing her loyalty. *Cats.*

Her phone rang.

231

She had exchanged numbers with Brendan before leaving. Would this be his *"just checking to see if everything is okay at your place"* courtesy call? She pulled the phone from her pocket.

It was not Brendan Knight.

The caller was Obadiah Ben-David.

She answered.

"Sorry if I'm interrupting something," he said. "Where are you?"

"I just got home."

"Do you have power?"

"It went out, but I've got a generator."

"Listen carefully. Get out of the house right now. Run to Christine's."

"What?"

"Quickly. You may not be alone."

Her eyes darted around the room as she backed toward the front door. "What's going on?"

"Go! I just need to make sure you're safe right now."

"Look, I'm inside my house. It's like a tornado outside, and I'm not going anywhere until you tell me what you know."

There was a moment of silence. Then, he said, "Someone killed Ben tonight. We might be getting close to the murderer."

"My God, your poor dog. I—"

"No time for that now. Call me when you get to Christine's."

"Okay," she said, hanging up the phone.

She grabbed Hemy and ran for the front door.

25

Rachel Roberts sat on top of the queen-sized bed in Christine Harper's guest bedroom. The down comforter was powder-blue colored, and its fluffiness reminded her of her own bed back home. Hemy was curled up on her lap and purring; she'd thrown the old boy underneath her jacket on her way to Christine's to avoid getting him wet. She had taken a cold shower and slipped into a pair of sweatpants and a t-shirt that Christine had loaned her, and her wet clothes were being washed and dried by her friend.

She yawned and took a sip from the bottle of water she'd taken out of the refrigerator downstairs. The room's walls were painted jade, and she could tell that the tan carpet was new because it still had a fresh smell and squished when she walked on it. There were two large windows that looked out over the stormy Lake Huron, and the room was bathed in a soft glow from the candle on the nightstand—Christine's house did not have a generator. The room's other furniture was minimalist and lived-in: one dresser and a full-length mirror opposite the foot of the bed. There was no television set on the dresser, just a jewelry box, hairbrush, and a small plant.

She set the water bottle down and listened to the wind roar outside. She didn't think that there had been anyone in her house, but she'd been inside for less than a minute. Whether there was or there wasn't, she felt safe now. Christine had still been up and had reached the front door thirty seconds after Rachel had knocked. Rachel had then dialed Obadiah Ben-David to tell him that she was safe and that she'd call him once she was settled in.

She picked up her phone from the nightstand and dialed his number.

"Feeling better?" he said.

She gave him a quick recap of what had happened between Christine letting her in and right now.

"Good. Let's talk business."

"I am so sorry about Ben. You don't have to tell me what happened, but I will listen if you need me to."

The silence was long enough for Hemy to get up, walk across the bed, and jump to the floor.

"Thanks," Ben-David said. "I already buried him. Went out in this mess and dug a grave in the woods off to the right of my driveway." He exhaled into the phone.

Gathering himself, Rachel thought. She couldn't imagine what state she'd be in if someone had killed Hemy.

"Amos had left, and I noticed that Ben hadn't come in from outside in a while. I checked in my bedroom, and when I didn't find him, I went outside. Well, someone had shot him four times—had to have used a silencer because I didn't hear anything, and I've got sharp ears. The only good thing I can say is that it was over fast. Old Ben went right down and never got up. All the blood was pooled in one spot. Poor lad never had a chance. Doesn't look like there's any evidence out there, either. I already combed my lot with a flashlight and didn't find a damned thing. Fuckin' storm."

"Has anything like this happened to you before?"

"Nothing. I've had the occasional angry client come and knock on my door and give me a piece of his or her mind. There's also been a few of the people that my clients had hired me to catch cheating send me a hate letter or give me a nasty phone call. But, I've never had anyone destroy any of my property or hurt someone I cared about. So, when I went out and found Ben, I came right in and called you."

"Why?"

"Because this isn't ordinary. I wasn't sure about it before, but we're dealing with someone who is sick and unpredictable."

"Matty Joshua?" asked Rachel.

"He's still the number one suspect, but—" He paused. "The way I figure it, Ben's death could mean a couple of things. One. It's a warning to stop investigating, which means we're getting close. Two. The person or persons who killed Kaj Reynard are taking out any early warning systems I have at the house. I have always figured that my dogs are the best security system, and so I've never invested in any other one. With Ben gone, now I'm a little more vulnerable to someone approaching my house. My neighbors are pretty far down the beach on both sides, and no one's got a security camera out here. They could come at me from the road or the water. Anyway, I couldn't remember if you had a security system, so I had to call you right away and make sure you were safe. Decided that if our suspect or suspects are malicious enough to kill my dog, then they might be insane enough to try and do something harmful to you."

"You thought my life was in danger?"

"I didn't want to take any chances," he said. "I'm just glad that you're safe at Christine's."

"What about the rest of tonight?"

"I don't think they'll try anything more. They sent their message, and now they'll wait to see what we do."

She swallowed. This adventure of hers had now left the "new experience" category and entered the "dangerous and out-of-hand" category. What good was *Dark After Midnight* if there was no Riley Cannon to write it? Then, she weighed something she had never thought about before. *What if something happens to me? Would Topaz find a ghostwriter to take my notes and finish the book?* She did not like what her conscience told her. "What are we going to do tomorrow?" she asked.

"I'll pick you up at Christine's at nine in the morning. We'll take a look at your place—make sure it's okay. Then, we'll go have a look at Kaj's boat. Might be something there that Ritter missed." There was a long pause. "After that, I'm not sure. Maybe we take another run at Ingrid Bara or head out to Shelby's Marina. I've gotta sleep on it."

It sounded like the phone call might end, but then Ben-David said, "Anything to report from your dinner?"

"I can't think of anything. The case didn't come up much." She was sliding down the headboard. So, she sat up, placed another pillow behind her, and leaned back. "He did tell me that he was sad about the loss of Kaj."

"He ask you anything?"

"Not really."

"His sister show up at all?"

"No. I didn't see her. However, at one point, we did discuss her. Brendan told me that he thought that Daria saw me as a threat."

"Interesting," was all Ben-David said.

There was silence again, and Hemy jumped back on the bed. "So, tomorrow at nine?" she said.

"I wouldn't blame you if you wanted out right now," Ben-David said.

"While you sleep on the case, I'll sleep on that. Fair enough?"

"Fair," he said. "How's Hemy?"

And at that moment, she decided that she would forever like Obadiah Ben-David. Any man who just lost his dog and was still nice enough to ask about her pet was good with her for life. "He's right here on the bed with me." She petted the giant furball as he sat down next to her and stared up at her face. "Obadiah, I'm sorry about Ben. If I lost Hemy—I—"

"He was a good dog—a family member and someone I trusted. You've probably noticed, but I don't have many people in my life. I've only let a few get close since—well, you rest up, and I'll see you in the morning."

The call ended, and Rachel got under the covers and then blew out the candle. Lightning lit up the sky, and she listened as the rain pounded the windows. *What would tomorrow bring?* As she closed her eyes and pondered the question, Hemy's purring and her exhaustion eventually took her into a deep sleep.

And because of her plunge into darkness and heavy, slow breathing, she did not see the figure standing on Christine's beach, looking at the house…and up at the room that Rachel was sleeping in.

PART III

The Beacon

Landon Beach

26

id-morning the next day, Rachel Roberts and Obadiah Ben-David walked down the small dock toward Kaj Reynard's boat *Coca-Cola Classic*. Behind them was the owner of the dock, Mac Schmidt—Hampstead's version of George R.R. Martin, complete with the faded captain's hat upon his head. Everything outside was still wet from the storms that had continued throughout the night as if a planet-sized bucket of water had been emptied directly over Hampstead, Michigan. The worn dock boards were dark brown and slimy and creaked with each step they made. With Ben-David's weight, she thought he might break through and disappear into the water below at any second. The same could be said for Schmidt, and she imagined hearing a snap and a yell behind her, turning around to see a gaping hole where the old dock owner had stood. The sun had been shining for the past hour, but the storm clouds on the horizon were inching their way toward the shore as if someone was threatening to pull a black sheet over the sky in an hour. There had been no mention of Ben, and Rachel had decided not to bring it up. Let Ben-David deal with it in his own way.

They reached the red-hulled cabin cruiser with white trim, and Rachel could see *Coca-Cola* **CLASSIC** painted on the transom in white letters with

Hampstead, Michigan underneath, painted in smaller, black letters. Since learning the boat's name from Baby Lloyd, Rachel's mind had been working on why Kaj would choose the name Coca-Cola Classic. She remembered the story well from her childhood because her father had gone into a fit when the new Coke formula—much sweeter than the original—had been launched. Thankfully, in 1985, when she was in elementary school, Coke had brought back the old formula and called it Coca-Cola Classic, a name their favorite drink would carry until phasing it out in 2009. Sharing a coke with her dad had been one of her favorite traditions growing up. He would come home on Friday night after work with takeout from Pizza Hut and a six-pack of Coca-Cola Classic bottles. In the summer, they would sit out on their small deck and enjoy their meal, talking about the week; in the winter, they would sit in the living room with their meal on T.V. trays and enjoy the roaring fire in the hearth. To this day, she still kept her refrigerator stocked with Coca-Cola bottles, which she had to special order. Thinking about this, she felt a remote kinship with Kaj Reynard. *Maybe the guy just really liked Coke*, she thought.

"Like I told you up at the house," Mac Schmidt said as they all stood on the dock, looking down into the stern of Kaj Reynard's boat, "I saw him take this puppy out after midnight a few times." He put his foot on the starboard gunwale. His feet were so wide that Rachel thought his green-colored Crocs were going to split. "No idea what he was doing, but when I would wake up the next morning, the boat would be neatly tied up right here like it is now."

"Did Ritter say anything else to you when he inspected the boat a few days ago?"

Schmidt scratched the gray chest hair that was sprouting from his unbuttoned shirt. "Just that everything below was ship-shape, which struck me as odd."

"Why?" Ben-David asked.

"Because Kaj Reynard was a slob. Used to park his old Pontiac Firebird in my lot, and every time, *every time* he opened his door to get out, shit would fall on the ground, and he would never pick any of it up. I complained to him about it, but he'd always blow me off. That is, until I told him that he'd have to take his boat someplace else. Then he started picking the stuff up and either stuffing it back into his car, or if it was fast food bags and paper cups, he'd throw it in the trash can I put right in front of his usual parking spot. I'd go down and take a look in his car every now and again after he headed out to sea, and the inside of his car looked like the Huron breezes we had last night had gotten in there and stirred up a mess." Schmidt paused, looking back at the small gravel parking lot. "But, when he got that new Bronco, he kept the inside as clean as the outside. Don't know what happened. But when Ritter told me that the interior spaces of Kaj's boat were clean as a whistle, I was suspect of it because Corey Ritter is a bit of a packrat too, and what's clean to him might be filthy to most people. So, I went down there and couldn't believe my eyes. Nothing was out of place. And," he said, frowning, "I shouldn't have done this, but I did open a few cabinets. Again, I was shocked. One cabinet was above his nav station—a nice row of books arranged left to right and tallest to shortest. The other cabinet was next to the head—toilet paper, towels, and other cleaning supplies all neatly stowed and secured."

Ben-David had his notepad out and was writing.

Rachel anticipated his question and asked, "Are those the only two cabinets you opened?"

Ben-David gave her a nod.

"Yeah," Schmidt said. "I'm assuming that Ritter poked around a bit, but I didn't get the feeling that he had stumbled onto anything of importance. His short debrief to me felt like he had just checked off another box in the investigation, 'Examined dead guy's boat and found nothing' or something like that." He took his foot off the boat, and the starboard fenders squeaked as they rubbed against the hull and dock while the craft settled. "Well, I'll be up at the house if you need me."

Rachel and Ben-David nodded.

"Hope you find out who killed him soon. Between the storm last night and the murder, everybody around town is jumpy right now." He took a quick peek at the lake and clouds in the distance. "And it's looking like we might get hit again today." He turned away and started to walk back down the dock. The worn boards moaned as each heavy foot exerted pressure on them. Over his shoulder, he said, "But maybe it'll head north and miss us this time. Happened before."

When Schmidt was halfway up the dense and bright green grass of his backyard, they boarded the boat. Ben-David handed her a pair of plastic gloves and then put on a pair himself. There were only a few lockers to sift through in the stern and cockpit, and they found nothing out of the ordinary—life jackets, beach towels, a pair of binoculars, a whistle, flare gun, and flares. Underneath the port bench was a spacious cooler that still had a few cans of Budweiser sloshing around in a pool of water from the long-ago melted ice. They headed below.

"Let's start up forward and make our way aft," Ben-David said.

Rachel grinned as she watched the huge man bend down to avoid hitting his head as they moved past the small salon, past the head, and into the v-berth. So far, for all the talk of Kaj Reynard's messiness, she had to agree with Mac Schmidt's assessment: *Coca-Cola Classic* was an anomaly. The cushions in the salon were navy blue with cream-colored accent pillows on top. The hull was fiberglass, but the cabinets were made of varnished mahogany, giving the interior a more natural feel. In her second book, *Late-Afternoon Associates*, she'd written a scene where Adrienne Astra had to climb aboard a fifty-foot yacht in Key West and roar off into the night to escape a deadly assassin. For that section of the book, she had had to research boats, which she knew nothing about, in order to make the scene ring authentic. *"If you don't study up, the boat and gun readers will murder you in the reviews, Captain Cannon,"* Topaz had warned.

In the v-berth, Kaj Reynard had added a few nice touches. The comforter on the berth was scarlet with gray pillowcases. There was a gray throw blanket draped off of a corner, and there was a row of paperbacks on the port-side mahogany shelf. The starboard-side shelf was empty. She glanced through the paperback titles. *No Riley Cannon, but guess who?* Judge Macy Ashberry and the Green Beret Colonel, along with nearly every other book that Christine Harper had recommended in the past year's blogs in Harper's Highlights. She'd have to tell Christine later, whom she had not had many words with last night or this morning. Her friend had been up almost all night trying to make an editing deadline for one of her bigger clients. They had given each other a hug over coffee in the morning, and Rachel had headed out with Hemy and Ben-David while Christine was back to hacking away at her laptop's keys at the kitchen table. When they arrived at Rachel's house, they had found nothing. No broken windows or opened doors. No signs of footprints around the house, but Ben-David had been skeptical of finding them anyway after not being able to find any around the perimeter of his fenced-in side yard where he'd found Ben.

They pulled open the two large drawers underneath the v-berth and found a stack of shorts, underwear, socks, and t-shirts in one drawer and a scattering of *Playboy* magazines in the other. Rachel rolled her eyes.

"I'll bet a few of those disappeared with Corey Ritter," Ben-David said, closing the drawers.

In the v-berth stateroom closet, they found a windbreaker, hooded sweatshirt, and flip-flops. The check of the head and the closet that Schmidt had told them about took only a minute, and then they were back in the salon. Underneath the small port bench was another life jacket, some neatly coiled line, and two extra fenders.

"I'll check the galley cabinets and this aft cabinet," Ben-David said.

Rachel headed toward the nav station. "I'll see if there's anything of interest around here."

First, she checked the cabinet above the nav station and found the neat row of books that Schmidt had told them about. Next, she sat down behind the small desk and opened the desk drawer. Inside were two rolls of masking tape, a compass, a rolling ruler, pencils, a calculator, a pair of dividers, a cigar tube, a lighter, matches, a folded chart, a pad of paper, and a worn copy of the United States Coast Guard's *Navigation Rules*. She picked up the pad and book and set them on the table. Then, she slid the chart out, opened it up, and spread it out on the table. She recognized the area immediately. Near the bottom was the Hampstead coastline—specifically the Lakeview Village's coastline—and up a third of the way from the coastline was Beacon Island. The rest of the chart was the water east of the island. And this is the area where her eyes found the only markings on the chart.

Presumably using a pencil and ruler, Kaj Reynard had drawn a large box east of Beacon Island. She leaned in to get a better look when Ben-David said, "Hey, come here and look at this."

She turned her head and saw him standing in the aft-most part of the galley, almost out of view. He then backed up into the galley.

She got up from the nav station and entered the galley, squeezing by him to get a look into the aft cabinet. "I don't get it," she said. "It's just a bunch of spices and cooking supplies." She picked up a bottle of Pam. "Shelves look pretty standard, maybe a foot deep."

Then, a large arm reached past her head and gave the entire shelving unit a push.

She was startled as the entire deck-to-overhead set of shelves swung aft, exposing a large storage room.

"Hidden compartment," Ben-David said and then used the flashlight on his phone to illuminate the space.

Rachel could now see scuba tanks, a wet suit, dive knife, regulator assembly, pressure gauge, fins, mask, snorkel, a spear gun, and, hanging on the starboard bulkhead, a large amount of what appeared to be orange parachutes. "What are those?" she asked.

"Lift bags. You fill them with air underwater to bring stuff up to the surface from the bottom."

"There are at least a dozen of them," she said. "What would Kaj need so many of them for? And why hide your dive gear in a secret compartment?"

"Can you fit in there?" Ben-David asked.

"I think so," Rachel said.

"Would you feel comfortable going in and poking around a little for us?"

"Sure," she said and entered the compartment. She now had her phone out and was using the flashlight to inspect the space. "How did you do it?" she asked.

"Do what?"

"Discover this hidden space?"

"I was studying the layout when we were in the stern. Then, when we got below, I found it odd that there was a cabinet that seemed to close off the access to the stern. Usually, there is access to a nice little aft stateroom tucked in there. So, when I opened the cabinet door and saw the shelves and noticed that they weren't deep, I felt around for some sort of latch. Found it right underneath the shelf with the spaghetti noodles and sauce." He pointed to it, and Rachel ran her hand underneath the shelf until she felt the small lever.

"Do you think Ritter discovered this place?"

"He doesn't know shit about boats. Knowing Corey Ritter, he probably took some food out of those shelves. Plus, if he *had* found the hidden room, he'd have blabbed about it already. That is, unless—"

She finished his sentence. "—he didn't want anyone else to know about it. But wasn't your friend Amos with him when he searched the boat?"

"He was. But Amos could have been searching topside when Ritter was still below. Doesn't matter. One call to Amos will clear everything up."

"What about Kevin Shelby? Kaj's boat was at his marina for months. Wouldn't he know about it?"

Ben-David scratched his beard. "It's a fair question, but if Kaj wanted to keep this room hidden, my guess is that he built it after the boat was at Shelby's."

"Unless Shelby and Ritter both know about it, and the three of them were up to something. But then again, why would Kaj want to hide a dive locker?"

"I'm not sure. A lot of people scuba dive around here, including Baby Lloyd. Remember him telling us that he likes to anchor out, dive down, and sit on the bottom for an hour to clear his head?"

Rachel nodded. "And, according to Baby Lloyd, he was only out with Kaj once, which means they probably didn't spend the night on the boat and probably weren't out long enough for either of them to go anywhere near Kaj's galley."

"Agree. I don't think Baby Lloyd knows anything about the compartment."

She was just about to start searching again when Matty Joshua's words entered her mind. "Hey, do you remember what Kevin Shelby told us about the fight that Kaj and Matty had in the marina parking lot?"

Ben-David's eyes got a little bigger. "Yes," he said and hurriedly took his notepad out of his pocket and began flipping pages. A few seconds later, he said, "Shelby told us that Matty asked Kaj, 'What's out there?'" He shined his phone's flashlight on the lift bags. "So Kaj Reynard has a secret dive locker and an army of lift bags, which are used to bring stuff up from underwater. No one apparently knows about it, and no one goes out on his boat with him. A year ago, Mac Schmidt gets up in the middle of the night to take a leak and sees Kaj heading out to sea. Then, you've got Matty 'Hollywood' Joshua asking Kaj, 'What's out there?'"

"I have an idea," Rachel said, "but let me check this place out first."

"Okay," Ben-David said, watching her as she began to lift up dive gear and shine her flashlight underneath.

She moved a few tanks and placed the wetsuit on the floor on the opposite side of the small room. Then, she shined her light in the back corner, which had been out of sight because of the gear. "That's odd," she said.

"What?" Ben-David asked.

She moved a little further in. "Well, there's a small pile of torn plastic wrapping back here. And, I'm no plastic expert, but it looks old."

"Let me see."

She moved out of the way, and together they shined their lights on the pile.

"Hand me a piece," Ben-David said.

She grabbed one of the smaller pieces—about the size of a Ziploc freezer bag—and handed it to Ben-David.

While he examined it, she started to pick up the pile, then stopped. "Huh," she said. "Shine your light right here."

He did as she told him.

"There's a good amount of what looks like white dust down here." She lifted up the pile of torn plastic further. "Even more on the floor in the corner. What is this stuff?"

Ben-David wiped his forehead. "What do you think it is?"

White dust. Torn plastic bags. "Cocaine?"

"That would be my guess," Ben-David said.

Rachel finished her search, but it yielded nothing more. After snapping a few dozen photographs that gave them a layout of the entire space, she stepped out of the small compartment and into the galley. Ben-David slid past her and pulled the shelves closed until he heard a *click* and then shut the cabinet door.

"You said you had something," he said.

"Come over to the nav station."

She sat back down behind the table and pointed at the hand-drawn box east of Beacon Island. "I think Kaj drew this."

Ben-David suddenly had an intensity that she had never seen before, and he brought his head to within a foot of the chart.

Then, as if they saw it at the same time, Rachel said aloud a hand-written note on the southwestern corner of the box. "LH's search box."

Their eyes literally searched the box. Sure enough, just before the eastern-most side of the box, and almost to the southern edge, which was south of Beacon Island, there was an asterisk circled with an exclamation point next to it.

Ben-David quickly ran his index finger south from the edge of the search box, paralleling the coastline. He was taking quick breaths, almost hyperventilating—and perspiration was dripping off his forehead and onto the chart. Suddenly, his finger stopped, and his whole hand began to shake.

She looked at where his finger was. It was in an area of Lake Huron just off Au Gres. Written on the chart was an **X** with the words **Boyd: Sparky #1**. Ben-David stood up.

"Who is LH? And what in the hell does Boyd, Sparky number one mean?" She looked up at Ben-David. His face was ghost white, and his body was starting to wobble. "My God, are you okay?"

He went to speak, but then his eyes closed, and his body went limp—and crumpled to the deck with a loud thud.

27

Hampstead, Michigan, Friday, June 16, 1989

*T*wenty-eight-year-old Obadiah Ben-David carried a tray full of food and a large glass of Vernors into the small master bedroom that he shared with his wife, Isabella. It was seven in the evening—she was starting to take dinner later and later because of a lack of appetite—and the warm glow of the fading sunlight streamed in through the open blinds of the room's west windows.

"Here's your supper, dear," Ben-David said, setting the tray across her lap. She needs to eat—she looks so tiny and fragile, he told himself.

"Thank you," Isabella whispered.

Ben-David opened the ice-cold can of Vernors and put a plastic straw through the opening. She was getting weaker by the day, and the straw was a small gesture to try and help her from having to move any more than necessary. He watched as she sucked the amber-colored liquid through the straw.

She swallowed and gave him a small grin of relief.

251

He was not an emotional man, but he had cried more in the last three months than he had during the rest of his life. She had been diagnosed with breast cancer earlier in the year, but the bombshell had arrived in March. The cancer had spread, well, everywhere. She had handled it better than he had; she was stoic, dignified, and instead of sinking into depression, asking for pity, she had focused her attention on his needs. He tried to stop her but soon realized that this was her way of dealing with what was thought to be a likely death sentence. But, there was one option that might make a difference—an option that he had to try. And tonight, he would.

After graduating from Central Michigan University in 1983, Ben-David had decided to become a professional investigator back in his hometown of Hampstead. He liked justice. He liked working with people. And he liked being home. He had also figured that job security was a given because, last time he checked, human beings continued to make poor decisions that had consequences. And he had been right, but, unfortunately, the job security, satisfaction, and the freedom it provided had one drawback: poor health-care coverage. But in the glory years of prime youth—the real roaring twenties—a person feels invincible, and health-care coverage is given about as much thought as a colonoscopy. That is, until your wife, who is a pre-school aide at your local church, feels lumps in her breast when she is two months pregnant, he thought.

She'd miscarried in April. Then, in May, after more tests than they thought were possible, the doctors had told them that the only chance Isabella had was to start treatment in Boston at the best cancer center in the world. So, for the past month, Ben-David had spent sleepless night after sleepless night trying to think of a way to foot the bills that would come with treatment in Boston—travel, hotel, the whole damn program. Neither of their parents had any money, and until three nights ago, he had come up with zero options.

But on the night of Tuesday, June 13th, 1989, his—and he prayed that Isabella's—fortune changed. Depressed and drunk at a local bar, Ben-David watched as the Detroit Pistons climbed the mountain and won the NBA Finals against the legendary Los Angeles Lakers four games to zero. The bar had gone bananas as the Bad Boys closed out the series with a 105-97 game four win. He hated to admit it, but he'd gotten swept up in the emotion of the event, and for a few meaningless minutes, he'd forgotten about the wife he was soon to lose because he couldn't do anything to save her. He'd toasted the T.V. set that hung over the bar when Joe

Dumars, the most fundamentally sound guard he'd ever watched, was named series MVP. Then, the music had come on, on-the-house pitchers were distributed, and the real celebration had started. About to get up from his seat and leave, his luck changed.

Two hands had grabbed his shoulders, and Ben-David had turned around to see his high school classmate, Boyd Hawkins, who now went by "Hawk." The wiry classmate had been the Salutatorian of their graduating class, but he'd only lasted two years at the University of Michigan. A capitalist by nature, Hawk had been introduced to the joys of cocaine in college and the even greater joys of the profits that soared once he started dealing Santa's snow. Soon, he told Ben-David that night, he was making more money in a month than his professors were in an academic year. Whereas most people, including Ben-David, had viewed Hawk as a golden boy gone astray, Hawk viewed himself as an entrepreneur who was headed for early retirement. And for some reason, on that magical World Championship night, Hawk listened as Ben-David poured his heart out about the cruel situation with his wife and his inability to do anything to help her.

Hawk had listened over a few pitchers and, to Ben-David's surprise, had said, "Meet me at Hampstead Park tomorrow morning at ten," before leaving the bar. To Ben-David's greater surprise, Hawk kept his word and met him there the next day at exactly ten o'clock. While they watched children play in Lake Huron and adults read paperbacks on the beach, Hawk told him that he had a way to help Ben-David. Naturally, the professional investigator had prodded for details, but Hawk had said, "No details until you show up on Friday night, but if you do your job, there'll be enough money for you to get your wife treated in Boston. You'll need a gun. If you don't show up with a gun and on time, then I'll know you're not serious, and, well, your wife is going to die, right?" Ben-David had nodded, and Hawk had finished the meeting at that point with, "Beecher Hardware parking lot. Midnight. I'll pick you up. Don't leave your vehicle in the parking lot. Park down the block at the Hampstead Bar. Another car in the parking lot won't get noticed, and you're a P.I., so you can always say you were on a case."

Ben-David leaned over and gave the top of Isabella's head a kiss. The ceiling fan over the bed—that he was so proud of installing—blew cool air down on them, and he thought about

253

closing the open bedroom windows before leaving later. But, they did not have air conditioning, and it was still hot inside the house. Michigan summers lacked the humidity of a summer down south, but they were just as warm. Isabella was more comfortable wrapping herself up in an extra blanket with the fan on and the windows open than wearing a t-shirt and having the fan off. It would be more manageable if they lived where Ben-David's parents did—on the lake, just north of Hampstead. The house would one day be theirs, his dad had promised, but, now, it didn't seem to matter. Unless he was successful tonight, he wouldn't share many more days here in this small country house with his wife, let alone the Ben-David family lakefront home.

"I'll be out working a case tonight," he said with some certainty.

She chewed up the last bit of buttered toast in her mouth and then washed it down with a sip of Vernors. "A new case?" she asked.

"Yes, could be gone most of the night. Another divorce case."

She raised the piece of toast to her mouth.

My God, it looks so heavy for her to pick up, Ben-David thought.

"Anyone we know?" she said, taking a slow bite.

"No," he answered. "A summer visitor who thinks his girlfriend is cheating on him." It was a lie, and he felt horrible for deceiving her.

"Oh," she said, nodding. "When are you leaving?"

"Later, after you go to bed. Do you want me to bring the T.V. in here?"

She shook her head 'no.'

He'd built a small cart to wheel their one television set between the living room and bedroom. Some of their friends with more money had televisions in both rooms, but the Ben-Davids had never felt the need to bring that distraction into the bedroom. Their bedroom was for sleeping and for making love, and they had kept the room sacred for those things since they had married two years ago. But, when Isabella became sick and needed to be in bed more, he had built the cart and brought the set into the bedroom so she could relax and take her mind off the illness while he was away working during the day.

He walked to the window. "Still want these open?"

"Obadiah?" she said.

He turned and faced her.

"You've done all you can do."

He swallowed and felt his eyes start to twitch—a warning sign of the hot tears that were building, threatening to pour out. He had become aware of the signal and accepted it ever since he had wept when they were told the first biopsy results. He couldn't face her and turned back toward the window, trying to gather himself. How could she be so strong and he so weak? "I can't go there," he finally said. "Tomorrow, I'm going to visit the bank again."

"Don't," she whispered. "We already know the answer. What you need right now is rest."

He faced her again and then lowered his head. She was right. He hadn't been sleeping for more than a few hours each night—terrified that he would wake up and she'd be dead, and he'd have missed one last conversation that they were meant to have before he lost her forever. "Maybe I'll take the dog out and then come back in and close my eyes for a bit before I head out."

"I think you should," she said. Her tone was loving, concerned, and honest—all things he would miss about her.

He came over and gave her one more kiss before leaving the room.

For whom the bell tolls…it tolls for thee. And so it had for Obadiah Ben-David fifteen minutes ago at his house. He had thought about leaving a note in case he never returned but thought that it would just complicate things. Better to think that he'd be back with enough cash to carry his beloved wife out to the car, make her comfortable, and take off for the airport to Boston.

He pulled into the Hampstead Bar parking lot at five minutes to midnight. The onshore breeze was strong, bending the maple trees on the edge of the lot toward the cars parked underneath them. Ben-David backed the car in underneath the maples, giving him a view of the entire lot and bar. As he rolled up the window, he heard "Come on Eileen" blaring out the speakers on the bar's back deck. Some things never change.

He waited a few seconds to make sure that no one was around—no drunk classmates of his wanting to catch up or other townsfolk who knew him well by now as the local professional investigator. He was in no mood for small talk or town gossip, and he had a .357 Smith &

255

Wesson Magnum tucked into his shorts underneath his untucked black Dickies t-shirt. The gun had been a present from his father, Buford Josiah Ben-David, when he became an official professional investigator. Until this point in his career, he'd never had to use it.

Seeing no one, he got out of the car, locked the door, and headed toward the street. At six-eight and weighing two and a quarter, Ben-David knew that he would stick out if he walked down the sidewalk, so he climbed over a patch of bushes and went behind the ramshackle buildings that stood between the bar and Beecher Hardware. They need to level these, Ben-David thought as he moved through the shadows, hearing the breeze off the lake whistle through his ears as it blew his shirt up to his chest, exposing the gun. He pulled the shirt back down and held it with one hand as he reached the end of the building and turned right up the small alley between the building and Beecher Hardware. He didn't think he'd see the store owner, Tyee Beecher, tonight even though Tyee was known to keep late hours in the summer, sometimes coming in after being out on his boat, Magnum, all evening. But Ben-David had seen Magnum tied up to the dock behind the hardware store and figured that Tyee was either at home or out at his sister and brother-in-law's house, which was close to Ben-David's parents' home.

He reached the end of the alley and waited, watching the empty parking lot. He reached underneath his shirt and felt the handle of the gun. How quick could he pull it up and fire a round? he said to himself. He'd been to the range many times over the years, was a good shot, but had never had to threaten anyone with it or shoot in a hurry before. He swallowed, thinking of what might happen tonight. Then, he thought of Isabella —alone at the house, sleeping peacefully in their specially made gargantuan bed. Ben-David thought: Sometimes good people do bad things for the right reasons. That had been the saying he had repeated to himself over and over since Tuesday night when the Pistons had won it all and Dumars was headed to Disney World.

An old pick-up pulled into the parking lot, and when it came to a stop, the driver turned off the headlights, and Ben-David could see him.

It was Hawk.

He took quick steps toward the truck, gave a quick wave to Hawk, and got in.

"You got your gun?" Hawk said.

"Hello to you too," Ben-David replied.

"Forget hellos." His tone was cold. "You got it or not?"

"I've got it," Ben-David said, showing him the .357.

"Good. That's good for tonight," Hawk said. Then, he popped open the glove box and took out two straws and two small round Tupperware containers. He handed one to Ben-David and kept one for himself. Then, he did the same with the straws. "A little pick me up before the evening's festivities?"

Hawk took the top off of his container, and Ben-David could see the white powder inside.

He looked around, sure that the Hampstead police would drive up at any second and arrest them for possession of cocaine.

"What's got you bugged, big fella? No one's gonna bother us."

"I don't do any of that stuff, man," Ben-David said.

"Relax," Hawk said. "This amount is nothing. Just a little somethin' to take the edge off but keep us awake. You know?" Then, after quickly looking around, he took his straw and snorted up the cocaine in his container. He closed his eyes and nodded a few times. His eyes opened, and he said, "Nice, nice, real nice." He swiveled his head toward Ben-David. "Your turn, bubba."

"No," Ben-David said.

Hawk eyed the other Tupperware container and, after a few seconds of silence, grabbed it, opened it, and snorted the small amount. He did his eyes-closed-nodding routine again and then gave his passenger a grin. "Suit yourself. Let's roll."

Hawk turned on the headlights and put the truck into drive. They took a left and headed south on US-23.

As they reached the outskirts of town, the Hampstead lights grew dimmer and dimmer behind them as the thick trees rose up on both sides of the highway. The windows were down, and Hawk was playing Def Leppard, slapping his right hand on the dashboard. But, when they were perhaps a mile outside of town, he turned the music off, rolled up his window, and motioned for Ben-David to do the same.

"Okay, you ready for the deal?"

Ben-David was sweating. "Yeah."

"Well, here it is. Tooooonight, we are running the largest shipment of cocaine in Great Lakes history." He looked over and opened his eyes wide, the whites of them like two flashlights in the darkness. "Two hundred fuckin' bricks!" he yelled and gave a hoot.

"What's a brick?" Ben-David asked.

"C'mon." Hawk rolled his eyes. "Don't you know anything about drugs? I thought you were a P.I.?"

Ben-David said, "Seriously, Hawk. I don't."

"Okay, well, let old Hawk take you to school." He took a pack of cigarettes out of his shirt pocket, shook one out, and lit it. "A brick is one kilogram of uncut cocaine, which means that it's about ninety percent pure. Costs around two large to produce one kilo of cocaine in Colombia."

"Two large?"

"Christ, you really don't know anything about the biz, do you?" He inhaled on his cigarette, and the end glowed crimson like a tiny warning light in the truck's darkened cab. Hawk exhaled and then spoke with the cigarette hanging from his mouth. "Large means thousand. So, two thousand dollars to produce one brick in Colombia. Now, the usual path goes from South America to Miami to Michigan. And as the stuff travels north, the more expensive it becomes because of the greater risk. For instance, one brick in Miami would sell for around fifteen large. But, when it hits the Great Lakes State's border, it's worth about twenty-five large."

Ben-David did the math in his head. Two hundred bricks at twenty-five grand a piece was a shipment worth five million dollars.

"You add it up yet?"

Ben-David enthusiastically shook his head 'yes.'

"That's right. Five million big ones. Now, here's the kicker. The quality of the stuff we're transporting is only anywhere between thirty and sixty percent of what it once was. If you want the good stuff, you've gotta hang out down south and get it before they cut it and get it ready for distribution." Hawk took another drag and then blew the smoke up toward the inside roof

of the cab. *"Doesn't matter to me. The stuff I did in the parking lot was somewhere in that range, and it suits me just fine. Plus, it's all about the money, you get me?"* He did not wait for an answer. *"So, you're probably wondering what our percentage of the five mil is for transporting it, right?"* He put a hand on Ben-David's left shoulder. *"Well, old Hawk here negotiated for a five percent cut for us as a 2-man team. So, two-hundred and fifty large for us. Since I brought you along, I figure I'll take one hundred and fifty grand, and you'll bring home one hundred grand to your wife early this morning. Sound fair?"*

One hundred thousand dollars for a few hours' work? This could get Isabella to Boston. He'd have to figure out how to get the money into a bank, but he had a few friends who might help him because of Isabella's condition. It was a chance he'd have to take. Plus, if tonight went well, maybe he'd take a few more runs, and they'd really be set for long-term treatment. Immediately, he thought of all the problems and obstacles that would entail, but he reasoned that this is what happens when you are desperate. You don't think things all the way through, he told himself. However, if it meant saving his wife's life, then he'd do it as many times as it took to get her cured. *"More than fair,"* Ben-David said. *"One question, though."*

"Shoot," Hawk said.

"I would think that Detroit would be the end of the line for the drugs coming up from the south. I mean, isn't that where it would get distributed?"

Hawk let out a cackle. *"And here I thought you didn't know anything about this kind of work. Ha!"* He took out another cigarette and used the remaining part of his first one to light the second. Then, he flicked the old cigarette out the window he had cracked. *"You're right. Detroit usually is the destination. Tonight, we're making a special run. Some big cheese in the Upper Peninsula is working out a new distribution network in Canada with another head honcho who supposedly has a covert fortress up on the eastern shore of Lake Superior. I heard the guys gossiping about it on my last run. Anyway, the Hampstead Coast Guard station makes this leg of the journey the most dangerous, which is why we get the big bucks. The rest of the way is cake for these guys."*

"How many runs have you done?"

"This is my second. First one was a trial—ten bricks. I made it no problem. You ready for logistics?"

"Hit me with it."

"That's what I'm talkin' about! Startin' to relax and get excited at the same time, right?"

He was starting to relax. "Bum a smoke off you?" he asked Hawk.

"Sure thing!"

When he had lit up, Hawk continued. "Here's the plan. We park the truck at the Au Gres marina, hop aboard a fifty-foot cabin cruiser named, get this, The Big House. It even has a maize and blue paint scheme. You ever been to Michigan Stadium?"

"Always wanted to. Never had the chance."

"Massive," Hawk said. "Nothin' like seeing the band go across the field as an 'M' while playing 'The Victors.' Anyway, you've gotta get down there. This season we're supposed to win it all. Who knows how much longer Schembechler will stay as football coach now that he's the athletic director. Well, The Big House will be all fueled up and waiting for us—I've driven her before, smooth as silk—and we'll head out to sea. A mile or so offshore, we meet up with the delivery boat, Jolly, and load the powder. Each brick weighs a little over two pounds, so we're talkin' movin' north of four hundred pounds of the stuff. This is why I need you. For your strength. We gotta get the stuff loaded fast."

Ben-David took a heavenly haul of smoke into his lungs and then exhaled. He almost couldn't believe it, but Hawk was making perfect sense.

"Once we've got it stowed in the cabin, we'll take Beacon Island down our starboard side and head straight north all the way to Shelter Harbor." He gave Ben-David a hard stare. "That's the hard part." There was silence for a few moments, and then Hawk said, "When we're north of town, we'll anchor the boat and wait for someone to motor out to us. He'll go below with me, count the bricks, and if they're all there, which they will be, then we take his small motorboat in to shore. A big cabin is there, and inside we'll collect our pay." He snapped his fingers. "It's simple."

"How do we get home from Shelter Harbor?"

Hawk tapped the side of his head with his right index finger. "There's a car waiting for us. All we do is take our money and drive home. We'll stop at my house, unload my half in my garage, then drive out to your house and unload your half in your garage. After I drop you off at the bar for your car, I'll scoot down to the Au Gres marina, where someone will take this car. I'll hop in my truck, drive home, and get plastered. We're makin' history here, brother. Piece. Of. Cake."

It sounded straightforward, but Ben-David had been around long enough to know that something like this was never just straightforward. In fact, right now it was as if Mickey Rourke's character in Body Heat, a film that he had enjoyed watching with Isabella, was sitting next to him in the truck saying his famous lines from the movie, "I got a serious question for you: What the fuck are you doing? This is not shit for you to be messin' with. Are you ready to hear something? I want you to see if this sounds familiar: any time you try a decent crime, you got fifty ways you're gonna fuck up. If you think of twenty-five of them, then you're a genius...and you ain't no genius." He wiped his large, sweaty hands on his shorts. "So," he said, "why me?"

Hawk's eyes darted over to him and then focused back on the road. "What do you mean? I already told you. I need your strength."

"I mean, why me? Why cut me in?"

Hawk slowly nodded, like a professor working to understand one of his student's questions. "Because we go way back, and I know your lady's life is on the line. Jesus, man, I'm just looking out for you."

"But why the gun? You know the guys we're linking up with already, don't you?"

Hawk took a drag, exhaled, and then held the cigarette in his right hand while massaging the steering wheel. "That I do. But, let's be clear. The only reason I got that first opportunity was because their first choice screwed up the first run and almost gave away the entire show. The guy I've been talking to is the head honcho on Jolly—they call him Poor Paul. He told me what happened to the last guy." Hawk drew his finger across his throat and then shuddered. "Anyway, I'm not goin' down like that, and I ain't gettin' double-crossed either. With you *armed and how big you are, I figure I've got good back-up." He looked over at him quickly, "Understand?" and then looked back at the road.*

"You think they'd try anything tonight? What good would it do them to off us? We're the ones taking a major risk."

"What you're saying makes sense, big fella, but I've found that in this game, just when you think you've got it all figured out, you don't. That's why I'm bringin' you along tonight. Simply put…I don't trust Poor Paul."

"What about the guy in Shelter Harbor who is supposed to come out and meet us?"

"Mason Keach? Oh, he's good people. True professional. Won't have any trouble with him." Hawk flicked the cigarette out his window. "C'mon. Let's listen to some tunes and relax. We're all over this shit tonight."

28

Hampstead, Michigan, Friday, June 16, 1989

T he moonlight shimmered on the black water as Hawk slowed The Big House. The winds had died down, and the lake water was flat. Hawk killed the engine, and the boat began to drift. They had reached their destination for meeting Jolly.

Hawk took out a thermos of coffee and poured them each a mug. "Now, we wait."

"How long?" Ben-David said, looking at his watch. It was almost 2 a.m.

"All part of the game. We wait on them. They never wait on us." Hawk took a drink of coffee then removed a Ziplock baggie and a plastic straw from his pocket. In ten seconds, he had sniffed up the powder that had been in the bag. "They should be here soon. Can't wait too much longer if they want us to get loaded up and get to Shelter Harbor just before sunrise." He wiped his nose with the palm of his hand. "That's somethin' I'm lookin' forward to. The sunrise on Lake Huron later. When we hit Alpena, we'll know we're gettin' close. Ain't nothin' like it, is there? Red ball o' fire comes steamin' up from the deep and parks its ass on the horizon for a few precious minutes. We'll be countin' dough soon after that," he said, slapping Ben-David's shoulder.

Ben-David was impressed with Hawk's seamanship skills. He had quietly navigated the boat out of the *Au Gres* marina and punched buttons on the Loran to bring up their waypoint. The boat was new and beautiful and fast. Once they reached deeper water, Hawk had opened it up past fifty, and the boat had cut the waves with ease; they'd cruise between thirty and forty to reach their destination on time. The cabin below was spacious with all the modern amenities of luxury cruising. If ever stopped, the most the authorities would say was that the craft's paint job, name, and maize and blue everything in the salon announced that the owner was an obnoxious University of Michigan fan, and they would probably say that because they were envious, but no one would ever suspect that the boat was running drugs. Ben-David noticed that someone had staged the boat with fishing gear, bait, and even a cooler full of snacks, pop, and water. If for some reason, they were stopped, Hawk said that they were to say that they were starting out early to hit their spots on a day-long fishing trip. However, they would have notice. At that moment, someone with a VHF radio was hiding in the woods next to the Hampstead Coast Guard Station. He would call them on Channel 89 if any of the Coast Guard's boats left for sea. Why Channel 89? Well, the drug associates loved the Pistons too and picked the channel to pay homage to the championship that had just been won. And, Hawk had said, they had probably bet heavily on the Pistons too. Hopefully, if they got the call, they could just shut down and avoid detection. They'd already have their running lights off because they were not to use them at all during the run.

Hawk had shown him the large hold underneath the salon decking and then lifted the cushions of the long and deep benches in the salon to show him where half of the bricks would be loaded. Then, they had moved forward, and he had shown him an enormous storage locker underneath the king-sized berth in the master stateroom where the rest of their shipment would be stowed.

The sound of a motor could be heard, and Hawk stowed the thermos. "It's them," he said.

Ben-David went to stand up but then sat back down. "What in the hell are you doing?" he said to Hawk.

Hawk had pulled his gun out and was aiming it at Ben-David's chest.

"Now, listen. Almost everything I said before was true. Except they think I'm making the run alone. No one knows about you, okay? So, what I need you to do is hide in the head below. I'll help them get things loaded up, and if everything goes right, we'll be on our way shortly. However, if there's trouble, I want you to come up from below and surprise them. And I mean come out blastin'. The code word will be 'Zilwaukee' after that monster bridge that just got constructed over the Saginaw River. If I say Zilwaukee, then I'm in trouble. Got it?"

"You should have told me this before! And what about when we get to Shelter Harbor?"

"I'll drop you off before I reach the cabin, then I'll pick you up in the car after I have the money."

"But, I can't swim!" Ben-David yelled, pulling at the life jacket he had on, which Hawk had teased him about. It was embarrassing, but the Ben-David family had suffered a major catastrophe years ago when his uncle and cousin had been fishing, and their small boat had flipped over. Neither of them could swim, and they had taken off their life jackets. Before a nearby boat could reach them, they had drowned. And for that one reason, Ben-David had been raised to be afraid of the water, and he had never learned to swim, too horrified by the memory of the loss of his uncle and cousin.

Hawk scanned the horizon, searching for the boat. "No time for that now. Just get below."

"What if they see me?"

"Then we're both dead."

His stomach felt like a vise was squishing his insides together. He thought: What am I doing? But, as the boat's engine grew louder, he knew that he had no choice. "Fine. I can't believe you did this to me." He stood. "Just make sure they don't use the head."

"Oh, right. Yeah. I'll keep 'em out. It's all gonna be okay, man."

Ben-David left the cockpit and headed below. Once inside the head, he closed the hatch and pulled out his gun.

Ten minutes later, he heard Jolly pull alongside.

"Evenin', Poor Paul," Hawk said.

Ben-David heard a man with a deep voice say, "Evenin'. Right on time. You alone?"

"Yes, sir," Hawk replied. "You?"

There was no answer.

"Damnit," whispered Ben-David. Poor Paul must have just nodded or shook his head. Which one was it? he thought. Ben-David listened, trying to hear if anyone else was onboard Jolly.

Then, Hawk helped him out. "So we're both goin' solo tonight, huh? Well, I'm ready to load up."

Okay, so there's just Poor Paul, he told himself. Shooting and killing one man would be hard enough. He felt some relief that he wouldn't have to worry about more targets.

"Good," said Poor Paul.

There was shuffling on deck, then two thuds amidships, and he figured that Hawk had just put two fenders over the side.

He heard Poor Paul say, "Take this line," and he heard Hawk's footsteps on the deck, moving forward. Then, Hawk headed aft.

He thought: They're tying up.

A minute later, Ben-David heard the sound of the rubber fenders being squeezed between the boats and the popping sound of lines straining, and he knew that the boats were now tied up.

Then, the transfer began with no words between the men. Footsteps across the deck, down the companionway ladder, through the salon, and into the master stateroom. Over and over again, until he heard the deck compartment and salon benches opened up, and then it was just footsteps across the deck, down the companionway ladder, and back up again. For twenty minutes, he stood, .357 Magnum in hand and sweating in the cramped head.

Finally, he heard the benches close and the deck hatch secured.

We made it, he thought.

"Hey, I'm going to use your head, okay?" Poor Paul said. Judging by his voice, he was standing on the companionway ladder. Ben-David's hand started to shake, and he tried to control his breathing. He was going to have to shoot as soon as the hatch was opened. He raised the Magnum.

Forgive me, Isabella, he said to himself.

"Man, don't be usin' my head," he heard Hawk say from the cockpit. "C'mon up here. Got a little thanks for you, and then I gotta be on my way."

For a moment, no one moved on the boat, and only the sounds of the fenders and lines could be heard. Then, he heard Poor Paul's steps head up and out of the cabin.

Ben-David exhaled and then listened.

"To your health," Hawk said, and Ben-David heard two glasses clink.

"Twenty-one-year-old Glenlivet," Poor Paul said. "You remembered my weakness."

"When someone is a friend, I like to take care of them," Hawk said.

"Any questions?" Poor Paul asked.

"Nope," Hawk said. "Tell Mason I'm headed his way."

Five minutes later, both engines roared to life, and soon he felt the boat begin to move through the water. Then, he heard Hawk say, "Sparky."

What was that all about? he thought.

After another five minutes, he heard Hawk say, "C'mon up, Obadiah. We're all clear."

Ben-David put the gun back in his shorts and opened the hatch, sucking in breaths full of fresh air. He headed topside, feeling the anger rise from within.

"Good job, mate," Hawk said as he arrived in the cockpit and took a seat on the port bench.

"Stop the boat for a minute," Ben-David said. His tone was stern.

Hawk looked at Ben-David's hands. "I know you're pissed, and I'll stop this beast, but can it wait until we're near Beacon Island? I want to make sure I take us into deeper water. It's an evasion technique I used on the first run that I don't tell them about."

"Fine," Ben-David said. "But I thought we were supposed to take a straight shot north, which means that Beacon Island would be off our starboard side when we pass it."

"Exactly," Hawk said. "That's precisely what the associates expect us to do. But I do it my way. Every once in a while, on the way up, I deviate from hugging the coast and head for deeper water. So, I head east of Beacon Island, and then it's on our port side when we pass it. I also do this maneuver when we go by the Sanisstey Islands."

Hawk looked again at Ben-David's hands. What's he looking for? My gun? he thought. "You think I'm going to shoot you, Hawk?"

"What? Uh...oh, no. Just checkin—"

"Relax," Ben-David said. "I'm not going to do anything to throw away the money I need to help Isabella. I just want some straight answers."

Hawk seemed to relax a little. "Okay. That's good to hear. I just didn't know how you'd take my lie earlier. I really am sorry, man. I just had to make sure I had back-up in case Poor Paul tried somethin'. Last time, he had a mate and a helmsman that were with him. I guess this run is so important that they're only letting a few of us in on it." Hawk looked at the fathometer. "There we go, seventy feet. Nice, deep water. Just sit back and relax, okay? You want a scotch?"

"No."

"We'll be to Beacon Island shortly, and I'll bring this baby to a stop, and you can ask me all the questions you want. Sound good?"

Ben-David nodded, and The Big House sped up.

Ten minutes later, he could see the Beacon Island Light and watched as the light glowed for three seconds and then went dark. After around ten seconds, the light lit up for another three seconds straight and then vanished.

Hawk slowed the boat.

When it was barely making any forward progress through the water, Hawk suddenly said. "Damnit!"

"What?" Ben-David asked.

"I think we're fouled on something? Didn't you feel that vibration? Shit!"

Ben-David hadn't, but he'd been concentrating on what questions he was going to ask Hawk.

"Follow me," Hawk said, walking toward the stern.

Ben-David did, and they were now facing the stern, looking down into the ink-black water.

"See anything?" asked Hawk.

"No," Ben-David said, squinting at the water.

"I'll get the flashlight."

Ben-David heard Hawk take a step but then stop.

He turned around just in time to see Hawk aiming his gun at him. Ben-David lurched forward and knocked the gun out of Hawk's hand just before Hawk could pull the trigger. But his move had put him off-balance, and Hawk's left hand came crashing across his temple.

The last thing Ben-David remembered was maybe feeling wet, but he couldn't be sure as everything in his world went black.

Hawk cursed himself as he saw Ben-David's unconscious body floating away off the stern. If he didn't have a life jacket on, I could just leave him and let him drown! he thought. But that option was out of the question now. He had to kill Ben-David before heading north. It had been his plan all along, and he had told no one about it—not even his sister. Use him for security if anything went wrong with Poor Paul and then eliminate him on the way up to Shelter Harbor. There were cinder blocks and heavy line underneath the cockpit bench. After he shot and killed him, he would remove the life jacket, tie his legs to the blocks and dump Ben-David's body in the deep. He'd clean up any blood and then be on his way. Then, he'd pocket the entire two-hundred and fifty large.

"Okay, let's do this right." He glanced at his watch. Christ! I've got to hurry, though, he thought.

He looked at Ben-David's body floating just a few yards off the stern. I'm a good shot. Let's take care of that first, he told himself. He picked up his gun and then aimed at Ben-David's large head. He took one step closer, not seeing the water on the deck that had come on board as a result of Ben-David going over the side.

Whishhh.

Hawk's right foot slipped. As he fell forward, signals coursed through his brain, telling him he was in danger. The message, which would usually inform his reflexes and tell him to put his hands out to break his fall, took a different path and informed his trigger finger. Hawk squeezed off two rounds—that went into the deck...and through the hull.

His head hit the deck first, followed by his body, and it took several seconds to register where he was because of the shock. His shirt and pants felt wet, and it was then that he realized that the boat was starting to sink! He stood up, seeing Ben-David's unharmed body that was even farther away from the stern.

With the gun still in his grip, he shook in anger—and fired another round straight down into the deck. A new stream of water started.

"Fuck!" he yelled into the night.

And he thought: Okay, okay. I can still call my sister. Maybe I can plug these holes, and she can reach me, and everything will be fine. The cocaine. I better check it. Wait. Shut off the engine first. Calm down!

He threw the gun overboard.

Shit! Why did I do that? Okay, I need a sniff to clear my mind. Then, I'll radio in. But wait a minute. They could be listening. The hell with it. It's worth the risk, he thought.

The water was rising faster around his feet.

He said to himself: I could call Poor Paul! Yes, I'll tell him I got boarded and got into a shootout. He'd believe… The chill of the cold water interrupted his thought.

Hawk headed below and pulled the cabin hatch closed behind him. Don't want Ben-David sneaking up on me if he wakes up and then climbs aboard. Wait a minute. That's ridiculous, he thought. He looked up at the closed hatch. It was pitch black in the salon.

"Damnit!"

He needed to turn on the lights, which he was not supposed to do, but he wouldn't be able to take a sniff if he couldn't see anything, and right now, he did not trust his ability to do anything without a little extra help. He flipped a switch, which turned on the light over the salon table. Then, he fished the bag and straw out of his pocket. The bag had a ball's worth of white powder in it. It was the big hit to get him through the night once he passed by the Sanisstey Islands. He needed the white magic more than ever now.

He opened the bag and snorted the entire amount. After a few seconds, he felt everything speed up like he could kick his legs in the water and power the boat all the way up to Shelter Harbor himself. Shit's easy! he told himself.

But, as he had sat down behind the salon table and sniffed the coke, he hadn't noticed that the stern was sinking lower into the water. The salon deck was no longer level.

He thought: Time to check on the forward bricks. Just want to make sure everything is squared away. Then, I'll make the call to Linda. She'll be out here in no time with my boat, and I'll get this evening back on track. Life has its obstacles, and this is just one of them. You're being tested. Rise up.

He stood.

The deck's angle immediately made him lose balance, and he fell back toward the galley, where his head hit one of the metal countertop's corners. Blood squirted into the galley sink, and his body crumpled to the deck.

An hour later, The Big House settled onto the bottom of Lake Huron, seventy-seven feet below the calm surface. Inside the darkened, closed cabin, along with the ice-cold lake water, was the lifeless body of Boyd Hawkins—and two hundred bricks of cocaine worth five million dollars.

29

Hampstead, Michigan

Present Day

An hour after Obadiah Ben-David had passed out, Rachel Roberts sat next to him in his van, which was parked in the lot between Beecher Hardware and the Hawthorne Fish Company. Ben-David was on his second bottle of water that Rachel had purchased for him at a convenience store on the way over from Mac Schmidt's dock. She was working on a fresh coffee and kept her eyes on her partner as he came back to life after passing out. The van was in a spot with an unblocked view of Lake Huron, and Rachel thought that the late morning breeze had put a blindfold over the seas, confusing them. Their windows were down, and the air felt good. A few moments ago, two seagulls had flown by and landed on the back deck of the Hawthorne Fish Company building, looking for any scraps that may have fallen down from employee lunches that took place at the picnic tables back there.

"So that's how I ended up in the water that night," Ben-David said. "When I woke up, I was all alone, and there was no sign of the boat. No sign of anything. Like I said, I couldn't swim without a flotation device, but I'd seen enough movies to know that if I kicked my legs and paddled with my arms, I would move. So, I faced Beacon Island and dug in for all I was worth. I didn't know if Hawk would come back to try and finish the job—puzzled why he didn't finish it while I was unconscious. But I was alive. I paddled for a few hours until I made it ashore." He took a sip from his water bottle and then screwed the top back on.

She was worried about him. When he had fallen over in the salon of Kaj Reynard's boat, Rachel thought that he had had a heart attack and died. She still had to sort out her feelings from the event—specifically, why she had started to cry when he didn't immediately respond to her.

Memories of my father?

She had quickly opened the galley's refrigerator and found a bottle of water, which she had opened and then splashed some water on his face. At this, he had moaned, and his eyes had twitched open. Her emotions had then turned to the laughing-while-crying state as he looked up at her and said, "What happened?" After ten minutes of sitting on the salon deck and finishing the water, she had helped him to his feet and guided him back to the van. And it was then that he had started to tell her the story that he was continuing now. *"All these years,"* he had said, tearing up. *"I've kept it locked inside. I have to tell someone, and since it looks like it has something to do with this case, now is as good of a time as any. You ready?"* he had said.

"Back then, before the Knights owned Beacon Island, there were daily tours of the lighthouse during the summer. I waited until the mid-morning boat arrived, and I hid in the woods next to the path which leads from the dock to the lighthouse. As the groups spread out, I just joined in. Thankfully, no one saw me, and thankfully there were a few tall guys, so I didn't look so out of place. I'm not sure if anyone noticed. If they did, they didn't say anything because an hour later, I got on the boat with everyone and headed back toward the state dock." He looked into her eyes. "Lakeview Marina hadn't been built yet."

As a novelist, one of her favorite parts of hearing a story was to join in and move it along. She said, "And so you get back home, and…do what? You don't have the money."

"I arrive home and apologize to Isabella for being out longer than I had anticipated. I lie and tell her that I had to watch a house all night on the divorce case I was on. Being the most wonderful woman I've ever known, she accepted my explanation and never said another word." He wiped his eyes and took a drink of water. "I take a nap, and then Isabella takes a nap. I wake up, make a pot of coffee, and sit at the kitchen table, trying to anticipate what will happen next. The main thing that keeps nagging me is I can't figure out why Boyd Hawkins didn't finish me off. I was in the water and unconscious. Why didn't he just pull the boat around, get close, lean over the gunnel, put a few rounds in my head, and then take off? Makes no sense."

Rachel nodded. She had wondered the same thing.

"I start to worry because now I know what a loose cannon Hawk is and that he's hooked on the white powder." He turned toward Rachel. "It's horrible stuff. Absolutely ruins people. And all it takes is *one* time. On one of my former cases, I found out that a husband had not only been cheating on his wife but had become addicted to cocaine. The divorce was messy. But, when it was finally over, the husband got $100,000.00 in the settlement—they were both pretty well off. Wife calls me up a few months later and tells me that she still had access to his account and had watched the money disappear day by day until it was all gone. Really sad. Guy showed up at her house one night with his right ear missing. A week later, he was dead." Ben-David finished the bottle of water and opened the second. "Hence, I don't know what Hawk might be up to when he gets back in town with his $250,000.00—knowing that $100,000.00 of it is mine. In fact, I don't know at that point what I'm going to do. My gun had fallen out of my shorts when I went overboard, so I would have to purchase a new one. Do I go over to his house and threaten him? Does he ambush me and kill me because I know what he's doing and that I could turn him in? It was stressful."

"Well, you're sitting here next to me, so I know it worked out," Rachel said. "What happened?"

"That's the thing. *Nothing* happened. I sat in my living room every night with a shotgun for about a week, peering through the blinds at the street. Hawk never showed. Finally, after I wasn't able to sleep anymore, I decided to go to his house. He had a place out past the Hampstead Golf Course and Country Club. Pretty big joint, secluded, and lots of property—forty acres if I remember. So, I arrive at his house one morning, maybe a week and a half since the incident, and ring the doorbell. After five minutes of waiting, I walk around the side of his place, and then I start to see weird stuff. It looked like he'd been planning on re-sodding his side yard. He had black dirt down. But, in the dirt, I see all kinds of human footprints. Different sized shoes and boots. I head around back, and there I see that his back door had been forced open. I pull out my new Magnum and enter the house. It is absolutely torn to shreds. Couch cushions cut open, cabinet doors ripped off their hinges, drywall broken apart, the whole place. After I check every room, I figure that the drug partners had come a-callin'. This made me wonder why. Did he not show up in Shelter Harbor? Did he try and run over to Caseville, gas up, and then take the stuff across the lake to Ontario—maybe Kincardine or Port Elgin? I didn't know. Maybe it was his plan all along, and he had someone waiting there for him. Then, they could transport the stuff to Toronto, sell it, and take off to some beach in the Caribbean for the rest of their lives. Because they had stripped the shit out of his house, I figured that he never showed up with the shipment. Well, after a month, Hawk's mom and dad reported him as a missing person. Two months after that, they took care of his unpaid bills and then sold the house. A young couple lives in it right now." He paused to take a sip of water.

She drank her coffee and waited. He was a good storyteller.

"For over thirty years, Boyd Hawkins has never been found, and people have been searching for the legendary shipment. Problem is, though, no one knows where to look for it. I think the drug partners eventually gave up searching—that is, the ones who weren't executed for working with Hawk. I imagine Poor Paul disappeared shortly after that night. There is absolutely no way to search the entirety of Lake Huron, and that was even if they thought his boat had sunk. Plus, if you remember, I was the only one who knew that he had altered his route. And the partners *did* show up initially. I distinctly remember an unusual number of boats and divers around the area between where you live and Beacon Island. They also searched close to the Hampstead coast—probably all the way up to Shelter Harbor. Didn't find a thing."

"Did you ever go searching for it?"

Ben-David stared out at the water for a minute and didn't speak. She didn't push, but while she waited, her brain was scrolling through ideas for the new book. Perhaps Rose Varga had gotten into drugs on the side but had made some mistakes, which forced her to kidnap the President's daughter to get enough money to pay her debts. Maybe her assistant Kristy Cummings had gotten hooked on Santa's snow. This could be a nice layer. Not only would Rose be jealous of Adrienne Astra and want to take her down, but she would also be on the clock to pay off what she owed to the Cartels. *Good*, Rachel thought. This adds tension and complexity. She could write a great flashback chapter that showed the first time Rose got involved with the drug business. How she made a huge profit, got hooked, but then realized, too late, that she was now owned by the men down south. This would allow for Adrienne to not only fight Rose Varga, but she might also have to fight the Cartels. *Interesting.* She was about to open her notebook when Ben-David finally spoke.

"My wife died at the end of the summer. After I buried her and finished the Jewish tradition of Sitting Shiva—"

"What's that?" Rachel asked, not meaning to interrupt, but her heightened sense of curiosity and awareness had momentarily overridden her sense of tact. Before he could answer, she recovered with, "Sorry. I interrupted you."

Ben-David waved a hand. "No worries. I would have asked too. Sitting Shiva is a Jewish period of mourning where the immediate family of the deceased, which was only me, of course, stays home and receives guests, who usually bring over food. Well, they did that for sure because I gained fifteen pounds." He paused. "After it was over, I did a lot of stupid things. Cast off my religion, hit the bottle night after night, got sloppy in my work, and left the bar too many nights with women I didn't know. I was a wreck. But that's when Amos came and saved me. He started inviting me out to his house for dinner, where his wife would cook anything and everything to perfection. I must have put on twenty pounds over that winter. Then, that following summer, he took me to a secluded beach south of Hampstead where no one would know who I was, and he taught me how to swim. Once I was comfortable in the water, he signed me up for scuba diving classes, and by the end of the summer, I had my certification and had conquered my fear of the water. I'm now a certified cave diver," he said, shrugging. "The next summer, I purchased a small boat—nothin' special, just a good old Boston Whaler—and started my own search for the wreck of *The Big House*." He shook his head.

"What?" Rachel asked.

"Well, from the looks of this," he said, patting the chart from Kaj Reynard's boat that they had taken, "I looked everywhere but where it looks like Kaj found it. I probably went over that section once, but there was so much area to cover. I actually figured that he wrecked out by the Sanisstey Islands. The reefs out there will slit your hull in an instant." He picked up the chart, looked again at the point in the box where *The Big House* was probably located, and frowned. "I searched for ten summers." He threw the chart back down. "Obviously, I never found a thing."

"What would you have done if you had found the wreck?"

"I vowed to bring what was left of the cocaine up and destroy it. I went through a long period of guilt back then, thinking that I probably supplied some good person who had a fatal weakness with the means to destroy his or her family, or at least himself or herself. I miss my wife every day and don't know if getting her to Boston would have saved her. But, I still regret everything about that night."

"How did Kaj Reynard find out about it, though?"

"That's what we have to find out today. Thing is, I think I know who Aunt Linda is."

She took a long pull on her coffee. "Who?"

"She's what made me put two and two together when I saw that chart this morning. Boyd Hawkins had a younger sister named Linda." He chugged the rest of the water and then crushed the plastic bottle. "And she still lives here in Hampstead."

He started the van.

"Let's go talk to her."

30

It was just past noon when Rachel Roberts and Obadiah Ben-David stepped up onto the rickety front porch of Linda Hawkins's small country home. There was a rocking chair at the far end with a brown blanket draped over one of the armrests, but, other than the white Honda Civic that was parked in front of the garage, the chair was the only thing that gave the impression of occupancy. Rachel had noticed that the roof was missing shingles, the few shutters that remained hung at an angle, threatening to fall to the ground at any minute, and she guessed that the color of the house's siding had once been brown but was now tan.

Rachel arrived at the door first and knocked. Ben-David took a step to her right, the porch's floorboards creaking, and pushed the doorbell. On the car ride over, he had explained that he had gone to school with both Boyd and Linda Hawkins. Boyd had graduated a year ahead of him—Linda, a year behind. Remembering that Agatha Darwinger had told her that Obadiah was fifty-nine, she put Linda's age at fifty-eight.

A minute later, a young woman, perhaps in her mid-twenties, Rachel thought, opened the door. "May I help you?"

Ben-David showed her his credentials, introduced Rachel, and then asked to see Linda Hawkins.

"Oh," the young woman said, pulling her phone out from a back pocket.

They watched as her thumbs moved at light speed on the phone's surface. There was a pause, and then she moved her right index finger in a scrolling motion. She turned the phone off and put it back in her pocket. "I see," she said. "Are you investigating the murder? Everyone's posting about it. My mom said that she thinks Kaj may still be alive and that the whole thing's a cover-up. Like the government isn't telling us something." She shrugged. "I don't know. A lot of my friends won't leave their homes—think they're next. I mean, it could happen, right?"

I could write a book just about this person, Rachel thought. "Who are you, sweetie?" she asked.

"Oh, yeah. My name is Holly. I'm a hospice worker and have been hired by Ms. Hawkins' sister, Karen. You're more than welcome to come in, but I don't think Ms. Hawkins would be of much help."

"Why is that?" Rachel asked.

Holly pursed her lips. "Because she can't talk anymore."

"Can't talk?" Ben-David asked.

"She's a lifelong smoker and has emphysema. According to her chart, which I didn't even see when they hired me," Holly said, acting offended, "she has had multiple procedures to have her esophagus stretched. It's called a—a…" Holly's phone was out in seconds, and her thumbs were flying. "That's right, *esophageal dilation*. Takes about…yep, takes about twenty-four hours to recover from each procedure. However, when I got hired, her sister told me that she wouldn't give up the cancer sticks and had now lost the ability to speak." She started tapping away at the screen. "Here, let me show—"

"We don't need to see any pictures," Ben-David said, cutting her off.

Holly made an over-exaggerated tap on her phone. "Ooookaaaayy. I was just trying to show you what her throat looks like," she said, putting her phone away again.

"How do you communicate with her then?" Rachel asked.

"She has her smartphone. We just text back and forth. And if it's something more detailed, she has a laptop."

"Well, don't you think she could type her answers back to us?" Rachel asked, looking confused.

Holly shrugged. "Guess I never thought about it."

There was silence for a few seconds. Then, Rachel watched the transformation—the nervous eyes, the shaky hands, the shallow breathing. Holly had made a mistake, and instead of owning up to it, she was about to display all-out victim mode.

"Look, I'm freaked out about the murderer, okay? I'm trying to do my job, and then the two of you show up, and I don't know who you are, and I don't know what you want. I'm out here all alone, and everybody's just on edge. I'm under *a lot* of pressure here, all right? And you start asking me questions, and they were late delivering pizza last night—mom was *pissed*, and our Wi-Fi has been spotty, and Marcus hasn't texted me back, and I'm wondering, like, have I been canceled? Okay!"

"Do you still live at home?" Rachel asked.

"Of course. What kind of question is that?"

"Just trying to get to know you a little bit." Rachel took a few steps back, looked up at the blue sky, then over to the beautiful green hues of the forest that bordered Linda Hawkins' side yard, and finally to the small pond that was around fifty yards to the left of the other side of the house. She turned back toward Holly, who had somehow manufactured a few tears. "I think everything is going to be fine."

"Thank you," Holly said, not comprehending what Rachel had just done.

Ben-David looked like he was going to laugh at any moment.

"I think it's best if you take us in to see Ms. Hawkins," Rachel said. "She might be able to help us catch the murderer."

"You think so?" Holly asked.

"Maybe," Rachel said. And then she couldn't resist. "While we're in with her, though, I don't think it's a good idea for you to go outside alone."

"Because of the murderer? I knew it!" She took out her phone. "I've gotta let my friends know. This is hot stuff."

"No," Rachel said, putting a firm hand on the girl's wrist. "If word gets out that you were here and a part of this, and we don't catch the murderer, then he or she could come for you."

Holly froze and put her phone away. "Oh my God, you're right. How do I get myself into these things? I didn't ask for this. Ohhhh, Gooddddd."

"Just stay inside while we talk to Ms. Hawkins," Rachel said. *Well…one more.* "Is that your car?" Rachel said, pointing to the Civic.

"Yes. Why?" Holly asked, her eyes alternating between the vehicle and Rachel.

"Is it locked?"

Holly whipped out her keys and pressed a button on the fob. The horn beeped, and the lights flashed. Then, she did it again. And again.

"Good," Rachel said.

By this time, Ben-David had turned away and was looking in the direction of the rocking chair.

"I'll lock the front door after you come inside," Holly said.

"Good thinking," Rachel said. "I'm glad you're here."

"Got it," Holly said, the tears disappearing and the confidence returning.

They entered the house, and Rachel thought that she had just entered a life-sized ashtray. It was as if Yankee Candle had produced a line called "Smokey Ash" and Linda Hawkins had emptied the store. Holly immediately locked the door behind them. Then, Rachel heard the *honk* of Holly's car again before the young hospice worker walked past and led them down the narrow hallway.

It was a cheerless house with no pictures on the wall or anywhere that Rachel could see. The blinds were all closed, giving the interior an overcast-day feeling, and minimalist furniture looked like it hadn't been new for decades. She wondered if Linda Hawkins had any children.

They reached the end of the hallway, and Holly opened the door to the master bedroom.

It was dark inside except for the red, green, and blue pinpoints of light from the medical equipment next to the bed in the far corner of the room. After they had all entered, Holly adjusted a dimmer switch on the wall, and the room brightened enough for Rachel to see the frail body of Linda Hawkins laying in the center of a hospital bed. Her eyes were closed, and Rachel noticed that she was on oxygen and was being fed through a tube.

Holly approached the bed and gently woke Linda.

She appeared disoriented at first as if waking from a dream where she was falling from the sky. But, Holly bent over and gave Linda's hair a soft brush with her hands. "You have some visitors," Holly said.

Linda's eyes searched the room, still adjusting to the light, and eventually found Rachel and Ben-David. Rachel would categorize Linda's stare as confused, but as they approached the bed and Linda got a better look at Ben-David, she registered who he was. Her demeanor did not change to relaxed or even friendly, but it wasn't adversarial either.

Holly set up the laptop and helped raise Linda's bed so that she could face them. Then, the nervous hospice worker brought in two weathered chairs.

Ben-David and Rachel sat down, and Holly said, "Text me if you need anything," to Linda, and then, "I'll check the front windows every once in a while," to Rachel.

Beyond the teasing, there was one advantage to initiating Holly's primordial instincts to survive. Someone had killed Ben-David's dog, and that person was still out there. Having a lookout didn't hurt.

Holly exited, and when the door closed, Ben-David got right down to business.

"Hi, Linda," he started. "We graduated a year apart from Hampstead High School. Don't know if you remember me or not, but I was also friends with your older brother, Boyd, whom everyone later knew as 'Hawk.'"

Linda was able to give a small nod as if to say, "I recognize you. Go on."

"I understand from Holly that your sister, Karen, set up your hospice care. Is that correct?

Linda nodded 'yes.'

"Does she live around here?"

Linda kept her eyes locked with Ben-David's for a few beats, and then she started typing on her laptop. She finished quickly and turned the screen toward them. It said:

No. She hasn't been back to Hampstead since 1985. Ran off with a guy. But, we've kept in touch.

"We're investigating the death of Kaj Reynard, and I wondered if you knew him at all?"

I don't know him. Sorry.

Rachel continued to watch her, looking for signs that she was nervous or uncomfortable.

Ben-David pulled the folded chart from his pocket, stood, and unfolded it on Linda's lap. He pointed to the search box and to the writing. "Are you sure you don't know who Kaj Reynard is, Linda?" Then, he swung for the fence, pointing at the marker inside the box. "Looks to me like he found that shipment Boyd was running in 1989."

And that did it. Her defenses seemed to melt before their eyes as her head sunk back against the pillow and her arms dropped away from the keyboard. She closed her eyes for a good thirty seconds. And when she reopened them, she started to tear up but also became red in the face at the same time. Rachel understood the tears, but what was the anger all about?

Linda pulled a tissue from the box on the stand next to her bed and wiped her eyes with a rushed energy of annoyance. She finished and threw the used tissue onto the floor.

"Do you want to revise your statement?" Ben-David asked.

Linda started typing, and when she finished this time, she hit the screen with her index finger before showing it to them.

What is she going to say? Rachel looked at the screen:

I did know Kaj. And now that he's dead, it's time for me to tell someone everything. I don't know how in the hell you found out about what might be located in that area of Lake Huron, but I'll start with this:

Here it comes.

Boyd isn't my brother. He's my *half-brother*.

31

Half-brother! Rachel Roberts thought.

She looked to Obadiah Ben-David, who had tilted his large head and squinted, reacting to what Linda Hawkins had typed. "What do you mean, half-brother?" he asked.

Linda typed and then turned the laptop toward them.

I'm going to die soon, and I feel horrible about what happened to Kaj—you'll soon know why. I heard about his death on the news, and I wondered if someone would come see me. I thought it would be the police. Kind of glad it isn't. I hate Corey Ritter.

Well, now that you've shown me the chart, I have a lot to say. I've already written most of it down, so I'll bring up the file and let you read it.

"That would be a good place to start, Linda," Ben-David said.

"We just want to find out who killed him," Rachel added. "Anything that you can tell us that helps us do that will be appreciated."

Linda nodded and then turned the screen toward herself. A few more clicks, and she closed her eyes for a second. Then, she opened them back up and turned the screen toward Rachel and Ben-David.

They read.

If you're reading this, then I'm already dead, or I'm about to be, but if anything happens to my nephew or me prematurely, then I want someone to know the whole truth. I've kept most of it bottled inside since Boyd disappeared in June of 1989, but I can't hold it inside any longer. Here it goes:

My father, Charles Hawkins, fought in World War II. When he came back, he married my mother, Lois. Together, they had three children:

1. Joe Hawkins (b: 1954): Died Vietnam, 1973
2. Karen Hawkins (b: 1957): Ran off with older man to Hawaii and never came back
3. Me (b: 1962): I still live in Hampstead

Now, you'll notice the gap between Karen and myself, and if you know our family, you will think that I possibly have early dementia and have left off my brother Boyd Hawkins who was born in 1960. Yes, Boyd was raised by my mother and father, but he was not my father's son.

A man named Russell Reynard also fought in World War II, the pacific theater, to be exact, and saw unimaginable horror when he fought on Okinawa—lost his best friend. Well, he married a woman from Hampstead named Dorothy Scott, and together they had three children: Harold Reynard (b: 1948), Margaret Reynard (b: 1952), and Michael Reynard (b: 1955). However, in 1958, Russell and Dorothy started having marriage troubles, leading to Russell moving out for six months at the end of the year and into 1959. Mother thought that it had something to do with Russell's repressed emotions from the war; my father had them too. Anyway, Russell rented a room above our garage for that half-a-year and, you've probably guessed it by now, had an affair with my mother. Russell had already patched things up with Dorothy and moved back with his family when mother found out she was pregnant. She did not know whose baby it would be: my father's or Russell's. But, after she gave birth and Boyd started to get older, we all realized that he looked nothing like us. Looking back now, I think my mother became pregnant with me out of the guilt she felt for the affair. In any regard, my father and mother raised Boyd as their son. My mother told me that she and my father never talked about the affair, but my father had to have seen the resemblance between Boyd and Russell Reynard. My mother confessed to me that she never told Boyd who his real father was and that Russell Reynard never contacted Boyd.

Now, Russell Reynard's youngest son with Dorothy, Michael, had two children of his own: Melissa Reynard (b: 1982) and Kaj Reynard (b: 1986). Hence, Boyd Hawkins, my half-brother, was also Kaj Reynard's uncle. And you're about to find out why this is important.

But, first, Boyd's disappearance in June of 1989 is both a tragedy and, God forgive me for saying so, a result of the decisions he made. It is a tragedy because he was the brightest of all of us. He was also extremely close to his brother Joe. But when Joe was killed in Vietnam, Boyd was thirteen, and it messed him up. If our family had been closer, we could have seen it and helped him deal with his grief, but from what my father had seen in World War II, he was emotionally unavailable to all of us during that time. Now, I look back at this entire time frame in anger—especially after reading Robert Caro's books. It is clear now that Lyndon Johnson stole the 1948 election to become a U.S. Senator. This, of course, made it possible for him to become Vice President and eventually President of the United States. If Johnson didn't win in 1948, then it is possible that he never becomes President. And if he never becomes President, then perhaps Vietnam goes in a different direction, and my brother Joe never gets killed. And if Joe doesn't get killed, then more than likely, he continues to mentor Boyd and be a positive role model for him. And if that happens, then, perhaps, Boyd never does what I am about to detail in the following paragraphs.

To make a long story short, Boyd dropped out of college and started dealing drugs. He was mostly small-time until late spring 1989 when he got an opportunity to make some real money. We were always close, and I, regrettably, became a confidant of his and a partner. I will take the space here to apologize to anyone that may have been harmed by my actions.

Boyd made one successful run from Au Gres to Shelter Harbor and disappeared during the second one. Before the first run, we came up with a simple system. He told me that he was to take a boat from the Au Gres marina out to meet another boat where they would transfer the product to Boyd's boat, and then he'd head north all the way to Shelter Harbor. Boyd and I grew up Detroit Tigers fans, and we loved our manager, Sparky Anderson. So, we bought a radio and set up a huge antenna on top of my house. During the first run, we decided that he would radio me on channel 84 (the year that the Tigers won the World Series) at three specific points. First, when he had the product onboard after meeting the other boat offshore of Au Gres. Second, when he passed by Beacon Island. And third, when he passed by the Sanisstey Islands, north of Hampstead. Each time he would only say, "Sparky." The first run went perfectly and netted us both more money than we had ever had in our lives. He also must have gained his partners' confidence because they then trusted him with the largest cocaine run ever attempted: 300 bricks worth 7.5 million dollars.

She pretended to keep reading but, out of the corner of her eyes, watched Ben-David. When he reached the last line of the paragraph, he blinked at the numbers. She waited until his eyes tiptoed over to hers. They exchanged a quick glance, and she imagined him yelling, *"The sonofabitch lied to me!"* She went back to reading but couldn't stop wondering: *Just how much cocaine had actually been on The Big House?*

Unfortunately, the night of the run, Friday, June 16, 1989, he disappeared. The only thing I knew for sure was that something had gone wrong after he picked up the shipment from the boat off of Au Gres. I knew that he was alone, and he had radioed "Sparky" to me just like the run before.

Rachel stopped again. Well, that answered two of Ben-David's questions. One: Boyd had not told Linda about Ben-David's involvement that night. And, two, the mystery of Boyd saying "Sparky" while Ben-David was hiding in the head was now solved. She tried to make eye contact with Ben-David, but he was back to being engrossed in the document. She read on, not wanting to fall behind.

But that was the last thing I ever heard him say. I stayed by my radio the entire night and heard nothing. The next day, I went over to his house, and he wasn't there. I tried again the next day and the next day. Then, three days after the run, I was paid a visit one evening by men I had never seen before. They asked me where Boyd was and then threatened me that if I was hiding him that they'd be back. Thank God they never searched my house because they would have found the money Boyd gave me after the first run. Before they left, they said that they would be watching Boyd's house, my house, my parent's house, and my sister's house in Hawaii. I was scared to death. So, I never went back to Boyd's house. A few months later, my parents got notified that he wasn't paying his bills, and we all went over to his house. It was torn to shreds. My parents were dumbfounded because they had no idea what Boyd was doing. I, of course, did, and I slipped into a bathroom and cried until I got myself together. We had the house cleaned up, and my parents sold it. None of us ever saw Boyd again.

At that point, I went through all of the possibilities of what could have happened to Boyd. Did he run away with the cocaine? Did a rival surprise him at sea, kill him, and then take off with the drugs? Was there an accident and the boat sank? I didn't know. But, as the years went by and he was never found or seen again, I figured that if something did happen out on the lake, it must have happened somewhere between Au Gres and Beacon Island. However, out of fear and guilt, I never did anything about it. Eventually, I stopped feeling the presence of his drug partners. For a few years, every Friday, when I would come home from work from my job at the county courthouse, there would be a vehicle parked just off the road next to the end of my driveway. I would turn in, see two men sitting in the front seats of the car, and then continue down the driveway to my house. Five minutes later, the car would leave. Then, one Friday, the car wasn't there, and I never saw it again.

Now, fast forward to 2019. My mother is on her deathbed—my father had passed away in 1993—and she calls me at my house and asks that I come to see her in the hospital. I think she always suspected that I knew that Boyd was not my father's son, and so it makes sense to me when I arrive, and she tells me that she has had a secret that she needs to tell someone about before she passes away. I listen, and she tells me everything about the affair and who Boyd's real father is. She dies the next night.

Naturally, at that point, I start researching all I can about the Reynards, and, of course, I find out that Kaj is dating Daria Knight. I think about reaching out to him but decide against it. What good would it do? He's dating a rich girl and has it made. I also decide against reaching out to Michael Reynard. Nothing positive could come from me telling him that his father had a son with my mother. Around this time, my emphysema got bad, and I was diagnosed with cancer. So, I put the whole thing out of my mind while I concentrated on my health.

Then, I heard about Kaj's big breakup and that he wasn't doing well. I also heard that he might be mixed up with the local drug circle—Kevin Shelby is an idiot. This, of course, brings back memories of Boyd, and I feel for Kaj because it sounds like he's getting a raw deal. And, I know I shouldn't feel this way, but it burns me up that he's getting a raw deal from some rich bitch. I decided to contact him and invited him out to my house. Turns out, I loved the kid. He was like Boyd reincarnated, and I immediately had a soft spot for him. When I told him about his grandfather and my mother, he took it well. And then it all came together. He was down on his luck, I didn't know if I had long to live, so I decided to tell him about the legendary drug run and what my theory was. He became interested in an instant. So, he brought me a chart, and together we mapped out a search box between the coast and Beacon Island. I didn't have a lot of money, and we agreed that there should be no connection whatsoever between us if things went bad—no phone calls and only meetings at my place, which is outside of town. He told me he could borrow money from a friend to get his boat fixed by the upcoming summer, so we went with that. I'm guessing the friend might be Baby Lloyd Darwinger because Kaj slipped one time and said that he's the only guy he'll fish with. Sounds like the kind of friend you could borrow money from. Here again, I am ashamed of myself, but I also wanted things to be kept quiet in case we did find the cocaine and could sell it. Back then, there was still an outside chance that I could have surgery and prolong my life. What can I say, people do weird things when their life is on the line. Also, Kaj decided not to tell his parents anything about Boyd. I would have been fine if he had, but it did simplify things for us.

His boat got fixed, and he searched the entire 2020 summer and fall for the boat. Didn't find a thing. We continued to talk about it over the winter months, and then something occurred to me. Boyd always kept a few cards close to his chest. So, I took another look at the chart and tried to imagine what Boyd might have done. He had told me that the drug partners thought he was just a stupid mule who took orders. But I knew him, and they had underestimated his capabilities. I told Kaj that, perhaps, instead of following the coast, maybe Boyd had passed by the other side of Beacon Island. After mulling it over, Kaj thought it could have happened, and so we drew a new search box for the upcoming spring, summer, and fall.

And, the last time we met out at my place, I could no longer speak. I had to converse with him via this stupid machine. He told me that he had started searching but hadn't found anything yet.

Then, this morning happened. Kaj was murdered last night. From what I've heard, he stumbled onto the beach from the water with a knife in his back and, before he could say much, fell facedown and died. And where did this happen? On the beach directly ashore from Beacon Island. From what he told me over the past two years, he did have some enemies. But, as I sit here typing, I can't stop thinking that maybe he found the boat with the cocaine, didn't tell me about it, and then things unraveled from there. But that theory may be too poetic. Anyway, I'm in hospice and will most likely be dead before I ever find out what happened.

32

Rachel finished just before Ben-David. As her partner read the last few lines, she wondered what he would say to Linda Hawkins. Clearly, he now had answers to questions that had been on his mind for thirty years. However, regardless of that, there was nothing in the document that got them any closer to who killed Kaj Reynard. And that frustrated her.

Ben-David sat back down and then spoke. "I appreciate you letting us read this, Linda. You don't have to do what I'm about to ask you, but it might help us discover who murdered Kaj."

She maintained eye contact with him, giving no indication that she would help or not help.

"Would you be willing to e-mail that document to me?"

She didn't move a muscle for a few beats—just continued to stare into his eyes. Then, she pulled the computer back to her and, with a hand, waved him over. Rachel watched as Ben-David gave her his e-mail address and Linda sent him the document.

"Thank you," he said. Then, he held up the chart and pointed to the spot Kaj Reynard had marked inside the search box. "I'm assuming that you've never seen this mark before."

She typed:

Never seen it.

"Is that why you appeared angry when I showed it to you."

Yes.

"Do you think that he found the boat?"

Looks like it.

When they had left Beecher Hardware's parking lot earlier, Ben-David had said that Kaj Reynard must have found the boat. It was the only explanation for the mark on the chart coupled with the empty plastic bags and trace of white powder that they had found in his boat's secret compartment. This had led to a brainstorming session, and she had written down the questions they came up with in her notebook. She pulled it out, flipped to the correct page, and reviewed the questions.

How much of the cocaine had been salvageable?
How much of it had Kaj been able to bring up?
Was there anyone else in on the diving operation? *If not, then who found out about it and killed him?

Kaj's house had been thoroughly searched, and the drug dogs had been brought in. Nothing had been found other than a bag of pot in his nightstand drawer. This begged the final questions that she had written in her notebook:

What did Kaj do with the cocaine when he got it to shore?
Where is the cocaine now?

"And I'm assuming that because you never called each other, your information wouldn't be in his cell phone?" asked Ben-David.

No. He respected my rules about no phones.

Ben-David made eye contact with Rachel. "That's why Ritter hasn't been out here. Her number wasn't in Kaj's call log."

She nodded. And, she also wondered: *Where in the world is indispensable Police Chief Corey Ritter right now?*

"Any idea who would want to kill him and why?" Ben-David asked.

Linda started to tear up, but her fingers clicked away at the keyboard.

I don't know. Never talked much about his personal life. Just that he hated his mom and dad and didn't speak to his sister anymore.

"When's the last time you saw him?"

3 weeks ago. Told me he hadn't found anything yet. I feel so guilty right now. If I hadn't told him about Boyd and the drugs

Her hands stopped moving, and more tears poured out.

Ben-David looked frustrated, but he waited for her to compose herself. Then, he said, "Brendan Knight? Daria Knight? Ingrid Bara?"

Her hands didn't move.

Rachel picked up the list. "Kevin Shelby? Baby Lloyd Darwinger? Don Garvin? Matty Joshua? Did Kaj ever mention *any* of these people?"

She started typing.

The trip hasn't been totally wasted, Rachel thought. They now had a possible motive for why someone would want to kill him. And of the list of suspects, Kevin Shelby and Matty Joshua had skyrocketed to the top. Brendan and Daria Knight had the deep pockets and connections to get coke any time they wanted and would never be hurting for money. She doubted they knew anything about the cocaine. If anything, Kaj had shared some with them, and that had been it.

If Baby Lloyd Darwinger was storing any of the cocaine for Kaj, he could have gone out to sea the other night and dumped it, but unless he shredded the bags and dumped millions of dollars of cocaine into Lake Huron, some of the bricks would have shown up. *Was he fed up with running the family gas station business?* Maybe, but Agatha wasn't acting like someone who knew more than she was letting on—no paranoia from a burden of hiding something. No, Rachel's instincts told her that Baby Lloyd didn't know anything about the drugs.

Ingrid Bara was an interesting person because she was now dating Matty Joshua, and Matty had yelled, "What's out there?" to Kaj Reynard. Then, there was the other night where Matty was supposedly meeting up with someone on a boat. *Was it Kevin Shelby? Had Kaj's old drug partners figured out what he was up to and tried to get in on the deal?* That's where her thoughts were taking her. *Dory? No, it had to be Matty or Kevin.* But the solid logic of those conclusions bothered her, and she didn't know why.

Linda hit "enter" and showed them the screen.

I've lived in Hampstead long enough to know about Matty and Kevin. But they're small-time dealers. Only thing I've heard about the Knights is when I found out that Daria broke up with Kaj, and that was from my hairdresser. Don't know who Ingrid Bara and Don Garvin are. Baby Lloyd and Agatha Darwinger are friends, have been for years. Wait a minute, was it Baby Lloyd who gave Kaj the money to fix up his boat?

Ben-David nodded, and she pulled the computer back and started typing again. When she finished this time, she hit the "enter" key even harder and then swiveled the screen so they could see it.

Thought it was him. Anyway, I've said all I know. I wish I could help you out more, but it looks like my nephew was keeping stuff from me—the most important stuff at that! I wonder now if he was going to share any of the money with me after he found someone he could sell the cocaine to? All I know is that it would take someone who is connected to move that amount of product.

They met out in the hall while Holly went into the bedroom and assisted Linda. Ben-David's head was near the ceiling, and Rachel felt like she was in some dystopian version of *Alice in Wonderland*. She grasped the door handle and gently shut the door to Linda's room.

The veteran professional investigator folded his hands and blew into them. "*Three. Hundred. Bricks.* Well, it's now safe to assume that *no one* knows how many were on *The Big House* that night. I'll say this, though, someone had done a lot of work on that boat because the storage spaces were huge. I remember thinking that the couches and v-berth seemed to be raised like you'd have to climb up to get on them if you weren't tall. But, they weren't raised so high that they would attract much attention if you just took a quick peek at the salon and master stateroom. I think I just noticed them because I'm tall." He rubbed his hands together and then folded them again. "So, it could be less than two hundred bricks, or two hundred bricks, or three hundred bricks, or *more than* three hundred bricks."

"You surprised that he lied to you and maybe to his sister?"

"Not at all," Ben-David said with a smile of disgust. "But it still pisses me off."

Rachel told him her thoughts on the suspects before asking, "What's our next move?"

"We don't need to see the parents right away. So, he told Linda that he hated them. Big deal. They weren't fond of him either. That's not a new lead," he said. "We go visit Ingrid Bara. But, before we do that, I need to dive down and take a look at *The Big House*—confirm that it's there, where Kaj marked on the chart, and see if any bricks are left in the salon or v-berth. Of course, I don't know what kind of shape she's in because we still don't know how she sunk that night. Also, I keep coming back to the fact that he came in from the water when he showed up on Christine Harper's beach. The clothes he had on were normal summer attire, but I wonder what he was doing before then? Did he dive that night? But, if he did, then that's miles away from where he came ashore. Hence, he'd have to have fallen overboard or been pushed overboard closer to the Lakeview beach. We know he wasn't on his boat that night. So, whose boat was he on?" He glanced up at the ceiling and then back at her. "I guess there is one other crazy theory."

"What?" Rachel said.

"Look, chances are Boyd Hawkins died that night I was with him or died sometime after. No one's seen him for thirty-plus years, but there is always the possibility that somehow he survived and has come back."

"But why would he wait this long?"

"Don't know. It's so far-fetched that I won't even give it a second thought. Just had to put it out there 'cause it crossed my big noggin' while I was reading Linda's shitty dissertation."

Rachel hadn't even considered the possibility that Boyd Hawkins was still alive and had come back to Hampstead to...*do what? Take revenge on Ben-David? Dive down to The Big House and reclaim the lost shipment?* Ben-David was right—too far out there. She did want to solve the case, and for all of Kaj Reynard's faults, he still didn't deserve to be murdered. But, at that moment, she could just hug Ben-David for the idea he had just given her for the book. What if one of the old villains was still alive and plotting revenge on Adrienne Astra? And what if that super-villain was controlling Rose Varga? She thought about the first three books, and, as much as she hated to admit it, she thought of the characters as they had been portrayed on screen. Yes, they were *her* characters, and she would have to make them live in book #4, but because of Topaz's latest text about the saga's film dream team being reunited, the actors and actresses who had brought her creations to the big screen were on her mind. Mostly because her fiery agent would want to know who she was considering resurrecting and then start plotting to pull the A-lister back in—the woman was relentless. Another advantage to this line of thinking was that the directors had stayed true to the plot and characters from the books. *Now, who could the mastermind villain be?*

Donald Sutherland? No. His character, Geoffrey Cashmere, had been ripped to shreds by five tiger sharks he kept in a large pool on the edge of his property, where he usually disposed of victims. Kristy Cummings had seduced him, and he had thought he was meeting her by the pool for an important meeting when Adrienne Astra had surprised him. Their fight on the edge of the pool—

numerous reversals where one would almost fall in, and then the other would get the upper hand. Ejogo had slipped and actually punched Sutherland in the face during a take, but the old man gave a wicked grin, and the cameras kept rolling.

Second film. Catherine Zeta-Jones. Another no-go—Ejogo had thrown her character, Mercedes DiMera, off a rope bridge and watched her plummet two hundred feet until she hit the rocks below. The film had originally been given an NC-17 rating because of an overzealous special effect shot that showed Zeta-Jones's head exploding like a pumpkin that had been packed with dynamite. They toned it down a bit, and the rating had gone back to R.

What about the third film? Clooney's Aristotle Baron had apparently been blown up by his own bomb after being tricked into going back into his chateaux, where he had planned to leave Adrienne Astra to perish. The audience had pretty much bought that Clooney's character had met his end—Bogdanovich's close-up on George's face realizing what was about to happen had been talked about for months after—a masterclass in one shot. *So good!* But, in this day and age, anything was possible. Could they lure handsome George back for one more go of it? It had been almost a decade since he said he would only do one film. Maybe Aristotle Baron seduces Rose Varga! She liked it, but she'd have to speak to Topaz. *"I'll throw my own Lasso of Truth around him, darling! Get right to the bottom of it, find his vulnerability, and get him on board!"* With Clooney or without him, it would be a win because Clooney's character, Aristotle Baron, was a co-protagonist in the third book; if she revealed in *Dark After Midnight* that he had been the main antagonist all along, it would be a superb twist and add a mammoth layer of complexity to the character—just the kind of opportunity a writer looks for in a series. *Wonderful.*

"I understand," she finally said. "Since Boyd has never been found, it is a loose end. Just an unlikely scenario." She heard footsteps approaching the door. "Also, I'm diving with you," she said, and the door opened.

303

Holly shuffled out and eased the door shut behind her. "She's resting now. Did you both get anything out of her?"

Oh, Holly. "Nothing new, unfortunately," Rachel said, putting a reassuring hand on Holly's shoulder. "Thanks for letting us see her. We'll see ourselves out."

"That's it?" Holly said.

"How the business works," Ben-David added. "However, there is the possibility that we'll be back out here, so make sure you don't talk to anyone about our visit. Understand?"

"Okay," she said. "I didn't see anything out of the ordinary happen outside while you were in there with Ms. Hawkins."

"Good job," Rachel said.

They turned and headed down the narrow hallway.

A minute later, they were getting in the van when they heard Holly's car honk and the lights flash. Rachel turned back toward the house and saw the young hospice worker standing behind the living room window with her key fob raised.

She noticed Rachel and gave a thumbs up.

Ben-David said, "You got yourself a new friend."

Rachel gave Holly a thumbs up back.

As the van turned out of the driveway and onto the highway, Ben-David said, "Okay, since I can't talk you out of diving with me, let's get *Grizzly Adams* in the water and go find a drug-running boat—and maybe get closer to solving who in the hell stabbed and killed Kaj Reynard."

33

I t was mid-afternoon by the time they had anchored over the wreck site. The sun was at its peak, warming the navy blue and neon green neoprene wetsuit Rachel Roberts had on, and there was a two-mile-per-hour breeze from the west that felt refreshing as it blew across her face. The Huron breezes had shifted, and the bad weather had missed Hampstead.

Obadiah Ben-David's boat was an older cabin cruiser, but whereas Kaj Reynard's boat *Coca-Cola Classic* showed signs of advancement, the *Grizzly Adams* showed signs of experience and the love of its owner. The mahogany accents throbbed with layers of varnish, and there were personal touches—a built-in green Coleman cooler in the stern, a stainless-steel rack along the port gunwale that held four scuba tanks, and a dog bed with two bowls were secured to the aft cockpit deck. Since they had boarded the boat, Ben-David had not looked once at the dog station. As much as she wanted to find out who murdered Kaj Reynard, she wanted to find who had killed Ben. If there was one topic that she could still use to summon rage, it was pets. She finished strapping the dive knife to her right calf.

Get me within an arm's length of the person who killed his dog, and you'll see what I can do with this dive knife.

Ben-David emerged from the cabin, looking like he had been plucked from the pages of a 1960's edition of *National Geographic* that featured a scuba diver testing the perils of the deep–just a gigantic version of that diver. His wetsuit was black with a thin yellow stripe that ran down the arms, body, and legs. His hood was all black.

They had talked about contacting Corey Ritter and Amos before coming out here, but Ben-David had decided against it. He wanted to check out the boat first; they'd contact Ritter and Amos after their dive.

"I checked the fathometer again," he said, sitting down on the starboard gunwale. "Sometimes, it gets quirky. Still says around eighty feet, which matches the chart."

The boat continued to wander around its anchorage, and she could now see Beacon Island in the distance. She tried to imagine a twenty-eight-year-old Obadiah Ben-David paddling toward it in the middle of the night. Who cared if the Great Lakes didn't have any sharks in them? Swimming alone for miles in the dark water was enough to scare most people. She'd been afraid of the water when she was young, unsure why, just that there might be danger in a cold, wet place that engulfed her and was difficult to see below its surface. It was her dad that had taught her to respect the water and, later, how to scuba dive. It was this element that she had added to *Enemies in the Evening*, and it had separated her novel from the other thrillers. No one at the time was writing about a female spy who could scuba dive. And, sitting here in the baking sun and cool Huron breeze, she felt the creative spirit fill her and nudge her in the direction of including another scuba diving action scene in *Dark After Midnight*. Perhaps, she could use it to kick off the novel with an exciting opening scene of Adrienne and Rose conducting underwater surveillance, and then something goes wrong. Yes, that might be it. The operation goes wrong, and Adrienne and Rose escape. Then, when they're out of danger, they talk over how the enemies could have known that they were there. Her readers wouldn't know either because bitchin' superspy Adrienne Astra doesn't get ambushed. Maybe they would think she was losing her edge, which would be a great idea to put in the reader's head because then they'd think she was vulnerable and start to worry about how she's going to make it through the novel. But, Riley Cannon would, of course, know the answer: Rose Varga had set her up to be killed in the underwater ambush but had underestimated her friend's ability to handle the seemingly unwinnable situation. She filed it away, thinking she had the opening that would grab her readers—"By the *throat*!" Topaz would say—once more.

"Did you hear me?" Ben-David asked.

"Eighty feet. Right," Rachel said. "Sorry." She pointed at the island. "I was thinking about the swim you took thirty years ago."

"It was a long one," he said. "Let's gear up."

Rachel pulled her hood down and tucked the bottom into her wetsuit. After slipping their fins over their neoprene booties, they each put on a weight belt and then helped each other strap on a BCD and tank. Lastly, they each spat into their masks and rubbed the saliva around the glass, then dipped them in the water and put them on.

"Okay," Ben-David said, handing her an underwater light, "Let's go over it one more time. We'll follow the anchor line down. When we reach the bottom, I'll orient us with my compass, and then we'll kick northwest. The wreck should be less than a hundred yards away. We'll see what kind of shape *The Big House* is in and see if it's possible to penetrate the wreck. Sound good?"

"Got it."

They each scanned the horizon—not another boat in sight.

Ben-David gave her the 'okay' sign and then entered the water.

Rachel put her regulator's mouthpiece into her mouth and took a breath to make sure she had air. Then, she held her regulator in place with her right hand and, with the dive light in her left hand, rolled backward into Lake Huron.

After the bubbles created by her entrance had dissipated, she followed Ben-David at a depth of around ten feet toward the anchor line. It had been a few years since she had dived, but it felt natural, like connecting with an old friend. The water was cool but not uncomfortable. On the way down, she would generate heat by kicking.

They arrived at the anchor line and turned on their lights. Ben-David aimed his at the line, and Rachel did too. Then, they followed it into the dark water below.

She wondered what they would find. After spending the past six months cooped up in her second-floor writing room, she couldn't believe that she was scuba diving down to the possible scene of a crime. In an ironic way, her novels had paved the way for their creator to experience some first-hand intrigue and danger—she only hoped that it wouldn't be *much* danger.

At seventy feet, they slowed, and moments later, they reached the anchor, nestled into the bottom. If the color of the water on the surface could be described as turquoise, then the water down here could be described as nothing but black. The yellow beams of their lights were like small beacons cutting wedges into the darkness. It had been a smooth descent, and her excitement was now at an all-time high. During all of her scuba diving trips with her father, she had never once seen a wreck. In tropical waters, a wreck would usually mean a pile of ballast stones if the original ship had been wooden, the decking and structure eaten away by the voracious Teredo worms long ago. But in the Great Lakes, the fresh chilly water preserved wrecks to the point where they still looked like ships. Like her diving partner, she wondered what condition *The Big House* would be in.

Ben-David studied his compass and then pointed in the direction they were to go in. She verified the course with her own compass, and they exchanged the 'okay' sign once more. He shined his light in front of him, and they began to kick.

Soon, the far reaches of their lights illuminated the hull of an old cabin cruiser. They exchanged an excited glance and kicked. And the closer they got, the clearer it became that the wreck was indeed *The Big House*. They were approaching from just off the port bow, and the maize and blue hull stared at them as if ready to take off at any second and ram the two divers. The structure was supremely preserved, and Rachel thought that it was as if the boat had gently sunk straight down and was now anchored to the bottom in exactly the way it would be anchored on the surface—upright with no list.

When they were within ten yards of the wreck, Ben-David changed course and swam parallel to the port rail. Halfway to the stern, they kicked over to a set of cabin windows and tried to look in, but they were covered with grime. She followed him all the way to the stern, and that is where they discovered definitive proof. In faded letters on the transom was the name of the boat: *The Big House*.

For a moment, Ben-David sat motionless on the bottom, a few yards aft of the transom, and Rachel watched as he stared at the letters. *The memories this must be bringing up*, Rachel thought. The only parallel to his situation that she could make at this point would be if she was to visit a place where she had been a few months before her mother left. In a cruel way, the boat in front of Ben-David was a time capsule of one of the most painful periods of his life. And it was quiet in the deep—the only sound being their breathing, and the only sight besides the wreck, their rising streams of air bubbles heading to the surface. There were no distractions at eighty feet underwater to help him escape the memories of the horrifying night thirty years ago.

He tapped on her arm and pointed to his dive slate.

She focused her attention on it, and he wrote:

Congrats. We found it. Stay right here while I take a peek inside. Be right back.

She took the pencil from him and wrote:

Looks like the cabin doors are closed. Be careful.

He gave her the 'okay' sign and then swam up and over the stern and headed for the cabin. She positioned herself off the port quarter, aiming her light at the cabin to help him see. *For being down here for over three decades, the boat still looks fine,* Rachel thought.

Ben-David stopped and aimed his light on a section of the aft deck. She drew her beam away from the cabin doors and pointed it where Ben-David had focused his. She inched closer, and then he waved her over, and soon she was right next to him.

In the deck were two holes.

He searched the rest of the deck and found another. He wrote on his dive slate:

Maybe how the boat sank? These look like bullet holes.

She nodded, and they both shined their lights around the aft portion of the wreck, searching for anything else that didn't look right. After a minute of doing this, she took her station again off the port quarter and shined her light on the cabin doors.

Ben-David reached them and tried to pry them open with one hand. He was unable to. Setting his dive light on the deck, he got both hands on the cabin doors and adjusted his grip. Then, with one massive exertion, he got the doors open.

Their victory was short-lived, however, when a moment later, a dark figure emerged without warning.

All Rachel could do was watch in horror as a diver swam right at them.

34

Rachel watched Ben-David fall back as the diver came forward. He reached for his dive knife, ready to strike…but then the diver stopped moving.

On instinct, Rachel had pulled out her knife and swam toward the danger, and she was now next to Ben-David, examining the motionless diver.

It was Matty Joshua.

They grabbed hold of his arms and lowered the body to the deck. Now, past the initial shock, they noticed Matty's regulator and air hose floating away from his body. Everything seemed to be present. He had on a red wetsuit, yellow weight belt, mask, BCD, tank, fins, and his dive knife was still strapped to his calf. He didn't have on a hood, but one could still dive at this depth without one. Rachel and Ben-David had worn theirs for extra warmth.

Seeing that his gear was all accounted for, they searched his body for any signs of injury or foul play. They found none.

He must have drowned, Rachel thought. *What happened here?*

Ben-David wiped his dive slate clean with a Mr. Clean magic eraser that was hanging by a string from the corner of his slate. He began writing something new. When he finished, he turned it toward her:

Here's our prime suspect—underwater on a boat that was packed with drugs. Didn't get here by himself. Where's his boat? Did he dive with someone else? Who closed the doors on him? Was he dead before he got down here? Need to contact Ritter. He'll get an underwater crime scene investigator out here. We probably shouldn't touch anything else, but I've got to check the benches and v-berth. Be right back.

She gave him the 'okay' sign and watched him disappear into the cabin. Five minutes later, he emerged. After wiping his dive slate clean again, he wrote:

Opened the head and found a skeleton with remnants of clothing still on it. Pretty sure it's Boyd. Either he died in there, or Kaj stowed what was left of him in there—no idea how he died. No cocaine left in any of the holds. Rest of the salon, galley, head, cabinets, and master stateroom look the same as the last time I saw them.

She pulled out her dive slate and wrote:

If Matty killed Kaj, then he was in on it with at least one other person. Has to be the person he was meeting up with on the boat the night he went missing. Probably been down here a few days. No way he did all of this on his own—could have been double-crossed if they were in the process of bringing more of the stuff up. Wish we knew how much Kaj had brought up.

Ben-David wrote back:

Solid points. Let's put Matty back in the cabin and then head up.

Rachel sat on the port cockpit bench wrapped in a blanket. Ben-David had just brought up the anchor and was sitting behind the helm. He handed her a mug of steaming coffee that he poured from a thermos and then took a long pull from his own mug.

"I'll call Corey Ritter when we get to shore," he said. "In addition to telling him about Matty Joshua, I'll send him an e-mail that has Linda Hawkins's document, then let him know that there might be a whole lot of cocaine stowed somewhere in Hampstead but that the chances of that are unlikely. I think that whatever Kaj Reynard or Matty Joshua or someone else brought up from *The Big House* has already left the area, which means that someone has a whole ton of money socked away or there's no money at all because Kaj and Matty got killed before they could collect."

"Are you going to tell him about your connection?"

He turned on the engine. "I hadn't planned on it. Maybe one day after this all blows over, but it would just confuse things right now. Agree?"

"I do," she said, taking another sip. "Do you think Matty could have killed Ben?"

He put his hand on the throttle but did not push it forward. He looked to be staring at Beacon Island in the distance. "Maybe," he said. "Him or whoever he was working with."

"I still can't get a clear picture of Kaj's death that night. Why stab him in the back? Why not just shoot him or drown him? It was sloppy. If he had said the murderer's name instead of 'Help me' that night on Christine's beach, we wouldn't even be here right now."

"Yeah. I still can't put together what happened that night either." He pushed the throttle forward, and the boat gained speed, eventually coming up on plane. "Listen, we've had a lot of excitement for one day. Why don't I drop you off at home where you can rest and get something to eat. Baby Lloyd and Ingrid Bara aren't going anywhere. And if Kevin Shelby tries to skip town, then he sticks out like an adult sitting with a Kindergarten graduating class. I'll have to meet with Ritter, and, believe me, it's going to be boring. We're going to have to go over all of this stuff again, and then he's probably going to want me to go out with them to the wreck site."

She admitted to herself that none of that sounded particularly fun, but could she just go home and relax?

"I know what you're thinking," he said. "It is absolutely fine for you to take a break right now. And, I think you'll be safe at your place too. I'll walk through it with you when I drop you off and won't leave until I feel things are safe for you there. If I don't get a good feeling, then I'll take you and Hemy to Christine's. Sound like a plan?"

A hot shower, comfy clothes, and a good meal sounded like heaven to Rachel. And, really, what could she do right now but wait to see what happened after Ben-David spoke with and met with Ritter. It would also take some time before the autopsy results came back on Matty Joshua. And maybe Ben-David was right. A drug deal had gone horribly wrong for Kaj Reynard and then Matty Joshua, and the dealers were miles or states away right now with the whole load. "Okay," she replied. "But, I want to be with you when you interview the next person."

"Deal."

As the *Grizzly Adams* headed toward the Hampstead coast, a person in the lantern room of the Beacon Island Lighthouse lowered a set of binoculars and spoke into a cell phone. "They know about the boat."

There was a pause, and then the answer came back, "So what. Get back to shore, and don't get seen."

35

"So, how's Hemorrhoid?" Topaz Kennedy asked Rachel Roberts over the phone.

Rachel sat up on her couch and said, "Hemy, Topaz, *Hemy*."

"Oh, right, sorry dear. Never could remember the chubby ball of fur's name."

"He's named after a writer!"

She had yet to hear from Ben-David, who, after checking her house over earlier, had left to meet up with Cory Ritter and Amos Meyer. She had just meant to close her eyes for a short while on the couch after she had taken a hot shower, but Topaz's phone call had woken her up, and she had been shocked to see that it was nearly 7 in the evening. Rachel rubbed her eyes and yawned. *Wake up, girl.* Her stomach growled as she leaned over and grabbed the bottle of water that had been cold when she had set it on the coffee table earlier.

Topaz snickered. "Oh, right. Well, anyway, I approve of your plotting decisions. Really top-shelf stuff. Can't wait to see how the whole thing turns out."

"You think bringing Aristotle Baron back as the main villain will work? I keep going back and forth since I thought of it."

"Heavens yes, child. And Rose Varga's betrayal? Delicious. Also, like the drug angle. I'm afraid Kristy's hooked, and there's no turning back. Once I see it on paper, I'll approach dear George and have him signed up for the part in a jiff. It'd be wonderful to see him in that role again. Still haven't gotten over my hot flash from the first time."

Rachel heard the unmistakable ice clinking in a glass. Topaz was having her evening scotch on ice.

"How's the case coming along, Miss Fletcher?"

Rachel told her everything, except Ben-David's connection to the 1989 drug run. She shook her head after saying it all out loud. "I know," she said. "You can't make this stuff up."

"Oh, but you can, you licentious liar! You do it for a living."

Rachel let out a much-needed chuckle. She needed Topaz right now. If the world only knew what a good agent could do for a writer.

"Now, listen up because I've got it all figured out. Naughty boy Matty Joshua did it all alone. He killed Kaj, brought up the Christmas packages of snow from the lake bottom, has them hidden somewhere—don't worry, love, you'll find them—and then got caught below trying to destroy any evidence that would link him to the job. Ah, yes. It's all there for the trained eye to see."

She played along. "What about his boat? How did he get out to the dive site?"

The sound of ice sloshing back and forth could be heard again. "The *boat*! Almost forgot. Yes, you see it blew up or sunk or something. Either way, dear, it's gone forever, and no one's going to find it. Now, when do I collect my fee for solving the murder?"

They talked for another ten minutes, and then Rachel said she was going to get dinner and that if she didn't hear from Ben-David, she'd start writing pages tonight.

"Yes, capture the scuba diving mojo from this afternoon and slay that opening scene, Cannon."

She called her Cannon. This was a good thing—it meant she was getting invested in the project. Rachel felt a wave of relief pass through her. *This novel will get done.* "Well, I should get going. Need to check on Hemy's food supply because I've been gone a lot lately."

"Put that thing on a diet!" Topaz said. "Okay. Glad to hear the book is coming along. I'll call Hightower and tell him that pages should be along soon, so get cracking."

"I'll call you tomorrow."

"You bet your sweet forty-year-old buns you will, darling. Cheers. Night!" And Topaz ended the call.

Rachel set her phone down on the coffee table. It was now just past 7:30, and she was starved. Hemy was nowhere to be seen, but that was normal for this time of night when his mood determined when and where he showed up. She lifted up her Woolrich blanket and stretched. Maybe Ben-David was diving on *The Big House* right now. It was still light outside, but that wouldn't last much longer. The wind chimes made their presence known as a stiff breeze came off the lake and howled as it went around the house. *What to have for dinner?*

Her phone rang, vibrating the glass on the table.

Maybe an update. She reached over and picked up the phone.

It was Brendan Knight.

"Abernethy miss me?" she asked.

He laughed, then said, "Him and me."

"Good to know. What's up?"

"I know you're still working on the investigation, but can you get away for a few hours tonight? I'd like to see you again."

Rachel liked the thought. Would Ben-David need her? Since she hadn't heard from him, she decided that she would accept the invitation and keep her phone on in case he called her. However, her car was still at Darwinger's. *The hell with it. I can walk.* "I accept. But I haven't had dinner yet. Can I grab something really quick and then head over to your place?"

"Got a better idea. I'll come down the coast in our cabin cruiser, *Knight Dive*, and motor in with the dinghy to pick you up on your beach in half an hour. Then, we'll head out by Beacon Island and have a nice dinner on the boat. You game?"

"Yeah. What are we having for dinner?" she teased, not expecting him to have an answer.

"I'll think of something; don't worry. Also, bring your bathing suit. It looks like it's going to be perfect weather for an evening swim. Don't worry about a towel. We've got plenty on board."

"Okay. I'll be ready."

"See you soon."

She felt excitement rise within her. This was exactly what she needed right now. The vision of Matty Joshua's lifeless body, far beneath the waves, had haunted her when Topaz's phone call had woken her up. Ben-David was right: all the suspects weren't going anywhere tonight. Tomorrow would be a new day, and they'd do some more interviews. Someone had to be lying about something.

She glanced around the room. Nothing had happened while she had taken the nap. Her security system was working, and she had friendly neighbors on both sides of her beach house. She'd have to talk with Ben-David, but a thought had occurred to her when he was walking around her home earlier, making sure it was safe. Maybe the killing of Ben had nothing to do with the current case. Perhaps, it was someone from a past case or just random. She couldn't completely commit to that line of thinking, but it was a possibility. And nothing had happened to either of them since then. But, just to be safe, she called Ben-David to let him know where she'd be. He didn't answer, so she left a message.

Feeling confident that she had kept her partner in the loop, Rachel stood up and headed to her bedroom to change and grab her swimsuit.

* * *

Obadiah Ben-David surfaced next to the Hampstead Police boat—a Brunswick 250 Justice. "I'm heading back over to *Grizzly Adams*," he said to Corey Ritter, who looked down at him from the starboard gunwale.

"Thanks again for the help, Obadiah. Sorry it took so damn long to get out here. Like I said, our diver, Scott, lives two hours away." And now Ritter had given the same apology three times. The fat police chief put a foot on the gunwale and almost went overboard. "Whoa, shiiiiitttt," he said, miraculously regaining his balance. Then, he chomped down on a stick of beef jerky.

At that moment, Amos Meyer's hooded head broke the surface next to where Obadiah was treading water. "Scott'll be on his way up in a few minutes," Amos said to Ritter. Then, he turned to Ben-David. "Nice divin' with you again." He gave his old friend a pat on the shoulder.

"Yeah," Ritter said, pointing to the deck of the boat. "Never would've gotten Matty's body up here without your help."

It would take some time before the medical reports came back, giving them a better idea of how Matty Joshua had met his end, but at least he was onboard the boat and the process could begin. The only question Ben-David had was: *Where do I go from here tonight?* It was late, and he was tired. Maybe he'd go home and rest up. Ritter would have to notify Matty's girlfriend, Ingrid Bara, so they had agreed to let Ritter and Amos question her tonight. In the morning, Ben-David would start with Baby Lloyd again if he couldn't find or get a hold of Kevin Shelby. Maybe that's what he and Rachel needed right now—a good night of sleep and a fresh perspective tomorrow morning. "No problem." He started kicking toward *Grizzly Adams*, which was perhaps fifty yards away. "Call me tonight if you get anything from Ingrid Bara."

"Will do," Ritter said and then took another bite of jerky before helping Amos board the boat.

Five minutes later, just as Ben-David was climbing up onto *Grizzly Adams*'s swim platform, he heard Amos shout, "Obadiah! Come here! Scott found something down there!

36

en-David didn't answer back. He took off his weight belt, tank, and BCD and jumped back in. With strong, powerful kicks, he was back at the police boat in no time. At the rail were Amos and the underwater crime scene investigator, Scott Steele. Ritter hovered above, shining a light down at Scott's hand.

"I found this on my final sweep. It was on the deck underneath the ladder. Must've moved from someplace else because it wasn't there when I searched earlier."

In Scott's hand was a golden ring with an enormous purple stone.

"Oh no," Ben-David said. "I know whose ring this is." And Mickey Rourke's lines flooded his head again:

"...any time you try a decent crime, you got fifty ways you're gonna fuck up. If you think of twenty-five of them, then you're a genius...and you ain't no genius."

"Whose?" Ritter asked.

"Sonofabitch!" Ben-David said, slapping the water. "It's Daria Knight's."

* * *

Rachel sat next to Brendan in *Knight Dive*'s candlelit salon. They were alone and almost done with the Mediterranean chicken that Brendan had prepared for them, along with a fresh salad. They were also on their second bottle of wine, which had her feeling warm, relaxed, and adventurous.

Out the salon window, she could see the lights of the Knight estate on Beacon Island, for they were anchored only a few hundred yards offshore. The cabin doors were open, and the slightest of breezes were funneling down into the boat's interior, giving her constant reminders of Brendan's intoxicating cologne. He had only disappeared once during the evening to use the head, and she had taken advantage of his absence by closing her eyes and taking deep breaths. Would they take a swim after dinner as he had invited her to do? Or, would they do something else? The forward stateroom hatch was closed as if he was teasing her, waiting to guide her to the stateroom and open the hatch to reveal a berth with flower petals on the cushions and soft music playing.

Or, would they take a swim, and then she would be invited to stay out at the island estate this evening? Either option would be fine with her. His stock had gone up when she had watched him prepare the chicken, cook it to perfection, and make the salad. No chef. No Abernethy. Just Brendan Knight and his own skills.

She had also checked her phone when he had gone to use the head, but there were no calls.

"More wine?" Brendan asked.

She nodded and watched him pour. The French wine was an excellent match for the chicken, and she went to cut the last piece in half when her knife slipped and fell to the deck. "I'm sorry," she said, standing up.

"No, no, no. Sit down. I'll get you another one," Brendan said.

"Absolutely not," she insisted. "I'm the clumsy one. Which drawer is it?"

"The middle one," he said. "I'll be right back."

And she watched him head forward, open the stateroom hatch, and then close it behind him. *Getting things ready for us?* She let out a quiet laugh and walked over to the galley.

She noticed a brand-new knife block on the counter. Shun knives. Expensive. Beautiful. Not looking, she opened the wrong drawer. When she glanced down into the drawer, she saw not utensils but an old set of stainless-steel knives. She picked one up and looked at the brand.

Cuisinart.

A shudder ran down her spine as if each vertebra was a falling domino. She took inventory of the knives. *Please let there be an 8-inch chef's knife with an ergonomically designed handle.*

There wasn't.

She shut the drawer. Then, she heard the stateroom hatch open and close.

Ben-David watched the police boat continue to get farther away as it sped toward the Knight's Lakeview residence. He had just weighed anchor and now sat behind the helm, ready to race to Rachel's beach. But, before that, he wanted to make a call first and warn her.

His phone had died, and he had charged it while bringing up the anchor. He unplugged it now and saw that he had a message. As he listened to Rachel's voice, his facial expression turned to fear. He tried to reach Ritter and Amos, but no one picked up.

"Damnit!" he yelled and plugged the phone back in.

He slammed the throttle home and took off at full speed for Beacon Island.

She turned to see Brendan Knight wiping his nose and smiling. "Find the knife?" he asked.

Rachel gave him a nervous grin. "Um, no." She then looked down and opened the correct drawer, picking up a steak knife. "There it is."

Brendan squinted at her for a minute. "Wrong drawer?"

She recovered. "Yeah, wine must be getting to my head early tonight. We just might need to take that swim before the dessert you promised me." She sat back down and began cutting her chicken. But her hand was shaking, and she thought she saw Brendan notice it.

He did not sit back down behind the salon table but instead went into the galley and pulled open the drawer that had the old Cuisinart set in it.

She watched as he bit his lower lip and studied the drawer. Then, he sniffed and rubbed his nose again. "Well, shit. She can't do anything right," he said.

"Excuse me?" Rachel said.

He turned toward her and then looked past her at the stateroom door. "Come in here and bring it," he said loudly.

Rachel's hands began to shake. *What was going on? Who was in the forward stateroom?* She needed to act. In an instant, her phone was out of her pocket, and she had pushed the video record button with her right hand while taking a sip of wine with her left hand. Then, she put her legs together and let the phone slide down until it reached her bare feet. She let out a string of coughs while she parted her feet, and the phone dropped the last few inches to the deck.

Brendan hadn't noticed as he took a seat next to her, but he picked up her utensils and threw them across the room.

"Brendan, what are you doing?"

The hatch to the forward stateroom opened and out walked Daria Knight in a white bikini—holding a hardcover copy of *Enemies in the Evening*. She stumbled a little bit and then wiped her nose in a similar fashion to her brother. "God, that shit is pure," she said to Brendan.

"I know, right?" he replied.

Rachel looked at his glazed eyes. *The cocaine.*

"Hi, Riley Cannon," Daria said, running her hand across Rachel's cheek. She sat down across from them at the salon table.

Don't let her feet find the phone! Rachel thought. "What did you call me?"

Daria giggled.

In the light given off by the candles on the table, she could see that Daria's eyes were glazed too.

Brendan stroked Rachel's right shoulder.

She tried to move away, but he latched on to her neck and squeezed. "Don't make me squeeze harder."

Rachel stayed put.

"That's a good girl," Brendan said. "What my sister just called you was your pen name, right? We know you're Riley Cannon."

He snapped his fingers, and Daria slid him the book, then she picked up the wine bottle and drank straight from it.

"Look at this picture," he said, flipping the book over to the back cover. "I have to hand it to your publisher; they did a good job of changing just enough features to disguise you. But we nailed it. This is you. You're not a coder."

Stall for time. You'll figure something out. "I don't know what you're talking about," she said. "Now, can I finish my meal, or can you at least take me home? I think we're done here."

"Oh, we're not done here at all, bitch," Daria said. "We just introduced the catalyst to the evening. The real fun is about to start."

"What about the missing Cuisinart Chef's knife?" Rachel said.

Daria stopped smiling. "What did you just say?"

Brendan grabbed the wine bottle and took a long swig. "What she said is that you messed up, sis. I can't trust you with anything. I told you that night to get rid of the entire set of knives after you stabbed your ex-boyfriend in the back. But, no, you just threw them in the drawer after you bought the new block. You're so lame."

"Fuck you," Daria said. "What does it matter? Miss Cannon here isn't going to be telling anyone about any of it," she said, pointing at Rachel.

She knew what they had just admitted, but if her phone was still recording, she needed the evidence to be air-tight. "Why did you kill Kaj Reynard?"

The Knight's both exchanged a glance. Then, Brendan said, "You wanna tell her, or should I?"

"Set up another line while I tell her," Daria said. She stared into Rachel's eyes. "And when I say set up a line, it means set up *three* lines. We're all doing it. Get ready for some fun, missy."

Brendan rose and walked toward the forward stateroom. She heard him open and then close the hatch.

"You ready, bestselling author?" As if she could sense Rachel's fear, she said, "Oh, c'mon, we're not going to kill you. You're a celebrity. We just want to fuck your brains out tonight, that's all. No, no. Not together. We're not that sick. We just like to take turns. Flipped a coin earlier. I get to go first. Yay!" she said, stomping her feet.

Rachel was petrified.

"We killed Kaj Reynard because we wanted the massive shipment of cocaine he found. Can you believe it? Almost 300 bricks. Look, I know you know about the boat—Brendan saw you and that over-the-hill Boy Scout from the lighthouse today." She took a massive swig of wine, finishing the bottle. "Anyway, poor Kaj tried to use the stuff as a bargaining chip to get back into my life. Guess he missed me. But, after a few earth-shattering romps I gave him, he was right back in my hands. I got him that new Bronco, and then he finally spilled the beans about where the boat was located. So, we dove down with him and brought up the mother lode. Then, and this is the embarrassing part, we took a celebratory cruise down the coast, did too much coke that night, and after knockin' boots with him in the salon, I stabbed him in the back. Had it all planned out. However, because of the extra lines I did, I gotta give myself a lot of credit for remembering to put on the gloves I had brought for the job before I plunged that big chef's knife into Kaj." Daria gave Rachel a wicked grin and patted herself on the back.

"But, I had no idea that Brendan had brought us in so close to shore while we were down there having sex. Then, Kaj somehow summons the strength to push past Brendan and jump into the water. We're so gone at that point that after a few seconds of waiting for Kaj to come up, we quietly motor back home. I can see the wheels turning, Rachel. And the answer is, yes, we totally took advantage of the security system at our compound being down that night. Now, we've got all of the bricks stored and are getting ready to make a large transfer with the big boys from Detroit. Partnering up with them, in fact."

"Did you kill Matty Joshua too?"

She giggled. "Yeah, did you find him out there today? Ha! He was so easy to manipulate. We had dropped the hint to him a little while back that Kaj had found something out in the lake—kept it real vague, though, because we knew that we might have to use him the way that we ended up using him to clear us. Then, after Kaj's murder, we had him meet us on *Knight Dive*," she said, tapping the bulkhead, "and told him that we needed his help and that there was a ton of money in it for him if he would help us. We let him snort a few lines and then suffocated him to death. Never even saw Brendan sneak up behind him with the plastic bag he put over his head. Of course, that might have been because I was giving him a blow job at the time. That cat had one small dick. Regardless, the other night, we took him down and placed him inside the wreck. Brendan and I figure that when Ben-David and you don't find anything else, it'll all somehow get blamed on Matty. Well, that and we had Matty write out a confession with a gun to his head, right before I started going down on him—told him it was a fun little game—which we will make sure gets found by the authorities when the time is right." She leaned forward. "So, don't get any ideas, Rachel."

"What about Christine Harper?"

"What about her? We've got a date tomorrow night."

The hell you do.

"And Ben-David's dog?"

"I enjoyed assassinating that ugly hound. Didn't like how your dickhead partner treated me the day you came to our place and questioned us. No respect."

The master stateroom hatch opened, and Brendan Knight walked out carrying a tray. Both Daria and Rachel noticed that he was swaying,

"Jesus Christ, did you do another line in there?" Daria said.

"Shut up," Brendan said and made it to the table.

On the tray were three straws and three lines of white powder.

"Oh, and one more thing," Daria said. "We're going to videotape you doing cocaine and having sex with us. As long as you stay quiet, the video will never get shown, and you can continue to write bestsellers, which we will help you promote. You're my mom's favorite author. If I got half the attention from her that Riley Cannon did over the years, well, maybe things tonight would have worked out differently."

"That was never going to happen," Brendan said, laughing.

Daria squinted and put her index finger on her lips. "Yeah, you're probably right. Asshole. Okay, time to have some fun."

"We'll go first and then take a video of you snorting a line," Brendan said. "You'll *love* it. Just let me know if you want another one, and I'll get it ready. You're gonna feel like you could swim all the way across Lake Huron to Canada after this."

Daria snorted her line, and then Brendan snorted his.

Daria started tapping her hands on the top of the table. "Okay, give me the camera," she said to Brendan.

Her brother searched his pockets and then looked around, confused.

"Don't tell me you left your phone at home again?"

Then, his eyes lit up. "Be right back."

Daria looked at Rachel. "He'll be right back. This is going to be amazing. Just relax and let loose. You're *fine.*"

Brendan returned, holding his cell phone. "Here we are."

Then, he heard a noise.

"What's wrong?" Daria asked.

"Shh," he said, walking toward the opening hatch. From underneath his shirt at the small of his back, he pulled a Glock 22.

Rachel saw it and made eye contact with Daria. "You said I'd be okay."

Daria ignored her and swiveled her eyes back to her brother.

There was a *bump* topside, and then the boat heeled to starboard.

Brendan ran up the cabin ladder, and shots were fired.

Rachel seized the opportunity and slugged Daria Knight in the face. Blood erupted from Daria's nose and splattered all over the salon table. Rachel moved toward the ladder, but Daria recovered and leaped at her. Rachel kicked at her hands and broke free.

She was about to run up the cabin ladder when Brendan Knight appeared at the top. There was a large red stain in the center of his chest. He whispered, "Daria," and then fell backward. His figure was replaced by that of Obadiah Ben-David, who was limping toward the opening.

Her spirits rose as Ben-David reached the top of the ladder. His shoulder and arm were wet with blood. Then, she saw his eyes go wide, and he yelled, "Duck!"

She did as she was told and then heard two shots ring out, followed by a loud sound behind her.

She stood up, gathering herself, and then turned around. On the deck was the dead body of Daria Knight. The gunshot wounds were almost a carbon copy of her brother's—center of mass. Then, Rachel looked at Daria's right hand.

In it was a revolver; there was a cabinet by the salon table that had been opened.

She rushed up the ladder to Ben-David, who was now on his back and breathing heavily.

"I'm hit bad," he said.

She looked and could now see a shot in his thigh to go along with the one to his arm and shoulder. *He's lost a lot of blood already.*

"I got through to Ritter. He should be here any minute with Amos."

She thought she heard a motor roaring in the distance.

"You're going to be okay, Obadiah. Stay with me."

He swallowed and then rubbed her right hand. "You were a helluva partner."

And then his eyes closed.

EPILOGUE

Hampstead, Michigan

1 Year Later...

What was supposed to be the trial of the century, billionaire power couple Saul and Pamela Knight vs. Michigan Professional Investigator Obadiah Ben-David and Rachel Roberts, ended up never making it to court. Greedy Jayson Jasper had been licking his eternal scotch-wet chops, ready to first bankrupt Ben-David and Rachel, then ask for the death penalty, and if he couldn't get that, then life in prison for them both would do just fine, when the investigative duo's lawyer, legendary defense attorney T. Samuel Bond, entered the arena. After Jasper listened to the recording from Rachel's phone, he realized that he was in the ring with a different animal. Unbeknownst to Ben-David and Bond, Rachel had edited the recording, removing the part where she had been exposed as author Riley Cannon, before sending it to them.

Then, Bond delivered the knockout blow. After an *anonymous* tip, the feds invaded Beacon Island, combing every square inch of it. After a week, the search was all over—and the results were all over the news. The FBI had found two hundred eighty bricks of cocaine hidden in two locations: one was the basement of the old Beacon Island Lighthouse keeper's house, and the other was a hidden room off the Rene Library in the Knight's island estate. Daria and Brendan Knight's fingerprints were all over the bricks—all over everything. In fact, in the secret room off the Rene Library, a legal pad had been found on top of one of the stacks of bricks. On the legal pad were handwritten notes by Brendan Knight that detailed how the cocaine would be moved off of the island and into the hands of their new drug partners. Pallets were to be made so that the Knight's helicopter, *Knight Sky*, could pick them up in the middle of the night and drop them off on a ship called *In Memory of...I Forgot* that would be miles out to sea from Beacon Island.

At the bottom of the legal pad, there was a date, which was only a week after the deadly confrontation between Rachel, Ben-David, and Brendan and Daria Knight. How had the room been located? The drug dogs had gone crazy by a large bookshelf containing the top ten *New York Times* bestselling fiction books of each year from 1931, when the list only had five fiction books, to present. Of course, Riley Cannon was there too. After pressure from the Special Agents conducting the search, Abernethy had broken. With his head down in shame, the old butler had walked over to a life-sized bronze statue of Pamela Knight's grandfather and namesake of the library, Rene, complete in his French Resistance attire, and pulled Rene's arm down, which was holding a dagger. Machinery and gears had engaged, and the entire bookshelf of bestsellers had swiveled 90 degrees, exposing a passageway that led to the secret room.

Jasper and the Knights dropped the case. Then, in a stunning move of self-preservation and narcissistic victimhood—a bait and switch of epic proportions—Saul and Pamela Knight initiated a public scorched-earth campaign against their children for deceiving their parents and becoming involved in drug dealing. They pledged ten million dollars to the war on drugs and spent another ten million starting a special wing of a Detroit hospital that would treat teens who had been both arrested and become addicted to drugs. The ribbon-cutting ceremony had been held in May for the "Saul & Pamela Knight Restorative Justice and Rehabilitation Centre." Jayson Jasper had helped them cut the ribbon—and had gotten inebriated at the afterparty.

On Tuesday, July 5, 2023, *Dark After Midnight* was finally released and became an instant #1 *New York Times* bestseller. Rachel had only given one exclusive interview—an e-mailed document that contained her answers to five questions asked by…Christine Harper. When it was announced that the interview questions and answers would be released via Harper's Highlights' website and social media, Christine's following jumped to 100 million. She never knew that the answers had been sent from a computer a few houses down the beach.

The novel opened to rave reviews from the usual suspects:

"Cannon explodes back onto the thriller scene! After a 12-year wait, her main character Adrienne Astra returns with fanfare and is smarter, sexier, grittier, and stronger. A cultural phenomenon awakens…and delivers once again."
—*The New York Times*

"Everyone knows that it is dark after midnight, but when you find out why in Cannon's new thriller, you'll be up the rest of the night, begging for sunrise. This novel scared the hell out of me."
—Sherrilyn Masters, *The Washington Post*

"He knew it was coming—couldn't stop it—and now my husband officially hates me again because I ignored him for an entire day while reading *Dark After Midnight* in one sitting. Spectacular! The crew is back, and now I'm waiting like everyone else to get my tickets for the movie. *Ben*, hurry up already! Note: The hubs stole my copy of the book, and I haven't seen him in hours…"

—Gerry Romanoff, *ThrillerFeast*

"Her best book yet, and I never thought I would say that after I reviewed *Enemies in the Evening* over a decade ago. Like fine wine, Cannon and her main character have aged well. After inhaling *Dark After Midnight*, I was reminded why, every once in a great while, I still enjoy fiction."

—H.W. Wetherington, *The Wall Street Journal*

"By far, the *darkest* entry in the saga yet. Wait until you see who teams up to try and take Adrienne Astra out! Affleck, who has already signed on to direct the film adaptation, cannot be sleeping at night right now. If ever there was a definition of "beach read" in *Webster's*, the only words needed in the entry would be *Dark After Midnight*."

—*The Detroit Free Press*

"Adrienne Astra is back and better than ever in the latest nail-biting, up-all-night thriller from Riley Cannon, whose return to the genre comes at a time when her readers need her most . . . *Dark After Midnight* isn't just the best book since *Gone Girl*, it's *the* reading event of the decade."

—Ryan Steck, *The Real Book Spy*

The following Tuesday, the battle was joined as Judge Macy Ashberry, the retired Colonel, and Trisha Parker all released their new novels, which, of course, had been ghostwritten by other less-than-worthy writers. Boatloads of money were spent, television interviews were conducted, radio and TV spots launched, and a "break the internet" publicity campaign blasted off—that would forever become a case study in the annals of publishing warfare—to try and topple *Dark After Midnight*.

Macy Ashberry's marketing team even dusted off the slogan that had launched her legendary career in an attempt to reclaim her past glories: "John Grisham was a *lawyer*. Macy Ashberry was a *judge*."

None of it mattered.

Riley Cannon *crushed* all three authors.

By Labor Day weekend, the trend in complaints regarding the three former titans of the industry was clear:

"Not up to the rough-and-tumble Colonel's usual standard. What *happened* here?"
—*The New York Times*

"I hate to admit it, but after a strong comeback, Judge Macy Ashberry—queen to many of the legal thriller—has lost her golden touch. Ashberry's crown is forever tarnished; this book is a prisoner that should never have been allowed to escape her castle's dungeon. And now the prisoner has brought back an army to invade. The Judge dare not enter Riley Cannon's courtroom again."
—H.W. Wetherington, *The Wall Street Journal*

"Did Trisha Parker even *write* this?"
—Sherrilyn Masters, *The Washington Post*

It was 3 o'clock on Saturday afternoon during a perfect Labor Day weekend, as Obadiah Ben-David walked down his driveway toward the mailbox. The sun had been out most of the day, taking brief respites behind small cloud banks, and the temperature was just under eighty. His six-month-old bloodhound puppy, Ben, trailed behind him on a green leash, sniffing the ground and then running to catch up.

A car passed by, and Ben-David waved. No clue who was in it, but since last summer, he had started to open back up to the world. With the help of Amos Meyer and Rachel Roberts, peace had come to his battered soul. He had done what he had done to try and help his wife survive—a part of him would never regret it—but the three-decade-long burden had taken a toll on him that he had been unaware of until the day after he and Rachel had killed Brendan and Daria Knight. The whole matter had proven to him that you can never outrun your past; you can stay ahead of it for a while, dodge its trappings, but eventually, it *will* catch up with you. He was thankful that his deeds had not led to any harm for Rachel; that, he would never have been able to forgive himself for. The thought that a mistake that you made when you were twenty-eight could harm someone you cared about when you were near sixty was almost too much to comprehend, but it served as yet another humbling reminder that there will always be unintended consequences for people's actions.

Now, thirty pounds lighter and retired, he enjoyed small things that he had never taken time to notice before—like afternoon walks to the mailbox with his puppy while sipping from his favorite coffee mug, a Darwinger's special. Baby Lloyd had presented it to him in a retirement ceremony at the gas station, and Corey Ritter had given Ben-David the key to Hampstead. Even Kevin Shelby, who miraculously had been found to have nothing to do with Kaj Reynard, Matty Joshua, and the Knights' drug situation, had shown up and shook his hand. Rachel had been there and had stayed later than all of the other guests. Together, they had closed the joint down with Baby Lloyd and Agatha. Then, in the parking lot, he had met a spitfire of a woman wearing a Detroit Tigers baseball cap, who was there to pick up Rachel. She had been introduced as Aunt Jackie, and Ben-David had liked her.

He reached the mailbox and pulled open the aluminum door.

Inside, there was only one package.

Wasn't expecting anything.

336

He removed it, closed the door, and set his coffee mug on top of the mailbox. Then, he tapped the package with his fingers and continued examining it with his large hands. From the shape, size, and feel, he decided that there had to be a hardcover book inside. He searched for the return address.

There wasn't one.

Though there *was* postage, and his address was correct—printed on a white label.

He tied Ben up to the mailbox post and opened the package.

After wedging the mailing envelope under his left armpit, he beheld the glossy front cover of a thick book. The title, *Dark After Midnight*, ran across the bottom and seemed to vanish into the illustrated darkening water below it. Above the title was a female scuba diver with a spear gun, aiming it at a boat on the surface, which was close to the right-hand edge of the cover. Then, to the left of the boat was an island with a mansion on the beach and a seaplane above it shooting rounds into the water. Finally, above the seaplane and in letters that were twice the size of the title were the words RILEY CANNON.

Ben-David was puzzled. He was not a fiction reader and would have never ordered a book. If he had wanted something to read, he would have visited the local bookstore, *Hampstead Pages*, and talked to the friendly owner and bookseller Tilly Michaels, who had run the store for years and was a Hampstead treasure—especially for those who made Hampstead their summer home. You had to stop by and check in with Tilly. He frowned. Maybe those days were coming to an end, and he didn't like it.

He thumbed through the first couple pages and stopped at the dedication. It read:

TO THE 1989 DETROIT PISTONS.

Ben-David's eyes got wide, and he flipped to the back cover. There was a photograph of a young woman. Thirties? He couldn't tell for sure. Half of her face was hidden in the shadows. The hair was long and golden blonde. She was also wearing glasses that had the slightest tint, but the woman's eye color appeared to be brown.

She looks familiar, he thought. *Where have I seen this person?*

Then, his heart jumped.

Rachel?

He studied the eyes again. *Can't be.* Rachel had blue eyes and short, auburn-colored hair. Then, he saw the mole on the right cheek and knew it wasn't her because Rachel had no such mole. His heart rate started to calm back down. Whoever had taken this author photo hadn't done his or her job. *Should have touched up the mole*, he thought.

He opened the book back up and read the dedication one more time.

To the 1989 Detroit Pistons

Who would have sent this to me?

Then, as if originating from a far-off land, the day's cool Huron breezes reached him, and he shivered. He closed the book, studied the author's picture on the back one more time, and said, "Nah."

He untied Ben and strolled back toward the house—book under his arm, coffee in one hand, dog leash in the other.

From the nearby woods, Rachel Roberts watched as Obadiah Ben-David disappeared up his driveway. She grinned and then headed for her car, which was parked around the bend and out of sight of Ben-David's mailbox and driveway. The breeze felt refreshing, and she was contemplating a swim in Lake Huron before dinner. Good to get her energy up before attacking the evening pages. *3 a.m. Phone Call* was almost done, and Topaz was on fire after reading the last few chapters that Rachel had sent her. *"I'll give you a 3 a.m. phone call, darling, if you ever surprise me like that again!"*

Rachel stopped and looked back one more time at Ben-David's mailbox.

Maybe one day she would tell him who Riley Cannon was.

AUTHOR'S NOTE

Thank you for reading or listening to *Huron Breeze*. As an independent author, my success greatly depends on reviews and referrals. If you enjoyed the book, it would help me out if you left a quick review and then passed on the recommendation. If you would like more information on upcoming books and discounts, please sign-up for my email list through my website (landonbeachbooks.com) or follow Landon Beach Books on Facebook, Twitter, or Instagram.

Huron Breeze. Well, I was all prepared to start my last novel in The Great Lakes Saga, *The Bay*, when a dear friend in the publishing world challenged me to take a break and try my hand at writing a mystery. Like most readers, I enjoy mysteries, but I wasn't sure about writing one. He told me to think about it, so I decided that I would give it a week. If no ideas came to mind, I'd start in on *The Bay*. As I've mentioned before in interviews, my creative writing degree is in screenwriting, and one of my favorite decades of film to study is the 1970s. A few years ago, my best friend and I happened to come across a lost gem called *Night Moves* that was directed by Arthur Penn, written by Alan Sharp, and starred Gene Hackman. For some reason, during that week of searching for ideas, I put *Night Moves* in the DVD player one evening. As the end credits rolled, a rough idea for a mystery formed in my mind. I hopped off the couch, grabbed a pen and legal pad, and immediately started working through a possible plot and did some character sketches. By the next morning, I had enough for me to call my friend and tell him I was up for the challenge. Hence, in *Huron Breeze*, the Knight family name and their associated toys—ahem, the yacht *Night Moves*—are a nod to the film that set me on this journey, which ended up being the most fun I've ever had writing a novel. Because of the experience, I'm almost certain that I will write another mystery somewhere down the road.

Many thanks to MB, EL, JG, RR, DB, JT, AB, MM, KL, LD, and CG who all provided helpful comments on early drafts of the manuscript. To my fans: I hope you enjoyed this brief detour from the saga, and I continue to be amazed by your kindness and goodwill. For John Carroll, Kevin Allen, Roberta Smith, and Heather Miller: You are all living proof that small-town generosity, warmth, and support are still alive and well on the sunrise side. Finally, a mammoth thanks to my wife and two girls who made the writing of this book possible and welcomed me with open arms, understanding, love, and humor, each time I emerged from the writing room.

Happy Beach Reading!

L.B.

If you enjoyed *Huron Breeze*, expand your adventure with *The Wreck,* the first book in The Great Lakes saga. Here is an excerpt to start the journey.

THE WRECK

Landon Beach

PROLOGUE

LAKE HURON, MICHIGAN
SUMMER 2007

T he Hunter 49's motor cut, and the luxury yacht glided with no running lights on. Cloud cover hid the moon and stars; the water looked black. A man in a full wetsuit moved forward in the cockpit and after verifying the latitude and longitude, pushed the GPS monitor's "off" button. The LCD color display vanished.

Waves beat against the hull, heavier seas than had been predicted. He would have to be efficient or he'd need to reposition the boat over the scuttle site again. The chronometer above the navigation station read 0030. This should have been finished 30 minutes ago. Not only had the boat been in the wrong slip, forcing him to search the marina in the dark, the owner—details apparently escaped that arrogant prick—had not filled the fuel tank.

He headed below and opened the aft stateroom door. The woman's naked corpse lay strapped to the berth, the nipples of her large breasts pointing at the overhead. A careful lift of the port-side bench revealed black wiring connecting a series of three explosive charges. After similar checks of the wiring and charges in the gutted-out galley and v-berth, he smiled to himself and went topside with a pair of night vision goggles.

A scan of the horizon. Nothing.

He closed and locked the aft hatch cover. Moving swiftly—but never rushing—he donned a mask and fins, then pulled a remote detonation device from the pocket of his wetsuit. Two of the four buttons were for the explosives he had attached to the outside of the hull underwater, which would sink the boat. The bottom two were for the explosives he had just checked on the interior.

He looked back at the cockpit and for a moment rubbed his left hand on the smooth fiberglass hull. What a waste of a beautiful boat. How much had the owner paid for it? Three...Four-hundred thousand? Some people did live differently. With the night vision goggles hanging on his neck and the remote for the explosives in his right hand, he slipped into the water and began to kick.

Fifty yards away he began to tread water and looked back at the yacht. It listed to starboard, then to port, as whitecaps pushed against the hull. He pressed the top two buttons on the remote. The yacht lifted and then began to lower into the water; the heaving sea had less and less effect as more of the boat submerged. In under a minute, the yacht was gone. He held his fingers on the bottom two buttons but did not push them. The water was deep, and it would take three to four minutes for the boat to reach the lake bed.

At four minutes, he pushed the bottom two buttons, shut the remote, and zipped it back into his wetsuit pocket. He treaded water for half an hour. Nothing surfaced.

He swam for five minutes, stopped, scanned the area with his night vision goggles, and swam again.

After an hour of this, he pulled the goggles over his head and let them sink to the bottom. He continued his long swim to shore.

I

HAMPSTEAD, MICHIGAN
SUMMER 2008

The sand felt cool under Nate Martin's feet as he walked hand-in-hand with his wife down to the water. A bonfire crackled away on their beach behind them—the sun had set 30 minutes ago and an orange glow still hung on the horizon. The Martins' boat, *Speculation*, bobbed gently in her mooring about twenty yards offshore.

They parted hands and Nate stopped to pick up a piece of driftwood and toss it back toward the fire. Brooke Martin continued on and dipped her right foot into the water, the wind brushing her auburn hair against her cheek.

"Too cold for me," she said.

Nate took a gulp of beer before walking ankle deep into the water beside her.

"Not bad, but colder than when I put the boat in," Nate said.

"Glad I didn't have to help," Brooke said and then took a sip from her plastic cup of wine.

"Not up for a swim?" Nate joked.

"No way," Brooke said.

They started to walk parallel to the water, with Nate's feet still in and Brooke's squishing into the wet sand just out of reach of the lapping waves.

Four zigzagging jet skis sliced through the water off the Martins' beach. Two were driven by women in bikinis and the other two by men. They weren't wearing life jackets, which usually meant these were summer folk who spent June, July, and August in one of the beach castles smoking weed in mass quantities. These four were probably already baked.

One girl cut a turn too close and flew off.

"Crazies," Nate said.

She resurfaced and climbed back aboard. Her bikini bottom was really a thong and her butt cheeks slapped against the rubber seat as the jet ski started and took off.

"Should they be riding those things this late?" Brooke asked.

"No," said Nate, "but who is going to stop them?"

They continued to walk as the sound of the jet skis faded. A quarter mile later, they reached the stretch where the larger homes began. The floodlights on the estates' back decks illuminated the beach like a stage. The Martins turned around.

When they arrived at their beach, Nate placed a new log on the fire and sat down in his lawn chair. Brooke sat down but then rose, moving her chair a few feet further away from the heat.

"What are your plans for tomorrow?" Nate said.

"I think I'll lay out. I looked at the weather report and we're in for a few good days until rain arrives," Brooke said, "then I'll probably go to the bookstore." Her voice trailed off. She gathered her thoughts for a moment. "We need to make love the next four nights."

"Okay," Nate said.

"You could work up a little enthusiasm," Brooke said.

He had sounded matter-of-fact. "Sorry. It's just that scheduled sex sometimes takes the excitement out of it. We're on vacation. We should just let it happen."

"So, you get to have your strict workout regime everyday, but when I mention a specific time that we need to make love in order to give us the best chance at conceiving, it's suddenly 'We're on vacation'?"

She had a point. He thought about trying to angle in with a comment about her obsessive need to clean the house the moment they had arrived earlier today, but as he thought of it the vision of his freshly cut and edged grass entered his mind. If they really were on vacation, as he had put it, then the lawn being manicured wouldn't be so important to him. Damn.

"What is your plan for tomorrow?" She said.

A switch of topics, but he knew she was circling. "I'm going to get up, take my run, and then hit the hardware store for a new lock for the boat."

"What happened to the lock you keep in the garage?"

"It broke today," Nate shrugged.

"How does a lock break?"

"I put the key in, and when I turned it, it broke off in the lock."

"You mean our boat is moored out there right now without a lock?" Brooke asked, while shifting her gaze to the white hull reflecting the growing moonlight.

"Yep."

"Do you think someone would steal it?"

"Nah. The keys are in the house. If someone wanted to steal a boat worth anything, they'd go down to Shelby's Marina and try and take Shaw's *Triumph*." Leonard Shaw was a Baltimore businessman who had grown up in Michigan and now summered in the largest beach mansion in Hampstead. Once his two-hundred foot custom-built yacht was completed, he'd hired a dredging crew to carve out a separate berth in the marina to dock the boat. With the dredging crew working mostly at night, locals and vacationers complained of the noise and threatened to pull their boats out of Shelby's. Nate was glad he had avoided the hassle by keeping *Speculation* moored off of his beach.

Brooke swiveled her eyes between Nate and the boat. "Why didn't you get a new lock today?"

He moved behind her and started to kiss the back of her neck. *We're on vacation, relax, baby.* "Is that a hint? Do you want me to swim out and sleep on board tonight?"

"Of course not," Brooke whispered back, enjoying the foreplay. "Are you trying to get a head start on tomorrow night?"

"No. Just trying to enjoy *tonight*," Nate said. "Can we concentrate on that?"

She leaned her head back and he kissed her lips.

Ten minutes later, the fire started to die with two empty lawn chairs sitting in front of it.

2

Sun rays peeked around the edges of the horizontal blinds in the Martins' bedroom window. Nate opened his eyes and looked at his watch, eight o'clock. He was normally up by six. Brooke was snoring, and he eased out of bed and lifted one strip of the blinds. *Speculation* was in her mooring. He smiled and dropped the blind back into place.

After putting on a pair of shorts and a tank top, he grabbed a pair of socks and his running shoes and exited the bedroom. The hallway was dark as he made his way to the kitchen. He pressed "start" on the coffee pot, and the coffee he had prepared the night before began to brew as he put on his shoes.

The past year had been a revolving door of pain, uncertainty, and disappointment. They had been trying to conceive for six months when his father died. Only last month had it felt right to try again. He hadn't been himself in the classroom either. His ninth grade physical science lessons at W. M. Breech High School had wandered aimlessly, his tests were rote memorization, and the usual passion he brought to each day had been missing; his students let him know they knew it.

His mother had lasted in the beach house until Christmas. The original plan had been for Nate and his older sister, Marie, to share ownership when their parents were unable to handle the upkeep, but Nate had bought Marie's half and the house was now his and Brooke's. His mother had left in January to move in with his sister in St. Petersburg.

He pushed the brass button on the doorknob and closed the door behind him. After wiggling the knob to make sure it was locked, he hopped off the small porch onto the stone walkway, went past the garage, and followed the dirt driveway until he was parallel with their mailbox. After stretching, he looked at his watch and started to jog down Sandyhook Road.

Each lakeside house had some sort of identifying marker next to its mailbox. A red and white striped lighthouse carved out of wood. A miniature of the house painted on a three foot by three foot board. A post. A bench. Something with the owner's name and the year the house had been built on the marker. This five miles of beach, once sparsely populated with neighbors in similarly sized residences, was now dominated by beach mansions that looked more like hotels than houses. The lots were owned by lawyers, congressmen, real-estate tycoons, government contractors, Detroit businessmen (of the few businesses that remained), and a few others who had money. Some were migrants from the already overcrowded western shore of Michigan. White collar Chicago money had run north and was moving around the Great Lakes shoreline like a child connecting the dots to make a picture of a left-handed mitten.

The sun flickered in and out of Nate's face as he ran under the oak trees spanning the road. He thought of the advice his father had given him when he was searching for his first teaching job: "Make sure that you buy a house east of the school so that when you go into work you'll be driving west, and when you come home from work you'll be driving east. That way, you'll never be driving into the sun. Just a simple stress reliever that most people don't take into consideration—that is, until they rear-end someone for the first time." As with all of Nate's father's advice, it had sounded too simple but ended up being right.

Last June his father had been diagnosed with stomach cancer. Three months later, on an overcast September day, Nate had buried him.

Brooke heard the back door close and rose from bed. She turned off their box fan and opened the bedroom blinds. The entire beach was motionless, and their boat was still moored, surrounded by flat water. The aroma of coffee drifted into the bedroom as she put on her robe.

By the time she reached the kitchen, Nate had already filled his mug and was headed down to the water. She poured herself a cup and started a bacon and eggs breakfast.

The sand parted with each step as Nate walked toward the water. Bordering both sides of the Martins' property was a wooden fence; the spindles were flat, painted red, and held together by wire with a metal rod driven into the ground every fifteen feet or so. The fence was not only a "beachy" way to mark property lines but served its primary purpose of trapping sand. Nate took off his shoes and set his mug down by the end of the northern fence line. He began to walk south.

The water ran over his ankles and then receded. It was cool and felt good on his tired feet. The beach looked abandoned. No more than twenty yards from where he started, Nate stepped down with his right foot and felt something sharp. He stood, balancing on his left leg as he inspected the bottom of his right foot. No apparent cut. No bleeding. He rubbed in circles and the pain went away. As he stepped back down onto the wet sand, he saw something sparkle in the place he had stepped before. Glass? A toy left behind by some toddler? As Nate picked the object up, he saw that it was neither. He submerged the object, wiping the wet sand off it, and then dried it with the bottom of his tank top. He held the object a foot in front of his face and studied it. In his hand was a gold coin.

* * *

Brooke saw Nate returning from the water. Assuming that he was coming in to complete his morning routine of running three miles, taking a walk to the water with his coffee, and now eating breakfast and reading the newspaper, she rose to unlock the sliding glass door from the deck. However, he walked right by the deck and headed for the garage. She unlocked the door anyway and refilled her cup. She took a seat at the worn kitchen table, which she wanted to replace but didn't as it had been in the family since Nate was a child. She had plans to redo many parts of the house, but Nate was adamant that the table remained and that the bedroom he stayed in as a boy not be changed. When his father was alive, Nate would have coffee with him in the morning and read the paper at this table. Brooke would still be sleeping and his mother would be cooking breakfast. He had remarked to her that at times he still felt like a visitor, expecting his father to pull up a chair and start a conversation with him about the old days and family stories he'd heard over and over again.

Brooke finished the paper, breakfast, and her cup of coffee and Nate had not come in yet. What was he doing? His bacon, eggs, and toast were cold. She grabbed the coffee pot and headed to the garage.

Nate heard the garage door open as he stared at the coin through a magnifying glass, mesmerized by it.

His wooden writing desk sat in the middle of black carpeting that covered one-quarter of the garage's concrete floor. Two bookcases that he had constructed from odds-and-ends left over from the addition that his parents had done a few years ago rested against the wall behind the desk. Favorite authors had taken up permanent residence on the top two shelves of the first bookcase, and the remaining three shelves were full of paperbacks, read according to his mood at the time he had purchased them. On the top shelf of the second bookcase rested a pair of fins and a mask that he used when cleaning off the bottom of his boat. His father's dive knife was next to the mask.

The shelf below the diving gear contained books that Nate had almost worn the covers off: a Marine Biology desk reference set, half-a-dozen books by Dr. Robert D. Ballard from the Woods Hole Oceanographic Institute, a few by Jacques Cousteau, and five years' worth of magazines from his National Geographic subscription.

The bottom shelves contained books about Great Lakes ports, navigation rules and aids, and boating regulations. Next to one of the rows of books were rolled up charts and a navigation kit. Nate had taught himself how to navigate and routinely took *Speculation* out overnight.

Brooke arrived at Nate's desk and refilled his coffee mug. "Are we rich?" She asked looking at the coin.

"Very funny," Nate said, "I found this on our beach this morning."

"Is that gold?" Brooke asked, more serious now that she had a better look at the coin.

"Maybe. I don't recognize any of these marks or the language that is engraved on it." He put the coin and magnifying glass down and pointed to the bookshelf. "Hand me that book."

Brooke reached up to the top shelf and grabbed a heavy, hardcover book. She looked at the title—*The Golden Age of Piracy*—and tried to hide a grin.

Nate knew her expression meant: *only you would have a book like this, Nate.* "Thanks," he said, laughing at himself with her. "I'm glad to see that I'm still a cheap source of entertainment for you."

She giggled back, and then kissed him on the cheek.

Nate began to leaf through the book.

Brooke set the coffee pot down and picked up the coin and magnifying glass.

After checking the appropriate pages, he closed the book and looked up at Brooke. "Nothing in here that resembles the markings on this coin." He took a drink of his coffee.

Brooke passed the coin and magnifying glass back to Nate. "I can't make out anything on it either." She picked up the coffee pot. "Well, I'm going in to take a shower and then head out to do a little shopping. Your breakfast is cold, but it's on the table if you still want it," she said. "I looked down the beach this morning and I think the Gibsons are up."

Nate was once more absorbed in the mystery of the coin and only grunted in reply.

"I wonder if anyone will make us an offer on our place this summer," Brooke wondered aloud.

A few Hampstead locals had hung on to their homes, repeatedly declining offers that were made for their property. In some cases, it was enough money to bankroll them for a decade. The ink on the paperwork transferring ownership of the house from his mother to Brooke and him hadn't even dried yet when they had been approached. It was over Easter weekend, and they were at the beach house furnishing it with some of their own things. The doorbell had rung, and after five minutes of polite conversation, Nate and Brooke had said no; the prospective buyer and his trophy wife had stormed off.

Some of the mansion owners had even tried to sue the cottage owners, claiming that the cottages detracted from the beachfront's beauty. They wanted the locals out. Most of the locals wanted the castles bulldozed.

Nate set the coin and magnifying glass aside for a moment. "You think that the local kids have all the lawn jobs sewn up yet?" His father had once told him of an unofficial lottery held at the town barbershop to determine who would be allowed to apply for the summer mansion mowing jobs. It had been one of their last conversations.

"Probably," said Brooke. "I've felt stares at the dime store from Judge Hopkins and Sheriff Walker. I know they're wishing we would just sell our cottage already."

"How wrong is that?" Nate said. "The town leaders turning on the townspeople."

"What do they gain by us selling?"

"New mansions mean more opportunities for their sons or daughters to mow a summer resident's lawn," Nate said. "And if their kid does a good job, then maybe, just maybe, they'll get invited out for a summer party."

"Funny how some people get fooled into thinking they're moving up in the world," she said.

"If they only knew that they look like the person who walks behind a horse and picks up its droppings."

He couldn't help but laugh at the scene he was now picturing.

"What?" Brooke said.

He continued to laugh.

"Naaayyyyte," she said, poking him with her finger.

He gathered himself. "I started to envision some of the people we know who want to break into that circle walking behind the Budweiser Clydesdales at the Fourth of the July parade picking up piles of shit and waving to the crowd. Agree?"

"One hundred percent. Oh, the pictures you paint, Mr. Martin," Brooke said.

"You're the only one that can see the pictures I describe, sweetie."

"When are we getting our internet connection?" Nate said.

"They can't make it out until next week."

"Damned cable company. We're supposed to have cell phone reception out here next summer too. I'll believe it when I see it."

She kissed him and then left the garage.

He picked up the coin again and then looked out the window at the spot on the beach where he had found it. Where had it come from? Were there more? He put the magnifying glass and coin in the top drawer of his desk and reshelved the book. He stood with his hand resting on the dive gear for a moment. *Let's have a look.*

He entered the house through the sliding glass door and could hear the shower running as he walked down the hallway and grabbed a towel from the linen closet. He exited the house and as he stepped off the deck, he noticed that the blinds were now open on the lakeside windows of a house two down from them. No doubt the owner had his binoculars out and was watching to see what Nate was up to. The man spent more time prying into other people's lives than living his own. The beach mansion owners had one complaint that held weight: the locals were nosey.

Nate passed by the stack of unused wood in the sand and made his way to the water. The lake was placid and the sun had risen far enough to see the sandy bottom. He positioned himself at the approximate point where he had found the coin. He looked back toward the house to make sure it had been found on his property. It had.

After strapping the knife to his right calf, he pulled the mask down past his face so that it hung by its strap around his neck and rested on his upper chest. He entered the water holding the fins above the surface and probed the bottom with his toes for more coins as he walked out up to his waist. Feeling none, he put his fins on and pulled the mask over his head. He spit into the faceplate, rubbing warm saliva all over, and then dipped the mask into the cold water. After securing it to his face, Nate verified his alignment with the spot on the beach where he'd found the coin and dove under.

The water's temperature was probably in the high fifties, and Nate kicked to warm his body, seeing nothing on the bottom at first. Then, his own anchor auger, wire, and buoy appeared. He surfaced next to *Speculation*, took a deep breath, and dove to the bottom to test the auger. Holding onto the steel pole, he pulled from side to side, then up and down. Neither motion moved the mooring. He checked the wire which ran through the auger's eye to the buoy and back to the eye: they were secure.

A few summers back, he had applied for a job as a navigator on a yacht out of Shelby's. The local paper had advertised that a crew was needed for the vessel's summer voyage up Lake Huron to Mackinac Island, down Lake Michigan to Chicago, and then back to Hampstead. Perhaps "applied" was too strong a word. Thinking that mailing an item like a resume would be too formal, he had shown up at Shelby's to inquire about the job. The marina owner, Kevin Shelby, had finally opened his office door after Nate's third stream of knocking. Shelby had a cigarette and cup of coffee in one hand and was running the other hand through his greasy hair. There had been an open bottle of Baileys on his small desk.

After hearing Nate out, Shelby had said, "Fuck if I know. I've never even heard about the cruise, you sure you've got the right marina?"

And that was the end of his career as a navigator—and possibly berthing his boat there.

Nate swam under *Speculation* and after seeing that the hull was fine, he surfaced and kicked further out until the water was approximately ten feet deep. He took a deep breath and dove.

He traced the bottom and swam in a zigzag pattern out to a depth of twenty-five feet. Odds-and-ends were scattered across the sand: rocks, a tire, a rusted can but no coins. He surfaced. The sun hid behind a cloud making the water darker as Nate treaded. A breeze had started and *Speculation* wandered around her mooring. Where did the coin come from? Nate rotated in a slow circle watching the waves and hearing the distant cry of a seagull.

The sun came out from behind the cloud and the khaki colored bottom illuminated under his black fins. He dove and kicked back toward shore while hugging the lake bed. Had he hoped to find something? Sure. Did he really think that he would? No. At least he knew the boat wasn't going anywhere.

As he dried off on the beach, Brooke emerged from the house.

ABOUT THE AUTHOR

Landon Beach lives in the Sunshine State with his wife, two children, and their golden retriever. He previously served as a Naval Officer and is currently an educator by day and an author by night. Find out more at landonbeachbooks.com.